THE FLIGHT OF THE FALCON

THE FLIGHT OF THE FALCON

by

DAPHNE DU MAURIER

LONDON
VICTOR GOLLANCZ LTD
1965

Printed in Great Britain by
The Camelot Press Ltd., London and Southampton

AUTHOR'S NOTE

The Flight of the Falcon is a work of fiction. Although Ruffano was inspired by an existing Italian city the topography, the events described, the inhabitants and every member of the university are purely imaginary.

CHAPTER ONE

W<small>E WERE RIGHT</small> on time. Sunshine Tours informed its passengers on the printed itinerary that their coach was due at the Hotel Splendido, Rome, at approximately 1800 hours. Glancing at my watch, I saw that it wanted three minutes to the hour.

"You owe me five hundred lire," I said to Beppo.

The driver grinned. "We'll see about that in Naples," he said. "In Naples I shall present you with a bill for more than two thousand lire."

Our bets were continuous throughout the tour. We each kept a book, checked the kilometres against the time, and then settled up when either of us felt like paying. The latter generally fell to me, no matter who had come out on top with the betting. As courier, I received the larger tips.

I turned round, smiling, to my load of merchandise. "Welcome to Rome, ladies and gentlemen," I said, "the city of popes, emperors, and Christians thrown to the lions, not to mention movie stars."

A wave of laughter greeted me. Somebody in the back row cheered. They liked this sort of thing. Any facetious remark made by the courier helped to establish the relationship between passengers and pilot. Beppo, as driver, may have been responsible for their safety on the road, but I, as guide, manager, mediator and shepherd of souls, held their lives in my hands. A courier can make or break a tour. Like the conductor of a choir he must, by force of personality, induce his team to sing in harmony; subdue the raucous, encourage the timid, conspire with the young, flatter the old.

I climbed down from my seat, flinging wide the door, and saw the porters and pages hurrying from the swing-doors of the hotel to meet us. I watched my flock descend, sausages from a machine, fifty all told—no need to count the heads, for we had not stopped between Assisi and Rome—and led the way to the reception desk.

"Sunshine Tours, Anglo-American Friendship League," I said.

I shook hands with the reception clerk. We were old acquaintances. I had been on this particular route for two years now.

"Good trip?" he asked.

"Pretty fair," I replied, "apart from the weather. It was snowing in Florence yesterday."

"It's still March," he said. "What do you expect? You people start your season too soon."

"Tell them that at the head office in Genoa," I answered.

Everything was in order. We held block bookings, of course, and because it was early in the season the management had fixed my whole party on the second floor. This would please them. Later in the year we should be lucky to get the fifth, and tucked away in the rear of the building at that.

The clerk watched my party file into the reception lounge. "What have you brought us?" he asked. "The holy alliance?"

"Don't ask me," I shrugged. "They joined forces at Genoa on Tuesday. Some sort of club. Beef and barbarians. The usual treatment in the restaurant at seven-thirty?"

"It's all laid on," he said, "and the relief coach ordered for nine. I wish you joy."

We use certain code-words for our clients in the touring business. The English are beef to us, and the Americans barbarians. It may not be complimentary, but it's apt. These people were running wild on pasture land and prairie when we were ruling the world from Rome. No offence intended.

I turned to greet the respective leaders of my Anglo-American group. "Everything's fine," I said. "Accommodation for all on the second floor. Telephones in every room. Any queries ring down to the desk and they'll put you through to me. Dinner at seven-thirty. I'll meet you here. The reception manager will now show you to your rooms. O.K.?"

Theoretically, this was where I laid off for an hour and twenty minutes, found my own small lair, had a shower and collapsed, but it seldom worked that way. Nor did it today. My telephone buzzed as soon as I'd taken off my jacket.

"Mr. Fabbio?"

"Speaking."

"It's Mrs. Taylor here. Utter and complete disaster! I've left every package I bought in Florence in that hotel in Perugia."

I might have known. She had left a coat in Genoa and a pair of overshoes in Siena. She had insisted that these things, almost

8

certainly unnecessary south of Rome, must be telephoned for and forwarded to Naples.

"Mrs. Taylor, I'm so sorry. What were in the packages?"

"Breakables, mostly. There were two pictures . . . a statuette of Michelangelo's David . . . some cigarette boxes. . . ."

"Don't worry. I'll take care of it. I'll telephone Perugia right away and see that your packages get to our office in Genoa, and are waiting there for your return."

It depended on how busy they were at reception whether I left them to put through the call and make the enquiry, or dealt with it myself. Better do it myself. It would save time in the long run. I had sized up the Taylor woman as a package-leaver as soon as she joined us. She trailed belongings. Spectacles, head-scarves, picture postcards kept falling out of her outsize handbag. It is an English failing, a fault of the species. Apart from this, beef give very little trouble, though in their desire to seek the sun they blister more readily than other nationalities. Bare-armed, bare-legged, they're into cotton frocks and shorts the first day of the tour, turning brick-red in the process. Then I have to conduct them to the nearest chemist's shop for salves and lotions.

The telephone buzzed once more. Not my call to Perugia, but one of the barbarians. A woman again, naturally. The husbands never bother me.

"Mr. Fabbio?"

"Speaking."

"Guess what. It's a boy!"

I did a double-think. Barbarians give you their life history the first evening in Genoa. Which of them was it that was expecting her first grandchild, back in Denver, Colorado? Mrs. Hiram Bloom.

"Congratulations, Mrs. Bloom. This calls for a special celebration."

"I know it. I'm so excited I don't know what I'm doing." The scream of delight nearly broke my eardrum. "Now, I want just you, and one or two of the others, to meet Mr. Bloom and myself in the bar before dinner, to drink the little boy's health. Shall we say seven-fifteen?"

It would cut down my free time to half-an-hour, and that call from Perugia hadn't yet come through. Nothing to be done. Courtesy first and foremost.

"That's very kind of you, Mrs. Bloom. I'll be there. All well with your daughter-in-law?"

9

"She's fine. Just fine."

I hung up before she could read me out the cable. Time for a shave, anyway, and with luck a shower.

You have to be wary about accepting invitations from clients. A birthday or a wedding anniversary is legitimate, or the arrival of a grandchild. Nothing much else, or it tends to make bad blood and you are half-way to ruining your tour. Besides, where drinking is concerned a courier has to watch his intake. Whatever happens to his party, he must remain sober. So must the driver. This is not always easy.

I dealt with the Perugia call while still dripping from the shower, and after struggling into a clean shirt went downstairs to inspect the arrangements made for us in the restaurant. Two long tables in the middle of the room, each seating twenty-five, and in the centre of either table, dwarfing the flowers, the bunched flags of both nations, the Stars and Stripes and the Union Jack. This never fails to please—the clients feel that it gives tone to the proceedings.

A word with the head waiter, promising him to have my party seated by seven-thirty sharp. They liked us to have our main course finished and the dessert served before the other diners wandered in to their tables. It was important for us, too. We worked to a tight schedule, and were due to take off for our tour of "Rome By Night" at nine o'clock.

A final check on time, and then the short celebration drink in the bar. There were only a handful of them gathered to toast baby Bloom, but you could hear them from the entrance hall, where the excluded beef hung about in twos and threes, aloof, disdainful, their faces buried in the English newspapers. The extrovert barbarian roar had turned the Anglo-Saxons dumb.

Mrs. Bloom glided towards me, a frigate in full sail. "Now, Mr. Fabbio, you'll not refuse champagne?"

"Half a glass, Mrs. Bloom. Just to wish long life to your grandson."

There was something touching in her happiness. Generosity exuded from her person. She placed her arm through mine and drew me forward into the group. How kind they were, dear God, how kind . . . Epitomising, in their all-embracing warmth, the barbarian hunger for love. I drew back, suffocated, then, ashamed of myself, let the wave engulf me. Back in Genoa I had many tributes from Mrs. Bloom's compatriots. Christmas cards by the score, letters, greetings. Did I remember the trip two years ago? When would I visit them in the States? They often thought of me. They had named their youngest son Armino. The sincerity of those messages shamed me. I never answered them.

"I hate to break this up, Mrs. Bloom. But it's just on seven-thirty."

"What you say goes, Mr. Fabbio. You're the boss."

The two nations mingled in the entrance hall, halting momentarily as they greeted new acquaintances, the women appraising each other's dresses. Then through to the restaurant drifted my fifty head of cattle, lowing, murmuring, myself the stockman in the rear. There were cries of pleasure at the sight of the flags. For a moment I feared a burst into national song, "The Star-spangled Banner", "God Save the Queen"—it had happened before—but I caught the head waiter's eye and we managed to seat them before patriotism could do its worst. Then to my own small table in the corner. One lone male barbarian, middle-aged, swimmy-eyed, had placed himself at the corner of one of the long tables, from where he could watch me. I had him taped. I knew his kind. He would get no encouragement from the courier, but we might have trouble with him in Naples.

While I ate I did the day's accounts. This was my custom. I shut my ears to the sound of voices and the clatter of plates. If the accounts are not kept up to date you never get straight, and then there is hell to pay with head office. Book-keeping did not bother me. I found it relaxing. And then, when the figures were totted up, the notebook put away, my plate removed, I could sit back, finish my wine and smoke a cigarette. This was the real time of reckoning—no longer of sums to be forwarded every day to Genoa, but of my own motives. How long would it continue? Why was I doing this? What urge drove me, like a stupefied charioteer, on my eternal, useless course?

"We get paid for it, don't we?" said Beppo. "We make good money."

Beppo had a wife and three children in Genoa. Milan—Florence—Rome—Naples—they were all the same to him. A job was a job. Three days off duty at the end of it, home, and bed. He was satisfied. No inner demon broke his rest or asked him questions.

The babble of voices, topped by the barbarians, rose to a roar. My little flock was in full cry. Replete, at ease, their tongues

11

loosened with whatever had filled their glasses, expectant of what the night would bring them—and what could it bring them but a bedding down beside their spouses after peering at buildings old, remote and alien to them, falsely lit for their enjoyment, glimpsed briefly through the windows, steamy with their breath, of a hired coach?—they spilt themselves, for a brief moment, of doubt and care. They were no longer individuals. They were one. They were escaping from all that bound and tied them—but to what?

The waiter bent over me. "The coach is waiting," he said. Ten minutes to nine. Time for them to fetch coats, hats, scarves, powder their faces and relieve themselves. It was not until I had counted the heads, as they climbed into the coach at one minute after nine, that I realised we mustered forty-eight. Two were missing. I checked with the driver—not Beppo, who was free to spend the evening as he pleased, but a man native to the city.

"There were two signore in advance of the rest," he told me. "They walked off together, down the street."

I glanced over my shoulder towards the via Veneto. The Hotel Splendido stands one street away, in comparative peace and quiet, but from the pavement one can see the bright lights and the gay shop-windows, and watch the traffic surge towards the Porta Pinciana. Here, for most women, is greater lure than the Colosseum we were bound for.

"No," said the driver, "they went that way." He pointed left. Then, from around the block, into the via Sicilia, came the hurrying figures. I should have known it. The two retired school-teachers from south London. Forever enquiring, forever critical, they were zealous for reform. It was this couple who had bade me stop the coach on the road to Siena because, they insisted, a man was ill-treating his oxen. It was this couple who, finding a stray cat in Florence, made me waste half-an-hour of our precious time seeking its home. A mother, admonishing her child in Perugia, had been in her turn admonished by the school-teachers. Now, bridling and outraged, they clattered towards me.

"Mr. Fabbio . . . Someone should do something. There's a poor old woman, very ill, humped in the doorway of a church round the corner."

I contained myself with difficulty. The churches of Rome give sanctuary to all beggars, down-and-outs and drunks who care to sprawl upon their steps until such time as the police drive them away.

"Don't concern yourselves, ladies. This is quite usual. The police will see to her. Now hurry, please. The coach is waiting."

"But it's absolutely scandalous. . . . In England we . . ."

I took both women firmly by the arm and propelled them towards the coach. "You are not in England, ladies, you are in Rome. In the city of the emperors oxen, cats, children and the aged receive their just reward. The old woman is lucky in that refuse is no longer fed to the lions."

The school-teachers were still choking with indignation as the coach swept left, past the very church where the woman lay.

"There, Mr. Fabbio, look . . . there!"

Obedient, I nudged the driver. He slowed down, co-operative, to give me a better view. Those passengers who were seated on the right of the coach stared likewise. The streetlamp showed the figure in relief. I have had moments in my life, as has everyone, when something in memory clicks, when we are aware of a sensation of what the French call "déjà vu". Somewhere, some time, and God alone knew when, I had seen that bowed posture, the ample drapery spread, the arms folded, the head buried under the weight of shawls. But not in Rome. My vision lay elsewhere. The memory was childhood's, blotted out by the years between. As we swept forward to the floodlights and the tourist illusion, one of the lovers on the back seat produced a mouth-organ and broke into the strains of a song long stale to the driver and myself, but popular with barbarian and beef—"Arrivederci Roma".

It was some time after midnight when we drew up at the Hotel Splendido once again. My troupe of fifty, yawning, stretching and I trust satisfied, rolled out of the coach one by one and passed through the swing-doors of the hotel. They had by this time as much individuality as machines mass-produced off an assembly line.

I was dead, and longed above all things for bed. Instructions for the morning, last messages, thanks, good-night from all, and it was over. Oblivion for seven hours. The courier could pass out. When, as I thought, the lift doors had closed on the last of them, I sighed, and lit a cigarette. It was the best moment of the day. Then, from behind a pillar where he must have hovered unobserved, stalked the lone middle-aged barbarian. He swung from the hips, as they all do when they walk, in unconscious identification with their coloured brethren.

"How about a night-cap in my room?" he said.

13

"Sorry," I answered curtly, "it's against regulations."

"Ah, come off it," he said, "it's after hours."

He rolled forward, and with a half-glance over his shoulder slipped a note into my hand. "Room 244," he murmured, and went.

I turned through the swing-doors into the street. It had happened before, it would happen again; my rebuff and his consequent hostility would be a factor to be reckoned with throughout the tour. It must be borne. The courtesy I owed to my employers in Genoa forbade complaint. But I was not paid by Sunshine Tours to appease the lust or loneliness of clients.

I walked to the end of the block and stood a moment, drinking the cold air. A car or two passed by and vanished. The traffic hummed behind me in the via Veneto, out of sight. I looked across to the church and the figure lay there still, immobile on the doorstep.

I glanced down at the note in my hand. It was ten thousand lire. A hint, I supposed, of favours to come. I went across the street and bent over the sleeping woman. The furtive odour of stale wine, worn clothes, rose to my nostrils. I fumbled for the hidden hand under the enveloping shawls and put the note into it. Suddenly she stirred. She lifted her head. The features were aquiline and proud, the eyes, once large, were now sunken, and the straggling grey hair fell in strands to her shoulders. She must have travelled from some distance, for she had two baskets beside her containing bread and wine, and yet a further woollen shawl. Once again I was seized with that sense of recognition, that link with the past which could not be explained. Even the hand that, warm despite the cold air, held on to mine in gratitude awakened an involuntary, reluctant response. She stared at me. Her lips moved.

I turned, I think I ran. Back to the Hotel Splendido. If she called to me—and I could have sworn she called—then I would not hear. She had the ten thousand lire, and would find food and shelter in the morning. She had nothing to do with me, nor I with her. The draped figure, suppliant, as though in mourning, was an illusion of my brain, and had no connection with a drunken peasant. At all costs I must sleep. Be fresh for the morning, the visit to St. Peter's, the Vatican, the Sistine Chapel, the Sant' Angelo. . . .

A courier, a charioteer, has no time. No time.

CHAPTER TWO

I AWOKE WITH a start. Had someone called Beo? I turned on the light, got out of bed, drank a glass of water, looked at my watch. It was 2 a.m. I fell back into bed, but the dream was with me still. The bare impersonal hotel bedroom, my clothes flung on the chair, the account book and the itinerary of the tour beside me on the table were part of a day-by-day existence belonging to another world, not the one into which my dreaming self had inadvertently stumbled. Beo. . . . Il Beato, the blessed one. Childhood's name, given me by my parents and by Marta, because, no doubt, I was an afterthought, a later addition to the family circle, there being eight years between my elder brother Aldo and myself.

Beo. . . . Beo. . . . The cry rang in my ears as it had done in my dream, and I could not rid myself of the sense of oppression and fear. Sleeping, I had been a traveller in time, no longer a courier, and hand-in-hand with Aldo I stood in the side-chapel of the church of San Cipriano in Ruffano, staring above me at the altar-piece. The picture was of the Raising of Lazarus, and out of a gaping tomb came the figure of the dead man, still fearfully wrapped in his shroud—all save his face, from which the bindings had somehow fallen away, revealing staring, suddenly awakened eyes, that looked upon his Lord with terror. The Christ, in profile, summoned him with beckoning finger. Before the tomb, in supplication and distress, her arms bowed, her flowing garment spread, lay a woman, supposedly the Mary of Bethany who, often confused with Mary Magdalena, so adored her Master. But to my childish mind she resembled Marta. Marta, the nurse who fed and dressed me every day, who rode me upon her knee, who rocked me in her arms and called me Beo.

This altar-piece haunted me at night, and Aldo knew it. On Sundays and feast-days, when we accompanied our parents and Marta to church, and instead of going to the Duomo worshipped at the parish-church of San Cipriano, it so happened that we stood on the left of the nave, nearest to the chapel. Unconscious, like all parents, of the dread that possessed their child, they never looked to see that my brother, clasping my hand in his, urged me ever nearer to the wide-flung gates of the side-chapel, until I was compelled to lift my head and stare.

"When we go home," whispered Aldo, "I will dress you as Lazarus, and I shall be the Christ and summon you."

This was the worst of all. More full of terror even than the altar-piece itself. For Aldo, searching in the press where Marta kept the soiled linen before putting it to the wash, would drag out our father's night-shirt, limp and crumpled, and drag it over my head. To my fastidious mind there was, in this, some touch of degradation; and to be wrapped in worn clothes belonging to an adult turned my small stomach sour. Nausea rose in me, but there was no time to rebel. I was thrust into the closet above the stairs, and the door shut. This, oddly enough, I did not mind. The closet was spacious, and on the slatted shelves lay the clean, fresh linen, lavender-sweet. Herein spelt safety. But not for long. The handle of the closet turned. The door softly opened. Aldo cried, "Lazarus, come forth!"

So great was my dread, so disciplined to his commands my spirit, that I dared not disobey. I came forth, and the horror was that I did not know whether I should meet with the Christ or with the Devil, for according to Aldo's ingenious theory the two were one, and also, in some manner which he never explained, interchangeable.

Thus at times my brother, robed in a towel as Christ, bearing a walking-stick for crook, beckoned me with a smile, fed me with sweets, put his arms about me, was kind and loving. But at others, wearing the dark shirt of the Fascist Youth organisation to which he belonged and armed with a kitchen fork, he would represent Satan, and proceed to jab me with his weapon. I did not understand why Lazarus, the poor man raised from the dead, should so have earned the Devil's hate, and why his friend, the Christ, should so basely have deserted him; but Aldo, never at a loss, informed me that the play between God and Satan was unending, they tossed for souls as men in the world, and in the cafés of Ruffano, threw at dice. It was not a comforting philosophy.

Back in bed, in the Hotel Splendido, inhaling a cigarette, I wondered why I had been so suddenly transported to that nightmare world where Aldo was my king. It must have been that, as I drank the health of the small newborn barbarian, unconscious memory confounded him with myself, the timid Beato of a former world; and that, when I saw the woman lying on the church steps, the vision of the altar-piece in the San Cipriano chapel, with the Mary who loved both Lazarus and Christ prostrating herself in supplication before the open tomb, returned to me in undiminished force. Whatever the explanation, it was not welcome.

After a while I fell asleep once more, only to plunge into further torment. The altar-piece became associated with another picture, this time in the ducal palace at Ruffano, where our father held the post of Superintendent, a much respected office. This portrait, on display in the duke's bedchamber, and accounted a masterpiece by all lovers of art, had been painted in the early fifteenth century by a pupil of Piero della Francesca. It had for subject the Temptation, and showed Christ standing on the Temple pinnacle. The artist had composed the Temple to resemble one of the twin towers of the ducal palace, the most notable feature of the whole façade that reared itself in beauty above the city of Ruffano. Furthermore, the face of the Christ, gazing out from the portrait to the hills beyond, had been drawn by the daring artist in the likeness of Claudio, the mad duke, named the Falcon, who in a frenzy had thrown himself from the tower, believing, so the story ran, that he was the Son of God.

For centuries this picture had lain in the dusty cellars of the palace, until it was discovered at some period after the Risorgimento, when much reconstruction of the building took place. Forever afterwards it graced—or, as some scandalised inhabitants of Ruffano murmured, disgraced—the ducal apartment. The picture, like the altar-piece in San Cipriano, both shocked and fascinated me, as my brother Aldo was well aware. He would force me to climb with him, without our father's knowledge, the dangerous twisting stairway of the tower, and opening the ancient doorway leading directly to the turret would lift me, with what seemed superhuman strength, on to the encircling balustrade.

"This was where the Falcon stood," Aldo would say. "This was where the Devil tempted him. 'If thou be the Son of God, cast thyself down; for it is written, He shall give his angels charge concerning thee; and in their hands they shall bear thee up, lest at any time thou dash thy foot against a stone'."

Hundreds of feet below lay the city of Ruffano, the distant piazza del Mercato. The people, the moving vehicles, scurried about their business like ants on some lowly, dusty plain. I would cling to the balustrade, trembling. I don't know what age I was. Six, perhaps, or seven.

"Shall I tell you what the Falcon did?" asked Aldo.

"No," I pleaded, "no. . . ."

"He spread out his arms," said Aldo, "and he flew. His arms were wings, he had become a bird. He soared over the rooftops and the city that was his, and the people stared up at him in wonder."

"It isn't true!" I cried. "He couldn't fly. He was not a bird, he was not a falcon. He was a man, and fell. He fell and died. Father told me so."

"He was a falcon," insisted Aldo, "he was a falcon, and he flew."

In my dream the scene of terror I remembered was repeated once again. I clung to the balustrade, Aldo behind me. Then, with greater power than I had possessed as a child, I flung myself backwards, breaking from his grasp, and ran down, down the narrow twisting stair to where Marta waited, calling "Beo . . . Beo . . .". Her arms were there, ready to receive me, and she wrapped herself round me, holding me close, soothing me and comforting me. Marta, dear Marta. Why, though, in the dream, the odour of old, worn clothes? The smell of wine?

This time, on waking, I could feel my heart thumping in my breast, and I was sweating. The nightmare was too vivid to risk a third encounter. I switched on the light, sat up in bed, took up my notebook, and went over the accounts until, dizzy with exhaustion, I fell into a half-doze, and slept without dreaming until the knock on the door at seven announced the floor-waiter with my rolls and coffee.

The routine of the day began. The night, with all its horror, was a world away. The telephone started buzzing, as it always did, and within ten minutes I was involved in all the small technicalities of the hours ahead; the plans of those who wished to spend the morning shopping and join the rest of us at lunch; the queries of those who desired to see St. Peter's but did not want to walk up and down the long galleries of the Vatican. Downstairs to the coach and the waiting Beppo, whose evening, unlike mine, had been spent in the warmth and comfort of his favourite trattoria.

"You know what?" he said. "You and I should change places. You drive the coach, and I make love to the clients."

This was a dig at my morning face, haggard from want of sleep. I told him he would be welcome.

As our cargo mounted, refreshed and eager for the "Rome By Day" that offered herself for their pleasure, I noticed that the lone barbarian, my suitor of last night, now cut me dead.

Our chariot swept left, past the church that had, in fearful fashion, confounded itself with San Cipriano and turned a dream to nightmare. The step was bare, the peasant woman gone. She was even now, I hoped, indulging herself, renewing inward fires with the ten thousand lire I had given her. The retired school-teachers had forgotten her existence. They were already thumbing a guide-book and reading to their neighbours those contents of the Villa Borghese—first stop—that must on no account be missed. I was not surprised to discover them, some twenty minutes later, hurrying past the more conventional statuary, to stare with avid eyes at the reclining hermaphrodite.

On, on, the peace of the Pincio behind us, and so down to the piazza del Popolo, across the Tiber to Sant'Angelo, and thence to St. Peter's and the Vatican. Then, God be thanked, to lunch.

Beppo, wise fellow, ate his in the coach, read the newspaper, slept; but my part was always that of the conductor, and in the restaurant near St. Peter's there was little room or leisure to relax. Mrs. Taylor had already lost her umbrella, left, she thought, in the cloakroom at the Vatican. Would I please see to it as soon as possible? We were due to leave for the Baths of Caracalla at 2 p.m., then back on our tracks to the Forum and a long afternoon amongst the ruins. Here it was my policy to let my charges loose to their own devices.

This afternoon it turned out otherwise. I had rescued the lost umbrella, and was crossing the via della Conciliazione to assemble my group, when I noticed that a handful of them had preceded me and were clustered about Beppo, who was reading to them from an open newspaper. He winked at me, enjoying his role of interpreter. His listeners looked shocked. I observed, with misgiving, that the two school-teachers were in the van.

"What's the excitement?" I asked.

"Murder off the via Sicilia," said Beppo, "within a hundred yards or so of the Hotel Splendido. These ladies claim to have seen the victim."

The most vocal of the school-teachers turned to me, outraged. "It's that poor woman," she said, "it must be the same,

The driver says she was found stabbed on the church steps at five o'clock this morning. We could have saved her. It's too horrible for words."

I was shocked to silence. My aplomb deserted me. I snatched the paper from Beppo and read for myself. The notice was brief.

"The body of a woman was found at five o'clock this morning on the steps of a church on the via Sicilia. She had been stabbed. The woman appeared to be a vagrant, and had been drinking. A few coins only were found in her possession, and the crime would seem to be without motive. The police are seeking anyone who saw the woman, or noticed anything unusual in the vicinity during the hours of darkness, and who may be able to help their enquiries."

I returned the newspaper to Beppo. The group watched for my reaction.

"This is very regrettable," I said, "but not, I'm afraid, altogether unusual. Crimes of violence occur in every city. One can only hope the criminal will soon be caught."

"But we saw her," clamoured the school-teacher. "Hilda and I tried to speak to her, just before nine o'clock. She was not dead then. She was asleep, and breathing heavily. You saw her from the coach as we went by. Everyone saw her. I wanted you to do something then."

Beppo caught my eye and shrugged. He moved discreetly to the coach and climbed into his driving-seat. This was my business to sort out, not his.

"Madam," I said, "I don't wish to be heartless, but as far as we are concerned the incident is closed. There was little we could have done for the woman then. There is nothing now. The police have her case in hand. Now, we are already behind schedule. . . ."

But argument had broken out amongst the group. The remainder of the party joined us, asking what had happened. Passers-by paused, and stared.

"Into the coach," I said firmly. "Into the coach, please, everybody. We are holding up the traffic."

Once seated, babel reigned. The barbarians, Mr. Hiram Bloom their spokesman, were of the opinion that it never helped to meddle in other people's business. You only got abuse. The Anglo-Saxons glowered, especially the two school-teachers from south London. A woman had died on the doorsteps of a church, within a few hundred yards of the Pope's own Vatican City, within earshot of British travellers asleep in bed at the Hotel Splendido, and if the Rome police did not know how to do their job it was time a London bobby came to show them.

"So what?" murmured Beppo in my ear. "The police station, or the Baths of Caracalla?"

Beppo was fortunate. He was not involved. It was otherwise for me. No motive, the paper said, ignorant of the true facts. The woman had been murdered, not for the few coins found in her possession, but for the ten thousand lire I had put into her hand. It was as simple as that. Some roaming vagabond, himself with an empty belly, had stumbled across her in the small hours, pocketed the note, and perhaps arousing her, and suddenly terrified for his own life, had silenced her forever. Our petty criminals have small respect for human life. Who would shed tears over a vagrant, and a drunkard one at that? A hand over her mouth, a quick jab, and away.

"I insist," announced the school-teacher, a note of hysteria in her voice, "in reporting to the police. It's my duty to tell them what I know. It may help them to learn that we saw her in the church porch at nine o'clock. If Mr. Fabbio refuses to go with me, I shall go alone."

Mr. Bloom touched me on the shoulder. "What exactly would it entail?" he said sotto voce. "Any unpleasantness for the rest of the party? Or just a routine statement from you on behalf of these two ladies, and then finish?"

"I don't know," I answered. "Who can ever tell with the police, once they start asking questions?"

I told Beppo to drive on. Dissentient voices rose and fell behind me. Indifferent traffic hemmed us in on either side. Mine must be the decision, for good or ill. One false move and the harmony of my flock would dissolve, and a spirit of ill-feeling and resentment, so fatal to a tour, spring into being.

I reached for my pocket-book and handed a roll of notes to Mr. Bloom.

"If you will be so good," I said, "as to take charge of the party, both at the Baths of Caracallà and at the Forum. There are guides who speak English in both places. Beppo will interpret if there should be any difficulty. You are due at the English Tea Rooms near the piazza di Spagna at four-thirty. I will meet you there."

The school-teacher leant forward. "What are you going to do?" she demanded.

"Conduct you and your friend to the police," I told her.

We were for it. There was no retreat. I told Beppo to set us down at the first taxi rank. The two Samaritans and I watched the coach drive away to the Baths of Caracalla. I had seldom regretted a departure more.

Driving to police headquarters my companions were strangely silent. They had not expected so swift an acquiescence to their plans.

"Will the police officers speak English?" asked the more nervous of the two women.

"I doubt it, madam," I replied. "Would you expect your police officers to speak Italian?"

They exchanged glances. I could sense the hostility that froze them to their seats. Also a deep mistrust of Roman law. Police headquarters are forbidding in any city, but I disliked the mission far more than they, to whom, no doubt, it could be counted as an experience of tourism. The sight of uniform, any uniform, makes me want to run. The tramp of feet, the brisk word of command, the cold speculative eye, have disagreeable associations; they remind me of my youth.

We alighted at our destination and I told the taxi to wait. I warned him, speaking clearly so that my companions could understand, that we might be hours.

Our feet sounded hollow as we crossed the courtyard to the police-station within. We were passed from the enquiry-desk to a waiting-room, from the waiting-room to an inner office, where the officer on duty asked our names, addresses, and the nature of our business. On my informing him that the English ladies wished to give information about the woman found murdered on the steps of the church in the via Sicilia, he stared. Then he struck a bell and snapped an order to the man who entered. The atmosphere was chill. After a moment two more police officers entered. Notebooks were produced. All three stared at the now subdued school-teachers. I explained to the officer behind the desk that neither spoke Italian. They were English tourists, I the courier in charge of Sunshine Tours.

"If you have any information material to last night's murder, please give it," he said curtly. "We have no time to waste."

The elder of the two Englishwomen began to speak, pausing,

between sentences, for me to act as her interpreter. I used my own discretion as to what to omit in her somewhat incoherent tale. The remark that it seemed to her and her friend disgraceful that in these modern times there was no hospital or asylum in Rome for a starving woman to go to would hardly interest the police.

"You actually touched the woman?" asked the officer.

"Yes," replied the school-teacher. "I touched her shoulder and spoke. She grunted. I felt that she might be ill, and so did my friend. We hurried back to the coach and asked Mr. Fabbio here to do something. He said it was not our business, and we were keeping the coach waiting."

The police officer questioned me with a glance. I replied that it was true. And that the time was just after nine p.m.

"And when you returned from the tour you did not notice whether the woman was still there?" he asked her through my interpretation.

"I'm afraid not. The coach did not pass that way, and we were all very tired."

"In fact, the subject was not mentioned again?"

"No. Actually, my friend and I did bring it up when we were undressing. We said what a disgraceful thing it was that Mr. Fabbio had not called an ambulance or informed the police."

Once again the officer glanced in my direction. I thought I detected sympathy. "Will you please thank these ladies for having come forward?" he said. "Their testimony has been helpful. For the records, I must trouble them to identify the clothing worn by the murdered woman, if they can do so."

I had not expected this. Nor had my charges. They turned a little pale.

"Is it necessary?" faltered the younger of the two.

"It appears so," I said.

We followed one of the police officers down a corridor and through to a small room. A white-coated attendant came forward, and after a moment's explanation went to an inner sanctum and brought forth a bundle of clothing and two baskets. My charges turned paler still.

"Yes," said the elder hurriedly, turning aside her head, "yes, I feel sure those were the things. How very dreadful it all is . . ."

The white-coated attendant, officious in his capacity as ghoul, asked if the ladies wished to view the body.

23

"No," I said, "they are not required to do so. The clothes are identification enough. However, if it would help at all with the enquiry, I am willing to do so on their behalf."

The police agent with us shrugged his shoulders. It was up to me. Neither of the two school-teachers knew what was being discussed. I passed with the attendant into the mortuary. Drawn by some painful and disturbing fascination, I approached the slab on which the body lay. The attendant drew back the covering, revealing the face. It was noble in repose, and younger than it had seemed last night.

I turned away. "Thank you," I said to the attendant.

I informed the officer in charge, on returning to the interview room, that the ladies had recognised the clothes. He thanked them once again.

"I assume," I said, "that these ladies will not be required for further questioning? We leave for Naples tomorrow afternoon."

Gravely the officer noted the fact in his report. "I do not anticipate," he said, "that we shall need their presence again. We have their names and addresses. I wish the ladies and yourself a pleasant resumption of your tour."

I could have sworn that after bowing to the school-teachers his eyelid flickered for an instant in a wink; but not at them, at me.

"Any clue to the victim's identity?" I asked.

He shrugged. "There are hundreds such, as you know, who wander into the city from outside. They are hard to check. Nothing on her of value. The murderer may have been a fellow-vagrant with some motive of revenge, or else a prowler, doing it for kicks. We'll pick him up."

We were dismissed. We walked back, across the courtyard, to the waiting taxi. I handed the ladies in. "The English Tea Rooms," I told the driver.

I looked at my watch. I had judged the time correctly. My charges could settle peacefully to a cup of tea together before the remainder of the party came. When we arrived I paid the taxi off and escorted the pair inside the English Tea Rooms. I settled them at a corner table.

"Now, ladies," I said, "you can relax."

My automatic smile brought no response, save a stiff inclination of the head.

I went out, and walked down the via dei Condotti to a bar. I had to think. I kept seeing the aquiline features, sharpened by

24

death, of the murdered woman. Murdered because I had put ten thousand lire into her hand.

I felt sure now I had not been mistaken. There had been recognition in her eyes the night before, and she had called Beo as I ran away across the street. I had not seen her for over twenty years, but it was Marta.

CHAPTER THREE

WHEN THE POLICE officers were questioning the English school-teachers—I should have spoken then. The opportunity was given me. They had asked whether, when we returned from our tour, we had noticed that the woman was still on the doorstep of the church. This had been the moment. "Yes," I should have said, "yes, I walked to the end of the street and she was there, and I crossed over and put a note for ten thousand lire in her hand."

I could imagine the look of surprise in the police officer's eyes. "A note for ten thousand lire?"

"Yes."

"What time was this?"

"Shortly after midnight."

"Did any of the party see you?"

"No."

"Was the money your own, or did it belong to Sunshine Tours?"

"It had just been given me. A mark of favour."

"You mean a tip?"

"Yes."

"By one of your clients?"

"Yes. But if you ask him, he will deny it."

Then the police officer would have asked for the two English ladies to withdraw. The interrogation would have continued, harder pressed. Not only could I never summon a witness to the fact that the lone barbarian had given me the money and had asked me to his room, but I could not produce a motive for giving away the money that would make sense to the police officer. Nothing made sense.

"You say you were reminded of an altar-piece that frightened you as a child?"

"Yes."

"And because of that you decided to put ten thousand lire into an unknown woman's hand?"

"It happened so quickly. I did not have time to think."

"I suggest to you that you never did have a note for ten

thousand lire in your possession, and that you are now inventing this story of putting such a note into the woman's hand because you imagine it will give you an alibi."

"An alibi for what?"

"An alibi for the murder itself."

I paid for my drink and went into the street. It had begun to rain. Umbrellas sprouted like mushrooms to right and left. Girls with splashed legs bumped into me. Tourists, taken by surprise, stood huddled in doorways. My school-teachers were safe in the English Tea Rooms, and with this weather, which had threatened all afternoon, Mr. Hiram Bloom would have mustered his party from the Forum and taken them back to Beppo and the waiting coach.

I turned up my coat collar, pulled my hat low and threaded my way through side streets to the via del Tritone and the Rome office of Sunshine Tours. It was almost four, and with any luck my comrade Giovanni might be back at his desk, though he liked to spin out the afternoon break. I was lucky. He was at his usual place in the far corner, speaking down the inevitable telephone. He saw me, raised his hand in greeting and pointed to a chair. The office was comparatively empty, save for a handful of tourists pressing patiently against the centre grille, demanding changes of reservations, hotel bookings, the usual routine.

Giovanni hung up, shook hands with me, and smiled. "Shouldn't you be in Naples?" he said. "No—what am I saying—Naples tomorrow, happily for you and your little bunch. Rome becomes more impossible every day. Good trip?"

"So-so. I can't grumble. Barbarian and beef, all very amiable."

"Girls good-looking?"

"Nothing to raise the blood-pressure. Anyway, do we have time? You try a courier's job."

He laughed and shook his head. "Well, what can I do for you?"

"Giovanni . . . I want your help. I'm in trouble."

He expressed sympathy.

"I want you to find a substitute for me to take the tour on to Naples," I said.

He exploded. "Impossible! Quite impossible in the time. I have no one here in Rome. Besides, head office . . ."

"Head office needn't know. At least, not immediately. Giovanni, surely you can rustle up someone? Supposing I had appendicitis?"

27

"Have you appendicitis?"

"No, but I can invent one if it will help."

"It won't help. I tell you, Armino, there is nothing I can do—we don't have substitutes hanging about in the office here just because you want a vacation."

"Listen to me, Giovanni. I don't want a vacation. I want you to put me on a northern route. Work an exchange. Just a temporary one, of course. I must go north."

"You mean Milan?"

"No . . . Any tour going towards the Adriatic will do."

"It's too early for the Adriatic, you know that. Nobody goes to the Adriatic until May."

"Well, then, not necessarily a coach, a tour, but a private client, who might consider Ravenna, Venice."

"Too early for Venice too."

"It's never too early for Venice. Giovanni, please."

He began to ruffle through some papers on the desk in front of him. "I can't promise anything. Something may turn up before tomorrow, but time is short. You take off for Naples at 1400 hours tomorrow, and unless I can arrange a double switch it won't work."

"I know, I know. But try."

"It's a woman, I suppose?"

"Of course it's a woman."

"And she can't wait?"

"Let us put it that I can't wait."

He sighed, and picked up his telephone. "If I have any news I'll leave a message at the Splendido for you to ring me. The things we do for our friends. . . ."

I left him, and made my way back to the English Tea Rooms. The rain had ceased and the sun glittered on all of us pedestrians so suddenly reprieved. If Giovanni could not work the transfer, that was that. I had made the gesture. Gesture towards what? I did not know. Appeasement of the dead, perhaps, or my own conscience. I could still be wrong, the murdered woman not Marta. If so, although in my own mind I was an accessory to her death because I had placed the ten thousand lire in her hand, I was absolved from heavier guilt. If Marta, no. The cry of Beo made me a murderer too, in every sense as guilty as the criminal, as the thief who used the knife.

When I arrived in the piazza di Spagna I saw that my flock

had finished tea and were about to mount the coach. I went to join them. I could tell, by the inflated appearance of the school-teachers, that they had recounted their tale. They were the heroines of their brief hour.

No message from Giovanni that evening at the hotel, and after dinner, a replica of the preceding night, but this time with speeches, we crossed over in the relief coach to Trastevere, so that my little flock could glimpse for an hour or so the café life that it pleased them to think was native to the area.

"This is the real Rome," breathed Mrs. Hiram Bloom, seating herself at a cramped table in a side-street outside a taverna brightly lit with pseudo-lanterns for her innocent enjoyment. Six musicians, wearing breeches, stockings and Neapolitan caps, appeared with beribboned guitars as if by magic, and my little party swayed in sympathy to their rhythmic strains. There was something endearing in their innocence and pleasure. I felt almost sad that tomorrow, perhaps, they would all be in Naples, no longer in my care. A shepherd has his moments. . . .

No message from Giovanni at the hotel desk when we returned. Nevertheless I slept, and this night, God be thanked, without a single dream.

A call came through from Giovanni a few minutes after nine. "Armino," he said quickly, "look, I think I've fixed it. Two Tedeschi in a Volkswagen, going north. They want an interpreter. You speak German, don't you?"

"I do."

"Seize on to it, then. Herr Turtmann and his frau. Ugly as sin, both clutching maps and guide-books. They don't care where they go, as long as it's north. Sight-seeing fanatics."

"What about my substitute?"

"All arranged. You know my brother-in-law?"

"You have several."

"This one used to work in the American Express. He knows all the answers, and he's raring to go to Naples. He's all right. We can trust him."

I had a moment's doubt. Would Giovanni's brother-in-law botch the trip? Did he know how to handle people? And even if it worked, when the head office in Genoa learnt about the transfer would I lose my job?

"Listen, Giovanni, are you sure?"

He sounded impatient. "Look, take it or leave it. I'm doing

you a favour, aren't I? I don't care either way. My brother-in-law is all set, and he's coming up to see you right away so that you can brief him. And I must let Herr Turtmann know. He wants to be off by ten-thirty."

I had just under an hour-and-a-half to hand over to my replacement, get myself down to the office and meet my new clients. It would be a near thing.

"Agreed," I told Giovanni, and hung up.

I drank a second cup of cold coffee and threw my few things into their case. At twenty minutes to ten Giovanni's brother-in-law knocked on the door. I remembered him at once. Eager, with a fine show of talk, I doubted if he carried indigestion tablets for queasy Anglo-Saxon stomachs, or would take an interest in the Bloom grandson. No matter. A courier can't have everything. We sat down side by side on my rumpled bed and I showed him my notes and the itinerary of the tour, plus the passenger-list, to which I added a short description of the idiosyncrasies of each client.

We left the room together, and I let my replacement go over to the reception desk and explain his status. I shook hands and wished him a good trip. As I passed through the swing-doors of the hotel into the street I felt like a nurse running out on her charges. The sensation was peculiar. I had never ratted on a tour before.

A taxi dropped me at the office in the via del Tritone, and as soon as I entered I saw Giovanni wearing his official face, all smiles and courtesy, talking to what were clearly my future clients. There was no mistaking their nationality. Both were middle-aged. Both carried ciné-cameras. He was a large, square-shouldered fellow, with stiff hair like the bristles of a clothes-brush and gold-rimmed spectacles. She was sallow, with hair piled-up under a hat a size too small for her. She wore, for no good reason, long white socks that contrasted with her dark top-coat. I came forward. He shook hands.

"My wife and I are keen photographers," announced Herr Turtmann as soon as Giovanni had introduced us. "We like to photograph in motion, from the car. We understand you can drive."

"Certainly, if you wish it," I said.

"Excellent. Then we can be off at once."

Giovanni bowed at them both, all smiles. Then he winked at me. "I wish you a pleasant trip," he said.

We took a taxi to where they had parked the Volkswagen. The roof was piled high with luggage, as was half the rear seat. The Tedeschi never travel light, and they accumulate possessions as they go.

"You will drive," commanded Herr Turtmann. "My wife and I wish to take pictures as we leave Rome. I leave the choice of route to you, but we should like to pass through Spoleto. They give two stars in my guide-book to the cathedral square."

I settled myself in the driving-seat, Herr Turtmann beside me, his wife tucked away in the back. As we crossed the Tiber they both held ciné-cameras to their eyes, moving them slowly from side to side like a machine-gunner sweeping his field of fire.

When the shooting ceased, which it did from time to time, they fed themselves copiously from paper bags and drank coffee from an outsize thermos flask. They talked little, and the silence suited me. It needed all my attention to pass the lorries on the road, and we had some two hundred and sixty kilometres to cover before we reached the destination I had in mind.

"And tonight?" asked Herr Turtmann suddenly. "Where do we sleep tonight?"

"We sleep at Ruffano," I said.

He rustled the pages of the guide-book on his lap. "There are several monuments with three stars, Gerda," he said over his shoulder to his wife. "We can shoot them all. Ruffano will suit us well."

It was both fitting and ironic that, having left the city where I was born and had spent the first eleven years of childhood in the company of one German, I should return to it more than twenty years later with another. Now, in March, the rolling countryside was purple-grey, stark and uninviting, the sky threatening the snow that had fallen in Florence; then, in the glazed, hot July of '44, the roads north out of Ruffano had been dusty white. The army trucks and vehicles on our route had given way to the Commandant's Mercedes, the flag fluttering from the bonnet. At times, aware of the car's importance, the weary drivers in the trucks would stiffen themselves into a salute, occasionally acknowledged by the Commandant within. If he was too indolent, I saluted for him. It helped to pass the journey, prevented me from feeling sick, and spared me the spectacle of watching my beautiful slut of a mother feeding her conqueror with grapes. Her

31

frequent rather silly laughter, merged with his, offended my sense of what was due to adult dignity.

"I see," remarked Herr Turtmann to his wife, "that in the ducal palace in Ruffano they have the remarkable portrait of the Temptation of Christ, considered blasphemous until quite recently. I always thought it had been removed by our people in the war for safer housing."

I did not tell him that I had watched my father, the Superintendent, and his assistants crate the picture with great care and store it, with some others, in the cellars of the palace, for fear of any such eventuality.

My clients were amenable to a brief snack in Spoleto, with a swift shooting of the piazza and the Duomo façade, and we pressed on through Foligno and beyond, our road forever curling, twisting, amongst the rolling hills, while ahead the mountains, snow-covered, gave warning that my home, some five hundred metres high, might be in the grip of winter still. The first snow-flakes fell, or rather we ran into them as we came up from the south; they must have been falling all day. The sky became a pall. The rivers, swollen with the coursing mountain streams, roared through the ravines beside us.

It was nearing seven when I had my first sight of home. To the traveller coming from Rome the city suddenly emerges, cresting the two hills, dwarfing the valleys below. I could not remember ever seeing it under snow. It was magnificent. Forbidding also, as if to warn the intrepid traveller—enter at your peril. How little changed, dear God, how little changed.

Herr Turtmann and his wife, risking the drifting snow, held cameras to the open windows of the car, and for their benefit, as well as to satisfy my own pride, I circled the valley just beneath the walls, to enter by the western gate, the porta del Sangue—the Gate of Blood.

"And rightly so," my father used to say, "since it was through here that Claudio, the first duke, drove his captives to their death."

Snow banked the road as it curved upward, lay thick upon the roof-tops, made phantoms of the trees, and, crowning the minarets of the twin towers of the palace and the Duomo and campanile beyond, turned my city into legend, into dream. I had forgotten there could be such beauty still.

I drove up the via dei Martiri to the city's centre, the piazza

32

della Vita, and there braked. Nothing had altered, save the falling snow that had turned the city dumb, driving the inhabitants within doors. The buildings, a blend of ochre and musty pink, enfolded the piazza, their symmetry broken by the five converging streets. Blank windows above the colonnades stared down on the cobbled stones, their shutters fastened. The shops were closed. I recognised the names. The bookshop, the pharmacy, they were still the same. Dominating all, the shabby, sprawling Hotel dei Duchi, where, as a child, it had been a treat to lunch on Sundays. But later, when it was the Commandant's headquarters, entry was barred. Then, sentries had stood to attention before the door, or stamped their feet. Staff-cars and dispatch-riders' motor-cycles had been drawn up where now I parked Herr Turtmann's Volkswagen. Memory, dammed for over twenty years, was in full spate, and I was flooded by a wave of feeling.

I pushed open the door of the hotel and looked about me, hardly knowing what it was I sought—whether the office of the Commandant, the click of typewriters, or the reception lounge with stiff-backed chairs on which my father and his friends drank Cinzano after Mass. I think it was the last. And the last greeted me, though modernised into some semblance of a tourists' bar, with picture postcard racks, magazines upon the table, and a television-set in the far corner.

The silence was profound. I struck a bell that pealed alarmingly. In old days the proprietor, Signor Longhi, and his wife Rosa were always there to greet my father. He was bright-eyed, kindly, and walked—if I remembered rightly—with a limp; he had been wounded as a young man in the first world war. His wife Rosa, vivacious, plump, had been a redhead. She and my mother used to chatter trivialities, and when my mother was not present Signora Longhi would flirt, though mildly, with my proud father.

Now, in answer to my summons, a little maid appeared. Flustered, she said she thought we could have rooms, but she must first ask the padrona. A loud voice called from above. The padrona herself descended, slowly, because of excessive weight, and wheezing as she came. The eyes, darkly pouched, peered out at me from flabby cheeks; her hair was the streaky auburn of a poor provincial dye. I recognised, with a shock, a middle-aged Signora Longhi.

"You want rooms tonight?" she asked, looking upon me with indifference.

I explained the needs of the Turtmanns and myself and turned away from her, disenchanted. I went out into the snow to fetch my clients and their luggage. The flustered maid, the only apparent porter, followed me. It was out of season, of course, and yet. . . . Somehow the welcome had not been auspicious. The Turtmanns, unmoved, checked in and tramped upstairs, watched by the yawning padrona. The little boy to whom she had once fed sweetmeats was long forgotten.

I saw the Turtmanns settled into a room on the second floor and found the way to my own, a small room overlooking the piazza. Despite the falling snow I unfastened the shutters, opened the windows and stood a moment, drinking the sharp air.

I felt as a phantom would, returning after death. The indifferent buildings slumbered. Suddenly the campanile by the Duomo tolled out the hour. The note, deep-toned, was echoed in a moment by the varying notes from the other churches. San Cipriano, San Michele, San Martino, Sant'Agata, I knew them all, I recognised them all, with the thin high note of San Donato on the hill below the ducal palace the last to sound. This had been the moment when I said my prayers at Marta's knee. I fastened the window, closed the shutters, and found my way to the dining-room below.

CHAPTER FOUR

Herr Turtmann and his wife were already eating. They gave no sign for me to join them, and thankfully I sat down at a small table near the serving screen. Another maid, less flustered than her fellow, served as waitress, directed from time to time by the padrona herself, who would come from behind the screen to stare at us, rasp out an order, then disappear. Every mouthful that I ate, each draught of the rough local wine, raisin-coloured, which filled my carafe induced nostalgia. The centre table, laid for a dozen through long custom, was where Aldo had celebrated his fifteenth birthday. Handsome as a stripling god, he raised his glass to our parents, thanking them for the honour they had done him, while the surrounding guests applauded and I, the sibling, stared. My father, fated to die of pneumonia in an Allied prison-camp, toasted his first-born with a smile. My mother, radiant in a lime-green dress, preened her maternal feathers, kissing her hand to husband and to son. The Commandant had not yet loomed on her horizon.

I poured out the last of the wine from my carafe, and as I did so, like an echo to my thoughts, a little, white-haired old man came limping from behind the screen, bearing an illustrated magazine which he took to the Turtmanns' table. He pointed with pride to the leading feature, an article on Ruffano, and to a photograph of himself, the proprietor, Signor Longhi. He left the supplement with the Turtmanns and limped back to my corner.

"Good evening, signore," he said. "I hope everything has been to your satisfaction?"

He had a nervous tremor in his left hand, and this he tried to hide by placing the hand behind his back. It was, I supposed, an ailment of old age; the eager, bright-eyed Signor Longhi was no more. I thanked him for his trouble, and he bowed and disappeared behind the screen, his eyes sweeping over me without recognition. I could not expect otherwise. Why should anyone connect the insignificant courier of today with Signor Donati's youngest of long ago,—"Il Beato" whom adults patted on the head? We were all forgotten, we had all passed on. . . .

Dinner finished, and the Turtmanns escorted to their room, I fetched my coat, opened the front door of the Hotel dei Duchi, and went out into the piazza. Silence, white and still, enveloped me. There were footsteps in the snow, at first clear and firmly printed, the tracks of an individual which soon lost themselves against a drift and vanished. The biting air penetrated my light-weight overcoat. Winter's invasion of spring had caught me, like any other tourist, ill-prepared.

I looked to right and left, forgetting, after more than twenty years, how the main street divided into two on either side of the piazza, each branch to run, almost perpendicular it seemed, to its own summit. I struck left, hazarding a guess, past the great bulk of San Cipriano which loomed at me out of the snow, and immediately knew I was at fault, for the street ran broad and steep, and would emerge eventually on the north-western hill in front of the statue of Duke Carlo. Carlo the Good, the younger brother of mad Claudio, who in his reign of forty years, loved and respected, rebuilt his palace and his city and made Ruffano famous. I turned back to the piazza and struck south up the narrow twisting street to where it opened, suddenly, into the piazza Maggiore, and there, in all its majesty, stood the ducal palace of my boyhood, of my dreams, the rose-pink walls touched by the falling snow.

Idiot tears pricked my eyes—I, the courier, moved like any tourist by a picture-postcard print—and I moved forward, still in a dream, and touched the walls I knew. Here was the entrance door to the quadrangle within, used by my father the Super-intendent and ourselves, Aldo and I, but never by the visiting crowds. There were the steps on which I used to jump, and here, beyond, the massive façade of the Duomo, rebuilt in the eight-eenth century. Icicles had formed on the fountain in the piazza, hanging like crystals from the lips of the bronze cherubs. I used to drink at this fountain, inspired by a tale of Aldo's that it held all purity and many secrets in its clear waters; if there were secrets, I learnt none of them. I lifted my head to the palace roof and saw brooding there, above the entrance door, the great bronze figure of the Falcon, emblem of the Malebranche, the ducal family, his head snow-capped, his giant wings outspread. Then I turned from the palace and walked on, uphill, past the university, and turned left into the via dei Sogni, the Street of Dreams. No one stirred, not even a prowling cat. Now it was my footprints only that marked the fallen snow, and when I came to the high walls that enclosed my father's house, with the single tree crowning the small garden, a cold wind like a knife cut across the narrow street, so that the snow, still featherlight, drifted in front of me.

Once more I had the strange impression that I was a ghost returned, or not even a ghost, some disembodied spirit of long ago, and that there, in the darkened house, Aldo and I lay sleeping. We used to share a room, until he was promoted to one of his own. Not a chink of light showed tonight from the fastened shutters. I wondered who lived there now, if indeed the house was inhabited at all. Somehow it seemed to me forlorn, reproachful. And the garden wall I always thought so high had shrunk. I crept away like a furtive alley-cat, down past the church of San Martino, and took the short cut of the San Martino steps, descending abruptly to the piazza della Vita once again. I had not, on my reconnaissance, encountered a single soul.

I let myself in at the hotel and went up to my room, undressed, and so to bed. A hundred images raced through my mind, crossing and re-crossing like routes converging on an autostrada. Some memorable, some dim. The present intermingled with the past, my father's face became confused with Aldo's, the very uniforms they had worn when I had seen them last. The uniform which had graced Aldo at nineteen, with the pilot's wings, merged into those of my mother's lovers—the German Commandant, the American Brigadier in Frankfurt with whom we lived for two years. Even the head waiter at the Splendido, a passing acquaintance glimpsed a dozen times and never thought of, turned into the bank manager my mother eventually married, my stepfather Enrico Fabbio of Turin, who gave me an education and a name. Too many faces, too many passing strangers, too many hotel bedrooms, hired apartments; none of them mine, nothing I called home. Life an unending journey with no end, flight without purpose. . . .

A shrill bell ringing in the corridor awakened me, and when I turned on my light I saw that it was morning, eight o'clock. I flung back my shutters. The snow had ceased and the sun was shining. Below me in the piazza della Vita people were going about their business. Shops had opened up, the assistants were sweeping away the snow; the familiar long-forgotten pattern of morning in Ruffano had taken on its accustomed shape. The sharp clean smell of the piazza came to my nostrils, the smell I remembered. A woman shook a mat out of a window. A group of men, standing beneath me, argued. A dog, with tail erect, chased a streaking cat, narrowly missed by a swerving car. More traffic than of old, or was it that in war only the military moved? I had no recollection of police on point duty, but one of them stood there now with arm outstretched, directing the cars across the piazza to the via Rossini and the ducal palace. The young were everywhere, on vespas or on foot, all southward bound, up the hill, and it came to me, with surprise, that the small university of my childhood must have expanded and that the ducal palace, once Ruffano's pride, perhaps no longer reigned supreme.

I turned from the window, dressed, and went along to the dining-room for coffee, thinking to spare the flustered maid an errand. Signor Longhi brought me a tray himself, setting the coffee on the table with tembling hands.

"My apologies, signore," said the old man. "We are short-staffed, and are having alterations to the kitchen before the season opens."

I had been aware since waking of thuds and knocking, the voices of workmen calling to one another, the smell of paint, of mortar.

"Have you owned the hotel long?" I asked him.

"Ah yes," he answered, with some of the eagerness I remembered, "over thirty years, with a break during the Occupation. We had a staff headquarters here for a time. My wife and I went to Ancona. The Hotel dei Duchi was patronised by many well-known people in old days, writers, politicians. I can show you. . . ."

He limped towards a bookcase in the far corner, opened it and removed a visitors' book, which he carried back to my table as tenderly as he would a new-born infant. It opened automatically at a certain page.

"The English Minister, Stanley Baldwin, honoured us once," he said, pointing to the signature. "He stayed one night, was sorry not to stay more. The American film star Gary Cooper—there, on the next page. He was to have made a film here, but nothing came of it."

He turned the pages proudly for my inspection, '36, '37, '38, '39, '40, the years of my childhood, and an impulse rose in me to say, "And Signor Donati, the Superintendent at the palace, you remember him, and the signora? You remember Aldo at fifteen? Do you remember Beo, the small Beato, so small for his age that they took him for four, not seven? Well, here he is. Still small, still insignificant."

I controlled the impulse and went on drinking coffee. Signor Longhi continued to turn the pages of his visitors' book—omitting, I noticed, the years of shame—and so on to the fifties and the sixties, with no more ministers, no more film-stars, the pages filled with the names of a hundred tourists, English, American, German, Swiss, the passing clientèle who came and went, the kind I took under my wing on Sunshine Tours.

A rasping voice summoned him from behind the screen, and he limped away to do his wife's bidding. Furtively, my eye on the screen, I turned to '44, and there it was, bold, with a flourish, the signature of the Commandant, and the months when he made the hotel his staff headquarters. The remaining page was a blank. The Longhis had departed to Ancona... I snapped the book to and carried it to the bookcase. That was the place for mementos of the past. The Commandant, with his arrogant step, his bullying voice that swiftly, all too swiftly, thickened to sickly sentiment, he was better under lock and key. But for him and his symbolic presence—a conqueror conquered, a feather in her cap—my mother and I, with my father dead in a prison camp and Aldo shot down in flames, might have gone to Ancona with the Longhis. There had been talk of it. And then? Fruitless speculation. She would have picked another lover on the coast and wandered anyway, trailing her "Beato" with her.

"Are you ready?"

I turned my head. Herr Turtmann and his wife were standing in the doorway, overcoated, booted, strung about with their camera impedimenta.

"At your service, Herr Turtmann."

It was their intention to see the ducal palace and then drive out of Ruffano and pursue their tour north. I helped them stack the luggage and Herr Turtmann gave me the money to pay the bill. Signora Longhi counted the notes, returned the change and yawned. If my mother had not died of cancer of the womb in '56 she would have looked like Rosa Longhi. Her figure too had spread. Her hair was dyed also. Whether from disillusion or because of her illness, she used to scold my stepfather Enrico

39

Fabbio in much the rasping way that the padrona here scolded her lame husband.

"Do you have much competition in Ruffano?" I asked, folding Herr Turtmann's bill.

"The Hotel Panorama," she answered shrugging. "Built three years ago. Everything modern. On the other hill, near the piazza del Duca Carlo. How can we hope to keep going in this dump? My husband is old. I'm tired. The place is beyond us."

Her epitaph spoken, she slumped behind the desk. I went out to join the Turtmanns in the car, another slice of childhood written off.

We left the piazza della Vita and drove up the narrow via Rossini to park outside the ducal palace. Morning had brought reality to my dream world of the preceding night. Other cars were stationed between our destination and the Duomo, pedestrians came and went, vespas roared past us to the university beyond.

At the entrance, a uniformed attendant leant from a boxed-in office. "Do you want a guide?" he called.

I shook my head. "I know where I am," I said.

Our footsteps echoed on the stone floor. I led the way through to the quadrangle, once more a ghost, a wanderer in time. This was where I used to shout, my voice reverberating to the arched colonnade.

"Aldo? Aldo? Wait for me!"

Back would come the answering echo. "I'm here. Follow me. . . ."

I followed now, up the grand staircase to the gallery above, while in every niche and vault stood the Malebranche falcon and the letters "C.M." for the two dukes, Claudio and Carlo. The Turtmanns stumped after me. We paused a moment in the gallery for them to draw breath, and the bench was there, the bench on which Marta used to sit and do her knitting, while I ran backwards and forwards along the gallery in front of her, or sometimes, greatly daring—if Aldo was not there to pounce upon me—travelled the whole circuit, pausing now and again to stare through the great windows that looked down upon the quadrangle below.

"Well?" said Herr Turtmann, staring at me. I withdrew my eyes from the gallery, with its empty bench, and turned right, into the throne room. Oh, God . . . that musty, sullen smell,

40

redolent of ages past, of ancient feuds, of dukes and duchesses long dead, of courtiers, pages. . . . The smell of vaulted ceilings, ochre walls, the heavy, dusty scent of tapestry.

The dead were with me as I walked the familiar room. Not only the spectres of the history I had learnt, the mad Duke Claudio, the beloved Carlo, the gracious duchess and her retinue of ladies; my own dead were beside me too. My father, gracious as a duke himself, showing the palace to visiting historians from Rome or Florence; Marta, shushing if I raised my voice, coaxing me out of earshot of the distinguished guests; Aldo, above all Aldo. Advancing on tiptoe, his finger to his lips.

"He's waiting!"

"Who's waiting?"

"The Falcon. . . . To seize you in his claws, and carry you off."

A babble of sound came from behind me. A party of young people, students doubtless, escorted by a woman lecturer, noised their way into the throne room with us, filling the whole place with their presence. Even the Turtmanns were disturbed. I beckoned them on to the reception rooms beyond. A uniformed guide, stifling his yawn, approached my clients, scenting the prospect of largesse. He had a smattering of English, and took my Tedeschi for barbarians.

"Note-a the ceiling," he said, "the ceiling very fine. Restored by Tolomeo."

I left him to it and slipped away. Ignoring the duchess's apartments I headed for the Room of the Cherubs and the ducal bedchamber. They were empty. An attendant on a window-seat slumbered in a far corner.

Little was changed. Palaces, unlike people, withstand the years. Only the pictures had been moved, brought from their war-time sojourn in the cellars to be displayed now, so I grudgingly admitted, to greater advantage than in my father's day. They were placed more correctly, where the light could play upon them. The Madonna and Child, my mother's favourite, instead of hanging on the wall in comparative obscurity, stood upon an easel, alone in tranquil grandeur. The dull marble busts of a later age, which were in old days grouped about the room, had been removed. There was nothing now to detract from the Madonna. The attendant opened an eye. I went towards him.

"Who is the Superintendent here?" I asked.

"There is no Superintendent," he replied. "The palace is under

41

the supervision of the Arts Council of Ruffano—that is to say the ducal apartments, the pictures, tapestries, and the rooms above. The library on the ground floor is used by members of the university."

"Thank you," I said.

I passed on before he could point out to me the dancing cherubs on the chimney-piece. There was a time when I had names for every one of them. I entered the ducal bedchamber, searching instinctively for the picture on the wall, the "Temptation of Christ" of which Herr Turtmann had spoken to his frau. It was still there. No Arts Council could place this one on an easel.

Unhappy Christ, or, as the artist with ingenious candour had painted him, unhappy Claudio. . . . He stood in his saffron shift, one hand upon his hip, staring at nothing—unless it was at the roof-tops of his visionary world, the world that might be his, should Temptation master him. The Devil, in the guise of friend and counsellor, whispered his message. Behind him the rosy sky foretold a triumphant dawn. The city of Ruffano slept, ready to stir and wake and do his bidding.

"All these things will I give thee, if thou wilt fall down and worship me."

I had forgotten that his eyes were pallid like his golden hair, and that the hair itself, framing the pale face, resembled thorns.

A wave of voices sounded in the rear. The Turtmanns and their persuasive guide, the students and the lecturer were hard upon me. I slipped through to the audience chamber, knowing that the pursuing babblers would not only dally before the picture I had left, but would turn aside to visit the ducal study, the ducal chapel. By slipping a few hundred lire into the guide's hand the Turtmanns might even be permitted a glimpse of the spiral stair-case leading to the tower above.

Here in the audience chamber was the hidden entrance to the second tower. The spiral stairway of this one, though a replica of the other, was never in my father's day considered safe. Those tourists who were intrepid enough to brace their muscles and brave vertigo were conducted to the right-hand tower, through the ducal dressing-room.

I went to the wall and lifted the concealing tapestry. The door-way was still there, the key within the lock. I turned it, the door opened. Before me was the stair, curving ever upward to the tower above, below me the descent, three hundred steps or more, to the abyss below. How long was it, I wondered, since anyone had climbed this stair? Cobwebs smeared the little leaded window, and dead flies. The old fear, the old fascination gripped me. I put my hand upon the cold stone step, preparatory to climbing.

"Who is there? It is forbidden to mount the stair!"

I looked over my shoulder. The guide I had left sleeping in the Room of the Cherubs had followed and stood staring at me, his beady eyes narrowed in suspicion.

"What are you doing? How did you get there?" he asked.

I felt the guilt of years. For such an act my father would have commanded bed, and bed without supper, unless it was smuggled up to me by Marta.

"I'm sorry," I said. "I chanced to look behind the tapestry and saw the door."

He waited for me to pass. Then he shut the door, turned the key and replaced the tapestry. I gave him five hundred lire. Mollified, he pointed to the room ahead. "Room of the Popes," he said. "Round the wall are busts of twenty popes. All very interesting."

I thanked him, and passed on. The Room of the Popes had always lacked allure.

I skirted the remaining rooms, the ceramics and the stone reliefs. In old days they had been good for hiding in, for the echo came more clearly. I walked down the great stairway once again, traversed the quadrangle and the entrance passage and went out into the street. I lit a cigarette and leant against the columns of the Duomo, waiting for my clients. A postcard vendor approached me with his wares. I waved him away.

"When does the invasion start?" I asked.

He shrugged. "Any time now," he said, "if the weather mends. The municipality do their best to put Ruffano on the map, but we're poorly placed. Those who are heading for the coast prefer to go direct. We depend mostly on the students for selling this stuff."

He thumbed his postcards and the little bicycle-flags bearing the insignia of the Malebranche Falcon.

"Are there many of them?"

"Students? Over five thousand, they say. A lot of them come in by day, the town can't house them. It's all happened in the last three years. Plenty of opposition from the older folk, the place getting spoilt and so on, the students rowdy. Well, they're young, aren't they? And it's good for trade."

43

The intake at the university must have doubled, possibly trebled. I could not be sure. The students gave little trouble in the past, as far as I remembered. I had the impression then that they were all studying to be teachers.

My informant ambled off and as I waited for the Turtmanns, smoking my cigarette, I became aware, for the first time for months, for years, that the hour no longer pressed. I was working to no schedule. There was no Sunshine Touring coach drawn up in the piazza in front of me.

The snow was melting rapidly under the hot sun. Children were chasing one another round the fountain. An old woman came to the door of the baker's opposite, her knitting in her hands. More student groups of youths and young women passed into the ducal palace.

I stared up at the Falcon above the palace door, his bronze wings poised for flight. Last night, snow-covered, oblique against the sky, he had seemed menacing, a threat to all who trespassed. This morning, though still the guardian of the palace walls, the spread wings hinted freedom.

The deep-toned bell of the campanile by the Duomo struck eleven. Hardly had the last notes died away when the Turtmanns, gesticulating, slammed the Volkswagen door. They must have emerged without my seeing them, and were now impatient to be gone.

"We have seen all we want to see," barked my client. "We propose to leave the city by the opposite hill, after photographing the statue of Duke Carlo. This will give us longer in Ravenna."

"It's up to you," I said.

We climbed into the car, I in the driving seat, as yesterday. We left the piazza Maggiore and went downhill to the piazza della Vita, and so across the city's centre and up the northern hill to the piazza del Duca Carlo. I realised now why the Longhis had lost business. The new hotel Panorama, with its view of the city and surrounding country, its gaily-painted balconies, its grass verges and little orange trees, held more glamour for the tourist than the poor hotel dei Duchi.

"Ha!" said Herr Turtmann. "Look, that is where we should have stayed." He turned on me, angrily.

"Too late, my friend, too late," I murmured in my own tongue.

"What? What is it you say?"

44

"The hotel Panorama does not open until Easter," I said smoothly. I stopped the car, and they got out to film the statue of Duke Carlo and the surrounding view. This used to be the regulation walk on Sundays. The local dignitaries, their wives and children and dogs, would parade about the plateau, neatly laid out with trees and shrubs, and bedding plants in summer. Here there was some change, if nowhere else. New houses had been built below the summit, and the orphanage, that once had stood alone in its stark ugliness, was now hemmed in by smarter dwellings. This, I took it, was the affluent quarter of Ruffano, the modern challenge to the more famous southern hill. I got out of the Volkswagen, carrying my small grip, as my clients, having finished the morning's filming, came towards the car.

"This, Herr Turtmann," I said, holding out my hand, "is where I say goodbye. The road to the right out of the piazza will take you downhill to the Porta Malebranche, and so on your way north. Take the coast road to Ravenna, it's very fast."

He and his wife stared at me, and he blinked behind his gold-rimmed spectacles. "You are engaged as our courier and chauffeur," he said. "It was arranged with the agent in Rome."

"A misunderstanding." I bowed. "I undertook to escort you as far as Ruffano, no further. I regret the inconvenience."

I have some respect for the Tedeschi. They know when they are beaten. Had my client been a fellow-countryman, or a Frenchman, he would have burst into a tirade of abuse. Not so Herr Turtmann. He looked at me a moment, his mouth tightened, then he ordered his wife curtly into the car.

"As you please," he said. "I have already paid in advance for your services. The Rome office must reimburse me."

He got in, slammed the door, and started up the engine. In a moment the Volkswagen was on its way, across the piazza del Duca Carlo and out of sight. Out of my life as well. I was no longer a courier. No longer a charioteer. I turned my back on the good Duke Carlo, high above me on his pedestal, and stared south to the opposite hill. The ducal palace of the Malebranche, with its twin towers facing westward, adorned the summit like a crown. I started to walk downhill into the city.

CHAPTER FIVE

At noon the piazza della Vita earns its name. The women, their shopping done, have all gone home to prepare the midday meal. The men take over. Crowds of them were assembled there when I reached the centre. Shopkeepers, clerks, loafers, youths, men of business, all talking, gossiping, some merely standing still and staring. It was the custom, it had always been like this. A passing stranger might have thought them members of some organisation about to take over the city. He would have been wrong. These men were the city. This was Ruffano.

I bought a paper and leant against one of the pillars of the colonnade. I searched the pages for the Roman news, and found half-a-dozen lines about the murder in the via Sicilia.

"The identity of the woman murdered two days ago in the via Sicilia has not yet been discovered. It is believed that she came from the provinces. A lorry-driver has stated that he gave a lift to a woman answering to her description after leaving Terni. The police are pursuing their enquiries."

We had passed through Terni yesterday, before turning right to Spoleto. Travelling south from Ruffano to Rome a wanderer, a vagrant, would be glad to seize the chance of a lorry-ride for the remaining distance. Doubtless the lorry-driver had come forward and identified the body, but in any case the description of the dead woman would by this time have been circulated to every city in the country, so that the police could check with their list of missing persons. What, though, if the dead woman was not upon the list? What if, filled with a sudden wanderlust, she had simply left her home? I could not remember if Marta possessed relatives. Surely not. Surely she had devoted herself to my parents after Aldo had been born, and had remained with us ever after. She never talked of brothers, sisters. . . . Her devotion, her whole life, had been given to us.

I put the paper down and stared about me. No faces that I knew, not even amongst the old. Hardly surprising, when I had left Ruffano aged eleven. The day we drove away, my mother and

I, in the staff car with the Commandant, Marta had been at Mass. She always went to Mass each morning. Knowing her custom, my mother had timed our exit deliberately.

"I'll leave a note for Marta," she said, "and she can follow later, with all our things. There's no time to bother with them now. The Commandant has to leave immediately."

I did not understand what it was all about. Military persons were always coming and going. The war was apparently over, yet there seemed to be more soldiers than ever before. Germans, not ours. It was beyond me.

"Where are we going with the Commandant?" I asked my mother.

She was evasive. "What does it matter?" she answered impatiently. "Anywhere, as long as it's out of Ruffano. He'll take care of us."

I felt certain Marta would be dismayed when she returned from Mass. She might not want to go. She hated the Commandant. "You are sure Marta will follow?"

"Yes, yes, of course."

And so to leaning out of the staff car, saluting, watching the passing country, thinking of Marta less often each day, being fobbed off in the months to follow with more lies, more evasions. And then forgetting, finally forgetting. Until two days ago. . . .

I crossed the piazza to the church of San Cipriano. It was shut. Of course it was shut. All churches closed at noon. As a courier it was part of my job to reconcile the tourists to this fact. I must bide my time as they did until the afternoon.

Then, suddenly, I saw a man I recognised. He was standing in the piazza, arguing with a group of cronies, a cross-eyed fellow with a long lean face, hardly altered in old age from what he had been at forty-five. He was a cobbler in the via Rossini, and he used to repair our shoes. His sister Maria had been our cook over a period, and a friend of Marta's. This fellow, and his sister if she lived, would surely have kept in touch with her. The question was, how could I approach him without giving myself away? I lit another cigarette and kept my eye on him.

Presently, the argument finished, he moved away. Not up the via Rossini but to the left out of the piazza, threading along the via dei Martiri, and so across it to a narrow street beyond. Feeling like a detective out of a police novel, I followed him. Progress was slow, for he paused now and again to exchange a word with an acquaintance, and I, more furtive than ever, was obliged to stoop to tie a shoe-lace, or stare about me as if a tourist and lost. I could have done with the Turtmanns' cameras to save my face.

He ambled on, and at the further end of the narrow street turned left again. When I caught up with him he was near enough to touch, standing at the top of the steep steps beside the small oratorio of Ognissanti. The steps descend abruptly, almost vertically, to the via dei Martiri below. He stood aside for me to pass.

"Excuse me, signore," he said.

"Pardon me, signore," I countered, "I was simply following my nose, a stranger in Ruffano."

His gaze, cross-eyed, had always been disconcerting. I did not know now whether he looked at me or not.

"The steps of Ognissanti," he said, pointing, "the oratorio of Ognissanti."

"Yes," I said, "so I see."

"You wish to visit the oratorio, signore?" he asked. "My neighbour has the key."

"Another time," I said. "Please don't trouble yourself."

"No trouble at all," he said. "She is sure to be at home. Later on, in the season, she opens the oratorio at regular hours. At the moment it isn't worth her while."

Before I could prevent him he had called up at the window of the small house adjoining the chapel. It opened, and an elderly woman thrust out her head.

"What is it, Signor Ghigi?" she called.

Ghigi, that was it. That was the name above the cobbler's shop. Our cook had been Maria Ghigi.

"A visitor to see the oratorio," he called, then waited for her descent. The window slammed. I felt myself unwelcome.

"I'm sorry to make myself a nuisance," I said.

"At your service, signore," he said.

The cross-eyes were surely searching me. I turned my head. In a moment or two the door opened and the woman emerged, fumbling for her keys. She opened the door of the oratorio and motioned to me to pass. I stared about me, feigning interest. The attraction of the oratorio is a group of martyred saints, modelled in wax. I remembered having been brought here as a child, and being reproved by the attendant for trying to touch the models.

"Very fine," I observed to the couple watching me.

"It is unique," said the cobbler, and then, as if in afterthought, "did the signore say he is a stranger to Ruffano?"

"Yes," I said, "I come from Turin." Instinct made me give my stepfather's city, where my mother had died.

"Ah, Turin," he said, as though disappointed, and added, "You have nothing like this in Turin."

"We have the shroud," I told him, "the shroud that wrapped the Saviour. The marks of the sacred body are upon it still."

"I did not know that," he replied, rebuked.

We were all silent. The woman jangled her keys. I felt the cobbler's cross-eyes upon me, and grew restless.

"Thank you," I said to both. "I have seen enough."

I gave the woman two hundred lire, which she stowed away in her voluminous skirt, shook hands with the cobbler, and thanked him for his courtesy. Then I walked down the steps of Ognissanti, guessing they were staring after me. It was possible that I had reminded him of something, someone, yet there was nothing to connect me, a man from Turin, with a lad of ten.

I retraced my steps to the piazza della Vita and found a small restaurant in the via San Cipriano, a few yards from the church. I had lunch and smoked a cigarette, my head still empty of plans. The restaurant must have been popular—it was new since my time—for it filled rapidly and customers were obliged to share tables. Instinctive wariness made me bring out my newspaper and prop it against the carafe of wine in front of me.

Somebody said, "Excuse me, is this place free?"

I raised my eyes. "By all means, signorina," I said, making room, jarred by the sudden interruption to my thoughts.

"I believe I saw you in the ducal palace this morning," she said.

I stared, then swiftly begged her pardon. I recognised the woman lecturer who had been in charge of the crowd of students.

"You tried to escape us," she said. "I can't say I blame you."

She smiled, and the smile was pleasing, though her mouth was too large. Her hair was parted in the centre and drawn smoothly back, her age a possible thirty-two. She had a large mole close to her left eye. Some men find these marks attractive, enhancing sexual charm. To each his own taste. . . .

"I did not try to escape you," I said, "only your audience."

After mixing so much with nationalities other than my own,

especially Americans and Anglo-Saxons, and being always in a subservient position, I had lost touch with the women of my own country, who demand flirtation as a common courtesy.

"If you had wanted to know about the pictures in the palace," she said, "you could have joined us."

"I am not a student," I said, "and I dislike to be one of many."

"A private guide would be more to your choice, perhaps," she murmured. Gallantry, I saw, would be the order for the remainder of the meal. When I tired of it, I could always look at my watch and make the excuse of time.

"The choice of most men," I said. "Haven't you found it so?"

She smiled, a conspiratorial smile, and gave her order to the waiter. "You are probably right," she said, "but as a lecturer on the staff of the university I have a job to do. I must make myself agreeable to both boys and girls, and endeavour to put facts into their reluctant heads."

"Is that a hard task?"

"With the majority of them, yes," she answered.

Her hands were small. I like small hands in women. She wore no ring.

"What are your duties?" I asked.

"I'm attached to the Faculty of Arts," she said. "I lecture two or three times a week in class to the second- and third-year students, and escort the first-year batch to the palace, as I did this morning, and to other places of importance. It's quite interesting. I've been here two years now." The waiter served her, and after eating in silence for a few moments she glanced at me and smiled. "And you?" she asked. "Are you on a visit here? You don't look like a tourist."

"I'm a courier," I said. "I look after tourists, as you look after students."

She grimaced. "Have you your charges with you in Ruffano?"

"No. I wished the last god-speed this morning."

"And now?"

"You might say I'm open to offers."

She said nothing for a moment. She was busy eating. Then she pushed aside her plate and turned to her salad.

"What sort of offers?" she asked.

"You make them. I'll tell you," I answered.

50

She looked at me in speculation. "What are your languages?"

"English, German and French. But I've never given a lecture in my life," I told her.

"I didn't suppose you had. Any degree?"

"Degree in modern languages, Turin."

"Why, then, a courier?"

"One sees the country. The tips are good."

I ordered more coffee for myself. The conversation did not commit me.

"So you're on vacation?" she said.

"Self-imposed. I've not been sacked. I just wanted a few weeks off from my regular work. As I told you, I'm open to offers."

She had finished her salad. I offered her a cigarette, which she took.

"I might be able to help you," she said. "They're temporarily understaffed in the university library. Half our stuff is still housed in a room in the palace. Later it will be moved into new quarters between the university and the students' hostel, but our fine new building won't be opened until after Easter. For the time being chaos reigns. The librarian, a good friend of mine, could do with extra help. And with a degree in modern languages. . . ." She left her sentence unfinished, but her gesture implied that the rest was easy.

"It sounds interesting," I said.

"I don't know about the pay," she said quickly. "It wouldn't be much. And the job is only temporary, as I said, but that might suit you."

"It might indeed."

She summoned the waiter in her turn for coffee, brought out a card from her bag and gave it to me. I glanced at it and read the words, "Carla Raspa, 5, via San Michele, Ruffano."

I handed mine in return. "Armino Fabbio, Sunshine Tours, Turin."

She raised ironic eyebrows and put it in her bag. "Sunshine Tours," she murmured, "I could do with one. Ruffano can be very dead after working hours." She drank her coffee, watching me as she did so. "Think it over. I must leave you—I have a lecture at three. I'll be in the library myself after four, and if you want to take this up I can introduce you to the librarian, Giuseppe Fossi. He'll do anything for me. Eats out of my hand."

The look in her eye suggested that he did more than that.

Gallantly I returned the look. For courtesy's sake we were conspirators.

"You have your credentials on you?" she asked as she rose from the table.

I patted my breast pocket. "I carry them everywhere," I said.

"Fine. Goodbye for now."

"Goodbye, signorina. And thank you."

She disappeared through the restaurant entrance to the street. I glanced at the card once more. Carla Raspa. The name suited her. Hard as nails, with a soft centre, like a Neapolitan ice. I pitied the librarian Giuseppe Fossi. It might be my answer, though, for the next two or three weeks. Not her—the job. Possibly the one went with the other, but I should have to take care of that when the moment came.

I paid the bill and went out into the street, carrying my grip, feeling like a snail with the world upon his back. I crossed the street and tried the door of San Cipriano once again. This time it was open. I pushed my way inside and went into the chancel.

The smell brought back the past, as it had done at the ducal palace. Here the memory, though less intense, was more sombre, muted, connected with Sundays, feastdays, the necessity of silence, and an inner restlessness that mirrored my longing to be outside. I did not connect the church of San Cipriano with devout feelings or with prayer, only with an intense awareness of being small and hemmed in by adults, with impersonal priestly intoning, the puff of incense, the touch of Aldo's hand, a desire to urinate.

The church was empty, save for a sacristan who seemed to be busy with candles at the high altar, and I made my way up the nave on the left-hand side, tiptoeing as if by instinct, and so up the single step to the chapel. Hollow sounds came from the high altar in the church, as the sacristan went about his business. I looked for a light in the chapel and switched it on. The light fell upon the altar-piece. Small wonder I had been frightened as a child at that figure in his shroud, the wrappings from the face hanging in streamers, the eyes of terror staring out upon his Lord. I realised now that the painting was no masterpiece. Executed in the days when tortured expression and exaggerated form had been the vogue, the risen Lazarus, to my maturer eyes, now seemed grotesque. Yet the bowed figure of the supplicating Mary in the foreground was still Marta, still the humped woman on the steps of the church in Rome.

52

I switched off the light and left the chapel. Two nights ago, dreaming, I had been a child still, imagination vivid. Now there was disenchantment; the risen Lazarus had lost his power.

As I turned into the nave the sacristan came pattering down to meet me. A sudden thought came to me. "Excuse me," I said, "are the baptismal records kept here in the church?"

"Yes, signore," he answered, "the records are in the sacristy. They go back a number of years, to approximately the beginning of the century. Earlier than that, they are kept in the presbytery."

"Would it be possible for me to look up an entry for the year 1933?"

He hesitated a moment, murmuring something about the priest in charge of the records not being available. I slipped a note into his hand and told him I was passing through Ruffano, unlikely to return, and wished to consult a baptismal entry for a relative. He protested no more, and led the way into the sacristy.

I hovered while he searched for the book. The odour of sanctity was all about me. Stoles and surplices hung from hooks. The faint scent of incense mingled with floor-polish pervaded all. The sacristan approached me with a book.

"We have the entries here from 1931 to 1935," he said. "If your relative was baptised in San Cipriano, his name should be here."

I took the book and opened it. It was like turning back the pages into the past. How many of my contemporaries must be here, children born and baptised in Ruffano, now adult, scattered, or perhaps living in the city still, shopkeepers, clerks, yet in this book only a few days old. . . .

I turned to July the 13th, the day of my birth. Here was my baptism, on a Sunday two weeks later. "Armino. Son of Aldo Donati and Francesca Rossi. Godparents, Aldo Donati, brother, Federico Ponenti, Edda Ponenti." I had forgotten that Aldo, not then nine years old, had been my sponsor. He had written his name in a round, childish hand, that yet already had more character to it than the uniform scrawl of the second cousins who shared the responsibility. They had lived, if I remembered rightly, at Ancona. Now it all came back. The first communion. Aldo's eyes upon me, hinting eternal punishment should I, through fear or clumsiness, let fall the Host out of my open mouth.

"Have you found the entry?" asked the sacristan.

"Yes," I said, "yes, it's there."

I shut the book and gave it into his hands. He took it, and

replaced it in the cupboard amongst a row of similar volumes.

"Wait," I said. "Have you the entries for the 'twenties too?"

"The 'twenties, signore? Which year?"

"Let me see. It would be 1925, I suppose."

He took out another volume. "Here is '21 to '25."

I took the book and turned to November. November the 17th. The date had always held significance for me because it was Aldo's birthday. Even in Genoa, on autumn mornings, when I looked at the office calendar, the number 17 under the month of November was somehow dedicated.

Curious . . . Aldo must have been a sickly infant, for here he was, baptised within a day of his birth. "Aldo. Son of Aldo Donati and Francesca Rossi." No mention of godparents.

I turned the page, and to my surprise the entry was repeated a few days later. "Aldo. Son of Aldo Donati and Francesca Rossi. Godparents, Aldo Donati, father, Luigi Speca, Francesca Rossi."

Who was Luigi Speca? I had never heard of him. Nor, I felt sure, had Aldo. And why the double entry?

"Tell me," I said to the sacristan, "have you ever heard of an infant being baptised twice?"

He shook his head. "No, signore. Though if the child was ailing, and the parents feared it might die, it is just conceivable that it might be baptised on the day of birth and the ceremony repeated later, when the child was stronger. Has the signore finished with the book?"

"Yes," I said. "Take it."

I watched him replace the book amongst its fellows in the cupboard, and turn the key. Then I came out into the sunlight, crossed the piazza della Vita and walked up the via Rossini. It was strange that Aldo should have been baptised twice. It was the sort of story, had we known it, that he would have turned to good advantage. "I was doubly blessed," I could imagine him telling me.

Marta would have known about the baptism. . . . So thinking, I was reminded of the cross-eyed cobbler, and I looked about me for his shop, situated, to the best of my recollection, halfway up, on the left-hand side. There it was. . . . But larger, smartened, and with rows of shoes to sell. No longer shoes with tickets and up-turned soles, advertising repairs. A different name, too, above the door. My cross-eyed Ghigi of the morning must have retired, to live beside the oratorio. He was the only likely link with Marta, or

54

his sister if she lived, and short of admitting my identity I did not see how I could approach him.

The same held good for the Longhis, at the hotel dei Duchi. It would be so easy to go back, to say, "I meant to tell you last night. I am the younger son of Aldo Donati. You remember my father, the Superintendent at the ducal palace?" Even the flabby face of the signora would have creased into a smile, the first shock over. And then, "You remember Marta? What happened to Marta?"

It was no good. It would not work. Anyone returning from the past, as I was doing, must remain anonymous. Otherwise it meant useless involvement. Alone, in secret, I could unravel the threads of the past, but not with identity known.

I passed the ducal palace once again and then turned left, coming, after a moment, into the via dei Sogni. I wanted to look at my old home by day. The snow had melted, as it had done elsewhere in Ruffano, and the sun must have filled the house all morning, for behind the tree I could see the windows of the first floor, opened. This had been my parents' bedroom, in early days a sort of sanctum in my eyes, but later shunned.

Someone was playing the piano. There had never been a piano in our time. The player had the touch of a professional. A torrent of sound rippled from the keys. It was something I knew, heard probably on the radio, or more likely still from the music rooms in the university at Turin when I used to hurry past to lectures. My lips framed a silent echo to the sound as it rose and fell, half gay, half sad, a timeless melody. Debussy. Yes, Debussy. The well-worn "Arabesque", but with a master touch.

I stood beneath the wall and listened. The music ebbed and flowed, changed mood and entered the more solemn phrases, and then again that first light-hearted ripple, higher, ever higher, confident and gay, but at last with a descending scale, dissolving, vanishing. It seemed to say: All over, nevermore. The innocence of youth, the joy of childhood, leaping from bed to welcome a new day . . . all gone, the fervour spent. The repetition of the phrase was only a reminder, an echo of what had been. So swift to go, impossible to hold.

The music ceased before the closing bars. I could hear the telephone. Whoever played must have gone to answer it. The window was closed, then all was still.

The telephone used to stand in the hall, and if my mother was upstairs she had to run to answer it, arriving breathless. I wondered if the player did the same. I looked up at the tree that shrouded the small garden like a canopy. Somewhere in the branches should be a rubber ball that I had much prized, kicked aloft one day in an idle mood and never recovered. I wondered if it lay there still, and with the wonder came resentment, a strange antagonism to the present owner of my home. Theirs the right to wander through the rooms, open and shut the windows, answer the telephone. I was just a stranger, staring at the wall.

The playing was resumed. This time a Chopin Prelude, mournful, passionate. The pianist's mood had changed with the telephone call, nerves were unleashed to sombre melancholy. And none of it my business.

I went on walking up the via dei Sogni, and so out into the via dell'8 Settembre, in front of the university. It was like walking into another age. The young were everywhere, pouring out of lecture rooms, laughing, talking, getting on to vespas. The old building which had always been known as the House of Studies boasted new wings, the windows glowing not only with fresh paint but with vitality. There were new buildings too across the way, and yet another in construction—the new library, possibly— topping the hill. This university was not the crumbling, rather faded seat of learning I remembered from childhood days. Austerity was banished. The young, with all their fine contempt for dusty ways, had taken over. Transistor radios blared.

I stood, clutching my grip, a wanderer between two worlds. The one the via dei Sogni of my past, with all its memories, but no longer mine; and this other, active, noisy, equally indifferent. The dead should not return. Lazarus was right to feel foreboding. Caught, as he must have been, betwixt past and present, he evaded both in horror, seeking the anonymity of the tomb—but in vain.

"Hullo," said a voice in my ear, "have you made up your mind?"

I turned, and saw Carla Raspa. She looked cool, confident and self-possessed. No doubts for her.

"Yes, signorina. Thank you for your trouble. But I have decided to leave Ruffano." This was my intention, but the words were left unsaid. A youth, straddling a vespa, swerved past us, laughing. He had a small flag fixed to his machine which fluttered in the breeze, just as, years back, the staff car of my mother's

56

Commandant carried his hated emblem. The student's flag was tourist junk, perhaps, bought for a few hundred lire in the piazza Maggiore, but it had for design the Malebranche Falcon and so was, to my nostalgic eye, a symbol.

Adopting my habitual mask of courier, of courtier, I bowed to the signorina, sweeping her from head to foot in a caressing glance that she knew, and I knew, meant precisely nothing.

"I was on my way to the ducal palace," I told her. "If you are free, perhaps we could go together?"

I had reached the point of no return.

CHAPTER SIX

THE UNIVERSITY library was housed on the ground floor of the ducal palace, in what had been the banqueting-hall of long ago. It had been used for manuscripts and documents when my father was Superintendent, and I gathered was so still, on shelves separate from those temporarily loaned to the university. My new acquaintance led the way, with all the assurance of someone on home ground, while I followed, assuming a stranger's ignorance.

The room was vast, larger even than I remembered, with the musty smell inseparable from books, many of which were stacked high upon the floor. A certain confusion prevailed. One clerk knelt upon the floor, inserting printed slips into some of the volumes. A second was halfway up a ladder, busy among the higher shelves. A third, a harassed female, was taking notes, dictated by the individual whom I gathered, correctly, to be the librarian, Giuseppe Fossi. He was short, stout, with an olive-green complexion and the wandering, bulging eye I associate with clandestine appointments. He hurried forward at the sight of my companion, leaving his minion in mid-note.

"I've found you an assistant, Giuseppe," said Carla Raspa. "Signor Fabbio has a degree in modern languages, and would be grateful for temporary work."

The bulging eye of Giuseppe Fossi appraised me with some hostility—was I perhaps a rival?—then, stalling for time, he turned back to the object of his admiration.

"Signor Fabbio is a friend of yours?"

"A friend of a friend," she answered promptly. "Signor Fabbio has been working in Genoa for a touring agency. I know the manager."

The lie was unexpected, but it served. The librarian turned back to me.

"I certainly need help," he admitted, "and anyone with languages, who could catalogue the foreign books, would be invaluable. You see for yourself the mess we are in." He waved an apologetic gesture about the room, and went on, "I warn you, the remuneration is small, and I shall have to press a point with the university Registrar if I take you on."

I gestured a willingness to accept whatever was offered, and he looked from me to Carla Raspa. The response she gave him with her eyes was similar to that already given me in the restaurant in the via San Cipriano, but more compelling. Excitement filled him.

"Well, now . . . I will see what I can do with the Registrar. It would naturally leave me freer if I had your help. As it is, the evenings . . ."

The same conspiratorial glance passed between them. He turned to the telephone. I had understood what she meant when she told me that Ruffano could be dead by night; nevertheless, she must be easily pleased.

We feigned deafness while Giuseppe Fossi carried on a rapid conversation on the telephone. The receiver clamped. "All fixed," he said. "It's the same throughout the university at the moment. Nobody has any time to spare for other people's problems—we must all make our own decisions."

I expressed my thanks, with a certain wonder that even a temporary increase in staff could be such an easy matter to arrange.

"The Rector is away sick," explained Giuseppe Fossi. "Without him, authority is non-existent. He *is* the university."

"Our beloved Rector," murmured the signorina, and I thought I detected irony in her voice, "suffered a thrombosis, alas, after attending an assembly in Rome, and has been in hospital there ever since. We are all lost without him. He has been ill for weeks."

"Does nobody take over?" I asked.

"Professor Rizzio, the Deputy-Rector," she answered, shrugging, "who happens to be the Head of the Department of Education, and spends his time arguing with Professor Elia, the Head of the Department of Economics and Commerce."

The librarian expostulated reprovingly. "Come, Carla," he said, "gossip, like smoking, is forbidden in the library. You should know better." He patted her on the arm indulgently and looked at me, shaking his head. The head-shake suggested dissociation from her views, the pat on the arm possession. I smiled, remaining silent.

"I must leave you," she said, and which of us she addressed remained in doubt. "I have another lecture at five."

59

She raised her hand to me, saying "Be seeing you," and was on her way to the door. Signor Fossi hurried after her, calling, "One moment, Carla . . ." I waited for instructions, while one of the clerks glanced up at me and winked. After a murmured consultation with the signorina, Giuseppe Fossi returned and said briskly, "If you care to start work right away it will help us all."

I spent the next two hours learning my work under his direction. Special care had to be taken because certain of the volumes which were part of the university library had become mixed up with others which, belonging to the ducal palace proper, were in the care of the Arts Council of Ruffano.

"Gross inefficiency," said Signor Fossi. "It happened before my time. But there will be an end to these troubles when we have all our own stuff in the new university library. You have seen the building? It's almost finished. All due to the Rector, Professor Butali. He has achieved wonders for the university"—he lowered his tone, with an eye on the clerk within earshot—"against much opposition. The usual thing, in a small centre such as ours. There is rivalry amongst the Departments, and jealousy too between the university and the Arts Council. Some want one thing, some another. The Rector has the thankless task of keeping the peace between them all."

"Was that the reason for his heart attack?" I asked.

"I would think so," he said, and then, with a knowing look flickering an instant in his bulging eye, "he also has a beautiful wife. Signora Butali is several years younger than her husband."

I continued sorting books until, at a little after six, Giuseppe Fossi gave an exclamation and looked at his watch. "I have an appointment at seven," he said. "Do you mind remaining here for another hour? And when you leave, will you please go to the Registrar's office to sign in? They will, if you wish, give you a list of addresses where you can find lodgings—the university has first call on a number of rooms and small pensioni in the city. Signorina Gatti will assist you if there is anything else you wish to know."

The female clerk, some fifty odd, peered at me dourly through her spectacles as Giuseppe Fossi bustled off, bidding us all good-night. Then she continued to make notes, her sour expression unchanged, and the younger of the two clerks—I had already heard him addressed as Toni—moved across the room to help me.

"He'll lose some weight this evening," he murmured.

"With the lady who went out earlier?"

"They say she's tireless. I've never tried my luck."

Signorina Gatti called him sharply to remove some books from the desk in front of her. I hid my face in an enormous ledger. The hour ticked by. At seven precisely I approached her desk and, after obtaining her grudging admission that there was nothing more I could do, made my way towards the Registrar's office. The young clerk, Toni, followed me, and we walked through the silent quadrangle towards the outer entrance.

I paused by the great stairway leading to the ducal apartments on the first floor. The lights were on, and I could hear the sound of voices.

"What's happening above? Don't they close at four o'clock out of season?"

"To the public, yes," said Toni, "but the Director of the Arts Council comes and goes as he pleases. Besides, he's particularly involved just now with all the arrangements for the Festival."

There was an attendant on duty by the side door. We bade him goodnight and went out into the piazza Maggiore.

"The Festival?" I enquired.

"Why, yes, don't you know about it? It's our great day. Inaugurated by the Rector, Professor Butali, really to put the university on the map, but now the whole of Ruffano takes a pride in it and the people flock in from miles around. The students give a fine display. Last year the performance took place here in the ducal palace." He walked to a vespa leaning against the wall and wound a scarf about his throat. "Got a date?" he asked. "If you haven't, my Didi will fix you up. She works in ceramics, down in the town, but she knows a lot of the C and E students, and their girls are a lively bunch."

"C and E?"

"Commerce and Economics. It only started three years ago, but soon it'll outnumber the other Faculties. The C and E students mostly live in the town, or come in by day, hence the fun! They aren't stuck away in the students' hostels like the rest."

He grinned, and started up his machine. I shouted above the din that I had to go to the Registrar and sign in, as well as find somewhere to sleep. He waved his hand, and was off. I watched him swerve away, feeling about a hundred. Anyone over thirty appears a dotard to the young.

I walked up to the university building. There was a door on the left marked "Registrar, Private", and beside it a sliding window-panel, with a clerk on duty behind it.

"The name is Fabbio," I said, pushing through my credentials. "The librarian, Signor Fossi, told me to call."

"Yes, yes. . . ."

He seemed to know about me, and scribbled something in a book. He handed me out a pass and a form to sign. Also a list of addresses.

"You ought to be able to find a room from one of these," he said. "They make a special price for us."

I thanked him and turned to go, but paused a moment. "By the way," I asked, "can you tell me who lives at No. 8, via dei Sogni?"

"No. 8?" he repeated.

"Yes," I said, "the house with the high wall, and the single tree in the small garden."

"That is the Rector's house," he said, staring, "Professor Butali. But he's away sick. He's in hospital in Rome."

"I knew that," I said, "but I had not realised that he lives in the via dei Sogni."

"Oh, yes," he replied. "The Rector and Signora Butali have been there for some years."

"Who plays the piano there?"

"The signora. She teaches music. But I doubt if she is at home. She's been in Rome with the Rector during the past weeks."

"I thought I heard music," I said, "when I passed the house this afternoon."

"She must be back, then," he answered. "I wouldn't necessarily know."

I wished him good evening and left. So . . . My home was honoured by being the residence of the Rector himself. In old days the head of the university had lived next door to the students' hostel. There had obviously been many changes, as the fellow selling postcards and flags had told me, and what with the boys and girls studying Commerce and Economics, many of them coming in by day, my quiet city of Ruffano would soon begin to rival Perugia or Turin.

I walked back downhill past the ducal palace and stood for a moment under the street lamp to study my list of addresses. Via Rossini, via dell'8 Settembre, via Lambetta . . . no, too close to the students. Via San Cipriano . . . perhaps. Via San Michele . . . I smiled. Wasn't that where Signorina Carla Raspa had her niche? I took out her card. Her address was No. 5; the address given me at the Registrar's office was 24. It was worth looking at. I picked up my grip once more and walked down to the piazza della Vita.

It must have been the snow of the preceding night that had driven the world indoors. This evening it was cold, but the stars glittered, the piazza was full, and unlike the midday session, when from long custom the middle-aged males took over, youth predominated. Girls, chattering and with arms interlocked, paraded before the colonnade, while the boys, hands in pockets, laughing, whistling, some of them straddling vespas, hung about in groups. The cinema, beneath the colonnade, was due to start. The lurid poster gave promise of passion under Caribbean skies. Across the way the Hotel dei Duchi looked forlorn and out of date.

I crossed the piazza, ignoring the glance of a little red-haired beauty—Commerce and Economics, I wondered?—and, turning right, found myself in the via San Michele. I looked for number 5. Discreet enough, with a small car parked outside. Guiseppe Fossi's? There were chinks of light coming from the shutters on the first floor. Ah, well. . . . Good luck to him. I continued down the street, looking for No. 24. It was on the opposite side, but from the windows one would have a fair view of No. 5. Seized with sudden amusement, coupled with schoolboy malice, I decided to inspect the house. The door was open. Light flooded the hallway. I looked at the name on the list . . . Signora Silvani. I walked in and looked about me. It was clean, newly decorated, and an enticing smell of fégato alla salvia came from a hidden kitchen. Someone ran down the stairs, calling over her shoulder to the floor above. It was a girl of about twenty, with small elfin features and enormous eyes.

"Are you looking for Signora Silvani?" she asked. "She's in the kitchen—I'll tell her."

"No, wait a moment." I liked the atmosphere, I liked the girl. She might tell me what I wanted to know. "They gave me this address at the university," I said. "I'm a temporary assistant at the library, and I want a room for a week or two. Anything going?"

"There's one vacant on the top floor," she answered, "but it may be booked. You'll have to ask Signora Silvani. I'm only a student."

"Commerce and Economics?" I asked.

"Why yes, how did you know?"

"I'm told they enroll the best-looking girls."

She laughed, and arrived in the hall beside me. It is always a gratification to me when a girl is smaller than myself. This one could have been a child.

"I don't know about that," she said. "At least we're alive, and let the others know it. Isn't that true, Paolo?" A boy, equally handsome, had followed her down the stairs. "This is my brother," she said. "We're both C and E students. We come from San Marino."

I held out my hand to each of them. "Armino Fabbio," I said, "from Turin, though I work in Genoa usually."

They answered in one breath, "Caterina and Paolo Pasquale."

"Look," I said, "would you advise me to try for a room here?"

"Certainly," answered the boy. "It's clean, comfortable, she feeds you well," he jerked his head towards the kitchen, "and she doesn't bother you about time. We come and go as we like."

"We're an easy crowd," said the girl. "Whoever wants to work can work. Whoever wants to play can play. Paolo and I do a bit of both. Yes, you try for that room."

Her smile was comradely, inviting. So was his. Without waiting for my answer she went off down the hallway, calling for the signora. The door of the kitchen opened and Signora Silvani emerged. She was a broad, middle-aged woman with a high bosom and enormous hips, good-looking in an engaging, friendly way.

"You want a room?" she said. "Come and look at it."

She pushed past the boy Paolo and myself and began to climb the stairs.

"You see?" laughed Caterina. "It's all so simple. Well, I hope you take it. Paolo and I are off to the cinema. Be seeing you."

They left the house together, chatting and laughing, and I followed Signora Silvani up the stairs.

We reached the top floor and she threw open the door of a room, the windows of which looked out on the street below. She switched on the light and I crossed the room to throw back the shutters. I like to know where I am, what I can see. I looked up the street, and saw the small car still parked before No. 5. Then I glanced round the room. It was not large, but it had the essentials.

"I'll take it," I said.

"Good. Make yourself at home. Board is optional. Give warning in the morning if you want to eat out, but I'm not particular if you forget. We're serving dinner now, if you want a meal tonight."

The casual greeting, the informal atmosphere with no questions asked, this suited me exactly. I unpacked my small grip, washed, shaved, and went downstairs. Voices led me to the dining-room. Signora Silvani had already installed herself at the head of the table, and was ladling out the soup. There were four others present, a middle-aged man whom she immediately presented as her husband, as ample and well-fed as herself, and three students, all of them male, harmless in appearance, none of them as striking as young Paolo.

"Our new boarder, Signor Fabbio," called my hostess, "and these are Gino, Mario and Gerardo. Sit down, now, and make yourself at home."

"No formality, please," I said. "My name is Armino. It is not so very long ago that I was studying for my own degree in Turin."

"Arts?"

"Foreign languages. Do I look like Arts?"

There was an immediate chorus of "Yes" at this, and general laughter, while Gino, next to me, explained that it was a joke of the household—anyone new was immediately accused of being Arts.

"Well, I'm a courier in the tourist business usually," I told them, "but being temporarily attached to the university library I suppose I come under Arts?"

There was a universal shout of disapproval, all of it good-natured.

"Take no notice of them," smiled my host. "Just because these lads study Commerce and Economics they think they own Ruffano."

"But we do, signore," protested one of them—Gerardo, I think it was. "We're the new life-blood of the university. None of the others count."

"So you say," said Signora Silvani as she served my soup, "but I've heard differently. The Arts students, and most of the others too, for that matter, look upon your lot as a pack of hooligans."

She winked at me mischievously as another howl greeted her remark, and the whole table plunged into university politics, all of it over my head. I ate, and was amused. This was a Ruffano I had never known.

Gino, my neighbour, explained to me that the new Faculty of

Commerce and Economics was already a thriving concern. Because of the additional fees which the students brought in the university had more money to spend than ever before in its long history—hence the additions to the various buildings, and the new library.

"They couldn't have afforded any of it but for us," he said passionately, "and then the rival Faculties, the Education saps, and the Arts, look down their noses and treat us like dirt, or try to do so. But we've nearly outnumbered them already, and in another year we'll flood them out."

"I tell you," said Mario, "one of these days it will come to a fight, and I know who'll win."

My friend Toni in the library had called the C and E students a lively crowd. He was certainly right.

"You know what it is," observed Signor Silvani, when the students were arguing amongst themselves, "these lads have never known war. They have to let off steam. Inter-Faculty rivalry is one way of doing it."

"Perhaps," I said, "but doesn't it suggest a want of tact amongst the professors?"

He shook his head. "The Rector is a fine man," he said. "There is no one more respected in Ruffano than Professor Butali. But you know he's sick."

"Yes, they told me so at the library."

"They say he nearly died, but he's on the mend. Signora Butali, too, is a very gracious lady. Highly respected, both of them. This silly rivalry has grown much worse while he's been away—once he's back it will soon be squashed, I can tell you. I agree with you, though. I blame much of it on the older professors, or so the chat goes where I work, at the prefettura. The Head of the Department of Education, Professor Rizzio, and his sister, who is in charge of the hostel for women students—they're both narrow and set in their ways, and perhaps naturally resentful of the Head of C and E, Professor Elia, who is what we call a thruster—rather too sure of himself, he comes from Milan."

I thought, as I did justice to Signora Silvani's excellent cooking, that to be in charge of a coach-load of tourists, all of them strangers, must be an easier matter than keeping the peace amongst a group of students like these. I had no recollection of such intensity of feeling at Turin.

Dinner over, our small party dispersed, the students to the

66

piazza della Vita while I excused myself from joining the Silvanis in their parlour for coffee and cigarettes. They were affable and kindly, but I had had enough chatter for the evening.

I went up to my room to fetch my coat, and then left the house. The car had not moved from No. 5.

The young people of Ruffano were still parading in the piazza della Vita, but with numbers thinned. Many must have gone into the cinema to watch the Caribbean film, and the rest had wandered home to their lodgings, or to convenient dark corners. I passed the hotel dei Duchi and walked down into the piazza del Mercato. High above me, on my left, loomed the western façade of the ducal palace, the twin towers thrusting to the sky. As a child I had always been in bed at this hour. I had never seen the towers so late at night, or understood their beauty and their grace. The silhouette might be that of some fantastic backdrop at a theatre, revealed suddenly to an amazed audience when the curtains parted. Fragile, ethereal at first view, the true impact came later. These walls were real, forbidding, with all the ingenuity of a fortress, concealing the strength within. The twin turrets above their encircling balustrades pierced the darkness like sharpened blades. Beauty was paramount, menace lurked within.

The via delle Mura surrounding the whole city of Ruffano stretched before me, curving gently, while immediately to my left were the steps leading up to the palace and to the city above. I decided to climb them. My foot was on the first step when I heard the sound of running. Someone was coming down the steps towards me, but in headlong flight. The descent was steep, and to run at speed was to court disaster.

"Watch out," I called, "you'll fall."

The running figure emerged from the darkness, stumbled, and I put out an arm to break the fall. The runner was a lad, a student possibly, and as he struggled in my hold, trying to break away, his startled eyes stared up at me in terror.

"No . . ." he said. "No. . . . Let me go."

Surprised, I relaxed my grip. He ran from me, sobbing, down the last of the steps. The hollow ring of his clattering feet rose to me where I stood.

Watchful, listening, I continued my climb. The steps were all in shadow, lighted only by one solitary lamp above. I saw a figure move back into the shadows.

"Anyone there?" I called.

There was no answer. I went warily, and when I reached the top paused and looked about me. The precincts of the ducal palace were to the right of me, the nearest of the twin towers darkly ominous. I noticed then that the small door close to the ever-barred portico between the towers was open. Someone was standing there. As I moved forward the figure vanished, the door was softly shut.

I continued up the rise, past the silent, shrouded palace, until I came out into the alley-way leading to the Duomo and the piazza Maggiore. The sight of the frightened boy had been disturbing. He might have broken his neck. The open door, the motionless figure, were somehow sinister. I walked on across the piazza. Everything was still. I took the side street leading into the via dei Sogni as I had the night before, seized with the same desire to look at my old home.

There was no one about. I stood for a moment under the wall staring up at the house. Light came from the chinks in the shutters of the room on the first floor, but I could hear no music. Then I heard footsteps coming down the street, following as it were in my wake, from the direction of the ducal palace. Some instinct made me hide myself behind an angle of the wall, and wait. The footsteps came on, purposeful and clear. No furtiveness about this pursuit, if pursuit it were.

Behind me the sombre bell of the campanile sounded ten, echoed a moment later by the other, more distant churches. The footsteps ceased. They had come to a halt by the door in the wall leading to the garden and to the house beyond. I leant forward and saw the figure of a man. He looked up at the house as I had done, and then moved forward and turned the handle of the door. The Rector's lady, like her predecessor in my home some twenty years before, perhaps sought consolation.

As the man paused a moment, opening the door, the street lamp by the side of the wall shone fully upon his face. He passed through, and closed the door behind him. I stood motionless, drained of all energy, all feeling. The man was surely no stranger, but my brother Aldo.

CHAPTER SEVEN

I BRUSHED PAST the group of students who were hovering, chatting, before No. 24, via San Michele, the Pasquale brother and sister amongst them, and went straight upstairs to my room. I sat down on the bed, staring in front of me. It was an illusion, of course, a trick of the light. Unconscious association with our home. Aldo had been shot down in flames in '43, my mother had received the telegram. I remembered it coming, and when it arrived she stared down at the envelope—for it must contain bad news of some kind—and then she went into the kitchen and called Marta, and they stayed in there together, the door closed.

Children have an instinct for knowing when news is bad. I sat on the stair and waited. Presently my mother came out again. She was not crying; she had the bruised, stunned look that adults wear when deeply moved or shocked. She said, "Aldo's dead. Killed flying. The Allies shot him down," and went upstairs to her room. I crept into the kitchen and Marta was sitting there, her hands in her lap. Unlike my mother she was not mute in her grief; the tears were flowing freely down her cheeks, and she held out her arms. I burst into tears instantly and ran to her, and the pair of us rocked together, crying, mourning our dead.

"My little Beato," she said, "my lamb, my Beato. You loved him so, you loved your brother."

"It isn't true," I kept saying between sobs, "it isn't true. They can't kill Aldo. Nobody can kill Aldo."

"Yes, it is true," she said, holding me close, "he has gone as he would have wished. He had to fly, he had to fall. Aldo, your Aldo."

Memory is merciful. There came a blank in time after that first day, and I had no further feeling. The weeks must have passed, and I must have gone daily to school with my companions, and worn a mourning armband, and have said to them, even with pride, "Yes, my brother's dead. Shot down in flames," as though to go thus added to his glory. I played. I ran up and down the stairs. It was around then that I kicked the ball into the tree. Incidents, isolated at the time, merged into others of wider implication: the surrender, the Armistice, which I did not understand, the arrival in Ruffano of the Germans, and the Commandant. Life, as I had known it, had come to an end.

Now, sitting on the bed in the Pensione Silvani, I lived those first moments once again, and told myself that he whom I had just seen was indeed a living person, but wrongly identified with a man long dead. This was hallucination. This was what had happened to the disciples when they looked, as they thought, upon their Lord, the risen Christ. . . .

There was a sudden knocking on the door. Startled, I called out, "Who's there?" I don't know what I expected. Perhaps the phantom stranger. My shout was taken for permission to enter the room. The door opened and the Pasquale brother and sister stood there, their faces concerned.

"Excuse us," said the girl, Caterina, "but you looked so ill when you came in just now. We wondered if anything was wrong."

I sat up on the bed. Made the supreme effort to appear at ease.

"It's nothing," I said, "absolutely nothing. I walked rather fast, that's all."

My poor reply was met by silence. I could see curiosity struggle with courtesy in their expressions.

"Why did you walk so fast?" asked Paolo.

I thought his question odd. It was as if he guessed . . . but how could he guess? I was a stranger. We were all strangers.

"I happened to do so," I said. "I made a tour round the ducal palace and the neighbouring streets and so back here. It turned out to be further than I had thought."

They exchanged glances. Again, it was as though they guessed, they knew.

"Don't think we want to pry," said Paolo, "but were you by any chance followed?"

"Followed?" I echoed. "Why . . . no. Who would follow me?"

I felt as if I were on the defensive. What could these children know about the past, about my home? What could they know of my dead brother Aldo?

"It's like this," said Caterina, and she spoke softly, shutting the door. "People do get followed, from time to time, if they prowl round the palace at night. There are all sorts of rumours. It never happens if you go in a group. Only to individuals."

I remembered then the running boy. The figure at the top of the steps. The softly closing door.

"It could have been," I said, half to myself and half to them, "it could have been that I was followed."

"Why, what happened?" asked Caterina quickly.

I told them about the boy and his headlong, breathless flight. I told them about the shadowed figure, and the withdrawal inside the palace door. I did not tell them about my return down the via dei Sogni, and how I stood outside my home. Once more they looked at each other, nodding.

"That's it," said Paolo decisively, "they were out."

"Who?" I asked.

"You're new to Ruffano, you wouldn't know," said Caterina. "It's a secret society within the university. We none of us know who the members are. They could be Arts, Education, C and E, Law, or a mixture of them all, but it's part of the oath they take, never to split on one another."

I handed them cigarettes. Already I was feeling more at ease. The past receded, and I was back in the world of university pranks.

"Don't smile," said Paolo. "It isn't amusing. We thought as you did, at first, that it was just ragging. It isn't so. Students have been hurt, and not only students but kids from the town. Seized and blindfolded . . . and, so rumour has it, even tortured. But nobody knows, that's the point. The victims don't tell. Something will slip out days later, a student will say he's sick, not turn up at lectures, and then the rumour spreads, *they've* got at him."

Brother and sister sat down on the bed on either side of me, their faces serious, yet eager. I felt it a compliment that they trusted me.

"Can't the authorities do something?" I asked. "Surely it's up to the university to stamp it out?"

"They can't," said Caterina. "You don't understand the power of these people. It's not like an ordinary society within the university, with its members known. This thing is secret. And it's evil too."

"For all we know," broke in Paolo, "it may include professors as well as students. And although all of us C and E students feel it's directed against us, we can't be sure we have heard there are members of our own group acting as spies for the society."

"So you see," said Caterina, "that's why we were worried, when you came in. I said to Paolo—it's them."

I patted each upon the shoulder and got up from the bed.

"No," I said, "if they were out, they weren't after me." I crossed to the window and opened the shutters. The car had gone from No. 5. "Sometimes," I said, addressing both brother and sister, "one can suffer from hallucinations. I've done so myself. You think you see something which is, frankly, out of this world, and then, later, it has an ordinary explanation. Your society may exist, it obviously does, but its importance could have been worked up in your minds, so that it appears more threatening than it is."

"Exactly," said Paolo, also rising to his feet. "That's what all the scoffers say. But it isn't so. You wait and see. Come on, Caterina."

His sister shrugged, and followed her brother to the door. "I know it sounds foolish," she said to me, "like a trick to scare children. But I'm sure of one thing. I would never walk about Ruffano by night without at least half-a-dozen others. It's all right round here, and in the piazza della Vita. Not up the hill, not by the palace."

"Thank you," I said. "I accept the warning."

I finished my cigarette, undressed, and went to bed. The tale of the "secret society" had proved an antidote to shock. Common sense told me that the encounter on the steps, the withdrawal of the figure to the open door of the ducal palace, had stimulated imagination already tensed because of the past, and when I came to my old home the natural consequence of this was to conjure, out of darkness into light, a living Aldo. The experience was, I now believed, the second of two. The first had been to confuse the murdered woman in the via Sicilia in Rome with Marta. No proof, hallucination. The second experience, the vision of my brother. Appeased, and in a strange way self-absolved, I fell asleep.

When I awoke in the morning, clear-headed, hungry, full of energy for the day ahead, I told myself that it was time to kill all phantoms, and put a final end to the shadows that had haunted me. I would search out the cross-eyed cobbler and ask him if Marta lived. I would even boldly ring the bell of my old home in the via dei Sogni and ask the Rector's lady, Signora Butali, the identity of her late-night caller. This last would, in all probability, produce a well-deserved rebuff, a complaint to the university Registrar, and an end to my temporary job. No matter if it did. My ghosts would then be truly laid, and I at liberty.

My young friends the Pasquales and the other students had dispersed to their various lectures before I left the house at a quarter to nine and walked up the via Rossini to the ducal palace. Ruffano wore her shining morning face, and the noise and bustle of the day were all about me. No shadowy figures now to lurk in doorways and scare the passers-by. I wondered how much truth there was in the students' story, whether the half of it was not a myth born of mass hysteria. Rumour, like infection, spreads rapidly.

I checked in at the palace library as the Duomo struck the hour, and so beat my superior by about three minutes. Giuseppe Fossi looked, I thought, subdued, and it could be that his activities of the preceding night had, in more ways than one, deflated him. He wished me and the others a brief good morning, and I was put at once to sorting and separating those volumes written in German and belonging to the university which had, by error, become mixed up with the palace possessions. The task, because it was so different from checking itineraries and figures, absorbed me, particularly so as one work in four volumes called *The History of the Dukes of Ruffano*, written in the early part of the nineteenth century by a German scholar, was, according to Giuseppe Fossi, extremely rare.

"There is a dispute between the Arts Council and ourselves as to its ownership," he told me. "Better put the books aside for the time being and not pack them with the rest. I shall have to check with the Rector."

I decided to stack the volumes carefully on a shelf by themselves. The leaves stuck together when I opened them. I doubt if they had ever been read. The Archbishop of Ruffano, who must have possessed them before the Risorgimento, either spoke no German or was too shocked by their contents to turn the pages.

"Claudio Malebranche, first Duke of Ruffano, was known as the Falcon," I read. "His brief life is shrouded in mystery, for contemporary authorities do not enable us to pronounce with certainty on the enormous vices wherewith tradition and innuendo have blackened his memory. A youth of outstanding promise, he became intoxicated by good fortune, and casting off his early discipline he surrounded himself by a small band of dissolute disciples, and dismayed the good citizens of Ruffano by licentious outrages and revolting cruelties. No one could walk by night for fear of the Falcon's sudden descent into the city, when, aided by his followers, he would seize and ravage. . . ."

"Signor Fabbio, a hand with these entries, if you please." My

73

superior's voice, a little tired, a little testy, summoned me from the fascinating disclosures promised by the German scholar. "If you want to read the books in the library," he said, "you must do so in your own time, not in ours."

I apologised. He brushed the matter aside, and we concentrated upon the ledgers. Either the signorina's cooking, or her demands, had proved excessive. I ignored the by-play of Toni, who, behind our superior's back, cradled his head upon his hands in mock exhaustion, but I was not surprised when Giuseppe Fossi, shortly before noon, pronounced himself unwell.

"I must have eaten something last night," he said, "that disagreed with me. I shall have to go home and lie down. I'll return later in the afternoon if I feel better. In the meantime, I should be extremely obliged if you would carry on."

He left hurriedly, his handkerchief to his mouth. Signorina Catti remarked that it was well known that Signor Fossi suffered from his stomach. Also he was overworked. He never spared himself. Once again the irrepressible Toni gestured, once again I ignored the pantomime, this time more obvious, of an athlete at play. The telephone rang, and being closest to it I answered. A woman's voice, soft and pleasing, asked for Signor Fossi.

"I'm sorry," I replied, "Signor Fossi is not here. Can I help you?"

She asked how long he would be absent, and I said I was not sure. He had felt unwell, and had gone home. The enquirer was not Carla Raspa—the voice was pitched too low.

"Who am I speaking to?" came next.

"Armino Fabbio, temporary assistant to Signor Fossi," I replied. "May I ask who it is enquiring after him?"

"Signora Butali," she answered. "I have a message for him from the Rector about some books."

My interest quickened. The Rector's lady in person, speaking from my home. My courier's well-trained courtesy took over.

"If there is anything I can do, signora, you have only to ask," I said smoothly. "Signor Fossi left the library in the charge of Signorina Catti and myself. Would you perhaps entrust your message to me?"

There was a moment's hesitation before she replied. "The Rector is in hospital in Rome, as you know," she said, "and during a conversation on the telephone I had with him this morning he asked me to request Signor Fossi for the loan of some rather

74

valuable books about which there is a trifling dispute between the university and the Arts Council. He would like to examine these books himself, with Signor Fossi's approval, and I could take them with me to Rome on my next visit."

"Of course, signora," I said. "I am quite certain Signor Fossi would raise no objection. What books are they?"

"*The History of the Dukes of Ruffano*, in German," she answered.

The secretary was making signs to me. I explained, my hand over the mouthpiece, that I was speaking to the Rector's lady. Her sour disapproval vanished. She rushed forward and snatched the receiver from me.

"Good morning, signora," she exclaimed, her voice all sugar. "I had no idea you were back from Rome. How is the Rector?" She smiled and nodded, hushing me to silence. "Naturally anything the Rector asks for he shall be given," she continued. "I will see that the books are delivered to you at the house today. Either I, or one of our assistants, will hand them to you personally."

Further assurances followed, with an added explanation that Signor Fossi was, as usual, overworked. More smiles. More nods. Then, apparently thanked and dismissed, she replaced the receiver.

Quickly I said, "I'll deliver the books to Signora Butali this afternoon."

Signorina Catti stared, her sourness returned. "There is no need to go yourself," she said. "If you will wrap the books for me I can take them. It won't be out of my way, and the signora knows me."

"Signor Fossi gave me instructions," I said, "not to let these books out of my sight. Also, I am more easily spared from the library than you."

Furious, but acknowledging defeat, she returned to her desk. A falsetto cough from the high ladder told me that Toni had been listening. I smiled, and went on with my work. Entry had been secured to my home in the via dei Sogni. For the moment this was all that mattered.

I did not return to the pensione for lunch. I found a small restaurant in the via Rossini which, though filled with students, sufficed for my hasty meal. I went back to the library while the other assistants were still lunching, and packed up the books for the Rector's lady. It intrigued me that the very volumes that had caught my fancy should be those demanded by the Rector from his sick bed. There was no time to linger over the life history of the Falcon. This I regretted. His madness I remembered, and his death. The intervening details had been glossed over by my father. Certainly they were not mentioned in the Ruffano guide-books, nor in the printed pamphlets issued to tourists in the ducal palace.

". . . The excesses were of so singular a nature that only the Devil could have inspired them. When accusations were made against him by the outraged citizens of Ruffano, Duke Claudio retaliated by declaring that he had been divinely appointed to mete out to his subjects the punishment they deserved. The proud would be stripped, the haughty violated, the slanderer silenced, the viper die in his own venom. The scales of heavenly justice would thus be balanced."

And so on for several pages. The picture of "The Temptation" in the ducal bedchamber above the library took on new meaning for me.

"Duke Claudio was undoubtedly insane. Excuses were thus made for him, after his appalling death, by the good and gentle brother who succeeded him, the great Duke Carlo. No such consideration can be afforded to the Falcon's followers. This small band of debauchees did not believe themselves to hold divine appointment. Their mission was to sully and destroy. So great was the hatred and fear which they inspired amongst the populace of Ruffano that when the final massacre took place, and the Falcon and his band were slaughtered, it is said that the corridors and state rooms of the ducal palace ran with blood, and that atrocities, impossible to name, were committed upon the fallen victims."

These pages would certainly while away the Rector's hours of leisure in a hospital bed.

I packed the books and left the library as soon as the second assistant returned from lunch. Then I set forth for the via dei Sogni. My excitement increased as I approached the garden wall. No hovering in the shadows today. I was going home. As I drew near I could hear, as yesterday, the sound of piano-playing. It was a Chopin Impromptu. The notes rang out, up and down the scale, with almost savage intensity. It was like an argument, passionate and fierce, that would brook no interference but must sweep everything before it, then rippled, suddenly, to melting protestation. No music for a sick bed. But, of course, the Rector was some hundred and fifty miles away in Rome.

I put my hand on the garden door and entered. Nothing had changed. The single tree dominated the small enclosure as it had always done, though the grass was closer trimmed than in our day. I walked the short flagged pathway to the door and rang the bell. The music ceased. A sense of schoolboy panic came upon me. I nearly dropped the books before the door and fled. I heard, as I had heard a hundred, a thousand times before, footsteps descending the stairs. The door opened.

"Signora Butali?"

"Yes."

"Forgive me for disturbing you, signora. I have brought you the books you asked for from the palace library."

There is a picture in the audience room of the ducal palace known officially as the "Portrait of a Gentlewoman", though my father called her the Silent One. The face is grave, withdrawn, the dark eyes look out upon the man who painted her with indifference, some say disapproval. Aldo had it otherwise. I remember him arguing with my father that the Silent One had hidden fires, and that the mouth, supposedly so pursed, deceived the watcher. Signora Butali might have posed for that same gentlewoman. Her beauty was of the sixteenth century, not ours.

"Was it you I spoke to on the telephone?" she asked, and, taking the answer for granted, added, "It's good of you to come so soon."

She put out her hand for the books, but I was looking past her to the hall. The four walls were the same, but that was all. The alien shapes of chairs, not ours, and a tall mirror seemed to alter the perspective. My father, fond of reproductions of his favourite pictures at the palace, used to display them in abundance, doubtless a dated fashion, but because of this we came to know them well. Today there was but one picture hanging in the hall, and that contemporary—glazed fruit, too large, splurging beside a sheet of music. The staircase wall leading to the floor above, white in our time, was now dove grey. These things I perceived in a single flash, and with it came unreasoning resentment that anyone should dare to walk into our home and so despoil it to suit their taste, disturbing, as it were, the layer of habit underneath. Had the walls and ceilings that knew us no feeling in the matter? Must they stay dumb?

"Excuse me, signora," I said, "I did not come only at your

77

request, but because I felt myself drawn to the house. I passed here yesterday and heard the piano. Being fond of music I stayed to listen. At that time I did not even know that this was the Rector's house—they told me later at the library. When you asked for the books this morning. . . ."

Like the gentlewoman in the portrait, the mouth remained unsmiling, but the eyes softened. "You decided that this was your chance," she interrupted.

"Frankly, yes," I said.

I put the books into her hands. Once again my eyes travelled up the stairs. The last time I descended them I was running. My mother was calling from the garden, holding her travelling-case, which she handed to the Commandant's orderly. The staff-car was waiting in the via dei Sogni.

"Do you play yourself?" asked the signora.

"No. No, I never had the gift. But yesterday . . . yesterday you were playing, I believe, the 'Arabesque' of Debussy, which God knows can be heard often enough from any radio station, but somehow it sounded different. It brought back memories of childhood and old forgotten things, why, I can't say . . . nobody played the piano in our family."

She looked at me gravely, as though considering a prospective pupil, and then she said, "If you can spare the time, come up-stairs to the music-room and I'll play the 'Arabesque' for you."

"Spare the time?" I repeated. "It doesn't concern me whether I can spare the time or not. Can you?"

Once again the eyes softened. Even the mouth relaxed. "I would not invite you in if I could not," she answered. "It's early anyway. I don't expect my next pupil until three."

She closed the door, and leaving the books on a chair in the hall led the way upstairs, and so directly into my mother's bedroom. This was transformed. I recognised nothing. It was just as well, because as I entered I expected to see the tumbled double bed with all the sheets overturned, as they had been on the day we left, the wardrobe with its doors opened and the shelves awry, discarded clothes, unwanted by my mother, left to hang, tissue paper on the floor, the breakfast-tray with the cold dregs of coffee.

"I love this room," said the signora. "I find it peaceful. As soon as we came here I told my husband, 'This is where I shall have the piano'."

The walls were green. The chairs, stiff-backed, were padded in some striped material. The floor had a high polish. Another contemporary picture hung upon the wall, this time of monstrous sunflowers. The signora wandered to the piano, which stood on the exact site of my mother's double bed.

"Smoke if you wish," she said. "It doesn't worry me. Now, the 'Arabesque'."

I went and stood by the window, looking down through the branches of the tree to the garden below. The tree had spread. The branches stretched like wings, and nearly touched the walls. The ball, if it was still there, was deeply hidden.

The ripple of the music started, the rapture and the pathos and the pain. The hot July sun baked the flagstone path, and the orderly's feet rang out as he marched backwards and forwards for the luggage. Marta was at Mass in San Donato. "Hurry . . . hurry . . ." called my mother, "the Commandant won't wait." I had to find the snapshot of Aldo. Aldo, before he was shot down. Aldo in his uniform, wearing his pilot's wings.

"Come without it. Marta can send it on."

"No. I have it. It will go in my pocket."

And so running down the stairs. And so also the signora, higher, higher up the scale, and down, repeating the phrase, once more, again, carelessly, gaily. There was nothing emotional in an "Arabesque". Unless, like the listener, you were a courier, a charioteer, on and on and endlessly on, flying from the present to the past.

She said, "I was playing Chopin when you rang the bell."

It could be that we get the death we deserve. That my mother, with her cancerous womb, paid for the doubtful pleasure of that double bed, and that the Commandant, yes, and my father too, surfeited with what they had once had, doomed themselves to ultimate starvation, the one in a Russian, the other in an Allied prison camp. But why the knife for Marta?

I sat down in a chair and stared at Signora Butali. Her piano playing brought her to life, colour had come into her too pale face. Here, I supposed, she found release, and was able to forget her sick husband. I studied her dispassionately. My own age, or a few years older. Thirty-five to thirty-six. The age for regret, for sudden love, for drama. The age for opening the door to callers after ten.

The music was interrupted, as yesterday, by the shrill summons of the telephone. She rose from the piano and went to answer it, excusing herself with a glance. I noticed that it was in this room now and that she did not have to run downstairs, as my mother had done.

"Yes," she said, down the mouth-piece, "yes, I have them."

Something told me that she was referring to the books. The Rector must be anxious. He also, I surmised, asked his wife if she were alone, for she replied, in the voice one uses when others are present, "No, no, not just now. Call me later." She replaced the receiver rather quickly.

Following my train of thought, and foolishly, I asked her if the Rector was better. She looked confused, then instantly recovered.

"Ah, yes," she said, "very much better. I had many things to see to here at home, otherwise I should never have left Rome."

Did she think I was accusing her of neglect? Perhaps. In any event, I suspected that the brief telephone call, just ended, had not come from Rome.

The spell was broken, and she made no move back to the piano. I had stood up when the telephone rang. Now I glanced at my watch.

"You've been very kind, signora," I said. "You've given me much pleasure. Now I must not take up any more of your valuable time."

"Nor I yours," she answered. "You must come again. What did you say your name was?"

"Fabbio," I told her, "Armino Fabbio. I'm working at the library on a temporary basis."

"I feel sure they are very glad to have you," she said. "I hope Signor Fossi will soon recover. Please give my regards to him, and to Signorina Catti."

Already she was walking to the door. The telephone call had destroyed all magic. I followed her out to the landing. She must use for bedroom the room that we reserved for the occasional guest. It looked south-east beyond the via dei Sogni to the precincts of the old monastic buildings, used now as the city hospital. My room had lain beyond.

"Thank you again, signora," I said.

The smile she gave me was gracious but mechanical.

"It's nothing," she answered. "I like to play to anyone who is fond of music."

I followed her downstairs. When we reached the hall she picked up the books, the action suggesting that she would take them back upstairs with her after I had gone.

"You will find them interesting," I observed. "That is, if you can read German."

"I don't," she said, leaving it at that.

There was no further excuse for delay. I was a stranger, she had had enough of me. The house, my house, was equally indifferent. I smiled, bowed over her outstretched hand, and left. The door closed. I walked down the flagged path to the garden gate, and so into the street. An old, bent woman walking in the distance, the vanishing skirts of a priest, a dog sniffing at the wall, even the bright day, all of these belonged to the present time, to the Ruffano that was not mine.

They say, in English, that you should kill two birds with one stone. I might as well lay my second ghost hard upon the first. Instead of returning immediately to the ducal palace and the library, I walked downhill towards the oratorio of Ognissanti. The cross-eyed cobbler must be braved in his own domain. Before I reached the corner of the street I saw that a small crowd had collected there. People were leaning out of windows, amongst them the dour guardian of the oratorio. A car was drawn up short of the steps. A police car. A man and a woman were being bundled inside it. I drew back and waited for it to turn and pass. My view of the car and of the couple within became blocked by the chattering crowd in front of me. The crowd broke up, still talking, gesturing. I turned to one of them nearby, a round-eyed woman carrying a crying child.

"Were they arresting someone?" I asked.

She turned to me eagerly, desirous, like all women in a crowd, of imparting information to a passer-by.

"It's Signor Ghigi and his sister," she said. "No, they are not being arrested, mercifully for them, but the police have come for them all the same, to identify a body. They say it's the body of that woman murdered in Rome, it was in the newspapers, and it may be the body of the Ghigis' lodger, that's what they say, a woman who had been lodging with them for some months. She used to drink, and she disappeared days ago, saying nothing to either of them, and now they wonder, the police wonder, everybody in the quarter is wondering, can it be the same, can it be poor Marta Zampini?"

She was still talking, the child was still crying, as I turned away and walked back along the street, my heart pounding.

CHAPTER EIGHT

I bought a newspaper in the piazza della Vita and stood a moment under the colonnade, searching the pages. There was no mention of the murder. The police had obviously been working on information about missing persons in the provinces, and now they were taking the Ghigis to Rome to identify the body. Or perhaps not even that. Perhaps the police in Rome had sent items of clothing to be recognised, the shawls, the baskets. These would probably be enough.

And then? No nearer to a solution of the crime. No motive for robbery. The police would never find out that someone, just after midnight, had put a note for ten thousand lire into the victim's hand. By now it was spent, by now it had passed from the thief and murderer to a dozen other hands. The thief and murderer would not be caught. Nor the planter of the note. Both were guilty. Both must carry the burden of that guilt.

When I entered the library the secretary and the clerks had all long returned from lunch. It was mid-afternoon. Everyone stared at me. It was as though they must know I had come from the oratorio of Ognissanti, and my purpose in going there.

Taking no notice, I walked to the bookshelves and busied myself with sorting the remaining German books, but this time without interest. The face of the dead Marta, allowed to lapse into darkness during the past three days, revealed itself once more. It could no longer be denied. The Marta of the past would never torment me, only the huddled drunken figure she had become. Why the sour, stale smell? She who had been clean, fastidious, forever washing, pressing, folding clothes and fresh linen and laying them away in closets? Only two people could give me the answer now—the cobbler and his sister, our ex-cook. They would know. They could recount for me, interminably, with every sordid detail, the disintegration through the years.

It was our fault, of course. My mother's first, then mine. Living at Turin we could have written. I could have written. Enquiries could have been made. Or later, from the agency in Genoa, I could have contacted Ruffano by telephone, demanded information. I did not do so. Twenty years had passed. Marta had had to disintegrate through twenty years.

Later in the afternoon the telephone rang. Signorina Catti answered it. She spoke for a few moments in a honeyed voice, then put the receiver down.

"Signor Fossi is still unwell," she announced to the rest of us abruptly. "He will not be back today. He has asked us to carry on until seven o'clock."

Expostulation came from Toni. "It's Saturday," he protested. "Signor Fossi always lets us go by six on Saturday."

"Perhaps," replied the secretary, "but that is when he is here himself. Today is different. Signor Fossi is at this moment in bed."

She turned again to her ledger, and Toni clasped his hands to his belly in mock anguish. "When a man is past forty," he murmured, "he should restrain his appetite for bodily pleasure."

"When a man is under twenty-three," said the secretary, "he should have some respect for his superiors."

Her ears were sharper than I thought, perhaps her wits too. We returned to our business, but I think all four of us were surprised when shortly before seven the cause of Giuseppe Fossi's ills walked through the library door. She was wearing a red suit that became her well. Small gold earrings pierced her ears. A dark coat swung from her shoulders. Nodding casually to the secretary, ignoring the two clerks, Carla Raspa strolled across the room and made for me.

"Hullo," she said.

"Hullo," I answered.

"How are you doing?"

"I'm doing well."

"Like the work?"

"It's a change from tourists."

"That's what I thought. You can't have everything." She glanced up at the bookshelves, humming under her breath. The secretary, bending over the desk, might have been made of alabaster. "What are you doing this evening?" asked Carla Raspa.

"What am I doing?"

"That's what I said."

The eyes, like bitter almonds, appraised my person. I tried to

83

remember what it was, whether bird or reptile, whose love-making ended always in the female devouring the male. It was an insect—the praying mantis.

"I have a date with a couple of students from the pensione where I am staying," I invented promptly. "We're all eating and then going to the cinema."

"Which pensione is that?"

I hesitated. "Signora Silvani's," I said.

"At 24, via San Michele?" she exclaimed. "Why then, we're neighbours!"

"I believe we are."

She smiled. The smile suggested that we were both of us engaged in some conspiratorial game. "Are you comfortable?" she asked.

"Very comfortable. The students are a pleasant bunch. All C and E."

"C and E! I'm sorry for you, then. You won't be able to sleep for the noise. They're a rackety crowd."

"They were quiet enough last night," I told her.

She continued to appraise me. I could see Toni listening from his ladder. "Where are you going to eat?" she asked.

"At the house," I said. "The food's very good." And, to make my alibi the more convincing, I added, "My young friends are called Pasquale, Paolo and Caterina Pasquale."

She shrugged her shoulders. "I never come in contact with the C and E students."

It was Toni who let me down. "Did you say the Pasquales?" he asked, zealous to show camaraderie.

"Yes."

"Then you must have got your date mixed up. They always go home to San Marino on Saturdays. In fact, I saw them depart this afternoon when I was returning from lunch. Bad luck!" He grinned, and crossed the library to fetch his coat, believing he had done me a service.

"Good," said my pursuer, "that means you're free."

I had a momentary vision of Giuseppe Fossi on his bed of sickness, then remembered, with relief, that he was my senior by several years. And it could have been the cooking. I flashed my courier's smile.

"Yes, I'm free," I murmured. "We'll eat at the Hotel dei Duchi."

She raised her eyebrows. "Why waste your money?" she said. "Anyway, they'll be closed down for the night by the time we're ready to eat."

The remark was ominous. It suggested an exhausting session without even an aperitivo to give appetite. I was not sure I should be equal to the strain. But if the remark was a pleasantry—well, I like to choose my moment for such things, and this was not one of them.

"So?" I questioned.

She allowed her eyes to drift towards the departing clerks and the retreating Signorina Catti, who still hovered by the door.

"I have plans," she said, her voice guarded.

We moved together towards the entrance. Signorina Catti, eyes averted, closed the door of the library behind us and wished us a cold good evening. She disappeared along the quadrangle, her heels tap-tapping on the stone floor. My companion waited until the last sound died away. Then she turned to me, smiling, and I became aware of a certain tense excitement that exuded not from her eyes and her mouth alone, but from her whole person.

"We're in luck," she said. "I've got two passes admitting us to the ducal apartments. I begged them from the Director of the Arts Council himself. It's an honour. He's very particular."

I stared at her. This was a strange volte-face. Or perhaps I had taken her choice of an evening pastime too much for granted.

"The ducal apartments?" I repeated. "But you can see them any time you like. You take parties of students there every day."

She laughed, and motioned me to give her a cigarette. I obliged, and lighted it for her.

"The evenings are different," she said. "No general public, no outside students, nobody from the town or from the university whom the Director does not personally invite. I tell you, we're honoured."

I smiled. It suited me. What must seem to her a great occasion was something my father had done in the past week after week. I was gratified that one at least of the forgotten customs should be continued. As a child I had, now and then, accompanied Aldo or my mother, and watched my father display to his friends the notable features of a room or a picture.

"What happens?" I asked. "Do we stand about hushed, in groups, while the Director expounds some theory?"

"I could not tell you," she answered. "This is what I am intrigued to find out. I imagine that this evening he will give us a pre-view of the Festival."

She glanced down at the two passes in her hand. "It says seven-thirty," she said, "but I think we might go up. We can always wait in the gallery if the doors are not open."

It amused me that an invitation from the Director of the Arts Council of Ruffano should produce such an impression upon a lecturer at the university, and so sophisticated a one as Signorina Carla Raspa. She must be lower in the ranks of the hierarchy than I had thought. She reminded me of those tourists who obtain tickets to a papal audience at the Vatican. Only the veil was missing. We mounted the stairs to the gallery above.

"What exactly is this Festival?" I asked.

"The Rector initiated it a few years ago," she answered. "The Department of Arts in the university here is small and with no titular head, and he keeps it under his own jurisdiction. He runs the Festival in conjunction with the Director of the Arts Council. It has been a terrific success. Each year they choose an historical subject and the students act it out in the ducal apartments, or in the quadrangle, or in the former theatre below the palace. This year, because of the Rector's illness, the Festival is entirely the responsibility of the Director of the Arts Council."

We had arrived at the head of the stairs. There was already a small group of people waiting outside the closed door leading to the throne room. They were all young—students, doubtless, mostly male. They were chatting amongst themselves quietly, even soberly, with none of the hilarious, rather forced jocularity that I associated with a student body. Carla Raspa moved forward and shook hands with two or three. She introduced me and explained their status to me.

"All third- and fourth-year students," she said. "Nobody gets an invitation before the third year. How many of you will be performing in the Festival?"

"We've all volunteered," replied one of them, a shock-headed lad with the side-whiskers that my friends the Pasquales would undoubtedly have dubbed Arts, "but the Director has the final choice. If you don't measure up to standard you're out."

"What's the standard?" I enquired.

The shock-headed student looked at his companions. They all smiled.

86

"Tough," he answered. "You have to be physically fit, for one thing, and able to fence. Why? Search me! It's a new regulation."

Carla Raspa intervened. "Last Festival, when the Rector was in charge, it was really beautiful. They enacted the visit of Pope Clement to Ruffano, and Professor Butali himself played the Pope. They had the main door opened to the quadrangle and the students, dressed as the Papal guard, had to bear the Rector in, where he was received by the Duke and Duchess. Signora Butali played the Duchess, and Professor Rizzio, Director of the Department of Education, the Duke. Then they went in procession through the apartments. The costumes were magnificent."

We all moved towards the door of the throne room at the sound of the key turning in the lock. The double doors were flung wide open. A student—I supposed he was a student—stood at the entrance to scrutinise our passes. He must have passed the physical fitness test. He was lean, hard-looking, and reminded me of one of our professional football players from Turin. Perhaps, if we did not behave ourselves, he would be employed by the Arts Director as chucker-out.

We passed into the throne room, and across it to the Room of the Cherubs, whence came a murmur of voices. Others were before us. The atmosphere became more like that of a papal audience than ever, and at the entrance to the Room of the Cherubs there stood a second scrutineer, who this time took our passes from us. I felt bereft, for the passes were like badges, giving status. Then, a little startled, I saw that the electric lights in the Room of the Cherubs had been extinguished. The room was illuminated by flares and torches, which, throwing monstrous shadows upon the fluted ceiling and saffron walls, gave to the whole an eerie, sombre flavour, mediaeval and at the same time strange, exciting. A huge log-fire was burning on the open hearth beneath the priceless chimney-piece, sacrosant in my father's time. The leaping flames of the fire drew all eyes like a magnet.

The torch-light and the flames, reflecting shadows on the ceiling, threw little light upon our neighbours, and which of them were fellow-guests and which were the hosts it was impossible to tell. All seemed to be young, and nearly all were male. The sprinkling of young women present would appear to be of the company on sufferance.

Slowly the great room filled, yet never for one moment becoming crowded, and as my eyes grew accustomed to the torchlight I saw that we, and some of the rest of the company who must also be newly admitted, stood about in groups, a little uncertain what to do, whereas others, moving more freely and with an air of authority, crossed and recrossed the vast room, now and then turning to stare at the rest of us with the indifferent, slightly contemptuous amusement of the habituated.

Suddenly the scrutineer at the entrance closed the door. He stood against it, his arms folded, his face expressionless. There was an instant silence. One of the women, nerves on edge, broke into a half-laugh, which was immediately hushed by her male companions. I glanced at Carla Raspa. She put out her hand to mine and held it, her fingers tense. The muted atmosphere communicated itself from one to the other, and I felt trapped. Escape, for anyone with a tendency to claustrophobia, would be impossible.

The door leading to the Duke's bedroom, closed hitherto, was flung open. A man entered, followed by six companions, who ranged themselves about him like a bodyguard. He advanced into the room, and putting out his hand immediately began to greet his guests, who, tension breaking, pressed forward eagerly to be amongst the first. Carla Raspa, her eyes shining, forgetting me, jostled in the queue.

"Who is it?" I asked.

She did not hear me. She had passed on. But a young man near to me, throwing me an astonished look, said, "Why, Professor Donati, of course, the Director of the Arts Council."

I stepped back out of the torchlight into the shadows. The figure with his bodyguard came on. A word to one, a laugh to another, a pat on the shoulder to a third—and there was no way of breaking from the line, no possible escape, the movement of those behind me urged me forward. Somehow I had caught up with my companion, and I heard her say, "This is Signor Fabbio. He is helping Signor Fossi in the library." I held out my hand and he shook it, saying, "Good, good. I am very pleased to see you," then, barely looking at me, passed on. Carla Raspa began talking excitedly to the neighbour on her left and not, thank God, to me. For me the tomb had opened. The heavens roared. Christ had come again in all his majesty. The stranger in the via dei Sogni the night before had been no phantom after all, and, if

I still dared to doubt it, the name alone was now conclusive.

The Director of the Arts Council. Professor Donati. Professor Aldo Donati. Twenty-two years had brought maturity to the broadened figure, the assured step, the arrogant angle of the head, but the high forehead, the full dark eyes, the mouth with the imperceptible droop at the right corner, and the voice, deeper now but casual, always casual—these things belonged to my brother.

Aldo lived again. Aldo had risen from the dead, and my world was rocking.

I turned my face to the wall and began staring at a tapestry. I saw nothing, heard nothing. People moved about the room and talked, a thousand aircraft could have hummed about me in the air, it would not have signified. One aircraft two-and-twenty years ago had never crashed, this was all that mattered. Or if it crashed it had not burnt, or if it burnt the pilot had come out of it unscathed. My brother lived. My brother had not died.

Someone touched my arm. It was Carla Raspa. She said to me, "What do you think of him?"

I said, "I think he's God."

She smiled, and putting up her hand she whispered, "So do they all."

I drew back against the wall. I did not want her to see that I was shaking. My dread was that I might collapse, fall, draw attention to myself and Aldo discover me here, before all these people. Later, of course, later. . . . But not now. It was impossible to think, to plan. I must not give myself away. I must stop shaking.

"Inspection over," murmured Carla Raspa. "He's going to speak."

There was one chair in the room, the fifteenth century stool with the narrow back that usually stood before the fireplace. One of the bodyguard stepped forward and placed it in the centre of the room. Aldo smiled, and gestured with his hand. Everyone sat down upon the floor, some of us with our backs to the wall, others huddled close together, nearer to the speaker. The torchlight still threw shadows on the ceiling, now more grotesque than ever because of the massed heads. How many of us there were I could not tell—eighty, perhaps a hundred, perhaps more. Aldo sat down in the chair, the firelight flickered, and with a supreme effort I tried to still my shaking hands.

"Five hundred and twenty-five years ago this spring, the people of Ruffano killed their Duke," he said. "You won't find how they drove him to his death in the guide-books or in the official history of the times; the censors, you see, even then, stepped in to hide the truth. I am referring, of course, to Claudio, first Duke of Ruffano, known as the Falcon, despised and rejected of men because they feared him. Why did they fear him? Because he had the ability to read their souls. Their petty lies, their small deceits, their competition one with another in the commerce of the day—for all the Ruffanesi ever thought about was to enrich themselves at the expense of the starving peasantry—were condemned by the Falcon, and rightly so. They understood nothing of art, nothing of culture, and this at a time when a new age was dawning, the age of the Renaissance. The bishop and his priests allied themselves with the nobles and the merchants to keep the people ignorant, little better than beasts, and to obstruct the Duke by every possible means within their power.

"It was his intention to gather around him at his Court young men of distinction—birth did not matter, if they had intelligence and wit—who by their personal courage, force of arms, and single-minded devotion to Art in all its branches should form themselves, as it were, into an élite—call them fanatics if you will —who by their example would act as a torch, a fire to every dukedom in the country. Art would reign supreme, galleries filled with beautiful things be of more account than banking houses, a bronzed statuette of greater price than bales of cloth. He raised for this purpose taxes, which the merchants refused to pay. He held tournaments and knightly exercises at the Court, thereby to train his young courtiers, and the people vilified him as a debauchee.

"Five hundred and twenty-five years have passed, and I believe the time has come to reinstate the Duke. Or rather, to do honour to his memory. That is why, since it has fallen to me, in the absence of the Rector of the university, Professor Butali, whom we all revere and honour, to arrange this year's Festival, I have decided to enact the uprising of the city of Ruffano against their much misunderstood lord and master, Claudio, first duke, and called by all—the Falcon."

He paused. I knew this pause. He had employed it in the past when we were lying beside one another in the bedroom that we shared and he was telling me a story.

"Some of you," he continued, "know about this already. We have had our rehearsals. You must remember that the flight of the Falcon, which will be the name of this season's celebration—for such was the manner of Claudio's passing—has never before been acted, and probably never will be again. I want it so to live in all your minds, and in the memories of everyone who sees it, that it will endure for all time. What has been enacted up to the present in our Festival plays will be as nothing compared to this. I want to stage the greatest production that this city has ever seen. Because of this, I am going to ask for even more volunteers than we have had in previous years."

A murmur rose from the seated ranks below him on the floor. Every hand shot up into the air. The faces, pale in the flickering light, were turned to his.

"Wait," he said. "Not all will be chosen. I shall choose later those whom I think fit. The point is this. . . ." Once again he paused. He leant forward in his chair, watching their faces. "You know my methods," he said. "We used them last year, and the year before. It is essential that every volunteer should believe in the part he plays, should think himself into his creation. This year you will be the courtiers at the Falcon's palace. You will be that small body of dedicated men. You, the Arts students of the university, will, by your very nature, become the élite. You are so already. For this you are here in Ruffano, for this you have your reason for living. Yet you are a minority in the university, your ranks are small, the immense numbers swamping the other Faculties are barbarians and Goths and Vandals who, like the merchants of five hundred years ago, understand nothing of art, nothing of beauty. They would, if they had the power, destroy all the treasures we possess in the apartments here, perhaps even pull down the palace itself, and put in its stead . . . what? Factories, offices, banks, commercial houses, not to give employment and an easier life to the peasant who lives no better now than he did five centuries ago, but to enrich themselves, to better themselves, to own more cars, more television sets, more biscuit-box villas on the Adriatic, thus breeding ever greater discontent, poverty and misery."

Suddenly he rose. He held up his hand to silence the burst of applause that echoed to the fluted ceiling.

"That's enough," he said, "no more from me tonight. What we are going to do now is to give you a short display of the sort of training we have already carried out with volunteers. Keep back from the square, or you may get hurt!"

The applause, checked, turned to instant silence. The crowd leaned forward, intent on what was to follow. Two of the body-guard came and took away the chair. Four more advanced, holding flares in either hand, and formed a square in the centre of the room, lit by the flames alone.

Aldo took his place beside one of the flares. As he did so two figures leapt into the square. They wore white shirts, the sleeves rolled to the elbow, and black jeans. Their faces were masked, not for protection but to conceal their features. Each carried a naked sword. They fought as duellists fought in days gone by, in earnest, not in play. There was no feint in parry or thrust, no pretence in the crouching stance of the competitors. The steel blades rang as they clashed and struck and dived, and when one of the duellists soon proved himself to have a longer reach than his adversary and in pursuit drove him to his knee, pointing the blade at his throat, a gasp rose from the huddled ranks as the half-fallen man, panting, stared through the narrow slits of his mask and the sharpened tip drew blood. A scratch, no more, perhaps, than a razor's slip might do, but the sword had done it, the drops of blood ran down his throat and stained the white shirt below.

"Enough!" cried Aldo. "You have shown what you can do. Well fought, and thank you."

He threw his handkerchief to the fallen man who, rising to his feet, staunched the wound. Both men left the lighted square and disappeared through the door to the Duke's bedchamber.

The spectators, stunned by the realism of the display, were too shaken to applaud. They waited, breathless, for Aldo to speak again. Once more I was reminded of my boyhood days and the effect he had had upon me then. This was the same power, but maturer, dangerous.

"You have seen," said Aldo, "that mock battles are not for us. Now, will the few women amongst us leave the room, and any of the rest who do not wish to volunteer? It will not be held against them. Those who care to offer themselves as volunteers, remain."

One girl pushed forward, protesting, but he shook his head. "I'm sorry," he said, "no women. Not for this. Go home and learn how to bandage, yes, but fighting is for us."

The door leading to the throne room was flung open. Slowly,

reluctantly, the few women passed through it, followed by some dozen men, no more. I was amongst them. The scrutineer in the throne room waved us on. We walked silently to the gallery outside, and the door was closed behind us. We were, I suppose, about eighteen to twenty all told. The girls, contemptuous, did not even wait for escorts. Those who knew each other well linked arms and clattered down the stairs. The men, shamefaced, defensive, offered each other cigarettes.

"I can't swallow that stuff," said one. "It's fascism all over again, that's what he's driving at."

"You're crazy," said another. "Didn't you realise he was pitching into the industrialists? He's a Communist, it's obvious. They say he's a member of the Communist Party."

"I don't think he cares one hell for politics," said a third. "He's just a magnificent hoaxer, that's all, and that's the way he gets his Festival company to work. He did the same last year, when he dressed up the Papal Guard. I was ready to volunteer until I saw that fight. No Arts Director is going to hack me to pieces."

Nobody raised his voice. They argued, but in fierce whispers. We all tramped down the stairs in the wake of the girls.

"One thing's certain," observed somebody. "If this leaks out to the C and E crowd there'll be murder."

"Whose murder?"

"After the show we've just seen? Why, theirs. The C and E."

"Then I shall volunteer. Anything to have a go at that lot!"

"Same here. Up with the barricades!"

Loss of face had been recovered. They stood in the piazza, still arguing, discussing, and it was plain that bitterness ran dangerously high between the C and E students and the other Faculties. Then they drifted uphill towards the university and the students' hostel. I waited until the figure I had noticed standing on the Duomo steps came to join me.

"Well?" said Carla Raspa.

"Well?" I answered.

"I never wanted to be a man until tonight," she said. "Like the American song, I thought 'Anything they can do I can do better'. Except, so it seems fight."

"Perhaps there will be parts for women, too," I said. "He'll recruit you later. There are always women in a crowd, to scream and throw stones."

"I don't want to scream," she said, "I want to fight." Then,

93

looking at me with no less contempt than the student girls, she
said, "Why didn't you volunteer?"

"Because," I answered, "I'm a bird of passage."

"That's no reason," she answered. "So am I, if it comes to that.
I can leave at any time, take my lectures elsewhere. Get a transfer.
Not now, though, Not after what I've heard tonight. It could
be . . ." she paused, while I lighted her cigarette, "it could be that
this is what I'm looking for. A purpose. A cause."

We started walking down the via Rossini.

"Would acting in a Festival play give you a purpose?" I asked.

"He wasn't talking about acting," she said.

It was still early, and because it was Saturday evening the
people were strolling up and down the street, in couples or family
parties. Not many students, or so I judged. They had gone home
until Sunday evening. The young who strolled the streets came
from the shops, the banks, the offices. These were the native
Ruffanesi.

"How long has he been here?" I asked.

"Professor Donati? Oh, some years. He was born here, fought
in the war as a fighter-pilot, was given up for dead, then returned
and took a post-graduate course. He stayed on as lecturer and
finally became adopted by the Ruffano Arts Council as their
bright boy, until a few years ago they voted him Director. He's
the darling of some of the powers that be, and bitterly resented
by others. Not by the Rector. Professor Butali believes in him."

"And the Rector's lady?"

"Livia Butali? I wouldn't know. She's a snob. Keeps herself to
herself and thinks of nothing but music. She comes of an old
Florentine family and won't let you forget it. I hardly think
Professor Donati would have much time for her."

We had come to the piazza della Vita. I had forgotten, until
that moment, my promise to take my companion out to dinner. I
wondered if she had forgotten it too. We crossed over in the
direction of the via San Michele, and stopped outside the door of
Number 5.

Then abruptly she held out her hand. "Don't think I'm un-
friendly," she said. "The truth is, I want to be alone. I want to
think about what we saw tonight. I shall heat myself some soup
and go to bed. Have I let you down?"

"No," I said, "I feel exactly as you do."

"Another time, then," she nodded. "Perhaps tomorrow, it all

depends. . . . Anyway, you're a neighbour, you're just down the street. We can always find each other."

"Naturally," I said. "Good night. And thank you."

She let herself in at the door of Number 5, and I continued down the street to 24. I entered cautiously. No one was about. I could hear the sound of television coming from the Silvanis' living-room.

I took up the telephone directory lying on a table in the hall beside the telephone, and searched the pages. Donati. Professor Aldo Donati. The address, 2, via dei Sogni.

I went out again into the street.

CHAPTER NINE

MY WALK TOOK me past our old home and nearly to the top of the via dei Sogni, before it curved to the right into the via dell'8 Settembre above the university. Number 2 was a tall, narrow house standing on its own, looking down towards the church of San Donato and the long via delle Mura that encircled the city. In former days this had been our doctor's house, good Dr. Mauri, who came and visited me whenever I coughed and wheezed—I was said to suffer from a weak chest—and I remember that he never used a stethoscope for the purpose of listening to my breathing but always laid his ear flat against my naked chest, gripping my small shoulders as he did so, a sudden proximity which I found distasteful. He was middle-aged even then, and must now be dead, or long past practising his medicine.

I came close to the house and saw the name-plate—Donati—on the right-hand door beneath the double entrance. This double entrance gave access both to the via dei Sogni and, through a half-passage, to the grassy slope beyond and the stone steps descending to the church of San Donato. To the left was the porter's domain, used in the old days by Dr. Mauri's cook.

I stared at the name-plate. We had had a similar plate at Number 8. It had been Marta's pride to keep it polished, and it could, with a little imagination, be the same. There was a bell beside it. I put my finger on the button and pressed. I could hear the summons within. No one answered. Aldo must live alone, or, if not alone, whoever lived with him was now in the Room of the Cherubs at the ducal palace in his company.

I rang once again to make sure, but there was nothing. I turned and looked opposite at the porter's door. I hesitated a moment, and then rang that instead. After a moment the door opened, and a man asked my business. The bushy eyebrows, the hair en brosse, though grizzled, were familiar. Then I remembered. He had been a comrade-in-arms of my brother's, one of the ground-crew at the aircraft base. He had attached himself to Aldo, and once my brother had brought him home on leave. Save for turning grey, he had not changed. I had. Nobody, look-

96

ing upon a man of thirty-two, would remember the boy of ten.

"Professor Donati," he told me, "is not at home. You will find him at the ducal palace."

"I know that," I answered. "I've already seen him there, but not in private. My business is personal."

"I'm sorry," he said, "I cannot tell you when the professor will be back. He hasn't ordered dinner. If you care to leave your name you could always telephone him for an appointment."

"The name is Fabbio," I said, "but he would not know it." I was not sure whether I cursed the anonymity of my step-father's heritage or blessed it.

"Signor Fabbio," answered the man. "I will remember. If I do not see Professor Donati tonight I will tell him in the morning."

"Thank you," I said, "thank you. Good night."

"Good night, signore."

He closed the door. I stood by the double entrance looking on to the via dei Sogni. I had remembered his name. Jacopo. He had been ill-at-ease when my brother brought him home on leave, believing himself out of place. Marta had seized the situation at a glance and taken him into the kitchen with herself and Maria Ghigi.

I wondered whether it would be any use going back to the ducal palace and looking for my brother there. No sooner thought than instantly dismissed. He would be attended by his bodyguard, perhaps by the whole crowd of adulating students.

I was about to step out of the porched entrance when I heard footsteps approaching. I looked and saw that it was a woman, and the woman Carla Raspa. I withdrew through the double entrance and stood behind the open doorway on the eastern side. She could not see me, but I could see her. When she came to Aldo's door she did as I had done and rang the bell. She waited a moment, glancing over her shoulder at Jacopo's entrance, but made no attempt to ring his bell. Then she felt in her bag, and bringing out an envelope pushed it through the letter-box to the floor within. I could sense the disappointment in her drooping shoulders. She went out once more into the via dei Sogni and I heard the patter of her high heels die away. Getting rid of me had been an excuse. No bowl of soup and bed for Carla Raspa. She must have had this in mind as soon as we left the ducal palace. Now, frustrated, she would find the soup more welcome, but she would have to drink it alone.

I waited until I judged her well ahead and out of sight and then I, in turn, returned to the via San Michele. This time I penetrated to the Silvani sanctum and explained to the signora that I had not eaten. Anything would do. Switching off the television she got up, protesting hospitality, and pushed me into the dinning-room, her husband following to keep me company. I told them I had been to the ducal palace by invitation. They seemed impressed.

"Are you going to take part in the Festival?" enquired the signora.

"No," I answered, "no, I think not."

"You should do so," she insisted. "It's a great thing for Ruffano, this Festival. People come for miles to see it. Last year many had to be turned away. We were lucky. My husband managed to get seats in the piazza Maggiore and we watched the procession of the Papal Guard. It was so realistic that I said afterwards we might have been living in those times. When the Rector blessed me, in his guise as Pope Clement, I felt I had been blessed by the Holy Father himself."

She bustled around, helping me to food and drink.

"Yes," agreed her husband, "it was magnificent. They say this year it will be even better, despite the Rector's illness. Professor Donati is a great artist. Some feel he has missed his vocation. He ought to be a film director, instead of giving up his time to the Arts Council here. After all, Ruffano is only a small city."

I ate, more from emptiness than hunger. Excitement and emotion were still at fever-point.

"What sort of a fellow is he, this Professor Donati?" I asked.

The signora smiled and rolled her eyes. "You saw him tonight, didn't you?" she said. "Well, you can judge for yourself what a woman thinks of him. If I were half my age, I wouldn't let him alone."

Her husband laughed. "It's his dark eyes," he said. "He has a way with him, not only with the women, but with the munici-pality too. Whatever he asks for, he gets. Seriously, though, he and the Rector between them have done great things for Ruffano. Of course, he's a native. His father, Signor Donati, was Super-intendent at the palace for many years, so he knew what was wanted. Do you know that he came back here, after the liberation, to find that his father had died in a prison camp, and his mother had run off with a German general, taking the younger brother with her—his whole family, you may say, wiped out? It takes guts to accept that. He stayed. Gave himself to Ruffano, has never looked elsewhere. Now, you can't help admiring the man for that."

Signora Silvani pushed fruit upon me. I shook my head.

"No more," I said. "Coffee only." I took one of the signore's cigarettes. "Then he never married?"

"No. You know what it is," said the signora. "When a young man comes home in a state of shock—he was a pilot, and he was shot down and joined the Resistance—and hopes to rejoin his family, it doesn't make him love the opposite sex better to learn that his mother has decamped with a German. My opinion is that it sickened him with women for good."

"Ah, no," said her husband, "he's recovered. After all, he was only a boy at the time. Professor Donati must be forty now. Give him time. He'll find himself a wife when he's ready for marriage."

I drank my coffee and stood up.

"You look tired," said Signora Silvani with sympathy. "They are working you too hard at the library. Never mind, it's Sunday tomorrow. You can stay in bed all day if you feel like it."

I thanked them and went upstairs. I flung my things off, my head still bursting, and lay down on the bed. But not to sleep. Only to see Aldo's face in the flickering firelight of the Room of the Cherubs, that pale, unforgettable face, and to hear again the loved, the feared, the well-remembered voice.

After tossing for two hours I got out of bed, opened the window and stood there, smoking a cigarette. The last loiterer had gone home, and all was still. I looked up the street and saw that the shutters on the first floor of Number 5 were open, as mine were. A woman was leaning out, also wakeful, also smoking a cigarette. If I could not sleep, neither could Carla Raspa. We were wakeful for the same cause.

The church bells roused me next morning from the fitful sleep into which I had eventually fallen. First at seven, then at eight. The Duomo, San Cipriano, then the others. Not the chimes for the hours, but the summons to Mass. I lay in bed and thought how we used to go, the four of us, my father, my mother, Aldo and myself, to High Mass in San Cipriano. Those were the early days before the war. We would set forth, dressed for Sundays, Aldo resplendent in his uniform of the Fascist Youth organisation. The girls had an eye for him even then. We would walk down the

99

hill to San Cipriano, and my martyrdom near the altar-piece of Lazarus would begin.

I got up and threw wide the shutters I had closed last night. It was raining. Rivulets of water ran in the gutters. A few people hurried by bent under umbrellas. Down the street the shutters on the first floor of Number 5 were tightly closed. I had not been to Mass since my schooldays in Turin. At least, not by intention. Sometimes I would escort a flock of tourists bent on sight-seeing, and, pausing near the high altar in whichever church we were visiting, be obliged to stand and stare. Now I would go of my own volition.

I was half-dressed when a knock on the door announced Signora Silvani's arrival with rolls and coffee. "Don't move," she said. "Look at the weather. There's nothing to get up for."

I had said the same thing to myself over the years when chance brought me a free Sunday, wet or fine. Nothing to get up for in Turin or in Genoa. Now the world had changed.

"I'm going to Mass in San Cipriano," I said.

She nearly dropped the tray. Then she put it carefully on the bed. "Amazing," she said. "I thought nobody went to Mass any more, except old people and the very young. I'm glad to hear it. Do you always go?"

"No," I said, "but this is a special occasion."

"It's Lent," she said. "I suppose all of us should go in Lent."

"My Lent is over," I said. "I'm going to celebrate the Resurrection."

"You'd do better to stay in bed and wait for Easter," she told me.

I drank the coffee and finished dressing. My head no longer reeled. Even my hands were still. The rain did not matter, poor Marta's death did not matter despite the manner of it. Later in the day I would see Aldo. For the first time in my life I held the cards; I was prepared for it and he was not.

I went out of the house into the rain, the collar of my light overcoat that had to do duty for a raincoat turned high up to my ears. The shutters were still closed at Number 5. Crossing the piazza were a few stragglers, bent on the same mission as myself. Others stood huddled under the colonnades waiting for the bus that brought the Sunday papers, or waiting for another bus to take them out of Ruffano. A few young people, braving the weather, were setting forth on vespas.

"It won't last," somebody shouted above the roar of his machine. "They say the sun is shining on the coast."

The summons from San Cipriano rang forth. Not so deep as the Duomo, but for me more solemn, more compelling, with a sudden urgency before the hour struck as though to hurry laggards to their knees.

Once inside, moved by the familiar sombre smell, I was struck by the paucity of people. In childhood days we had arrived early because my father wished to take his accustomed place. The church had been full, with the people standing in the side aisles. Not so today. The numbers were halved. Mostly family parties, women and young children. I went and stood near the side-chapel, feeling that I was fulfilling some age-long rite. The gates of the chapel were open, but no light above the altar-piece shone upon the face of Lazarus. The picture was veiled by the dimness. So were the other pictures in the church, and the statues, and the crucifixes. Then I remembered that it must be Passion Sunday.

I heard the sung Mass through, letting the thin voices of the boy choristers seep through me without pain. My mind was empty. Or perhaps I dreamed. A middle-aged priest I did not recognise gave a twenty-minute sermon warning us of perils past, of perils still to come, that the Lord, the Christ, still suffered for our sins. A child close to me yawned, his small face white with fatigue, and a woman who might have been my mother nudged him to attention. Later, the few communicants shuffled to the rails. They were mostly women. One woman, well-dressed, her head covered with a black lace veil, had knelt throughout the Mass. She did not go to the rails. Her head was bowed in her hands. When it was all over, when the priests and the choristers had gone, the people dispersing with their faces solemn still yet somehow eased, their duty done, she rose to her feet and turned, and I saw that it was Signora Butali. I walked ahead, and waited for her outside the church. The boy on the vespa had been right. The rain had stopped. The sun that had been shining on the coast had broken through to Ruffano.

"Signora?" I said.

She looked at me with the blank eyes of someone far away brought back unwillingly to a less pleasant world. "Yes?" she answered.

I saw that I meant nothing. I had left no trace. "Armino

Fabbio," I said. "I called at your house yesterday with some books."

Recognition dawned. I could read the thought passing through her mind. Ah, yes, the assistant librarian.

"Excuse me, of course," she said. "Forgive me. Good morning, Signor Fabbio."

"You were in front of me at Mass," I said. "At least, I thought it was you. I was not sure."

She walked down the steps at my side. She looked up at the sky and saw that the umbrella she carried was not necessary.

"I like to go to San Cipriano," she said. "It has more atmosphere than the Duomo. Is it going to be fine?"

Absently, she looked about her, and I felt a momentary hurt that she should feel so little interest in the man who stood by her side. A beautiful woman is usually aware of admiration, whatever the source. Effort is made. There is implicit understanding that homage is being paid. Signora Butali seemed unaware of these things.

"You have a car?" I asked.

"No," she said. "They're working on it at the garage over the weekend. I had trouble with it coming back from Rome."

"Would you object, then, if I walked with you up the hill? That is, if you are going home?"

"Not at all. Please do."

We crossed the piazza della Vita and began walking up the via Rossini as far as the prefettura, when she turned left and took the steps leading up to the via dei Sogni. Here we paused for breath, and for the first time she looked at me and smiled.

"The Ruffano hills," she said. "It takes time to get accustomed to them. Especially if, like me, you are a Florentine."

It made all the difference when she smiled. The mouth that seemed taut, disapproving, the mouth of the gentlewoman in the portrait my father loved, relaxed to femininity. There was even humour behind the eyes.

"Are you homesick?" I asked.

"Sometimes," she replied, "but what's the use? I knew what I was in for when I came here. My husband warned me."

She turned abruptly, and we set ourselves to climb the steps.

"It's not an easy life then, signora," I said, "to be wife of the Rector of a university?"

"Far from easy," she answered. "There are so many jealousies,

102

factions, to which I have to shut my eyes. I am less patient than my husband. He has given his life, literally, to his work here. If it were not so he would not be in hospital now."

She bowed and wished good morning to a couple descending the steps, and from the gracious inclination of her head, without a smile, I understood why Carla Raspa had spoken in feminine spite. Signora Butali, consciously or not, exuded breeding. I wondered what effect she had upon the professors' wives.

"Last night," I said, "I was lucky enough to get a pass to the ducal palace for a session given by the Director of the Arts Council."

"Indeed?" she replied in sudden animation. "Do tell me about it. Did it impress you?"

"It impressed me very much," I answered, aware that she had turned now to look at me. "Not only the setting, lit with flares and torches for the occasion, but the duelling display that followed, and above all Professor Donati's address to the students."

A spot of colour had come into her cheeks, due, I felt, not so much to her exertion in climbing the steps as to the turn in the conversation.

"I must go to one of the sessions," she said, "I really must. Something always seems to prevent me."

"Last year," I said, "they were telling me you performed at the Festival. Are you going to do the same this year?"

"No, impossible," she answered, "with my husband in hospital in Rome. In any event, I doubt if there would be a part for me."

"You know the subject?"

"Poor Duke Claudio, isn't it? I'm afraid I'm a little vague. I just know there was an insurrection, and he was murdered."

We had reached the via dei Sogni, and in the distance I could see the garden wall. Imperceptibly I slackened my steps.

"Professor Donati seems to be a very remarkable man," I said. "They told me at the pensione where I am lodging that he is himself a Ruffanese."

"Very much so," she said. "His father was Superintendent at the ducal palace, and in fact he was born and spent all his boyhood at the house we live in now. It's one of his ambitions to have it back from us. That is not very likely, unless my husband's health forces us to retire. Professor Donati loves every room in the house, as you can imagine. I gather he was immensely proud of his father, and his father of him. The family history is quite a tragedy."

"Yes," I said, "yes, so I heard."

"He used to speak about it," she said, "but not any longer. I hope he's beginning to forget. After all, twenty years is a long time."

"What became of his mother?" I asked.

"He never discovered. She disappeared with the German forces which occupied Ruffano in '44, and since there was fighting in the north shortly afterwards it is almost certain that she must have been killed in the bombing, she and the little brother."

"There was a brother?"

"Yes, a small boy of ten or eleven. They were very devoted. I sometimes think that it is because of him that Professor Donati gives so much thought to the students."

We had reached the garden wall. I glanced furtively at my watch. It was about twenty-five minutes after eleven.

"Thank you, signora," I said, "it was very good of you to let me walk home with you."

"No," she said, "it is for me to thank you." She paused, with her hand on the garden door. "Would you like to meet Professor Donati personally?" she said. "If so, I should be delighted to introduce you."

Panic seized me. "Thank you, signora," I said, "but I wouldn't in any way wish . . ."

The smile returned. "No trouble." She cut me short. "It's a custom of the Rector's to ask a few of his colleagues to the house on Sunday mornings, and in his absence I do the same. Two or three people may call this morning, and Professor Donati is sure to be one of them."

I had not planned it thus. I had planned to go alone to his house in the via dei Sogni. Signora Butali took my panic for embarrassment, an assistant librarian at the palace library feeling himself out of place.

"Don't be shy," she said, smiling. "It will be something to tell the other assistants about tomorrow!"

I followed her into the garden and to the house door, still thinking of an excuse to get away.

"Anna will be busy preparing lunch," she said. "You can help me set out the glasses."

She opened the door. We entered the hall, and passed through to the dining-room on the left. It was no longer a dining-room. It was lined with books from floor to ceiling, and there was a large desk near the window.

"This is my husband's library," she said. "When he is at home he likes to entertain here, and when we are many we fling open the double doors to the small dining-room beyond."

The small dining-room beyond had been my playroom. She opened the double doors and I saw, astonished, how the table was set there in the centre, stiff and formal, laid for one. I thought of the mess I had left the room in, with my fleet of small cars scattered over the floor and two tins, upturned, for the garage.

"The vermouth is on the sideboard," said Signora Butali, "and the Campari. The glasses are on the trolley. Wheel the trolley into the library, will you?"

She had arranged things to her satisfaction and put out the cigarettes when the bell rang.

"Probably the Rizzios," she said. "I'm glad to have you here, she's so very formal. Professor Rizzio is Head of the Department of Education, and his sister is in charge of the hostel where the women students live."

She looked suddenly vulnerable, and younger than her age. Perhaps when her husband was at home he shouldered the burden of social responsibility.

I slipped into my courier guise and waited by the trolley, ready to pour vermouth at her command. She went to the door to greet the callers, and I heard the murmur of the usual compliments. Then she ushered her guests into the room. They were middle-aged, grey-haired and angular. He had the worn and harassed appearance of one perpetually up to the eyes in work, with in-trays piled upon a desk that never cleared. I could picture him baying ineffectual commands to streams of tired subordinates. His sister had more authority, holding herself like a matron of old Rome. I pitied the luckless students who lived under her rule. I was introduced as Signor Fabbio, temporary assistant at the library. The signorina bowed, turning immediately to her hostess to enquire after the Rector.

Professor Rizzio peered at me with a puzzled air. "Forgive me," he asked, "but I don't recollect your name. How long have you been working at the library?"

"Since Friday," I told him. "I was engaged by Signor Fossi."

"Then your appointment went through him?" he said.

"Yes, professor," I answered. "I applied to Signor Fossi and he spoke to the Registrar."

"Really!" he commented. "I am surprised he did not consult me."

"I imagine he did not want to burden you with such a small matter," I murmured.

"Any appointment, however small, is of interest to the Deputy Rector," he said. "Where are you from?"

"I have been working in Genoa, professor," I replied, "but my home is in Turin. I graduated at the university there. I hold a degree in modern languages."

"That, at least, is fortunate," he said. "It is more than the other temporary assistants possess."

I asked him what he would have to drink, and he said a small glass of vermouth. I poured it for him and he moved away. His sister said she would take nothing, but when Signora Butali protested Signorina Rizzio was pleased to accept a glass of mineral water.

"So you are working at the library?" she said, dwarfing me with her presence.

Tall women bring out the worst in me, as they do in most men of less than average height. "I pass the time there, signorina," I said. "I am taking a vacation, and the job happens to suit me."

"You are fortunate," she replied, staring. "Many students in their third or fourth year would be glad to avail themselves of such an opportunity."

"Possibly, signorina," I said in smoothly courteous tones, "but I am not a student. I am a courier who speaks several languages, and I am accustomed to conducting parties of international repute through the more important cities of our country— Florence, Rome, Naples. . . ."

Dislike of my impertinence formed upon her features. She sipped at the mineral water, and her throat quivered as the liquid passed. Another ring at the front door spared her from further distress. My hostess, ears only for the bell, turned towards me, a tell-tale spot of colour in her cheeks.

"Answer it for me, will you?" she said. "It's probably Professor Donati."

She continued her rapid conversation with Professor Rizzio, her unwonted animation covering inward stress. A courier seldom drinks. He dares not. Now, however, I quickly swallowed a glass of vermouth under the disapproving eyes of Signorina Rizzio and, excusing myself, made for the front door. Aldo had opened it already, being, no doubt, persona grata in the house, and was frowning at the sight of Professor Rizzio's raincoat thrown down upon a chair. Then his eyes fell upon me. Without recognition. Without even a flicker of interest.

"Signora Butali is expecting you," I stammered.

"So I believe," he said. "Who are you?"

"My name is Fabbio," I said. "I had the honour of meeting you last night at the ducal palace. I was with Signorina Raspa."

"Oh, yes," he said, "yes, I remember. I hope you enjoyed yourself."

He did not remember. It mattered not at all what I thought of the evening. He moved forward into the dining-room, or rather the library, and at once the room became alive. Signora Butali called "Hullo", and he retorted with "Good morning", the morning a little emphasised. He bent over her hand and kissed it, then turned immediately to Signorina Rizzio. Signora Butali, without asking him what he wanted, filled a glass half-full of Campari and gave it to him.

"Thank you," he said, taking it from her, not looking at her.

The front-door bell rang once more, and questioning my hostess with a glance I went to open it. These menial duties kept me occupied, and served to steady the threatening tremor of my hands. Signor Fossi stood before me on the doorstep, accompanied by a lady. He looked taken aback at the sight of me, and immediately presented the lady as his wife. Somehow I had not thought of him as married.

"Signor Fabbio is helping us temporarily in the library," he explained to her, and, on my asking how he did, told me quickly that he had quite recovered.

I took up my stance once more behind the trolley, and poured them drinks. The conversation turned to health, our hostess touching upon her distress at the reason for Signor Fossi's absence from the library the day before.

"Luckily," she said, "Signor Fabbio was able to oblige me with the books I asked for."

The librarian, anxious to turn discussion away from his own past indisposition, did not dwell upon the loan of books, but immediately enquired after the Rector. Talk about Professor

Butali became general, everyone hoping that he would be able to leave hospital in time for the Festival.

Behind me I could hear Signorina Rizzio complaining to Aldo about the rowdy behaviour of the C and E students, who had taken to circling the city in the evenings on their vespas.

"They even have the insolence to roar their machines beneath the women students' hostel," she said, "as late sometimes as ten o'clock at night. I have asked my brother to speak to Professor Elia, and he assures me he has done so, but the Professor takes no action. If it continues I shall bring the matter up before the university Council."

"Perhaps," suggested Aldo, "your young women encourage the vespa enthusiasts from their windows?"

"I assure you they do not," retorted Signorina Rizzio. "My young women, as you call them, are either engaged in reading up their notes for the next lecture or they are safely tucked up in bed with the shutters closed."

I poured myself out another glass of vermouth. Then, looking up, I perceived Aldo's eye upon me, puzzled. I moved away from the trolley and stood by the window, staring down into the garden. The voices hummed. The bell rang. Somebody else went to answer it. This time I did not bother to come forward to be introduced, and I think my hostess had forgotten me.

Presently, while I was still staring into the garden, I felt a hand on my shoulder. "You're an odd fellow," said Aldo. "I keep asking myself what you are doing here. Have I seen you before somewhere?"

"It's possible," I said, "that if I disguised myself in a winding-sheet and hid in the linen closet upstairs you might recognise me. My name is Lazarus.'"

I turned and looked at him. His smile vanished. His features dissolved. I was aware of nothing but two enormous eyes blazing from a pale face. It was my supreme moment. For the one and only time in his life the disciple had shocked his master.

"Beo . . ." he said. "Oh, my God . . . Beo."

He did not move. The grip on my shoulder tightened. It seemed to me that his eyes engulfed his whole person. Then, with a terrible effort, he controlled himself. His hand fell away.

"Make some excuse and go," he said. "Wait for me outside. I'll follow you. There's a car there, an Alfa-Romeo; get into it."

Like a sleepwalker I crossed the room and, murmuring an

apology to my hostess, thanked her for her kindness and said goodbye. I bowed to the rest of the company who might have noticed me. I left the house, and passed through the garden to the street outside. There were three cars parked by the garden wall. I got into the Alfa-Romeo as he had bidden me. I sat there, smoking a cigarette, and later watched the Rizzios depart, then the Fossis, and others that I had not met. Aldo came last. He got into the car without saying a word and slammed the door. We drove away. Not to his own house, but downhill and so out of the city by the Porta Malebranche. Still he said nothing, and it was not until Ruffano lay behind us, and he had driven the car into the hills, that he pulled up suddenly, switched off the engine, and turned and looked at me.

CHAPTER TEN

His eyes never left my face. It was the old inspection I remembered. He used to do this when he took me out, to see if my hair was brushed, my shoes were clean. Sometimes he sent me back to change my shirt.

"I always said you wouldn't grow," he said.

"I'm five foot five," I told him.

"As much as that? I don't believe it."

He gave me a cigarette and lit it for me. His hands were steady, mine were not.

"Your curls have gone. I'd have known you otherwise," he said.

He tugged at my hair, a savage gesture that invariably hurt me in old days. It hurt me still. I shook my head.

"It was the Frankfurt barber," I said. "He started the rot, and it grew straight ever after. I wanted to look like the brigadier, and succeeded for a time."

"The brigadier?"

"A Yankee. We lived with him two years."

"I thought it was a German."

"The German came first. He only lasted six months after we left Ruffano."

I unwound the car window and looked out at the blue hump of the mountain that lay ahead. It was Monte Cappello. We could see it from the house at home.

"Is she alive?" he asked.

"No. She died three years ago of cancer."

"I'm glad," he said.

A bird, a hawk of some sort, came into my line of vision and poised, hovering, against the sky-line. I thought he was going to dive but he soared higher, in a widening circle, and hovered once again.

"What set it off?" said Aldo.

He might have meant, how did the disease take her, but knowing my brother I understood him to be referring back to '44.

"I've often wondered," I said. "I don't think it was father's death or the news of yours. She accepted both as fate like anyone else. Perhaps she was lonely. Perhaps she just liked men."

"No," said Aldo, "I'd have known that. I can always tell." He did not smoke. He sat with his arm along the seat behind me. "The spoils of victory," he said, after a moment, "that's what she felt herself to be. For a woman of her sort, basically conventional and submissive to her husband, it would act like an aphrodisiac. First the German Commandant, in her home town, then the Yankee after the German myth exploded. Yes . . . yes . . . I see the pattern. Very interesting."

I supposed it was, to him. Like reading history. Not if, like myself, one had been involved.

"Why Fabbio?" he asked.

"I was going to tell you. That was later, in Turin, when the Yankee brigadier left Frankfurt for the States. We met Enrico Fabbio in the train. He was polite and helpful with our baggage. In three months—he was a bank employee—she had married him. He couldn't have been kinder. And it was all part of the break with the past that I should take his name. After all, he paid."

"That's right. He paid."

I glanced at my brother. Did he resent the advent of our step-father? The inflection in his voice was strange.

"I'm grateful to him still," I said. "I continue to look him up if I'm in Turin."

"And that's as deep as it goes?"

"Why, yes. What else? He never took the place of father or of you. He was just a kind little man with a sense of family."

Aldo laughed. I wondered why my description struck him as funny.

"Anyway," I said, "we had nothing in common beyond sharing a roof and eating the same food, and after I took my degree at Turin I cut loose. I didn't fancy a job in the bank, which he suggested, so with my languages I entered the tourist trade."

"What as?"

"Junior clerk, clerk, guide, and finally courier."

"Tout," he said.

Well, yes. . . . Put bluntly, I was a tout. A superior tout. One degree higher than the fellow in the piazza Maggiore who hawked his picture-postcards.

"What firm employs you?" he asked.

"Sunshine Tours, Genoa," I replied.

"Good God!" he said.

He moved his arm from the back of the seat and started up the car. It was as though my admission had brought his interrogation to an end. No further questions needed. Case dismissed.

"They pay well," I protested in self-defence, "and I meet all sorts of people. It's experience, I'm travelling all the time. . . ."

"Where to?" he asked.

I did not answer. Where to, indeed. . . . He let in the clutch and the car roared ahead, climbing the surrounding heights, the road twisting and turning upon itself like a serpent's coils. The country spread out below us, the soil a patchwork quilt of dun and olive, and away westward the city of Ruffano, poised on her two hills, gleamed, a narrow circlet under the sun.

"And you?" I asked.

He smiled. Used as I was to Beppo's handling of the coach in Tuscany and the Umbrian undulations, where speed, of necessity, was second choice to safety, my brother's disrespect for his native Marches seemed to me profound. He courted death at every hairpin bend.

"You saw last night," he said. "I'm a puppeteer. I pull the strings, the puppets dance. It requires great skill."

"I believe you. But I don't see why. All that training, and that propaganda, for one day in the year, for a students' Festival?"

"Their day," he said, "this Festival. It's a world in miniature."

He had not replied to my question, but I let it go. Then abruptly he put to me the enquiry for which I had no answer. "Why didn't you come home before?"

Attack is the best method of defence. I forget who first coined the phrase. The German Commandant used to quote it.

"What was the use of my coming when I thought you were dead?" I said.

"Thank you, Beo," he replied. He seemed surprised. "Anyway," he added, "now you've come home I can make use of you."

He might have put it differently, after two-and-twenty years. I wondered if this was the moment to tell him about Marta. I decided not.

"Hungry?" he asked.

"Yes."

"Then we'll go back. To my house, 2, via dei Sogni."

"I know it. I called on you last night, but you were still out."

"Probably." He was not interested. He was thinking of something else.

"Aldo," I asked, "what are we going to say? Do we tell everyone the truth?"

"What truth?"

"Why, that we're brothers."

"I haven't yet decided," he replied. "It might be better not. How long are you here for anyway? Did Sunshine Tours give you the sack?"

"No," I said, "not the sack. I've taken a vacation."

"That's easy, then. We'll think of something."

The car turned from the hills to the valley below, and sped like an arrow towards Ruffano. We entered the city from the south, and climbed steeply to the via dell'8 Settembre, past the students' hostel, and then right. He drew up before the double entrance to his house.

"Out," he said.

I glanced about me, half hoping we might be seen, but the street was empty. Everyone was within doors having lunch.

"I saw Jacopo last night," I said as we entered the doorway together, "but he didn't recognise me."

"Why should he?" asked Aldo.

He turned the key and pushed me through into the hall. I went back twenty years. The furnishing, the decor, even the pictures on the wall, were those we had had at home. This was what I had sought for and had not found at Number 8. I looked up at Aldo, smiling.

"Yes," he said, "it's all here. What was left of it."

He stooped to pick up an envelope that was lying on the floor. The envelope that Carla Raspa must have pushed through the slit the night before. He glanced at the handwriting and threw the envelope on a table, unopened.

"Go on in," he said. "I'll call Jacopo."

I passed through to what must be his living-room. The chairs, the desk, the stiff-backed divan on which my mother used to sit, I recognised them all. Our father's portrait hung upon the wall, next to the bookcase. He seemed to have grown younger, to have shrunk in stature, but his air of benign authority was still there to humble me. I sat down and looked about me, my hands on my knees. The only concessions to a later age were pictures of aircraft on another wall. Aircraft in battle. Climbing, diving, smoke pouring from the tail.

"Jacopo will bring lunch directly," said Aldo, coming into the room. "It will be a few minutes. Have a drink."

He went to a table in the corner—I recognised that also—and poured out two Campari into glasses that were ours as well.

"I never knew, Aldo," I said, gesturing to the room, "that all this meant so much to you?"

He downed his Campari in a draught. "More, evidently," he replied, "than the surroundings of Signor Fabbio meant to you."

Cryptic, but what of it? It did not worry me. Nothing worried me. I was realising to the full the warmth of Easter-tide. Our own.

"I've told Jacopo who you are," said Aldo. "I think it's best."

"Just as you like," I answered.

"Where are you lodging?"

"In the via San Michele. No. 24, with Signora Silvani. She has a houseful of students, but not, I'm afraid, of your persuasion. All Commerce and Economics, very bigoted."

He smiled. "That's good," he said, "in fact, it's very good."

I shrugged. The rivalry between the two factions was still beyond me.

"You can be a go-between," he added.

I considered this, staring into my glass of Campari. I seemed to remember similar errands in the past, not always successful, when he was a scholar at the Ruffano liceo. Messages smuggled into schoolmates' pockets that sometimes went astray. The role had disadvantages.

"I don't know about that," I said.

"I do," said Aldo.

Jacopo came in to set the lunch. I called "Hullo," and he put down his tray and stood to attention like an orderly.

"I apologise for not having recognised you yesterday, Signor Armino," he said. "I am very glad to see you."

"Don't be pompous," said my brother. "Beo is only five foot five. Still small enough to put across your knee."

Which he had done, in '43. Egged on by Aldo. I had forgotten that. Marta had protested, and shut the kitchen door. Marta. . . .

Jacopo produced our meal, and a large carafe of wine made from the local grapes. Later I asked my brother if Jacopo did everything for him.

"He manages," said Aldo. "A woman comes to clean. I

employed Marta until she took to drink. Then it was hopeless. I had to send her packing."

The time had come. I had finished. Aldo was busy eating.

"I've something to tell you," I said. "I'd better tell you now because I'm involved. I believe Marta's dead. I believe she was murdered."

He put down his fork and stared at me across the table. "What the hell do you mean by that?" he said harshly.

His eyes, accusing, never left my face. I wiped my mouth, pushed back my chair and began walking up and down the room.

"I could still be wrong," I said, "but I think not. I'm afraid not. And if it's true, then it's my fault. It's because of what I did."

I told him the whole story. From start to finish. The English tourists, the lone barbarian and his ten thousand lire tip, my nightmare in the small hours and its connection with the altar-piece in San Cipriano. The newspaper item the following day, the visit to the police, my recognition, as I thought, of the body, and the impulse that drove me to Ruffano. Finally, the sight of the cobbler Ghigi and his sister Maria disappearing yesterday in the custody of the local police.

Aldo heard me through to the end without a single interruption. I did not look at him as I told my tale. I just walked up and down the room, speaking much too fast. I could hear myself stammering as I might stammer to a judge, and I kept correcting myself in small particulars that did not matter.

When I had finished I sat down again in the chair. I thought his accusing eyes must be upon me still. But he was peeling an orange, unperturbed.

"You see?" I said, exhausted. "You understand?"

He put a large segment of the orange into his mouth and swallowed it. "Yes, I see," he said. "It's easy enough to check. I'm on very good terms with the Ruffano police. All I have to do is to lift the telephone and ask them if it's true that the dead woman is Marta."

"And if it is?"

"Well, it's just too bad," he said, reaching for another segment. "She'd have died anyway, in the state she was in. The Ghigis couldn't control her. Nobody could. You ask Jacopo. She was a drunk."

He had not understood. He had not seen that, if it was Marta who had been murdered, she had been murdered because I had put ten thousand lire into her hand. I explained this to him for the second time. He finished his orange. He dipped his fingers in the bowl of water beside the plate. "So what?" he said.

"Isn't it something I ought to have told the police in Rome? Wouldn't it explain the motive for murder?" I repeated.

Aldo stood up. He went to the door and shouted to Jacopo to bring coffee. After it had been brought and the door was closed, he poured out coffee for us both and began stirring his slowly, thoughtfully.

"A motive for murder," he said. "It's something we all have, at some time or other. You as much as anyone else. Run along to the police if you like, and tell them what you've just told me. You saw an old woman lying on the doorstep of a church, and it reminded you of an altar-piece that was your peculiar horror as a child. Fine. So what do you do? You bend over the woman and she lifts her head. She recognises you, the child who fled with the German army twenty years before. You recognise her, and something cracks in your brain. You kill her, a blind impulse to kill a nightmare memory that haunts you, and then, to stifle conscience, you put a note for ten thousand lire in her hand."

He swallowed his coffee and went across the room. He picked up the telephone. "I'll get on to the Commissioner," he said. "He'll be at home on a Sunday, very probably. At least he'll be able to give me the latest news."

"No, wait, Aldo . . . wait," I burst out, in sudden panic.

"What for? You want to know, don't you? So do I." He asked for a number. It was out of my hands. It was no longer my secret, my inner turmoil. Aldo now shared it, but in sharing it he made my confusion worse. I could have committed the murder as he described it. I had no witnesses to prove an alibi. The very motive he suggested made a desperate sense. Protestations of innocence would be in vain. The police would not believe me—why should they? I might never be able to prove that I was guiltless.

"You're not going to involve me, are you?" I asked.

He raised his eyes to heaven in mock despair, and spoke into the mouthpiece. "Is it you, Commissioner?" he said. "I hope I haven't dragged you from your lunch. It's Donati here, Aldo Donati. Very well, thank you. Commissioner, I've been very disturbed by a rumour going round Ruffano, brought me by my servant Jacopo, that my old family nurse Marta Zampini, who has apparently been missing for some days, may turn out to be

this woman who was murdered in Rome. . . . Yes . . . yes. . . . No,
I'm a very busy man, as you know. I rarely read a newspaper,
and in any event I saw nothing about it. . . . The Ghigis, yes. She
had lodged with them for some months. . . . I see. . . . Yes. . . ."
He looked across at me, nodding his head. My heart sank. It was
going to be true, and I was still further enmeshed. "So there's no
doubt about it, then? I'm very sorry. She had completely gone to
pieces, you know. I used to employ her until it became impossible.
The Ghigis can't tell you anything, I suppose? Why Rome? Yes,
some impulse, perhaps. . . . And you hope to make an arrest soon.
Good. Good. Thank you, Commissioner. Yes, I shall be extremely
obliged if you would contact me as soon as you have more news.
Meanwhile, confidential, naturally. Thank you . . . thank you."

He replaced the receiver. He took an unopened packet of
cigarettes from a box and threw them across to me.

"Calm down," he said, "you'll soon be out of the red. They
expect to make an arrest within twenty-four hours."

His assumption that fear for my own skin was at the root of my
distress was so reminiscent of his attitude to me of old that it was
not worth denying. Guilty, yes. Guilty of putting the money into
her hands and not turning back. Guilty of passing by on the other
side.

Conscience, tortured, drove me to attack. "Why did she
drink?" I asked. "Didn't you look after her?"

His passionate reply startled me. "I fed her, clothed her,
cherished her, and she collapsed within," he said. "Why? Don't
ask me why. A reversion to type, to her drunken peasant ancestry.
When someone is bent on suicide you can't prevent them."
Once again he shouted for Jacopo. The man entered and removed the coffee tray. "I'm in to nobody," Aldo said. "Beo and I
are missing twenty-two years. It will take more than a few hours
to wipe them out."

He looked at me, then smiled. The room, familiar now and
personal because of its possessions, closed in upon me. Responsibility for the world and all its ills was mine no longer. Aldo would
take charge.

CHAPTER ELEVEN

We sat there talking, letting the day go by. Sometimes Jacopo entered with a fresh brew of coffee, and went out again without a word. The room filled with the smoke from my cigarettes, mine, not Aldo's. He had given it up, he said, he had long ago lost the urge. I drew from him, indirectly, sparked off by questions fired at random, the story of his immediate post-war years. How, after the Armistice, he joined the partisans. Even then he knew nothing of the fateful telegram that had told us of his death, and he assumed that we believed him to be a prisoner of war. It was not until he found his way back to Ruffano, some months after we ourselves had fled from it with the Commandant, that he learnt the truth from Marta. They, in their turn, heard the rumour that while travelling north to the Austrian border our convoy had been bombed, and our mother and I killed. So, in our separate ways, our worlds had disintegrated.

He a young man of twenty, I a child of twelve, each had to face a new existence. Mine was to look, week after week, upon a woman without roots who daily, nightly became more superficial, more lacking in discrimination, faded, stale; his to remember her as she had bidden him goodbye when last he came on leave, warm-hearted, loving, full of plans for future meetings—and then to have this image crack when not only Marta but all who knew her in Ruffano told him of her end. The gossip there had been, the shame, the scandal. One or two had even seen her drive away, laughing, beside her Commandant, while I waved a swastika flag from the window of the car.

"That was the final thrust," said Aldo, "you, with your flag."

I began to live it once again, and through his eyes her shame became my shame and I suffered for her. I made excuses. He would have none of them.

"No use, Beo," he said, "I don't want to listen. Whatever she did in Frankfurt or Turin, what life she made for the man Fabbio whom you call your stepfather, whether she was ill or unhappy or in pain, does not count. She died for me the day she left Ruffano."

I asked him if he had seen our father's grave. He had. He had been to the prison-camp where he lay buried. Once. Never again. He did not want to discuss that either.

"He hangs there on the wall," said Aldo, gesturing towards the portrait, "that's all I needed of him. That and his possessions, here in this room. Besides the legacy of all he had achieved at the ducal palace. I made it my business to carry on where he left off, but, as you see, with more authority than he ever had. That was my goal."

He spoke with a strange bitterness throughout as though, despite his standing in Ruffano and his swift rise to his present position, the years were wasted. Something eluded him still. Not the satisfaction of personal ambition, nor money, nor fame. He spoke of himself continually in the past tense. "I wanted this. I wanted that. I determined to carry out such-and-such an undertaking." Never once did he talk in the present, or in the future. Later, in one of the pauses in conversation, I said to him, "Don't you plan one day to marry? To start a family? So that you too will leave something behind you when you go?" He laughed. He was standing by the window at the time, looking out on the distant hills. From the window one could see Monte Cappello, beneath which we had driven in the morning. Now, with the approach of evening, it stood humped and clear against the sky, blue like a mandarin's coat.

"Remember?" he said. "When you were very small, I sometimes took infinite pains constructing a house of cards on the dining-room table, the table we've been eating at today. I would have the whole space covered—I must have used half-a-dozen packs. Then came the moment of triumph. When, with one breath, I blew the whole edifice flat."

I remembered it well. The fragile cards tremblingly balanced like a giant pagoda, the effect, with the last card poised, strangely awe-inspiring and beautiful to a staring child.

"Yes," I said. "What's that to do with my question?"

"Everything," he answered.

He crossed the room, took down one of the sketches of aircraft that were hanging on the wall, and brought it over to me. The sketch was of a fighter plane falling to the ground in flames.

"This wasn't mine, but it could have been," he said. "That's how I saw others go. Comrades, whom I'd flown beside. Mine wasn't a true flamer, I baled out before she flared, then she scorched to earth like a sizzling kite. The point was that at the moment of impact, when she was hit—I was climbing at the time, and I knew what it was—the explosion and my release in the sky happened almost simultaneously, and the moment of triumph, of ecstasy, was indescribable. It was death and it was power. Creation and destruction all in one. I had lived and I had died."

He replaced the picture on the wall. I still did not see what it had to do with marriage or with founding a family, unless it was that the experience he had undergone, which I tried to imagine and into which I followed him in vain, still staring at the picture on the wall, made all things valueless. To have known and rejoiced in death belittled life.

Aldo glanced at the clock. It was a quarter to seven. "I must leave you," he said. "I have a meeting at the ducal palace. It may not take more than an hour. Further discussions about the Festival."

We had not touched on the Festival all day. Nor any of his present activities. The past had been with us all the time.

"Have you a date later?" he asked.

I smiled, and shook my head. What should I want with a date now we were together?

"Good," he said. "Then I'll take you to dinner with Livia Butali."

He went to the telephone and called a number. Instantly I stood in fancy outside our old home further down the via dei Sogni. I heard the sound of the piano, Chopin again, and the music suddenly stopping, and I saw the player cross the room to answer the telephone, the ring of which she had been waiting for all day.

Aldo spoke into the mouthpiece. "Two of us," he said. "Say a quarter-past eight."

He cut short her query and hung up. I could imagine her standing there, frustrated, wondering, then returning to the piano to burst into a passionate Etude.

"Did you say you had a knowledge of German," he asked me suddenly, "amongst your other superficial expertise?"

"Yes," I said, "the legacy of the Commandant."

He ignored the thrust, and going to a chair behind the divan picked up the volumes I had brought Signora Butali from the library the day before.

"Take a look at these, then, while I'm away," he said. "I was going to give them to one of my boys, a German scholar, but you'll do even better. Translate for me anything you consider especially appropriate, and write it down." He threw the books on the table beside my chair.

"I think I should warn you," I said, "that what I've read in them already—only a rough glance, I admit—suggests that the Falcon was not the misunderstood genius you described to your élite last night but something very different. If Signora Butali is really going to take them to Rome for her husband to read he'll have another heart attack."

"Don't worry," said Aldo, "he won't read them. She got the books for me, because I asked for them."

I shrugged. As Director of the Arts Council of Ruffano he evidently had the right.

"That German writer was prejudiced, of course," Aldo continued. "Those nineteenth century scholars always were. The early Italian manuscripts I read in Rome last week gave a somewhat different angle to certain aspects of his life. Jacopo?" He opened the door and shouted across the hall. Jacopo appeared. "I'll be gone for an hour," said Aldo. "Let no one in. Beo and I will be dining later at Number 8."

"Yes, signore," said Jacopo, and then he added, "A lady called twice during the afternoon. She gave her name. Signorina Raspa."

"What did she want?"

Jacopo's poker face flickered to a smile. "Evidently the signorina wanted you," he replied.

I pointed to the envelope still lying unopened on the hall table. "That came last night," I said. "I watched her put it through the door. I was standing beyond the double entrance."

Aldo picked up the envelope and threw it at me. "You read it," he said. "She's as much your friend as mine."

He went out of the house, slamming the door behind him. I heard him start up the Alfa-Romeo. It was not more than four minutes' walk to the ducal palace, but he had to use the car.

"A pilot still?" I asked Jacopo.

"Never anything else," he replied emphatically. "Arts Council?" He snapped his fingers in the air in a superb gesture of contempt, then, pouring out a glass of vermouth, set it before me with a flourish. "May you dine well," he said, and left me.

I opened Carla Raspa's letter without compunction. It began formally, thanking Professor Donati for his extreme kindness in allowing her and her companion passes for the evening session at the ducal palace. The experience had affected her profoundly. She wanted to discuss the many implications of his address to the students with the speaker himself. She would be in all evening should he return before midnight, and she was free all Sunday, should he have an hour to spare at any time throughout the day. She would be delighted to call upon him, or conversely, if he had nothing better to do, she would be honoured to offer him a drink or a meal at her apartment at No. 5, via San Michele. It ended with the same formality, offering salutations. The signature, Carla Raspa, looped its way across the page, the letters intertwined like amorous limbs. I replaced the letter in the envelope, wondering if the writer was waiting still, and turned, not without relief, to the Falcon's ploys.

"Duke Claudio's precocious gallantry," I read, "was a scandal to the more staid of Ruffano's citizens, and proved ruinous to his own constitution. His follies and his vices attained a dangerous height, so alarming the older members of the Court that they feared greater excesses would threaten their ruler's life. The Duke's evil genius brought him into the company of strolling players, and, delighting in their loose manners, he threw himself among them without reserve, appointing the younger of them to high places in his Court."

Well, Aldo had asked for it. I found a piece of paper and a pencil, and, sipping my vermouth, scribbled a translation of the more forceful passages.

"The Falcon's casual acquaintance with the comedians ripened into intimacy, gradually monopolising his time and thoughts. These persons, belonging to the vilest classes, became the Duke's associates in public and in private. Conforming his morals to theirs, he defied decency, advancing from one extravagance to another, and producing spectacles of so shameless a nature before his subjects that . . ."

The German writer, shuddering, turned to Greek. My Turin degree had not covered the classics. Perhaps, from the point of view of the Festival, it was just as well, but I felt frustrated. I flipped back over the pages to those I had read in the library the day before. Someone, Aldo's young student doubtless, had forestalled me. My brother must have called for the books soon after I left them with Signora Butali, and brought them back for his translator to skim through. A slip had been inserted to mark the passage I remembered.

". . . When accusations were made against him by the outraged citizens of Ruffano, Duke Claudio retaliated by declaring that he had been divinely appointed to mete out to his subjects the punishment they deserved. The proud would be stripped, the haughty violated, the slanderer silenced, the viper die in his own venom. The scales of heavenly justice would thus be balanced. On one occasion a page neglected to provide lights for the Duke's evening repast. He was seized by the Falcon's bodyguard, who enveloped the wretched lad in sear-cloth coated with combustibles, and after setting fire to his head drove him through the rooms of the ducal palace to die in agony."

A pretty tale. A little rough for heavenly justice. I read on.

"The citizens, indignant at the dishonour which nightly violated their domestic circles, finally rose at the instigation of the leading citizen, whose handsome wife had been profaned by the Falcon himself. It was in the riot that followed that the unhappy Duke met his end. The buffoonery he had learnt upon the stage with his low followers decided him to execute a feat, hitherto unattempted, of driving eighteen horses from the fort on the northern hill of Ruffano through the centre of the city and up the further hill to the ducal palace. He was set upon and pursued by almost the entire populace, after having trampled many of them to death beneath his horses' hooves. This last ride, known to the Ruffanesi in after years as the Flight of the Falcon, ended in the Duke's massacre."

I poured myself another glass of vermouth. I thought the Duke had flung himself from the topmost pinnacle of the tower, declaring that he was the bird whose name he bore. The German scholar said none of this. Perhaps the Italian manuscripts were more explicit. Laboriously I copied down the details for my brother. Somebody else would have to decipher the Greek.

When he returned a few minutes before eight, in excellent spirits, having cast aside the more sombre mood of early afternoon when together we revived the past, I handed him my notes and left him reading them while I washed my hands. I came back after a few minutes to find him smiling.

"This is good," he said, "very good indeed. It tallies with what I had read earlier."

I told him, in American fashion, that he was welcome. He stuffed the notes into his pocket. Then he called goodbye to Jacopo and we left the house. This time, I noticed, he did not use the car. We walked down the via dei Sogni to our former home. "How do you explain me to Signora Butali?" I asked.

"I told her," he answered, "before I left this morning. She's as safe as Jacopo."

He led the way into the garden, and up the pathway to the house. The door was open for us. We might have been the pair of us, returning from some foray in the past, with our parents awaiting dinner, he to make the excuses, myself to be sent immediately to bed.

Our hostess had changed for the occasion. She looked, so I thought, more beautiful by evening light, the dark blue dress becoming her. She came towards me first, smiling and holding out her hand.

"I should have known," she said. "It wasn't Chopin or Debussy that drew you here. You wanted to see your home."

"It was all three," I said, kissing her hand. "If I seemed very rude and abrupt I ask forgiveness now."

I was no longer the assistant librarian who had walked home with her from church. I belonged, because of Aldo.

"It is fantastic," she said, "and very wonderful. I still can't believe it's true. This is going to make such a difference to both your lives. I'm so happy for you." She looked from one to the other of us, and tears, that possibly had been near the surface all day, rose to her eyes.

"Emotion," said my brother, "is wasted. Where's my Campari? Beo prefers vermouth."

She shook her head at him, protesting at his lack of feeling, and handed us the waiting glasses, filling one for herself.

"To you both," she said. "Long life and every happiness," and then to me, "I've always loved your name. 'Il Beato'. I think you fill it well."

Aldo shouted with laughter. "You know what he is?" he said. "He's nothing but a tourist tout. He scrambles around the country in a loaded coach showing the Anglo-Saxons Rome by night."

"Why shouldn't he?" she answered. "I'm sure he does it well and the tourists adore him."

"He does it for tips," said Aldo. "He dives into the Trevi fountain with his trousers off."

"Nonsense," she smiled, and to me, "Take no notice of him, Beo. He's jealous because you see the world and he is stuck in a small university city."

Beo came well from her. I liked it. And the teasing exchange between them put me at my ease. All the same . . . I glanced at my brother. He was walking about the room flipping at books, picking up objects and putting them down again, his restless manner, which I remembered from the past, suggesting suppressed excitement. Something brewed.

The double doors opened into what was now the dining-room, revealing the table set for three, lighted by candles. The girl who had put the food on the sideboard withdrew for us to help ourselves. My old playroom, subtly transformed with the curtains drawn and the candlelight playing upon the polished table and our three faces, had lost its morning strangeness. It was mine again, but warmer, intimate, and I had the impression that I was my boyhood self, promoted out of due time to join in one of Aldo's adult games.

It was my fortune often in the past to play the third, the aider and abetter of my brother's whims, whether to foster some budding friendship at the liceo where he spent his days, or to damp one down. He would prepare phrases for me first, and at a given sign I must out with them, to cause confusion, perhaps a furious argument, even a battle. His methods had not changed. Only the fish he wanted to play was now a woman, and to watch her rise to the flies he cast afforded him a double satisfaction with me as witness. I wondered how far he had gone; whether the banter that passed between them—myself frequently a butt for her to defend—was a ritual flight before the final act or if, already lovers, their secret increased in intensity and excitement by being flaunted before a supposedly innocent third.

There was no talk of Signora Butali's husband. The sick man in his hospital bed in Rome was no absent skeleton at the feast; he might not have existed. I wondered, had he been present, how it would have altered the behaviour of all three of us; our hostess withdrawing into her shell and becoming simply the doyenne of her dinner-table, whilst Aldo, flattering his host in a way that only I might possibly discern—he had done it as a boy with our father—would lead him on to self-disclosure, no matter whether interesting or tedious, as long as the undercurrent of intrigue remained unseen.

Dinner over, Signora Butali led the way upstairs to the music-room, and while we drank coffee and liqueurs the conversation turned upon the Festival.

"How are rehearsals?" she asked my brother. "Or is the whole thing to be as secret as last year to those who don't take part?"

"More so," he said, "but to the first part of your question, the rehearsals are going well. Some of us have been at it for months."

She turned to me. "You know, Beo," she said, "last year I played the Duchess Emilia, who received Pope Clement. Professor Rizzio, whom you met this morning, was the Duke. So lifelike were the rehearsals, and the coaxing methods of your brother who directed us, that I truly believe Professor Rizzio has imagined himself a Duke of Ruffano ever since."

"His manner to me this morning was certainly royal," I said. "I did not connect it with the Festival of a year ago. I thought perhaps that as Deputy Rector of the university and Head of the Department of Education he was simply aware of the great gulf between us."

"That's his trouble too," she agreed, and to Aldo, "but isn't it his sister's even more? I often feel sorry for the resident women students. They might be in a convent, shut up in that hostel with Signorina Rizzio."

My brother laughed, pouring himself cognac.

"Convents in old days were easier of access," he said. "An underground passage between the men's and women's hostels has yet to be constructed. Perhaps we might consider it."

He pulled the notes I had translated for him out of his pocket and, throwing himself in a chair, began to study them.

"There are many problems," I said to my hostess, "that have to be surmounted before the launching of this year's Festival."

"Such as?" she asked.

"Whether Duke Claudio was a moralist or a monster," I answered. "According to the historians he was a monster, and mad at that. Aldo thinks otherwise."

"He would," she said. "He likes to be different from everyone else."

Her voice was mocking, but the look she gave in his direction stimulating. My hostess was ready poised for another movement of the ritual flight. I thought of the dead expression on her face when I had walked with her from church, and the comparison was not flattering to me, the third.

"Anyway," I said, "the people of Ruffano believed him a monster and rose in a bloody insurrection against him and his Court."

"And are we to have this in the Festival?" she demanded.

"Don't ask me, ask Aldo," I replied.

She strolled over to his chair, her liqueur glass in her hand, humming beneath her breath, and the way she moved, the way she bent above him sitting there in the chair, was, to me, somehow evident of desire. Only my presence there stopped her from touching him.

"Well," she said, "do we have an insurrection, and if so who's to lead it?"

"Easy," he answered, without looking up. "The C and E students. They're ripe for rebellion anyway."

She raised her eyebrows at me and set her liqueur glass on the piano. "An innovation," she said, throwing back the piano lid. "I thought the acting in the Festival was meant for the Arts students alone."

"Not this year," he said. "There aren't enough of them."

She took a final sip of her liqueur, nectar to the queen before the flight, and sat down on the piano stool. "What shall I play for you?" she asked. The question was for me, the smile for me. The intonation in the voice, the whole poise of her person, hands ready above the keys, were for my brother.

"The 'Arabesque'," I said. "It's sexless."

It had been the day before, with me, a stranger, an alien in my own home, ghosts around me. Then the rise and fall, the ripple of descent, had spelt nostalgia, the shrugging reminder of the fleeting moment. Now it was night, and Aldo was in the house. The pianist, who yesterday had played from courtesy, now sought to woo my brother in the way instinctive to her. The "Arabesque", played throughout the country by a thousand pupils, became a dance of love, suggestive, shameless. I wondered that she should give herself away in this fashion, and sitting upright in my chair stared at the ceiling. From where she sat behind the raised lid of the piano she could not see the man she hoped to charm. I could. He had found a pencil and was adding to my translated notes, oblivious of the music. Debussy, Ravel, Chopin failed to rouse him. Music had never been one of Aldo's obsessions. If his hostess played, to him it was background sound, hardly more personal than traffic.

I could hardly bear it that her efforts should be so wasted, and lighting a cigarette began to weave a fantasy that I was in his shoes, and when the playing ceased I would get up from my chair, and cross the room, and put my hands over her eyes and she reach up to me. The fantasy intensified as the tempo of the music quickened. It became unendurable that I should sit there, dumbly, and endure her message, which, alas, was not for me. That Aldo, though indifferent to the music, was aware of its message I never for a moment doubted, and I wished him joy and her fulfilment; but to share their intimacy thus was at best doubtful pleasure.

Perhaps she sensed my discomfort, for suddenly she slammed the lid and rose. "Well," she asked, "is the insurrection over and done with? Can we all now relax?"

The irony, if intended as such, was as much wasted upon my brother as her music. He glanced at her, observed that she had ceased playing and was addressing him, and laid aside his notes.

"What's the time? Is it late?" he questioned.

"Ten o'clock," she answered.

"I thought we had only just finished dinner," he said.

He yawned, stretched, and put his notes into his pocket.

"I hope," she said, "that you've completed your opening scene, if indeed that is what you have been working on all evening."

She offered me more liqueur. I shook my head, and murmured something about getting back to the via San Michele. Aldo smiled, whether at my discretion, or Signora Butali's lightly-spoken gibe, I could not tell.

"My opening scene," he said, "which in fact was devised weeks ago, takes place off-stage, or should do, if we wish to be discreet."

"The thunder of horses' hooves?" I asked. "The Jehu act?"

"No, no," he frowned, "that won't be until the end. We must have the excitement first."

"Meaning just what?" enquired our hostess.

"The seduction of the lady," he replied, "what my German translator calls 'the profanation of the leading citizen's wife'."

Silence was prolonged. Aldo's quotation from my hastily scribbled notes was embarrassingly ill-timed. I leapt to my feet, my courier's smile too evident, and told Signora Butali that I had to be at the library next morning at nine. It was, so I thought, the only way to break the pause that threatened to turn oppressive, but after I had spoken I realised that my sudden departure was in itself a reflection on what had just been said.

"Don't let Signor Fossi work you, or himself, too hard," said my hostess, offering me her hand. "And come again whenever you feel like music. I don't need reminding, you know, that this house used to be your home. I'd like you to feel about it in the same way as your brother."

I thanked her for her graciousness, assuring her that if there were any books she wanted from the library at any time, either for herself or for her husband, she had only to reach for the telephone.

"It's very good of you," she said. "Later in the week I shall be in Rome. I'll let you know."

"I'll see you down," said Aldo.

See me down. Not leave, as I was doing. As we walked downstairs, with the door into the music-room still open, I chatted gaily and inanely about the many times he had chased me to the floor above. I did not want Signora Butali to think . . . exactly what she must be thinking. That I, the little brother, had my cue. The party was over.

Aldo came with me across the garden and opened the gate. The lamp above cast shadows down the street. The stars were brilliant.

"How beautiful she is," I said, "so sympathetic in every way, so restrained and calm. I don't wonder that you . . ."

"Look," he said, touching my arm, "here they come. See their lights?"

He pointed across the valley far below, where the main roads, entering Ruffano from east and north, were dotted with moving lights. The spluttering burst of vespas filled the air.

"What are they?" I asked.

"The C and E students returning from their weekend break," he said. "In a moment you'll hear them roaring up the via delle Mura like a herd of runts. They'll keep it up for another hour at least."

The city's peace was shattered. The Sunday quiet that in old days closed in upon Ruffano like a pall was interrupted.

"You have authority here," I said. "You could put a stop to it if it worries you so much."

Aldo smiled, and patted me on the shoulder. "It doesn't worry me," he said. "They can fart away all night for all I care. You're going straight back, aren't you?"

"Yes," I said.

"Don't hang about," he said. "Go there direct. Be seeing you, Beo, and thank you for today."

He went back into the garden and closed the gate. A moment later I heard him shut the door of the house. I walked off down the hill to my pensione, wondering what sort of reception he would get when he had climbed the stairs to the music-room once more. I wondered also if the girl who had brought in the dinner slept on the premises.

As I descended the hill the returning students were already converging upon the piazza della Vita. Small cars as well as vespas hummed and throbbed. Two coaches choked to a stand-still by the colonnade. I caught a glimpse of my young friends the Pasquales laughing and chattering with a score of others. To-morrow, possibly, but not tonight. Tonight I wanted to digest the day. I walked fast, so as not to be overtaken, and slipping through the open doorway of No. 24 ran upstairs and entered my own room. As I undressed I kept seeing Aldo standing in our mother's old bedroom with Signora Butali. I wondered if, being so used to the change in the room by now, the piano, the other furnishings, he no longer saw it as we had known it once, and as I saw it still.

The students were laughing and singing in the street outside, and at the far end, near the city centre, the gasp and splutter of the homing vespas warned the native Ruffanesi that the philistines had returned.

CHAPTER TWELVE

WHEN I WENT DOWN for breakfast the next morning I was given a rousing reception by the students. They were standing round the table drinking coffee and exchanging gossip about the preceding day. At sight of me there was a general uproar and Mario, whom I remembered from that first evening as being the most obstreperous, waved his roll of bread in the air and demanded how the Arts graduate had spent the weekend break.

"First," I said, "we librarians don't get a half-day on Saturday. I was kept sorting books until after seven."

A groan, half-ironic, half-sympathetic, greeted my remark. "Slaves, all slaves," said Gino, "tied to an out-worn system. It's typical of the way they run things up the hill. Now our chief, Elia, has some sense. He knows we put all we've got into a five-day week, and sets us free for forty-eight hours to do what we please. Most of us go home. He does the same. He has a villa on the coast and shakes the dead dust of Ruffano off his feet."

Signora Silvani, attending to the coffee-pot, handed me a cup with a morning smile. "Did you get to Mass?" she asked. "When you didn't come back for lunch my husband and I wondered what had happened to you."

"I met a friend," I said, "and was invited home to lunch and to spend the day."

"That reminds me," she added, "a lady called during the late afternoon. A Signorina Raspa. She said, if you returned, to look her up at Number 5."

Poor Carla Raspa! Having failed twice with Aldo she had turned in exasperation back to me.

"Did someone mention Mass?" asked Gino. "Did I hear aright, or were my ears deceiving me?"

"I went to Mass," I said. "The bells of San Cipriano summoned me, and I obeyed."

"It's all superstition, you know," said Gino. "The priests get fat on it, but no one else."

"In old days," said Caterina Pasquale, coming to join the

group, "there was nothing else to do but go to Mass. It was the morning's entertainment. You met your friends. Now there is so much more. Guess what we did, Paolo and I?" She smiled at me with her enormous eyes, biting a chunk out of her roll as she did so.

"You tell me," I said, smiling back.

"Borrowed our brother's car and drove to Venice," she said. "We went like stink and made it in four and a quarter hours. That's living, isn't it?"

"It could be dying too," I answered.

"Ah well, that's half the fun, taking the risk," she said.

Mario mimicked the action of Caterina at the wheel, banking, swerving, roaring the engine before a sudden crash. "You should do as I do," he said to me. "Run a vespa with a hotted-up engine."

"Yes," retorted Signora Silvani, "and wake us all with your noise. No one can sleep any longer on a Sunday night."

"Did you hear us?" laughed the student. "A whole crowd of us were coming back from Fano. Zup . . . zup . . . zup. . . . We hoped we'd enliven you all with our orchestration. Frankly, it's what you Ruffanesi need, a touch of exhaust music to melt the wax in your ears."

"You should have seen us," said Gerardo, "circling the city, up and round the via delle Mura, flashing our lights at the women's hostel to make them open their shutters."

"And did they?" asked Caterina.

"Not they. They were all tied down to their mattresses by nine o'clock."

Laughing, arguing, they scrambled off, but not before young Caterina, looking back over her shoulder, called, "See you this evening. The three of us might make a date."

Signora Silvani smiled after them, shaking an indulgent head. "What children!" she said. "No more sense of responsibility than babes in arms. And brilliant, every one of them. You'll see, in a year they'll all take Honours degrees, and then end up in some out-of-the-way provincial bank."

I left the house en route for the ducal palace, and saw that somebody was waiting for me higher up the street in the entrance of No. 5.

"Good morning, stranger," said Carla Raspa.

"Good morning, signorina," I replied.

"I thought," she said, turning with me towards the piazza della Vita, "that we had discussed the possibility of a Sunday date?"

"We did," I said. "What became of it?"

"I was in all day," she shrugged. "You had only to come for me."

"I was out," I said. "An impulse drove me to Mass at San Cipriano, where I bumped into no less a person than the Rector's lady, to whom I had taken some books the day before. I walked home with her and she invited me in for a drink."

Carla Raspa stopped and stared. "Which of course you accepted," she exclaimed, "and I don't blame you for it. One gracious nod from Livia Butali and you're there. No wonder you didn't bother to call on me after being given the entrée to her house. Who was there?"

"A flurry of professors," I said, "and amongst them my superior, Signor Fossi, with his wife."

I emphasised the wife. She laughed, and resumed walking.

"Poor Giuseppe," she said. "I can imagine him on his dignity, puffed up like a pigeon because of the invitation. What did you think of our Livia?"

"I found her beautiful. And charming. Very much more so than Signorina Rizzio."

"Heavens above! Was she there too?"

"Yes, with her brother. Both a little formal for my taste."

"Too formal for us all! You've done well for a newcomer, Armino Fabbio. There'll be no stopping you now. Congratulations. I haven't achieved as much in a couple of years."

We turned up the via Rossini. The pavement was crowded with morning shoppers and belated students hurrying to early lectures.

"I suppose," she said, "the Director of the Arts Council wasn't there by any chance?"

I had cut a good enough figure in her eyes without adding to my stature. Besides, it was better to be discreet. "He looked in for a moment, yes," I said. "I left before he did. I had a word with him while he drank Campari. He seemed amicable, and less imposing without his bodyguard."

Once again she paused and stared. "Incredible!" she exclaimed. "Only three days in Ruffano, and you have this sort of luck. You must be charmed. Did he mention me?"

"No," I said, "there was hardly time. I don't think he realised who I was."

"What an opportunity missed," she said. "If only I had known. You could have given him a message."

"Don't forget," I reminded her, "the whole morning was a fluke. If I hadn't gone to Mass. . . ."

"It's your baby face," she said. "Don't tell me that if I had gone to Mass and met Livia Butali she'd have bothered to invite me to an aperitivo. I suppose she likes to act the hostess amongst the university staff with her husband safe in hospital in Rome. Was Aldo Donati paying court to her?"

"Not that I noticed," I answered. "She seemed to have more to say to Professor Rizzio."

We parted, I to enter the ducal palace, she to continue up the hill to the university. A future date between us had not been mentioned. I felt, however, that it would come.

My easy Sunday had made me slow on schedule. When I arrived at the library I found that the others had arrived before me, including my boss, Giuseppe Fossi. They were standing in a group, talking excitedly. For some reason Signorina Catti was the centre of attention.

"There's no doubt about it," she was saying. "I had it from one of the students themselves, Maria Cavallini—she was locked in her room with four companions. It wasn't until the janitor came this morning to attend to the central heating that they, or any of the others, were released."

"It's outrageous, fantastic. There'll be a colossal row," said Giuseppe Fossi. "Have they informed the police?"

"No one could tell me that. I couldn't stay talking, I should have been late here."

Toni, his eyes on sticks, rushed across the room at sight of me. "You haven't heard the news?" he asked.

"No," I replied. "What news?"

"The women's hostel broken into last night," he said, "and the students locked in their rooms. No one knows what happened or who it was. The men were masked. How many of them, signorina?" He turned in excitement to the pallid secretary, who found herself so unexpectedly the bearer of strange tidings.

"A dozen or more, they say," she answered. "How they broke in nobody knows. It happened suddenly, just as all the C and E students were returning home. You know the appalling noise they

134

create with their machines? They served as cover, of course, to let their fellows in. Well, you may call it a rag. I call it an outrage."

"Come now," said Giuseppe Fossi, his eyes still bulging with excitement, "as far as we know none of the girls was hurt. To be locked in their rooms is no great hardship—I'm told it happens all the time. But if the place was burgled . . . well, that's another matter. They'll have to call in the police. In any event, Professor Elia will have to answer for it. Now, shall we get to work?"

He bustled towards the desk, with a nod to his secretary. She followed with notebook and pencil, her chin held high.

"Why blame Professor Elia?" murmured Toni. "It's not his fault if his C and E students enjoy a rag. I shall get the truth from my girl-friend later today. She'll know what really happened from her chums."

We settled to the morning's labours with lack of concentration. Whenever the telephone rang we lifted our heads and listened, but Signor Fossi's "Yes" and "No" revealed no secrets. Invasion of the women's hostel was not the library's business.

Halfway through the morning he sent Toni and me up to the new library with several crates of books. We took them in the small van which was used for the purpose. It was my first visit to the new library beyond the university, standing at the summit of the hill, close to the other recent buildings, the commercial schools and the physics lab. They had not the grace of the old House of Studies, but their lines were not unpleasing, and the big windows gave light and air to the students who would work within their walls.

"All thanks to Professor Butali," said Toni, "and the younger members of the university Council. Old Rizzio fought it tooth and nail."

"Why so?" I asked.

"Degrading the scholastic atmosphere," grinned Toni, "turning his scholars into factory hands. According to him the University of Ruffano was intended as a teaching university, pure and simple, where serious-minded young men and women would go out into the world after graduation to impart their classical learning to the boys and girls at school."

"They can do so still."

"They can, but what a grind! Why, a fellow with an economics degree can get a job in a big firm overnight, and make in three months what a teacher earns in a year. No future there!"

We heaved the crates out of the van and bore them into the new library. The decorators, Toni told me, had only been out of the place a week. High, light, with a raised gallery above lined with shelves throughout and a reading-room beyond, the building would offer many more facilities than the old banqueting-hall in the ducal palace.

"Where did they raise the money?" I asked.

"The C and E intake. Where else?" Toni replied.

We dumped the crates, which were to be unpacked by the assistant staff under the supervision of one of Giuseppe Fossi's colleagues, but not before the irrepressible Toni had gleaned further news of the women's hostel break-in.

"They say Rizzio's going to resign unless Professor Elia makes a public apology in the name of the C and E students," he said eagerly, following me from the building. "This will be a fight to a finish, I warn you. I don't think Elia will stand for it for a moment."

"I was told I'd come to a dead city," I replied. "Do you have this sort of excitement every day?"

"No such luck," he said, "but I tell you what it is. With the Rector away Rizzio and Elia will seize the opportunity to cut each other's throats. They detest one another, and this is their chance."

As we were parking the van outside the ducal palace, at about a quarter to one, I saw Carla Raspa come out of the side entrance with a bevy of arts students. She saw me and waved her hand. I waved back. She sent the students ahead and waited for me to join her.

"Doing anything for lunch?" she asked.

"No," I said.

"Go down to the restaurant where we first met," she said quickly. "Book a table for two. I can't stop now, I have to get my party home. No loitering allowed after what happened last night. You heard the news?"

"The break-in? Yes," I answered.

"I'll tell you more," she said. "It's unbelievable!"

She hurried after her flock, and I strolled off down the via Rossini. The restaurant, as before, was crowded, but I managed to get a table. There were no students. The place seemed to be the favourite rendezvous of those business-men of Ruffano who did not go home to lunch. Carla Raspa arrived soon after. She snapped her fingers at the waiter and we ordered lunch, then she looked at me and smiled.

"Out with it," I said. "I'm good at keeping secrets."

"No secret this," she answered, glancing, despite her words, over her shoulder. "It will be right through the university by now. Signorina Rizzio has been raped."

I stared in disbelief.

"It's true," she insisted, leaning forward. "I had it from one of her staff. These lads, whoever they were, didn't touch the girls. They locked the whole bunch in their rooms and set to work on the high and mighty one herself. Isn't it glorious?"

She was choking with laughter. I was not so much amused. The plateful of pasta placed in front of me by the waiter turned the edge off appetite. It looked like entrails.

"That's common assault," I said abruptly. "A matter for the police. Whoever did it will get ten years."

"No," she said, "that's it. They say the signorina's in a state of high hysteria and wants it all hushed up."

"Can't be done," I said, "the law won't allow it."

She attacked her own full plate with relish, covering the mashed-up brew with grated cheese. "The law can't take any action if nobody complains," she said. "The lads must have risked it, and guessed the reaction. Of course there'll be a row about the break-in, a terrific row. But what happened to Signorina Rizzio is her own affair. If she refuses to bring in a charge of assault, and her brother supports her, there's nothing anyone can do. Have you ordered wine?"

I had. I poured it out for her. She swallowed it down as though her throat was parched.

"It's not as though she had been knocked about," she continued. "I understand there was no question of that. No beating up. Just gently and persuasively shown what's what."

"How do you know?" I asked.

"Well, that's the tale. What the girls say at the hostel. Now that they have recovered from the fright of the masked men, and are themselves intact—those that were already, anyway—they can hardly contain themselves. That it should happen to her, the signorina! You have to hand it to those C and E boys. Imagine the nerve!"

"I still don't credit it," I said.

"I do," she answered, "and if the police are *not* summoned, and we're told the signorina is indisposed, you can bet your life it's true. Do you suppose she enjoyed it?"

Her eyes were gleaming. I felt slightly sick. Brutality in any form revolts me, and to commit violence upon the old or the very young was something I have never understood. I did not answer.

"She asked for it, you know," Carla Raspa continued, "treating her women students like novices taking their vows. No visits, even in the common room, from boys in the students' hostel, doors locked by ten. I know, because so many of the girls attend my lectures. They'd reached a breaking-point of exasperation. Of course one of the girls must have let the boys in, that's obvious. Then listened at the keyhole and spread the tale!"

I thought of the stately, formidable figure I had met the day before, sipping with mild distaste her mineral water. Imagination baulked.

Carla Raspa, facing the door of the restaurant, bent forward, touching my hand. "Don't turn now," she said. "Professor Elia has just come in. The Head of C and E himself. With a bunch of colleagues. What I ask myself is, will he have to resign?"

"Resign? Why should he?" I enquired. "How can anyone pin the break-in on his boys?"

"Because it's obvious," she said. "Signorina Rizzio has complained about the behaviour of the C and E students time after time. It was reported in the university journal. Last night was their answer."

I waited a moment for the party to settle at a table to the left of me, then half-turned in my seat to glance at them.

"The big man," murmured my companion, "with the shock of hair. More pleased with himself than anyone in Ruffano, and more self-opinionated, but he gets things done. He's a Milanese. He would be."

Professor Elia, eyes screened by thick-rimmed spectacles, black hair en brosse, had the large frame of one who can never fit into any sort of suit. Creases abounded in the impeccable cloth. He was talking rapidly, hunched over the table, allowing no one else to interrupt. Suddenly he threw back his undoubtedly fine head and uttered a thunderclap of laughter.

"Five of them," he said, "one after the other. That's what I'm told. And not a squeak in protest. Not a whimper."

The table rocked. His laughter filled the restaurant. Other people eating turned to stare. One of Professor Elia's companions motioned him to silence. The big man looked about him with contempt and caught my eye.

"Nobody here," he said. "They don't know what I'm discussing. But I tell you this. If anything's said officially against our crowd I'll not only make the lady the laughing stock of Ruffano but . . ." he lowered his voice, and we could hear no more.

"You see," murmured Carla Raspa, "the poor old Rizzios won't get much change out of him. They'd be well advised to let it go, or, better still, clear out. Anyway, after this shock the signorina can never show her face again. If she does, she'll only be greeted with the sort of guffaw we've heard at the next table." She accepted a cigarette, finished her wine, and summoned the waiter. "My treat," she said. "We both of us work for our living. You've still to take me out to dinner. When?"

"Not tonight," I answered, remembering the Pasquales. "Perhaps tomorrow?"

"Tomorrow it is."

We rose from the table and left the restaurant, resuming our walk together up the hill.

"Heard the latest?" whispered Toni from his ladder as I entered the library.

"What?" I asked guardedly.

"There's talk of the women's hostel being closed down and the students sent home," he said. "They'll have to take their examinations by post. They're saying there was another break-in three months ago and all the girls are pregnant."

Giuseppe Fossi, dictating letters to his secretary, looked up at the offender from his desk. "Would you please observe the rules?" he said icily, pointing to the notice SILENCE that hung upon the library walls.

Twice during the afternoon we drove to the new building with further crates. Each time we ran into fresh rumours. Students gossiped in droves, and Toni knew a dozen of them. The break-in was the subject of the day, the assault upon Signorina Rizzio common knowledge. Some said it had nothing to do with the C and E crowd at all, that there was, unknown to all save a favoured few, a passage between the men's and women's hostels which had been in use for years. The signorina had entertained nights without number every professor in the university, with preference given to the more muscular. Others, defending the lady's honour, declared that Professor Elia in person had led the

139

masked band of marauders into her sanctum, and that he had in his possession a captured nightdress belonging to the signorina which would bear witness to his feat.

Laughter was paramount then, but later in the day the mood changed. Word spread that the Authorities—whoever they might be—definitely put the blame for the break-in upon the C and E students, who, it was said, had returned from Sunday leave upon their vespas in a state of riot, and, circling beneath the windows of the women's hostel with songs and cat-calls, had fired the bolder amongst them to invasion.

Toni, looking over his shoulder, pointed out the first batch of angry C and E boys and girls emerging from the lecture-rooms allotted to them across the via dell'8 Settembre, not far from where we stood.

"Watch out," he called to me, "there's going to be trouble."

Somebody threw a stone. It shattered the windscreen of our van and the glass splintered. Another stone caught Toni on the side of the head. A shout went up from the small group of Arts students and others who were walking up the hill from the university proper. Some of them started running towards their supposed antagonists. In a moment there was shouting, yelling, more stones, more running, and two more boys, riding vespas, swerved into the midst of all of them, scattering students right and left.

"Come on," I said to Toni, "out of it. It's not our battle."

I pulled him into the van and started the engine. He did not say anything. He was mopping the side of his head, the blood flowing. We roared across the street, and avoiding the skirmish which students were running to join from all directions drove downhill past the university to the ducal palace.

I parked in our usual place and switched off the engine. "So much for university politics." I said.

Toni looked very white. I examined the cut. Not deep, but deep enough.

"Got a doctor you know?" I asked. He nodded. "Well, get along and see him. I'll make your excuses."

We climbed together from the van. He walked slowly to his vespa and straddled it, one hand still dabbing at his wound.

"You saw that fellow who threw the stone?" he said. "No ragging there, he did it deliberately, to start a fight. I'll get him later. Or my pals will."

He coasted slowly down the hill. I went into the library and reported the incident briefly to Giuseppe Fossi. He went off like a rocket.

"You had no business, either of you, to hang about the university buildings when the students are coming out of the lecture rooms," he exploded. "On a day like this, with rumours flying, it is asking for trouble. Now I shall have to put in a claim for the van, the matter will be reported back at the Registrar's office, Professor Rizzio may himself see the report. . . ."

"Of a bust wind-screen?" I interrupted. "Look, Signor Fossi, I'll get it seen to at some garage down the hill."

"There will be talk," he flustered. "Everyone knows the van, someone will have seen the incident. Trust Toni to tell all Ruffano."

I let him exhaust himself, then, when he quietened down, resumed my work. This was his probelem, not mine. I had something else to think about. The feeling of disquiet that had nagged at me all day had increased. If students cared to break in at the women's hostel it was their affair, and what they did there too. They would be either rounded up and punished, or permitted to go free. It was none of my business. But the timing bothered me. And my own translation from the German volumes.

". . . The citizens . . . finally rose at the instigation of the leading citizen, whose . . . wife had been profaned."

I was not the only one to handle the books and to read German. Aldo had shown them to one of his Arts students, a German scholar. The pages had been marked. Once again I heard my brother say, "We must have the excitement first. The profanation of the leading citizen's wife."

In retrospect I left the Butalis' house again, looked down from the street to the valley roads below, heard the throb of the returning vespas. Was it coincidence? Had the attack been planned?

It was difficult to keep my mind on sorting the more tedious works of German and English philosophers, and when the time came to close up for the evening I was the first to leave. Outside, I found the piazza Maggiore full of students. They were parading up and down in groups, some of them linking arms and all belligerent. What Faculties they represented I neither knew nor cared, but I realised they were stopping and challenging the casual passers-by. I hoped to escape notice, and had reached the steps of the Duomo when one big fellow happened to turn his head in my direction and swooped upon me.

"Hold on, shrimp," he cried, twisting my arm behind me. "Where are you sneaking off to?"

"Via San Michele," I said. "I lodge there."

"You lodge there, do you? And where do you work?"

"I'm an employee in the library."

"An employee in the library!" He mimicked my tone. "Well, that's a pretty dirty job, isn't it? Hands and face smothered in dust all day." He shouted down to others below the steps. "Here's a little Arts boy needs a wash. Shall we give him the water-treatment? What about dousing him in the fountain?"

A roar of laughter greeted the remark, some of it good-natured, but not all. "Hand him over! Clean him up!"

The fountain in the centre of the piazza was surrounded. Some of the students had already climbed the basin and were balancing, laughing and singing, upon the edge. There were many of them, fifty, a hundred. I felt very small, and very much alone. Suddenly a car, hooting high and long, swung into view from the direction of the university. The students fell back on either side of the piazza to let it pass. One fellow, losing his balance, stumbled into the fountain basin. There was a yell of laughter from the crowd, and as my captor, joining in the mirth, loosened his hold on me I ducked and slipped out of his hands. The car moved slowly on. It was the Alfa-Romeo, with Aldo at the wheel. Sitting beside him, waving his hand and smiling to the scattering students, who shouted and cheered at sight of him, was the Head of the Department of Commerce and Economics, Professor Elia.

I cut through the crowd of students to the passage leading from the via Rossini to the via dei Sogni. Here all was quiet. It might have been another world. No one roamed the street except for one lone cat that leapt on to the garden wall at sight of me. I opened the gate, walked up the pathway to the house and rang the bell. It was opened, after a while, by the girl who had brought in the dinner the night before.

"Signora Butali?" I enquired.

"I'm sorry, signore," she said, "the signora isn't at home. She left for Rome early this morning."

I stared at her blankly. "Left for Rome? I didn't think she was going until later in the week?"

"No, signore, nor did I. I found her gone when I came first

thing this morning. She left a note for me, saying she had decided to go suddenly. She must have been away by seven."

"Is Professor Butali worse, then?"

"I know nothing about that, signore. She didn't say."

I looked past her to the empty house. Already, because of the signora's absence, it lacked warmth and charm.

"Thank you," I said, "there is no message."

I walked the long way down to the pensione, avoiding the piazza della Vita. This way the streets were free of students, and the people I met were ordinary citizens going about their business. When I came to the via San Michele I saw that the entrance to No. 24 was blocked by Gino, Mario, and one or two others, and with them Paolo Pasquale and his sister. At sight of me she ran forward and, glancing up to me, took hold of me by the hand.

"Have you heard the news?" she asked.

I sighed. It was with me once again. There was no escaping it. "I've heard nothing else all day," I said, "even the books on the library shelves were full of it. There's been a break-in at the women's hostel. All the girls are pregnant."

"Oh, that," she said impatiently. "Who cares about that? I hope Signorina Rizzio has twins . . . No, the Director of the Arts Council has invited as many of the C and E students as care to do so to take part in the Festival, as a gesture to show his faith in all of us and that we were not responsible for last night's affair. Professor Elia has accepted on our behalf, and there's to be a meeting this evening, held in the old theatre above the piazza del Mercato. We're all going from here, and you must come with us."

She looked at me, smiling. Her brother joined her. "Do come," he said. "Nobody knows who you are. It's an experience nobody should miss. We're all mad to know what Professor Donati is going to say."

I had an intuition that I already knew.

CHAPTER THIRTEEN

THE DOORS OF the theatre were to be opened at nine. We had dinner first with the Silvanis, and set out at a quarter to the hour. The piazza della Vita was already crammed with students, converging upon the square from their various lodgings up and down the city, and now turning in a body down the narrow via del Teatro to the theatre itself. I soon lost sight of Gino and his companions, but the Pasquales held on to me firmly, one on either side, and I felt like a puppet, almost swung from my feet. The theatre in my father's day had never been much used. Concerts and oratorios were given at certain times, and occasionally there was a recitation by a visiting literary celebrity; otherwise it remained an edifice of architectural splendour, little known to the passing tourist or indeed to the citizens of Ruffano themselves. Today, so the Pasquales told me, all was changed. Thanks to the Rector of the university and the Director of the Arts Council, the theatre was in use throughout the year. Lectures, plays, concerts, films, exhibitions, even dances, all took place within its august walls.

We arrived to find a solid block of students waiting to pass in. Paolo, with a determined face, pushed and squeezed his way amongst them, Caterina and I hanging on behind. They were a good-natured crowd, laughing and chattering, pushing us in turn, and I wondered why the ugly mood of earlier on had changed, until I remembered that here there were no opponents —the students in this milling crowd were all C and E.

A great shout went up as the doors were opened, and Paolo, tightening his grip upon my arm, dragged little Caterina and me bodily through the entrance. "First come, first served," called some fellow at the door. "Those who are in first seize a seat and cling to it."

The auditorium was already filling rapidly, the crashing of seats as the flaps went down ricocheting to the roof, but this was drowned in turn by a group of students on the stage. Equipped with guitars, drums, and every conceivable form of rattle, they were singing the hit songs of the day, to tremendous applause from the surprised and delighted audience.

"What's on?" Paolo enquired of a student who was jiving in the aisle beside us. "Isn't anyone going to speak?"

"Don't ask me," replied the youth, shaking happily. "We're invited, that's all I know."

"Who cares? Let's make the most of it," laughed Caterina, and, taking up her stance in front of me, tapped and twisted with unexpected grace.

I should be thirty-two next birthday and I felt my age. As a student in Turin I had samba'd to perfection, but that was over eleven years ago. A courier gets no practice in the finer arts. I swayed to and fro, not to lose face before the present company, but I knew the figure that I cut was tame. The uproar was tremendous. Nobody seemed to care. I thought, with amusement, that Carla Raspa would have enjoyed it too, for all her scorn of the C and E students, but I could see no one in the auditorium who could even remotely come from the staff. All were students, all were impossibly young.

"Look," said Paolo suddenly, "that's surely Donati himself? There, taking over the drums."

I had my back to the stage, in an endeavour to follow the whirling of his sister, but at Paolo's exclamation I turned. It was as he said. Aldo, apparently unnoticed, had come on to the stage and taken the place of the student at the drums, and was now executing a fine performance on his own. The guitarists and the rattlers turned towards him, the singing and shouting grew louder still, the sound was deafening, and the audience, realising his identity with delighted clapping, pressed nearer to the stage. Nothing could have been more in contrast to the entry at the ducal palace which I had witnessed on Saturday. Tonight no flares, no silence, no body-guard, no element of mystery. Aldo, with a total disregard for status, had chosen to identify himself with the student throng. The gesture and timing were superb. I wondered when and how he had planned it.

"You know," said Caterina, "we've all misjudged him. I thought he was high and mighty like the rest of the professors. But look at him, just look! He might be one of us."

"I knew he wasn't really old," objected Paolo. "After all, he's barely forty yet. It's just that we've never had any contact with him, he doesn't belong to our crowd."

"He belongs now," said Caterina. "I don't care what anyone says."

The tempo increased. The whole audience swayed and shook to the throbbing of the guitars and the beating of the drums. Then suddenly, when exhaustion pitch was reached, came the final flourish. The sound went dead. Aldo came to the front of the stage and a student, one of the guitarists, pushed forward a chair from nowhere.

"Come on, all of you," said Aldo. "I'm through. Let's talk."

He collapsed into the chair, wiping his forehead. There was a burst of laughter and sympathy from the audience. He smiled and lifted his head, then beckoned those who were standing, or sitting in the front rows, to come nearer and gather round him. I noticed that the auditorium lights had dimmed, and an unseen light to the side of the stage threw his face and the group nearest to him into relief. Aldo had no microphone. He spoke clearly and distinctly, but in no sense did he declaim. It was as though he was chatting casually to the students closest to him.

"We ought to do that more often," he said, still mopping his forehead. "The trouble is that I don't get time. It's all right for you, you can work off steam any evening you care to, or at weekends—I'm not referring to last night, I'll discuss that later—but for an ulcer-ridden person like myself, spending half his days arguing with professors twenty years his senior, who steadfastly refuse to make one move that would bring Ruffano and the university up to date, it's just not on. Somebody has to wage war in this dust-ridden academy, and I'll continue to do so until I'm sacked."

A gulf of laughter greeted this remark, at which he stared about him, supposedly astonished.

"No, no, I'm serious," he said. "If they could get rid of me they would. Just as they would get rid of you, the whole fifteen hundred of you, if that's what you muster—I haven't the figures before me, but it's near enough. Why do they want to get rid of you? Because they're frightened. The old are always frightened of the young, but you represent a threat to their whole way of life. Any one of you who passes out of this university with a degree in Commerce and Economics is a potential millionaire, and, more than that, he will have a chance of helping to run the economy not only of this country but of Europe, possibly the world. You are the masters, my young friends, and everyone knows it. That's

146

why you're hated. Hatred is bred of fear, and your contemporaries who haven't your brains and your technical knowledge and your enthusiasm for life as it will and must be lived tomorrow are frightened of you. Frightened blue! No schoolteacher, no grubby lawyer, no chicken-livered so-called poet or painter—and that's what the students of the other faculties are trying to become—will stand a chance beside you. The future's yours, and don't let any half-baked set of decaying professors and their pathetic dwindling band of followers stand in your way. Ruffano is for the living. Not the dead."

Tumultuous applause followed the gesture of contempt with which he dismissed all, apparently, but his present audience. He waited for it to cease, then leant forward in his chair.

"I've no business to talk to you like this. As Director of the city Arts Council I don't mix myself up with university politics. My job is to look after the possessions in the ducal palace, which belong to all of you, and not to a minority, as some people choose to think. The reason I've got you here is because a clique—I'm naming no names—wants to destroy you. They want to make your Faculty, and all you stand for, so stink in the nostrils of the authorities that you will be chucked out, you, the Head of your Department, Professor Elia, the whole bag of tricks. Then, so they think, patrician rule will be resumed, and Ruffano fall asleep once more. The budding school-teachers, lawyers, poets, will have it their own way."

I flicked my eyes to Paolo on my right. He was watching Aldo attentively, his chin on his clenched fist. Caterina, on my left, was equally impressed. The mass of students with their upturned faces listened to him with as much intensity as the small élite in the ducal palace had done two nights before. But to a very different speech.

"Last night's break-in, and the outrage that followed," said Aldo softly, "if it was an outrage and not merely a trumped-up story, was a deliberate attempt to discredit you. This is the sort of game unscrupulous guerillas play in wartime. Commit an atrocity on your own people, and blame it on the enemy. Fine. Even admirable. It starts the bullets flying. Now, the university of Ruffano isn't geared to war at the present time, but, as you know, I run something called the Festival, which—if we like to make it so—can be used as your opportunity to take your revenge and show the enemy that you're as powerful and determined as

147

they are. The display this year will be the insurrection of the lively up-and-coming young citizens of Ruffano against the decadent Duke Claudio and his band of sycophants five hundred years ago. The merchants and the working people of the city outnumbered the courtiers by thousands, but the Duke had the law behind him, and the weapons. He destroyed by night, stealing into the streets in disguise and maltreating harmless individuals, just as—so they tell me—a certain nameless clique sometimes does today."

Caterina, gripping my hand, whispered under her breath, "The secret society!"

"Now," said Aldo, standing up, "I want you, the life-blood of the university, to play the citizens of Ruffano in the coming Festival. You won't need elaborate rehearsals, but I warn you it may be dangerous. The lads playing the courtiers will be armed—it's got to be authentic. I want you to get out into the streets with sticks and stones and any home-made weapon you can find. There'll be fighting in the streets and fighting up the hill and fighting in the ducal palace. Anyone who's scared can stay at home, and I for one won't blame him. But whoever is itching for a chance to get his own back upon the high and mighty, the snobbish inner circle who think they run the university and all Ruffano too—here's your chance. Come up and volunteer. I'll guarantee your victory."

He beckoned, laughing, and someone behind him on the stage started beating a tattoo upon the drum. The combination of this sound and the cheers from the audience and the crashing of seats as the students scrambled forward towards the stage where Aldo, still laughing, waited for them rang in my ears like the discords of hell.

I left Caterina and Paolo cheering and shouting amongst the others, and turned through the pushing crowd to the nearest exit. I was the only one amongst the packed and cheering students to attempt to leave. The guard at the door—I thought I recognised one of the scrutineers who had examined the passes on the Saturday evening at the ducal palace—put out a hand to stop me, but I managed to slip by. I walked up the street to the piazza della Vita, which by now was practically deserted save for the few city folk who promenaded still, and so back to my room.

It was no use doing anything tonight. The session in the theatre might continue until midnight, for all I knew, or even later. There

might be more pop music, more dancing, more talking, intermingled with another performance upon the drums. Aldo would
gather in his volunteers. Tomorrow I would go to his house and
get at the truth. My brother had not changed in two-and-twenty
years. His technique was the same now as then. The only difference was that, where he had once played upon the imagination
of a sibling and devoted ally, he was now playing upon the raw
and feverish emotions of fifteen hundred students. To train
actors for a Festival did not necessitate whipping them into rival
factions with all the risk of precipitating a real catastrophe. Or
did it? Was it Aldo's intention to launch his opposing teams into
conflagration so that the air should finally be cleansed? This had
been the theory of warlords of the past. It had not worked. Spilt
blood, like compost, fertilises the soil, brewing further strife. I
wished Signora Butali had not gone to Rome. I could have talked
to her. I could have warned her about Aldo and his multitudinous schemes, his magnetic power over the unsuspecting, the
vulnerable, the young. She might have reasoned with him, or
laughed him out of it.

When the students returned to the pensione, shortly after
midnight, I turned out my light. I heard the light step of Caterina
climb the stairs, and she opened my door, calling softly. I did not
reply. After a moment she went away. I was in no mood to
listen to the converted, or give an explanation of my own
behaviour.

The next morning, purposely, I waited until I had heard the
whole batch leave the house before I descended to the dining-
room. Signora Silvani was sitting at the table reading the newspaper.

"Here you are," she said. "I wondered if you had gone out
early, but the children thought not. Here's your coffee. Were you
as much impressed by the Director of the Arts Council as they
were?"

"He has a way with him," I said. "He's very persuasive."

"So I believe," she answered. "He's certainly persuaded our
lot, and I imagine most of the others. They're all to become
citizens of Ruffano for the Festival." She pushed the paper towards
me as I drank my coffee. "Here's the local paper," she said.
"There's a small piece about the break-in at the women's hostel,
but they say nothing was taken, and it was a simple student rag.
Signorina Rizzio has an attack of asthma—nothing to do with the

break-in—and has gone away for a fortnight for some mountain air."

I buttered my roll in silence and read the passage. Carla Raspa had been right. Poor Signorina Rizzio was unable to face her mocking world. True or untrue, to carry the stigma of an old maid deflowered brought the finger of scorn.

"Ruffano is in the headlines," went on Signora Silvani. "See at the top there, about the woman murdered in Rome? She came from Ruffano all the time, and the body's to be brought back for burial. They've caught the lad that did it. One of the underworld."

My eyes ran swiftly to the large type at the top.

"Last night the Rome police arrested Giovanni Stampi, a day-labourer, at present without employment, who has already served nine months for theft. He admitted stealing a note for ten thousand lire from the dead woman, but denies the murder."

I finished my coffee and pushed the newspaper aside. "He says he's innocent."

"Wouldn't you?" retaliated Signora Silvani.

I left the house and walked to work up the via Rossini. It was a week ago today that I had driven into Rome with my coach-party and that night had seen the woman, now proved to be Marta, sleeping in the doorway of the church. Only a week. A moment's impulse on my part had brought about her murder, my own flight home, and the encounter with my living brother. Chance or predestination? The scientists could not tell us. Nor could the psychologists, or the priests. But for that stroll into the street I should now be on the homeward route from Naples to Genoa, the shepherd of my flock. As it was, I had probably lost my courier's status for ever, exchanging it for what? A temporary job as an assistant librarian which I could not, dared not quit because of Aldo. He, returned from the dead, was my reason for living. We, my mother and I, had deserted him once, contributing, doubtless, to his present ambivalent mood. Never again. Whatever my brother chose to do, I must stand by him. Poor Marta's murder was no longer my concern, with the murderer caught; Aldo was my problem.

As yesterday, I found my fellow assistants in the library buzzing with rumour. The secretary, Signorina Catti, was busy denying the story spread by Toni that the unfortunate Signorina Rizzio had, after an X-ray at the local hospital, left Ruffano for an operation elsewhere.

"The story is malicious and entirely unfounded," she declared. "Signorina Rizzio was suffering from a bad cold anyway, and is asthmatic. She has gone with friends to Cortina."

Giuseppe Fossi dismissed the tale as students' gossip. "In any case," he said, "the whole unfortunate event will die a natural death, thanks to Professor Donati, who has brought about a reconciliation between Professor Rizzio and Professor Elia. He is giving a big dinner tonight at the Hotel Panorama for both of them. My wife and I have been invited, and all the professors. It will be an important affair, as you may imagine. Now, shall we stop all this nonsense and get to work?"

As I plodded away under his direction I felt easier in mind. A reconciliation between the Heads of the opposing Departments could do nothing but good. If this was Aldo's move, then I had misjudged him. Perhaps his address to the C and E students at the theatre had only been what it seemed to be on the surface—a wily bid for Festival volunteers and nothing more. Sensitive and intuitive to his every word and gesture I certainly was, but ignorant as to his achievements for the Festival up to date. Both Signora Silvani and Carla Raspa had been enthusiastic about the realism of previous occasions. The Butalis had taken part in last year's production, along with Professor Rizzio. Would this year's display be so very different after all?

I went back to the pensione for lunch, and was at once set upon by my companions of last night.

"Deserter . . . coward . . . traitor!" shouted Gino and his friends, until Signor Silvani, holding up his hand for silence, protested that he and his wife would put the whole lot out of the house.

"Shout yourselves hoarse at the Festival if you like," he said, "but not under my roof. Here I am master. Sit down and take no notice of them," he added for my benefit, and to his wife, "Serve Signor Fabbio first."

"If you want the truth," I said, addressing the table at large, "I came back early last night because I had a stomach ache." This was received with groans of disbelief. "Nor can I do the twist," I said, "or possibly it was that trying to do so made me ill."

"Forgiven," called Caterina, "and shut up, everybody. After

all, we forget he isn't a student. Why should he commit himself?"

"Because who isn't for us is against us," put in Gerardo.

"No," said Paolo, "that doesn't go for strangers. And Armino is a stranger to Ruffano."

He turned to me, his young face serious. "We won't let them bully you," he said, "but, all the same, you do see what a fine thing Professor Donati is doing by including every one of us in the Festival?"

"He wants performers," I answered, "that's all there is to it."

"No," said Paolo, "that isn't all. He wants to show in public that he's on our side. It amounts to a vote of confidence in every C and E student in the university, and from a disinterested observer like the Director of the Arts Council of Ruffano that puts us on top."

A chorus of approval rose from the whole table. Signor Silvani wiped his mouth and pushed back his chair.

"You know what they are saying at the prefettura?" he observed. "That the whole university is getting too big for its boots. A plague on all your Faculties, and we'd do better to be shot of the lot of you and turn the city into a nice big tourist centre with spas and swimming-pools on either hill."

This put an end to the argument. I was permitted to finish my lunch without drawing further fire. Before returning to the library I found that a note had been left for me in the entrance of No. 24, and I recognised the looped handwriting of Carla Raspa.

"I have not forgotten our date this evening," I read, "and I suggest that instead of your taking me to the Hotel dei Duchi we pool our resources and try out the magnificence of the Hotel Panorama. A big dinner is being given there by the Director of the Arts Council, and we can tuck ourselves away in a corner and watch the splendour. Call for me at seven."

Her persistence was untiring, but I doubted if it would win her admission to No. 2, via dei Sogni. The nearest she could get to Aldo was in the public restaurant of a hotel. I scribbled a note in answer, accepting the challenge, and left it in the doorway of her house.

The afternoon at the library passed without incident, and strangely enough without gossip either. The C and E bully who had sought to douse me in the fountain the day before had been right about the dust in the library. The shelves that Toni and I were now engaged upon were coated with it, and the books we removed could not have been taken out for years. One collection, right at the top, bore a name upon it that struck a chord in memory. Luigi Speca. Where had I lately heard or seen the name Luigi Speca? . . . I paused, and shrugged my shoulders. I could not remember. Anyway, the collection proved uninteresting. Uniform editions of Dante's *Divina Commedia*, Poems of Leopardi, Sonnets of Petrarca, all lumped together with other miscellaneous works. "Donated to the University of Ruffano by Luigi Speca." This proved possession, and they could go to the new university library. I packed them in one of the crates and left the box of papers for another time. Giuseppe Fossi was already becoming restive, with one eye on the clock.

"I can't afford to be late," he said shortly after six. "The dinner at the Panorama is at eight-fifteen for a quarter to nine. Dinner-jacket optional, but I shall dress, of course."

I doubt whether, if he could have exchanged his date with mine, he would have done so. He stalked from the library with all the bombast of a minor cleric bidden to partake of a papal feast. I followed him about twenty minutes later. Since I had no tuxedo with which to impress Carla Raspa, my one and only dark suit must suffice.

"Going to watch the fun at the Panorama?" asked Toni. "All Ruffano will turn out, so the boys are saying down in the town."

"I might do just that," I answered. "Look out for me."

Washed, changed and sleek, I arrived at No. 5 as the campanile struck seven. I climbed the stairs to the first floor and, seeing the card "Carla Raspa" inserted neatly in a slot beside the door, knocked upon it. It was opened immediately and my date for the evening stood there, immaculate in black and white—white top, low-cut, contrasting with the stiff black skirt—hair shining, drawn smoothly back behind her ears, lips bloodless. A vampire, before swooping to feed upon its victim, could not have looked more dangerous.

"I'm overwhelmed," I said, bowing. "The trouble is, if you set foot in the streets you'll be mobbed. We'll never get as far as the Hotel Panorama."

"Don't worry," she answered, drawing me inside the apart-ment. "I've looked after that. Did you see the car outside?"

I had noticed a Fiat 600 parked by the kerbside as I entered the building. "Yes," I said. "Is it yours?"

"Mine for the evening," she smiled, "borrowed from an obliging neighbour on the floor above. Have a drink. Cinzano from your home-town of Turin."

She handed me a glass and took one for herself. I glanced about me. The furnishings, which I supposed were standard, the apartment being let furnished, had been embellished with accessories of the tenant's choice. Bright and enormous cushions splayed upon the divan-bed. A wrought-iron lampstand—made in Ruffano?—stood beside it, the light subdued by a deep parchment shade. The small kitchenette beyond had a scarlet floor, and a corner of the room was set for dining, with a table and two chairs, all black. This was where Giuseppe Fossi must indulge himself before seeking satiation on the divan-bed.

"You seem very well installed," I said. "My congratulations, signorina."

"I like my comforts," she replied, "and so do the few friends who visit me. If you count yourself one, call me Carla."

I lifted my glass and drank to this distinction. She lit a cigarette and moved about the room, the aromatic perfume that exuded from her person too pungent for my taste. No doubt it was intended to whet the appetite and heat the blood. My vitals remained unmoved. She caught sight of herself in the mirror on the wall and pouted. It was a reflex action, signifying pleasure.

"What's the excitement," I asked, "of watching a formal party of professors and their wives?"

"You don't realise," she said. "It will be a sight in a million. They say Professor Rizzio and Professor Elia haven't spoken for a year. I want to see the impact. Besides, any party given by Aldo Donati is worth watching. Just to hover on the fringe will be a stimulant."

Her nostrils quivered in anticipation like a brood mare prior to stud. I expected her at any moment to paw the ground.

"You know," I told her, "that Giuseppe Fossi and his wife have been invited. What if he sees us? Will it spoil your delightful friendship?"

She laughed, shrugging her shoulders. "He must take what's offered," she said. "Besides, he'll be so blown-up with pride that he won't have eyes for us. Shall we be going?"

It was barely a quarter-past seven. Giuseppe Fossi had said something in the library about the party assembling at a quarter-past eight. I told this to Carla Raspa.

"I know," she said, "but my idea is this. That we ourselves should feed early, and then, when Donati's party assembles in the hall for drinks, slip out of the restaurant and join them. No one will realise we aren't amongst the invited until afterwards, when they go in to dinner."

It had been my function before now to arrange similar small deceptions for the pleasure of my touring clients. It made their entire evening if they could stand about in the proximity of film-actors or diplomats and indulge, even for five minutes, the fantasy of belonging to another stratum.

"Anything you wish," I said to my companion. "My only stipulation is that we do *not* follow the invited into the restaurant and then endure the humiliation of being turned from the big table."

"I promise to behave," she said. "But you never know. The numbers might be wrong, and if there should be vacant places I'd seize one without a qualm."

I doubted Aldo's party being so disorganised, but left her hope unchallenged. We descended to the street, and at Carla Raspa's suggestion I took the wheel of the borrowed car. We shot away down the street, and passing the church of San Cipriano climbed the northern hill towards the piazza del Duca Carlo, drawing up some two hundred yards short of it before the imposing Hotel Panorama.

We were too early for the city sightseers promised by Toni, but our arrival did not pass unnoticed. A doorman in uniform rushed to help us out of the car. Another, equally resplendent, swung the revolving doors. I thought with compassion of my old friend Signor Longhi at the Hotel dei Duchi.

The vestibule was large, stone-floored and pillared, set about with orange-trees in tubs and dripping fountains. Windows in the rear gave on to a terrace where during the hot weather, so my companion told me, the clientèle would lounge and also dine. The hotel, now in its second season, was run by a syndicate. Professor Elia, Director of Commerce and Economics, was said to be a member. I was not surprised.

"Don't worry," murmured Carla Raspa, "about the bill. I've plenty if you run short. The charges are staggering. It's intended, of course, for American and German tourists. No one else can afford it, except the Milanese."

We passed through to the restaurant, empty at the moment

except for ourselves. The enormous table in the centre, ready for the dinner-party later, reminded me of the set-up so frequently ordered by myself for Sunshine Tours. Only the flags were missing. The head waiter, with minions at his elbow, bowed us to the table which Carla Raspa had reserved beforehand, and handed us menus the size of proclamations. I studied mine in silence, thinking of my pocket. Carla Raspa, showing bravado, ordered for us both; the dish, a marriage-after-death of eel and octopus, presaged insomnia. Perhaps this was her intention.

"I should like," she said, "to live like this always. It won't happen as long as I remain a lecturer on the staff here."

I asked her the alternative. She shrugged her shoulders.

"A rich man somewhere," she answered, "preferably with a wife at home. Unmarried men tire sooner. They have so large a choice."

"You won't find one in Ruffano," I told her.

"I don't know," she said, "I live in hopes. Professor Elia has a wife who never emerges from Ancona. She won't be here tonight."

"I thought," I said, nodding at her ensemble, "all this was to attract Donati?"

"What's wrong with catching both?" she answered. "Donati is the more elusive. But they tell me Elia has a larger appetite."

Her frankness was disarming, and I felt myself secure. The table for two in the kitchenette and the divan-bed were not for me.

"Of course," she continued, "if a shrimp came along and offered marriage I'd accept him. But only if his bank balance were considerable." I got the message and affected a deep sigh. She patted my hand kindly. "As an escort you couldn't be better," she said. "Should I catch my fish and you stay on in Ruffano, you can share the pickings."

I professed myself obliged. We both of us became a little lit with a bottle of Verdicchio to smooth the passage of the eel and octopus. I found myself smiling for no reason. The walls of the hotel Panorama receded. The head waiter became less attentive, and kept peering out of the door towards the pillared vestibule.

"Have you had enough?" asked Carla Raspa. "If so, I think we'd better move. They're beginning to arrive—I can tell from the noise outside. Ask for the bill."

The bill was ready, folded upon a plate. We had eaten the one dish only, but from the figures I could tell we needed the support of that bank balance already discussed. I drew out my pocket-book, while my companion slipped assistance on to my knee beneath the cover of the tablecloth.

Haughtily, like a god who has eaten his fill before the arrival of lesser mortals, I paid, and escorted my companion from the restaurant. We entered the vestibule to find it already filling with the invited guests. Waiters were buzzing about proffering trays laden with glasses. The men, as Giuseppe had warned me, were in dinner-jackets, the women in every variety of evening dress. The hairdressers of Ruffano had been working overtime.

Carla Raspa unblushingly seized a glass from the tray that the nearest waiter offered her. I did the same.

"There he is," said my companion in dishonour. "He looks even more alluring in a tuxedo. I'd like to eat him!"

Aldo was standing with his back to us, but despite the babble of voices the rather clear tone of Carla Raspa, pitched in a key more suitable to the lecture-rooms she was used to than this formal gathering, reached his ears. He turned, and saw us both. For a moment he looked nonplussed, a rare thing for my brother. I imagined his lightning thought—had two of the invitations gone astray? My look of embarrassment must have reassured him, and my attempt to back away. He cut me dead, but nodded civilly enough to my companion. Then he moved forward to greet another arrival, Professor Rizzio, alone, without his sister. The Deputy Rector of the university looked weary and very strained. He shook hands with Aldo, and murmured something I could not catch in answer to my brother's solicitous enquiry as to his sister's health. His haggard appearance troubled me, and I could barely look at him. Discreetly I moved out of earshot and watched the other new arrivals, none of them known to me. Only Guiseppe Fossi, bursting out of his over-tight dinner-jacket, was recognizable amidst a hub of strangers, with his wife, more like an eager hen than ever, pecking and clucking at his side.

I squinted through the entrance to the line of cars outside, and beyond them to the chattering, gaping crowd. Not all Ruffano, certainly, but a fair proportion strolling to take the air, both city folk and students. I turned back to the hall. Giuseppe Fossi had noticed Carla Raspa, and was busy directing his wife in the opposite direction. Aldo, still engaged with Professor Rizzio, glanced frowning at his watch. My companion edged towards me.

"The other guest of honour is late," she said. "It's almost ten to nine. He's done it on purpose, naturally. To make a greater stir than Rizzio."

I had forgotten Professor Elia. The purpose of the party, of course, was to effect a public reconciliation. Aldo's triumph was to bring the two men together.

The voices rose deafeningly. Glasses clinked. I shook my head when offered a third martini.

"Can't we go?" I whispered to Carla Raspa.

"And miss the meeting of the giants? Not on your life," she answered.

The minutes dragged like hours. The hands of the hotel clock stood at three minutes to nine. Aldo had ceased talking to Professor Rizzio and was tapping an impatient foot.

"Does he have far to come?" I asked my companion.

"Three minutes in a car," she said. "You know the big house at the corner of the piazza del Duca Carlo? Oh no, it's obvious. This is his method of making the rest look small."

The telephone rang at the reception desk. I happened to hear it because I stood between it and the guests. I saw the reception clerk answer, listen, then reach for a memo pad and scribble a message. He looked bewildered. Waving aside the page who stood beside him, he hurried from the desk across the crowded floor towards my brother, and handed him the message. I watched Aldo's face. He read the message, then turned rapidly to the receptionist and questioned him. The man, troubled, obviously repeated what he had just heard on the telephone. Aldo raised both his hands and called for silence. There was an immediate hush. Faces swung towards him.

"I'm afraid something has happened to Professor Elia," he said. "A message had just come over the telephone from an anonymous caller suggesting that I should go to the Professor's house immediately. It could be a hoax, but very possibly not. If you'll all excuse me I'll drive there instantly. If all is well, I'll report back at once."

A gasp of consternation came from the assembled guests. Professor Rizzio, looking more drawn than ever, plucked Aldo by the sleeve. He was evidently asking to go with him. Aldo nodded, already moving swiftly through the crowded room. Professor

Rizzio followed. Others also broke away from their wives and turned towards the entrance. Carla Raspa, taking my hand, pulled me after them.

"Come on," she said. "It may be serious, it may be nothing. But whatever it is, we're not going to miss it."

I followed her through the swing-doors of the hotel. Already I could hear the roar of Aldo's Alfa-Romeo as it turned and spun away uphill towards the piazza del Duca Carlo.

CHAPTER FOURTEEN

WE FOLLOWED CLOSELY in our borrowed car, but others had the same idea. Those guests whose cars, like ours and Aldo's, had been parked in the space reserved for the hotel were soonest off. The crowd of watching students and city-folk, realising from the confusion that something was wrong, started running up the hill in their turn. Horns hooted wildly and there was a grinding and clashing of gears and much excited jabbering.

"That's Elia's house, there at the corner," pointed Carla Raspa. "The lights are on."

The Alfa-Romeo had already drawn up beside the house, which stood in its own garden on the right of the piazza del Duca Carlo. I saw Aldo spring from the car and dash inside, followed more slowly by Professor Rizzio. I slowed down, wondering what to do. We could not very well draw up behind Aldo's car. Cars hooted impatiently behind me.

"I'll circle the piazza," I said, "and come round again."

I shot ahead, but Carla Raspa, craning to look out of the window, said, "They're coming out again. He can't be there."

Chaos was piling up in my immediate rear, close to the house. I could see the lights of cars flashing in my mirror. People shouted.

"Donati's getting back into his car," said Carla Raspa. "No, he's not. Wait, Armino, wait. Park across to the right there, by the public gardens."

The piazza del Duca Carlo terminated in the formal municipal gardens laid out with gravel paths and trees and shrubs, with the statue of Duke Carlo dominating the scene. I parked the car close to some trees and we got out.

"Why the floodlights?" I asked.

"They are always switched on for the week of the Festival," said my companion. "Didn't you notice them last night? My God . . ."

She clutched my arm and pointed to the statue of Duke Carlo, who, serene and magnificent on his marble pedestal, gazed benignly down upon the gravel path below. Flood-lit, he was an imposing figure, but not so imposing was the man who sat immediately beneath him on the stone steps leading to the base. Sat, or rather straddled, for his hands and widely separated feet were bound to heavy weights, preventing movement. He was stark naked. Even from the distance where I stood, about twenty-five yards, I had no difficulty in recognising the powerful build, the shock of black hair, of Professor Elia.

As we stared, my companion choking back a cry half-frightened, half-hysterical, we saw Aldo, followed by some half-dozen men, run across the piazza towards the statue. In a moment the wretched victim was surrounded, masked from view by those who bent over him to set him free. I saw Aldo break away and wave his hand, shouting for a car. Another figure darted back across the piazza. Meanwhile more cars were approaching, drawing up, parking. The first of the running students swarmed up the hill. Everywhere people were calling, "What is it? Who is it? What's happened?"

We moved closer, drawn by the terrible instinct that pervades all humanity when witness to disaster. The instinct to be there. The desire to know. Being first upon the scene we had the advantage over our equally curious neighbours, although Aldo and the guests from the hotel who had followed hard upon him partially screened the unfortunate professor from our view.

Someone cut the thongs, the arms and legs sagged forward. The whole body drooped as though about to fall. The victim raised his head. He was not gagged. He could, had he so desired, have shouted for help before, and been freed the sooner. Why had he not done so? His eyes, without spectacles, searching the faces of those who in sympathy and consternation sought to screen him from the public gaze, gave me the answer. Professor Elia had not called for help because of shame. Shame at the lamentable, shocking and ridiculous figure he would cut before the inevitable strangers who must set eyes upon him first. As it happened, the man who stood before him, who looked down upon him with pity, even with anguish, and was the first to hand down the car rug that an eager helper thrust forward to envelop the naked frame, was his rival, the Deputy Rector of the university, Professor Rizzio, whose sister had been maltreated some forty-eight hours before.

"Help him to the car," called Aldo. "Screen him completely. And get all that rabble out of the way."

He and Professor Rizzio helped the victim to his feet. For a moment we caught a glimpse of him in all his drab disorder, his

161

ugly white limbs contrasting with his coarse hair; then the merciful rug cloaked him, the protecting arms enveloped him. His friends led him to the shelter of the car, and the bewildered watchers fell back on either side. I left Carla Raspa staring after the rescue party. I went behind one of the newly-planted municipal trees and vomited. When I returned, my companion was standing by the car.

"Come on," she called impatiently. "We'll go after them."

I looked across the piazza. The summoned car, pushing through the assembling crowd, had stopped once more before Professor Elia's entrance.

"We can't go to his house," I said, "we've no business there."

"Not after him," she said, swiftly getting into the car, "after the gang. The thugs who did it. They can't be far away. Hurry . . . hurry . . ."

Once again, those who had cars shared her idea. The victim could safely be left to the ministrations of his friends and a hastily summoned doctor; but for the perpetrators of the outrage the hunt was on.

Four roads led from the piazza del Duca Carlo, so the choice of route was varied. Those running left swung west and out of the city. To turn to the right would bring us downhill to the Porta Malebranche and the via delle Mura. Another street, running south from the gate, would take us uphill once more to the piazza della Vita and the city centre. I chose the route to the right, and heard a second car behind me. We cruised downhill to the gate and then I let the other car pass. It shot east along the via delle Mura. Two students, straddling a vespa, followed it. I had no doubt that other pursuers had gone westward from the piazza del Duca Carlo, and all would eventually meet up on the southern hill beyond the students' hostels.

I halted the car on one of the ramparts in the via delle Mura overlooking the valley below, and turned to my companion. "It's a useless chase," I said. "Whoever did it has gone to ground. They had only to dive into the side streets and get lost, then saunter out into the piazza della Vita like anybody else."

"How would they have taken Elia from the house and to the statue if they hadn't a car?" she asked.

"Covered him with rugs and carried him," I answered. "Everybody was so busy watching the guests arrive at the Hotel Panorama that the piazza del Duca Carlo at the top of the hill was deserted. The culprits knew this, and took a chance. Then they telephoned the hotel from Professor Elia's house and scampered." I reached for a packet of cigarettes and lighted one for her and for myself. "Anyway," I said, "they'll find them in the end. Donati will have to send for the police."

"Don't be too sure," said Carla Raspa.

"Why not?"

"He'll have to get Professor Elia's authority first," she replied, "and he won't want his nudity blazoned in the press and everywhere else any more than Rizzio wanted the world to know about the assault upon his sister. I'm willing to bet you a thousand lire that this second rag is hushed up like the first."

"Impossible! Too many people saw."

"A lot of people saw nothing at all. Only a group of men huddled round a figure covered with rugs. If the powers-that-be want to hush it up, they will. You realise that Friday is Festival day, when the students' relatives and outsiders come to Ruffano? What a moment to announce a scandal!"

I was silent. The incident had been well-timed. Short of expelling the students en masse, there was little the authorities could do.

"It could be one of two things," continued Carla Raspa. "Either a pay-back from the Arts and Education lads for the insult to the Rizzios, or a double-bluff from the boys in C and E to throw the blame on their opponents. I don't know that it matters much either way. As a rag, it was superlative."

"You think so?" I said.

"Yes," she said, "don't you?"

I was not sure which had distressed me most—the strained face of Professor Rizzio burying his pride and shaking hands with my brother at the Hotel Panorama, or the tortured, haunted eyes of Professor Elia when his nakedness had been revealed. Both were pathetic figures, shorn of lustre.

"No," I answered. "I'm a stranger in Ruffano. Both incidents revolt me."

She opened the window of the car, laughing, and threw out her cigarette. She seized mine from my lips and threw it out as well. Then she turned and, taking my face in her hands, kissed my mouth.

"The trouble with you is that you need firm handling," she said.

The sudden display of passion caught me off-guard. The thrusting lips, the entwining legs, the fumbling hands, were unexpected. The approach that doubtless delighted Giuseppe Fossi repelled me. If this was her moment it wasn't mine. I pushed her back against the handle of the door and slapped her face. She looked surprised.

"Why so violent?" she asked, not in the least annoyed.

"Love-making in a car offends my taste," I told her.

"Very well, then. Let's go home," she answered.

I started up the car once more, and we drove along the via delle Mura and into the city, and so by a side-street to the via San Michele. At any other time I might have been amused, even willing, to follow her lead. Not so tonight. Her advances sprang, not from our casual acquaintance and the light-hearted intimacy of an evening spent in each other's company, but from another cause—the scene we had just witnessed. I drew the car up with a jerk in front of No. 5. She got out and went into the house, leaving the door open for me. But I did not follow. Instead I got out of the car and made my way uphill to the via dei Sogni.

I wondered how long she would wait for me. Whether she would go to the window and look down at the parked car, and then, possibly unbelieving still, descend the stairs once more and peer in to see if I were still there. She might even cross the street to No. 24 and enquire of the Silvanis if by any chance Signor Fabbio had entered and gone to his room.

Then I dismissed her from my mind. I walked past my old home, darkly shuttered, and arrived at my brother's house. I rang the bell of the porter's entrance on the left, and after a moment or two Jacopo emerged. He broke into a smile at the sight of me.

"Could you let me in to wait for Aldo?" I asked. "He's out, I know, but I want to see him when he returns."

"Of course, Signor Beo," he said, and then, possibly guessing something from my heated appearance, for I had walked fast, he added, "Is anything wrong?"

"There was a disturbance," I said, "up in the piazza del Duca Carlo. It broke up the party at the hotel. Aldo's dealing with it."

He looked concerned, and leading the way across the passage opened Aldo's door. He switched on the lights. "The students, I suppose," he said. "They are always excited this week, with the

Festival. And then the break-in on the Sunday night. Was it something similar?"

"Yes," I said. "Aldo will explain."

He opened the door to the living-room and asked if I would like something to drink. I told him no. I could pour myself a drink if I needed one. He waited a moment, uncertain whether I was going to gossip with him or not, then, with the tact induced through long years with my brother, decided that I wished to be alone. He withdrew, and I heard him close the front door and return to his own domain.

I prowled about the room. Looked out of the window. Stared at the portrait of my father. Flung myself in a chair. The peace and the familiarity of home possessions were all about me, but I felt uneasy, sick. I got up again, and crossing to a table picked up the German volume of the *Lives of the Dukes of Ruffano*. It opened at the marked page, and I ran my eyes over it until I came upon the passage I remembered.

". . . When accusations were made against him by the outraged citizens of Ruffano, Duke Claudio retaliated by declaring that he had been divinely appointed to mete out to his subjects the punishment they deserved. The proud would be stripped, the haughty violated, the slanderer silenced, the viper die in his venom. The scales of heavenly justice would thus be balanced."

I closed the book and sat down again in another chair. Two faces were before me. That of Signorina Rizzio, haughty, unbending, hardly deigning to speak to me over her mineral water; and that of Professor Elia, lunching with his friends in the small restaurant off the via San Cipriano, guffawing at the rumour of assault, delighted, self-opinionated, proud. I had not seen Signorina Rizzio since Sunday morning. Whether she was with friends in Cortina or elsewhere hardly mattered. She had carried her shame with her. Professor Elia I had seen less than an hour ago. His shame was with him still.

The telephone started ringing. I stared at it, doing nothing. The persistent sound continued, and I got up and lifted the receiver. The operator said, "Will you take a call from Rome?" I answered, "Yes," mechanically. After a moment I heard a woman say, "Aldo, is it you?"

It was Signora Butali. I recognised her voice. I was about to tell her that my brother was out but she went on speaking, taking my silence for assent, or perhaps indifference. She sounded desperate.

"I've been trying to get you all the evening," she said. "Gaspare is adamant. He insists on coming home. Ever since Professor Rizzio telephoned him yesterday and told him what happened, he hasn't rested. The doctors say it would be better for him to return than to lie there, in hospital, working himself into a fever. Dearest . . . for God's sake, tell me what to do. Aldo, are you there?"

I put down the receiver. In about five minutes it rang again. I did not answer. I just went on sitting in Aldo's chair.

It was after midnight when I heard the key turn in the lock and the front-door slam. Jacopo may have heard the car arrive and gone to warn my brother that I was waiting for him, and then withdrawn to his own quarters, for there was no sound of voices. Soon Aldo came into the room. He looked at me, saying nothing, then went across to the tray of glasses and poured himself a drink.

"Were you up at the piazza del Duca Carlo too?" he asked.

"Yes," I said.

"How much did you see?"

"The same as you. Professor Elia naked."

He carried his glass to a chair and sprawled across it, one leg over the arm. "He wasn't even bruised," he said. "I called a doctor to examine him. Luckily the night was mild. He won't have caught pneumonia. Besides, he's as strong as an ox."

I did not comment. Aldo drank, then set down his glass and sprang to his feet. "I'm hungry," he said. "I haven't had any dinner. I wonder if Jacopo has left sandwiches. Be back in a minute."

He was gone about five minutes, and returned with a tray of prosciutto, salad and fruit, which he placed on the table beside the chair.

"I don't know what they did at the Panorama," he said, attacking the food. "I telephoned the manager to say that Professor Elia was unwell, that Professor Rizzio and I were staying with him, and would the others carry on without us? No doubt they did, or some of them. Most of the professors don't get a chance to eat up there on their salary, nor their wives. What in the world were you doing?"

"Watching the guests arrive," I said.

"Not your idea, I imagine?"

166

"No."

"Ah, well, she got her bellyful—that ought to keep her quiet for a couple of nights. Did she molest you?"

I ignored the question. He smiled, and continued eating.

"My little Beo," he said, "your homecoming hasn't been that easy. Who would think Ruffano could turn out to be so lively? You'd have a smoother passage in one of your touring coaches. Here, keep me company." He picked up an orange from his tray and threw it at me.

"I was at the theatre yesterday," I said, slowly peeling the orange. "You are quite a performer upon the drums."

He had not expected this. I could tell by the hardly imperceptible pause between his cutting a slice of ham and forking it to his mouth.

"You get around," he said. "Who took you there?"

"The C and E students from my lodgings," I answered, "who, like the mass of your audience, appeared as impressed by all you said as the élite on Saturday night at the ducal palace."

He waited a moment before answering. Then, pushing aside his plate and reaching for his salad, he observed, "The young are pliable."

I finished peeling the orange and offered him half. We ate in silence. I saw his eye fall upon the volume of the *Lives of the Dukes of Ruffano* lying on the further table where I had placed it. Then he looked at me. " 'The proud would be stripped, the haughty violated'," I quoted. "What exactly are you trying to do? Mete out heavenly justice like Duke Claudio?"

Appetite satisfied, he got up, removed the tray to a table in the corner, poured himself half a glass of wine, and stood with it beneath our father's portrait.

"My immediate job is to train actors," he said. "If they choose to identify themselves with the parts allotted to them, so much the better. We shall get an even finer performance on the day of the Festival."

The smile, disarming to the world, did not deceive me. I knew it of old. Too often in days gone by he had employed it to get his way.

"There have been two incidents," I said, "both highly organised. Don't tell me a bunch of students could, or did, plan either of them."

"You underestimate this generation," he replied. "They have

great powers of organisation, if they care to develop them. Besides, they are hungry for ideas. Give them a suggestion, and they're away."

He neither admitted nor denied association with what had happened on Sunday evening and tonight. I had no doubt that he had instigated both events.

"It doesn't disturb you," I asked, "to humiliate two people— three, counting Professor Rizzio—to such an extent that they are bound to lose authority forever?"

"Authority is bogus," he said, "unless it comes from within. Then it is inspiration and comes from God."

I stared. Aldo had never been religious. Our boyhood attendance at Mass on Sundays and feast days had been a routine affair, commanded by our parents, though frequently employed by my brother as a means to frighten me; the altar-piece in San Cipriano being an example of his powers to distort imagination to breaking point.

"Keep that for your students," I said. "It's the sort of thing the Falcon told his élite."

"And they believed him," he answered.

The smile, the tongue-in-cheek, were suddenly absent. The eyes, blazing in the pale face, were disturbing. I moved in my chair restlessly, and reached for a cigarette. When I glanced at him again the tension was over. He was finishing his glass of wine.

"You know the one thing that nobody in our country can endure?" he asked lightly, holding his glass against the light. "Not only our country but throughout the world, and right through history? Loss of face. We create an image of ourselves, and someone destroys the image. We are made to look ridiculous. You talked just now about humiliation, which is the same thing. The man, or the nation, who loses face either never recovers and so disintegrates, or learns humility, which is a very different thing from humiliation. Time will show how the Rizzios develop, and Elia, with the rest of the fry that make up this miniature Ruffano world."

I thought of someone who must have been losing face for the past three hours, and that was my companion of the evening, Carla Raspa. Perhaps she was too thick-skinned to admit it. Failure to come up to scratch would be blamed on me, not her. I did not care. She was welcome to whatever inference she chose to put upon my lack of gallantry.

"By the way," I said, "you had a telephone call from Rome at about ten-thirty."

"Oh?" said Aldo.

"Signora Butali, and she sounded anxious. The Rector insists on coming home, in connection, so I gathered, with Sunday night's incident."

"When?" asked Aldo.

"She didn't say. To tell you the truth, I hung up when she was still talking. She thought I was you, and I left it at that."

"Which was stupid of you," said Aldo. "I thought you had more intelligence."

"I'm sorry."

The information had disturbed him. I saw him eye the telephone. I took the hint and rose.

"Anyway," I said, "when Professor Butali hears about tonight . . ."

"He won't," interrupted Aldo. "What do you suppose Rizzio and Elia and I were discussing until midnight?"

"He may not hear officially," I said, "but don't tell me someone won't pass the word."

My brother shrugged. "That's a risk we have to take," he said.

I moved towards the door. I had achieved precisely nothing by coming to the via dei Sogni and waiting for Aldo, except confirmation of the suspicion nagging me. And to let him know I knew.

"If the Rector does come back," I asked, "what will he do?"

"He won't do anything," said Aldo, "there isn't time."

"Time?"

Aldo smiled. "Rectors are also vulnerable," he said, "they can lose face like other mortals. Beo . . ."

"Yes?"

He picked up a newspaper that was lying on the chair by the door. "Did you see this?"

He showed me the passage I had read at breakfast. The events of the day had put it completely from my mind.

"They've caught the murderer," I said. "Thank God for that."

"They've caught the thief," he interposed, "which apparently isn't the same thing. I had a call from the commissioner of police this morning. The fellow who took the ten thousand lire sticks to his story. He insists that Marta was already dead when he took the note from her, and the police have a hunch he's telling the truth."

"Already dead?" I exclaimed. "But then . . ."

"They're still looking for the murderer," he said, "which, for anyone hanging about the via Sicilia between midnight and the small hours last Tuesday night, might be unhealthy, or at least inconvenient." He put his hand on my head and rumpled my hair. "Don't worry, my Beato," he said, "they won't catch you. And if they did they'd soon acquit you. Innocence shines from your eyes."

What he had just told me knocked my composure sideways. The whole sick horror of the murder was with me still. I had thought it buried.

"What shall I do?" I asked desperately. "Shall I go to the police?"

"No," he said, "forget the whole thing. Come to my meeting tomorrow night and become one of the élite. Here's your pass." He felt in his pocket and brought out a small disk, bearing upon its face a falcon's head. "The boys will let you in with this," he said. "Entrance to the throne room at nine o'clock. And come alone. I don't propose entertaining Signorina Raspa or your playmates from 24, via San Michele. Sleep well."

He pushed me from the door and out into the street. It was after one, and everywhere was dark and still. I met no one between Aldo's house and the via San Michele. No. 24 was as quiet as the other shuttered houses. The door was unlocked and I went to my room without disturbing anyone, but judging from the sound of voices from Paolo Pasquale's room the whole company of students had gathered there, and were engaged in furious discussion. Tomorrow I might hear if they had been near the piazza del Duca Carlo.

I awoke about five a.m., not with any dream or nightmare, not with the vivid picture of the Head of the Department of Commerce and Economics seated in ignominious nudity beneath the marble pedestal bearing the bronze statue of Duke Carlo, but with the sudden recollection of where it was that I had read the name Luigi Speca—the problem which had puzzled me in the library during the afternoon. Luigi Speca had signed his name alongside my father's at Aldo's baptism. I had seen it written in the book of records kept at the sacristy of San Cipriano.

CHAPTER FIFTEEN

At eight o'clock there was a knock on my door, and before I could answer Paolo burst in, closely followed by Caterina.

"I'm sorry," he said, seeing I was in the midst of shaving, "but we want to know if you're coming with us. The whole of C and E are cutting lectures, and we're going to demonstrate outside the house of Professor Elia."

"What about?" I asked.

"You know. We saw you," broke in Caterina. "You were in a car, with the Raspa woman. We saw you leave the hotel and drive up to the piazza del Duca Carlo. You were in the thick of it."

"That's right," chimed in Gino, whose head appeared over Caterina's, "and later we saw the same car parked by the municipal gardens. You must have seen what happened. You were much nearer than any of us."

I laid down my razor and reached for a towel. "I saw nothing," I said, "except a crowd of professors around the statue. There was a lot of movement and excited talk, and then they carried someone, or something, away. Perhaps it was a bomb."

"A bomb!" everyone shouted.

"That's the best yet," said Caterina, "and do you know, he could be right. They could have tied Elia to a bomb timed to explode within a certain number of minutes."

"Well, what happened to it?"

"What sort of bomb?"

"The point is, was he wounded or cut about? No one will tell us."

The passionate discussion that must have been going on half the night promised resumption once again, and in my bedroom.

"Look here," I said, "clear out, the lot of you. Go and demonstrate if you want to. I'm not a student. I'm an employee."

"A spy?" suggested Gino. "You haven't been here a week, and look what's happened!"

The laughter from the rest was not spontaneous. It held an element of doubt. Caterina turned impatiently, pushing the others from the room.

"Ah, leave him alone," she said. "What's the use? He doesn't care." Then, to give me a final chance, she said to me over her shoulder, "The idea is to demonstrate in a body outside Professor Elia's house and get him to appear. If we're satisfied he's all right, and unhurt, that's good enough, we'll turn up for the morning sessions."

A few minutes later I heard them leave the house. The inevitable splutter of vespas followed, belonging, I thought, to Gino and Gerardo. I stood by the window and watched them disappear down the street. Then I looked across at the first floor of No. 5. The shutters were thrown back, the windows open. Carla Raspa had begun her day.

Signor Silvani was finishing breakfast when I descended for coffee, and he immediately asked me if I knew anything of the events of the night before. I told him I had been near the piazza del Duca Carlo and had seen the crowd.

"We only know what our young people here told us," he said, "but I don't like the sound of it. We've had ragging before, you get it in every university, but this sounds vicious. Is it true they tarred and feathered Professor Elia?"

"I don't know," I said. "I didn't see."

"I shall hear the truth at the prefettura," he said. "If anything serious was done last night, it will mean drafting extra police into Ruffano for the next few days. It's chaotic enough anyway on Festival day, without adding demonstrations to all our problems."

I looked about for a morning paper, but saw none. Perhaps it was in the kitchen, or had not arrived. I finished my coffee and walked up to the piazza della Vita to buy one. Unrest stirred in the air. The piazza was crowded with morning shoppers, and with the inevitable group of workless individuals who, idle not from choice but from necessity, came to the city centre to stand and stare. Students were everywhere, arguing, loquacious, most of them streaming out of the piazza up the northern hill to the piazza del Duca Carlo. Rumour, floating from one hill to the other, and then converging from all corners to the piazza della Vita, emerged in the small space like smoke from a steaming cauldron.

There was a Communist plot to blow up the university. . . . There was a Fascist plot to take over the municipality. . . . Guests at the dinner-party at the Hotel Panorama had been poisoned. . . .

The private residences of the Heads of Departments had been burgled. . . . A maniac from Rome, having murdered one of Ruffano's inhabitants, poor Marta Zampini, in the capital, was now loose in Ruffano itself, and had made an attempt on the life of Professor Elia. . . .

I bought a paper. There was nothing in it about last night's event, and only a brief statement about the murder. The police still held the thief in Rome pending further enquiries elsewhere. Elsewhere. Did this mean Ruffano?

There was a sudden movement in the crowd from the direction of the via dei Martiri. People fell back on either side to allow the passage of a priest and acolyte, and behind them four men bearing a coffin covered with a pall. In the rear came the mourners, a man with cross-eyes and a woman, heavily veiled, upon his arm. They made their way across the piazza to the church of San Cipriano. The gaping crowd closed in upon them. I followed, as in a dream, and stood within the precincts of the church in the midst of staring townsfolk, who participated out of curiosity. I listened for the opening words: "Requiem aeternam dona eis Domine: et lux perpetua luceat eis." Then I turned, and left the church.

As I pushed through the door I saw a man standing near the table where they sold candles. He was watching the crowd, and his eyes fell upon me. I thought I recognised him, and, from the momentary question in his eye, that he knew me too. It was one of the police agents who had been in the room taking notes when the English tourists made their statement at the police station in Rome. Today he wore plain clothes.

I ran down the steps and plunged into the piazza della Vita. Then darted along the via del Teatro and climbed the long ascending slope under the walls of the ducal palace. Instinct had made me run. Instinct had told me to take this devious way. If the agent had recognised me as the courier in Rome who had volunteered the statement about the murdered woman, he would remember that this same courier had been en route for Naples with his touring party, and he would ask himself, what was the courier doing in Ruffano? A word on the telephone to Sunshine Tours, a quick check-up with either the Rome or the Genoa office, would tell the agent that Armino Fabbio had asked to be released from the Naples tour and had gone north with a Herr Turtmann and his wife. Little doubt that further news would be elicited that

173

the courier had deserted Herr Turtmann in Ruffano, and nothing had been heard of him since.

I looked about me. The agent could not have followed me. Or, if he had, I had thrown him off. Strollers, shoppers, students, were walking past the piazza Maggiore on their lawful business. I went into the Duomo by the side-entrance, crossed the chancel and emerged at the further side, immediately opposite the ducal palace. In a moment I was inside the walls, and crossing the quadrangle to the library. It was only then, as I paused a moment to recover my breath, that I realised I had acted in foolish panic. It might not have been the police agent. If it had, there was no reason to suppose he had recognised me. My action, in fact, had been a classic example of the behaviour of a guilty man. I stood mopping my forehead, and at that moment the library doors opened and Toni and the other assistant staggered forth, bearing a crate of books.

"Hullo! Who's been chasing you?" asked Toni.

The question was apt. Stung by his enquiry, I thrust my handkerchief into my pocket.

"No one," I said. "I got held up in the town."

"What's happening, then? Have they gone on strike? Are they demonstrating?" they asked simultaneously.

I was so preoccupied with my own endeavours in eluding the possible police agent that I was slow to seize their meaning.

"On strike? Who?" I said.

Toni raised despairing eyes to heaven. "Do you live in this world?" he enquired. "Don't you know that all Ruffano is in a ferment because of what happened last night in the piazza del Duca Carlo?"

"They say the Communists got hold of Professor Elia," said his companion, "and tried to bash his head in. Fossi's given orders to shift everything we can from here to the new building in case an attempt is made to set fire to the ducal palace."

They staggered off along the quadrangle with the crate. I went into the library to find chaos. Books were piled high upon the floor, and Giuseppe Fossi, with Signorina Catti at his side, was lumping volume after volume pell-mell into another groaning crate. He raised his perspiring face at sight of me and burst into a torrent of reproaches. Then, sending the secretary off to the other end of the library with a pile of books, he whispered in my ear, "You have heard what they did to Professor Elia?"

"No," I replied.

"Emasculated!" he hissed. "I had it first-hand from one of the guests at last night's dinner. They say the doctors were with him throughout the night to save his life. There may be other victims."

"Signor Fossi," I began, "I'm sure nothing of the sort . . ."

He frowned me to silence, jerking his head towards the secretary. "They'll stop at nothing, nothing," he said. "Anyone in a position of authority may be threatened."

I murmured something about police protection.

"Police?" he almost screamed. "Useless! They'll be looking after the senior members of the staff. The backbone of the university, the men who do all the work, will have to fend for themselves."

Attempts to calm him were wasted. Green with fatigue after his sleepless night, he sat on one of the empty crates and watched me pack the books into another. I wondered which of us was the greater coward—he, who had turned to jelly through false rumour, or myself, because of the encounter in San Cipriano.

We did not break for lunch. Toni brought us sandwiches and coffee from the university canteen. The news was reassuring. The C and E students had called off the strike and attended the late morning sessions. Professor Elia had admitted a deputation to his house and received them in his dressing-gown. He had assured them that all was well. He had not been hurt. He refused to make any other comment, but implored the students, for his sake, to attend their lectures as usual. They must not think of taking revenge upon other students in the university.

"The lads agreed," murmured Toni in my ear, "just to keep him quiet. But it's not blown over. They're seething, every one of them."

Giuseppe Fossi left during the afternoon to attend a meeting of the university Council called for three o'clock, and I went up with Toni to the new building to help supervise the unpacking of the crates at that end.

It was as well for Giuseppe Fossi's reputation that I did so. The books had been stowed into the boxes with a total disregard for order, which meant double work not only for ourselves but for the clerks in the new library. I put Toni in charge of the van (in action again with a new windscreen), and stayed myself in the new library directing operations. One of the clerks, more thorough than the rest, soon had every volume dusted, sorted, and put in its allotted place in the bookshelves, while I busied myself with the catalogue.

The blowing and shaking of the dust by the energetic clerk brought various items to light which, after consultation with me, he disposed of in the waste-paper bin. Faded flowers, loose name-plates, forgotten letters, bills. It was almost time to knock off, and still no sign of Giuseppe Fossi, when the clerk brought me another letter to dispose of.

"Found this in a book of poems," he said, "but as it's signed by the Director of Arts, Professor Donati, perhaps it shouldn't be thrown away?"

He handed me the letter. I glanced at the signature. Aldo Donati. It was not my brother's handwriting, but my father's.

"All right," I said, "I'll take care of it."

As the clerk went back to his sorting I called, "Where did you say you found the letter?"

"In a collected edition of Leopardi," he replied, "belonging to someone called Luigi Speca. Or that at least was the name on the book-plate."

The letter was brief. The heading at the top of the page said 8, via dei Sogni, Ruffano. The date, November 30th, 1925. The faded black ink, the grey writing-paper, and my father's hand-writing moved me strangely. The letter must have lain between the pages of Leopardi's poems for nearly forty years.

"Dear Speca,

"All is well. We are remarkably proud of our young fellow. He is putting on weight fast and has a terrific appetite. He also promises to be extremely handsome! My wife and I can never thank you enough for your great kindness, sympathy and friendship in our moment of trouble, now happily behind us. We both of us look to the future with confidence. Please drop in on us and see the boy when you can spare the time.

"Your sincere friend,
"Aldo Donati.

"PS.—Marta proves to be not only a devoted nurse but an excellent cook. She sends her respects."

I read the letter three times, then put it in my pocket. The handwriting might be faded, but the message was as fresh as if it had been written yesterday. I could hear my father's voice, strong and clear, full of pride in his young son, now apparently restored to health after a dangerous illness. The baptismal entry was now plain. Luigi Speca must have been the doctor who attended him, a predecessor of our Doctor Mauri. Even the postscript about Marta was somehow poignant. She had entered our parents' service at this time and remained faithful to the end. The end . . . I had seen this morning in the church of San Cipriano. Requiem aeternam dona eis Domine.

The doors of the new library opened and Giuseppe Fossi entered, followed by Toni looking sullen. My superior had lost his haunted look, he was assured once more, and rubbing his hands briskly.

"All in order? Everything sorted?" he demanded. "What are those crates doing there? Ah, I see, all empty. Good." He cleared his throat, drew himself up, and bustled to the desk I had just quitted. "There will be no further trouble tonight," he announced. "The university Council has ordered a nine o'clock curfew for all the students. Any of them seen on the streets after that time will be reported and automatically expelled. This applies equally to employees on the university staff who may live in lodgings. Instead of expulsion they will lose their jobs." He looked pointedly at Toni, the other assistants and myself. "Special passes for those engaged on essential business can be obtained from the Registrar on application," he added, "and it will be easy enough for the authorities to check up, should they be abused. In any event, it will hurt nobody to spend an evening within doors. Naturally, the regulations will be relaxed tomorrow, the eve of the Festival."

I understood the reason for Toni's despondency. No encounter with his girl-friend in the piazza della Vita, or a trip round the via delle Mura on the vespa.

"What about the cinema?" asked Toni sullenly.

"The cinema by all means," answered Giuseppe Fossi, "provided you are back home by nine o'clock."

Toni shrugged, and muttering under his breath lifted one of the empty crates to bear it back to the van. Should I say anything to my superior about Aldo's invitation to the meeting at the ducal palace? I waited for the other assistants to move out of earshot, and then approached him.

"Professor Donati was good enough to give me a pass this evening for the ducal palace," I said. "There is to be a meeting to discuss the Festival."

He looked surprised. "Then that is the responsibility of Professor Donati," he replied. "As Director of the Arts Council of Ruffano he will be well aware of tonight's regulations. If he chooses to issue invitations to comparative strangers to the community it is his own affair."

He turned his back on me, obviously grudging the supposed honour done to me. I felt for the disk my brother had given me. It was safe in my pocket, alongside the forty-year-old letter from my father to Luigi Speca. I looked forward to showing this to Aldo. Meanwhile, I supposed that I too must obtain the late pass from the Registrar if I wanted to go to the ducal palace. It would not matter to my brother if I turned up or not, but my own curiosity was strong.

We closed down at the new building at seven o'clock and I walked across to the Registrar's office, which was already besieged by students applying for late passes. Most of them, accompanied by anxious relatives, had made plans for dinner which were now threatened with cancellation. The pre-celebration of the Festival would go by the board if the passes were not forthcoming, and the relatives would be left to languish in their lodgings and hotels. "It is completely childish," was the comment of one angry father. "My son is in his fourth year, and the authorities take it into their heads to treat him as an infant."

The patient clerk repeated for the second time that these were the orders of the university Council. The students had brought it upon themselves by disorderly behaviour.

The disgusted parent snorted in contempt. "Disorderly behaviour?" he said. "A little healthy fun! Haven't we all done the same in our time?"

He looked about him for approval, finding it. The parents and relatives queuing for passes were unanimous in blaming the authorities for being some twenty-five years behind the times.

"Take your son to dinner, signore," said the harassed clerk, "but have him back at the students' hostel by nine o'clock. Or in his lodgings, if he is quartered in the town. You will have all the opportunity you require for celebrations tomorrow and the day after."

One by one they turned away rejected, followed by their disgruntled and protesting young. I put my head in at the window of the Registrar with small hope of success.

"The name is Fabbio," I said, "Armino Fabbio. I'm an

assistant at the library, and have an invitation from Professor Donati for a meeting at the ducal palace this evening at nine o'clock."

To my surprise, instead of instantly rejecting me the clerk consulted a list at his side.

"Armino Fabbio," he said. "That's quite in order. We have your name on the list." He handed me a slip of paper. "Signed by the Director of the Arts Council himself." The clerk even had the courtesy to smile.

I took the slip and edged out of the queue before the parent behind me had time to protest. Next problem, where to eat? I had no intention of pushing my way into the already crowded restaurants in the town—what few there were—or of joining the Silvani dining-table. I decided to try my luck at the university canteen. Here there was standing-room only, but I did not mind. A bowl of soup and a plate of salami, a pleasant contrast to the octopus of the night before, soon took the edge off appetite. The mass of students were so busy eating and declaiming at the same time against the detested curfew that I passed unnoticed, or at any rate was taken for granted as a lesser member of the university staff.

The general intention, so I gathered, both ears alert, was to make up for this evening's treatment by painting the town red on the Thursday and the Friday nights. All hell would be let loose.

"They can't stop us!"

"We can't all be expelled."

"I've got my degree anyway, so shit to the lot of them."

One of the big-mouthed students was standing at the far end of the counter with his back to me. This was lucky, because it was the fellow who had wanted to douse me in the fountain on the Monday afternoon.

"I'm just not standing for it," he said. "My father can pull strings, and if there's any trouble he'll get some of these professors on the university Council sacked. I'm twenty-one, and they can't treat me like a child of ten. I shall ignore the curfew and stay on the streets until midnight if I feel like it. Anyway, the curfew isn't intended for the C and E students. It's for all these little teachers who study Latin and Greek and go bye-byes at the students' hostel."

He looked about him, hoping for trouble. I had caught his

179

eye on Monday and had no desire to catch it again. I slipped out of the canteen and made my way downhill to the ducal palace. The piazza Maggiore already wore an air of festival. Although it was barely dusk the palace was floodlit, and the Duomo too. The rose walls of the first had an incandescent quality, and the great windows of the eastern façade, luminous and marble white, came suddenly alive. The palace was no longer a museum, a gallery hung with tapestries and pictures round which the tourist would prowl his indifferent way, but a living entity. Thus the link-boys saw it five hundred years ago, under moonlight and with flares and torches. Horses' hooves rang on the cobbled stones, mingling with the clink of spurs. Harnesses jingled as saddles and trappings were removed, grooms and servants scattered, and through the great carved portico walked or rode the returning scion of the Malebranche, his gloved left hand upon his sword.

Tonight the students, with some twenty minutes or so still to spare before curfew, strolled up and down, arm-in-arm with visiting relatives. A group by the fountain began to whistle and call at two girls who pattered by, feigning the inevitable disdain. Somewhere a vespa spluttered, somewhere there was a shout of raucous laughter. I went to the side-entrance and pressed the bell, feeling like a wanderer between two worlds. Behind me lay the present, slick, proficient, uniform, the young the same the globe over, mass-produced like eggs; and before me stood the past, that sinister and unknown world of poison and rapine, of power and beauty, luxury and filth, when a painting could be carried through the streets and worshipped by the rich and by the rabble alike; when God was feared; when men and women sickened of the plague and died like dogs.

The door was opened, not by the night-guardian, but by a boy dressed as a page. He asked for my pass. I handed him the disk Aldo had given me and he took it, saying nothing, and lifting the flare from the stand beside him preceded me across the quadrangle. There were no lights. I had not thought how dark the palace would be without electricity. I had seen the torch-lit apartments above on Saturday, but here below, and on the stairs, the normal lighting had been switched on. Not so tonight. As we mounted the great stairs the torchlight turned our shadows into giants. The page who climbed before me, in his belted doublet and hose, did not seem to be in fancy-dress. I was the interloper. The gallery surrounding the quadrangle was black as pitch. One single flare, stuck in a bracket, cast a baleful stream of light upon the door of the throne room. The page knocked twice upon it. We were admitted.

The throne room was empty, lighted in similar fashion to the gallery outside, with two flares set in brackets, and we went across it to the Room of the Cherubs at the further end, where the session had been held on Saturday. This too was empty, and lit by torches. The doors leading to the Duke's bedroom, and to the audience room, were shut. The page knocked twice upon the door of the first. It was opened by a young man whose face I recognised as one of those guitarists who had made so merry upon the stage at the theatre on Monday. I recognised nothing else. He wore a jerkin of bottle green, the sleeves slashed with purple, and his hose were black. On his heart he wore the emblem of a falcon's head.

"Is it Armino Donati?" he asked.

My second name, unused for at least seventeen years, surprised me.

"Yes," I said cautiously, "sometimes known as Armino Fabbio."

"Here we prefer Donati," he replied.

He jerked his head for me to enter. I did so and the door was closed, the attendant page remaining in the Room of the Cherubs. I looked about me. The Duke's bedroom was half the size of the preceding room, and it was lighted, like the others, by flares in brackets, these flares placed on either side of the one great portrait on the wall to throw it into relief so that it dominated the room. It was the portrait of the "Temptation of Christ", Christ bearing the likeness to Duke Claudio.

There were twelve men in the room, including the guitarist who had admitted me. They were all dressed as courtiers of the early sixteenth century, and wore the insignia of the Falcon. The scrutineers who had examined our passes on the Saturday were amongst them, and the two duellists, and others I had seen on the stage on Monday evening. I felt, and no doubt looked, an idiot in my modern garb, and to give myself assurance strolled over to the picture to examine it. No one took any notice of me. All were aware of my presence, but they chose, perhaps from delicacy, to ignore it.

The Christ Duke Claudio, lit by flares, stared out with greater power from his frame than he did by day. The crudity of the modelling did not show, and the rather awkward stance, the hand upon the girdle, the inelegant feet, were now subdued. The eyes, deep-lidded, distant, stared into a troubled future that might have seemed imminent to the painter's mind, threatening his world, or else quiescent, not to erupt till centuries later. The tempter, Satan, was the same Christ in profile, suggesting, not a lack of models, but a rash attempt at truth. The portrait might have lost its power to terrify, but not to cause unease. I wondered that it had survived five centuries, to confound the vandals and to mock the Church. Today the tourist, with his eye upon his watch, the message missed, would pass it by unquestioning.

I felt a hand upon my shoulder. My brother stood behind me. He must have entered the room from the small dressing-room and chapel beyond.

"What do you make of it?" he asked.

"You knew once," I said. "I used to act him, as I acted Lazarus. But never willingly."

"You might do so again," he said.

He swung me round, showing me to his twelve companions. Like them, he was wearing the same period dress, but for the colour. Like the tempter, he was all in black.

"Here is our Falcon," he said. "He can play Duke Claudio at our Festival."

The twelve men looked at me and smiled. One of them seized a saffron-coloured robe that was lying on a stool near the chapel entrance and belted it around me. Another picked up a golden-curled wig and clapped it on my head. A third brought me a mirror. Time was no longer with me. Neither this time, nor the time of centuries past. I had gone back to childhood, to my bedroom in the via dei Sogni, and stood still to obey my brother's commands. The men who surrounded me were his companions of the liceo long ago. As then, protesting that I did not want to play, I stammered now, in what I hoped were adult words, "Aldo, I'd rather not. I came here to watch the rest of you. Not to take part."

"One and the same thing," said Aldo. "We are all equally involved. I'm offering you a choice. The part of the Falcon, one short hour of glory and adventure in your life which will never come again; or to be turned loose tonight in the streets of Ruffano without a pass, when you will be picked up and, your identity established, given a grilling by the local police, who, so I was told earlier today, have been continually in touch with the police in Rome."

None of the young faces crowded round me was hostile. They were friendly; they were also ruthless. They stood there, waiting for my answer.

"Here you are safe," said Aldo, "whether with me or with them. All these twelve lads have sworn to defend you whatever happens. If you go out of the palace alone who knows what may happen to you?"

Somewhere, either in the city centre, or parading in plain clothes up and down the via Rossini, or watching by the porta del Sangue or the porta Malebranche, could be my police agent from Rome, waiting to question me. Useless to tell myself that they could not prove me guilty. The question was—should I be able to establish my innocence? Both Aldo's alternatives appalled me, but the second frightened me the more. The voice that came from me was not my adult voice, but sounded to my ears like the ghostly echo of a child of seven, who, wearing the blanket robes of Lazarus, was thrust into his living tomb.

"What do you want me to do?" I asked my brother.

CHAPTER SIXTEEN

We went through to the audience room. It was here that the tapestry on the western wall concealed the door leading to the second of the twin towers, where the guardian had ejected me on my first visit nearly a week ago. Tonight there was no guardian, only Aldo and his bodyguard, and the tapestry hung as usual, with no suggestion that behind it lay the hidden door and the narrow twisting stairway beyond.

The audience room was lit by flares also, and to the left, upon its easel, stood the portrait of the gentlewoman which my father so much loved, and which put me in mind of Signora Butali. Someone had placed a long wooden table in the centre of the room, and upon it glasses and a carafe of wine. Aldo went forward and poured wine into a glass for each of us.

"You don't have to do anything," he said, answering at last the question which I had put to him in the other room, "except do as I tell you, when the time comes. Acting won't be required of you. As a courier you will play your part to perfection, because it will come naturally." He laughed, and raising his glass said, "Drink to my brother!"

One and all lifted their glasses, crying "Armino!", their faces turned to me. Then Aldo introduced them one by one, walking the whole length of the table, tapping each one upon the shoulder as he called his name.

"Giorgio, born near Monte Cassino, parents killed in the bombardment, brought up by relatives . . . Domenico, born in Naples, parents died of tuberculosis, brought up ditto . . . Romano, found abandoned in the hills after the German retreat, brought up by partisans . . . Antonio, ditto . . . Roberto, ditto . . . Guido, Sicilian, father killed by the Mafia, ran away from home, brought up by Sisters of the Poor . . . Pietro, parents drowned in floods in the Po valley, brought up by neighbours . . . Sergio, born in a concentration camp, mother living . . . Federico, ditto, but no surviving parents, brought up by an uncle . . . Giovanni, born in Rome, abandoned in a church, brought up by foster-parents . . . Lorenzo, born in Milan, father died, mother married again and stepfather a pervert, ran away from home, worked in a factory to save enough to enter university . . . Cesare, born in Pesaro, father drowned at sea, mother died giving birth to him, brought up in an orphanage."

Aldo came to the far end of the table and put his hand upon my shoulder. "Armino, known in the family circle as Beo, or Il Beato, because of his curls and his cherubic disposition. Born in Ruffano, father died in an Allied prison-camp, mother fled to Germany with retreating German officer, taking the boy with her, later married in Turin. And now you all know each other —or shall I say recognise one another?—for what you are. The lost and the abandoned. The despised and the rejected. Kicked along in the world to date by relatives and others who did what they had to but little else besides. I drink to you." He raised his glass and nodding to the twelve, and finally to me, drank his toast. "And now to business," he said, setting down his glass.

The lad nearest to him, Giorgio, brought forward a map, which Aldo spread upon the table in front of him. It was a large-scale map of the city of Ruffano. I drew near, with the others. The introductions, totally unexpected and fantastic, had the effect, temporary, perhaps, of making me lose my identity. I was not Armino, a lone courier without aim or mission, hunted possibly by the police, but another Giorgio, another Lorenzo.

"The course will run, as you know, from the piazza del Duca Carlo to the piazza Maggiore," Aldo said. "In other words, from the northern hill down to the city centre at the piazza della Vita, and uphill by the via Rossini to the ducal palace. The course will be clear until the piazza della Vita, and then the fun will begin. The citizens, represented by the C and E students, will converge upon the piazza from all five roads, with the exception of the via Rossini, which will be held by the Court, in other words by the Arts and Education students. The fighting will start immediately the cortège of the Falcon has passed the piazza della Vita and has begun to ascend the hill. You, and the courtiers on guard here at the palace, will keep the citizens back until the Falcon has passed safely through your ranks and has crossed the quadrangle and ascended the stairs to the ducal apartments. Is that clear?"

"Perfectly," agreed Giorgio, who seemed to be spokesman for the rest.

"Good," said Aldo. "Then all we have to do is to assign a given spot on the via Rossini to every courtier, which you can arrange with the volunteers, and hand over the plan of the side-streets to the C and E leaders. We shall be outnumbered by about three to one, but that's the glory of it."

He folded up the map. I hesitated before speaking. The query was so obvious as to seem absurd.

"What about the general public? Who will clear the streets?" I asked.

"The police," said Aldo. "They do it every year. But this year their instructions will be more explicit. No one but performers allowed in the area after a stated time."

"And where will the public watch from?" I persisted.

"From every available window," answered Aldo, smiling, "beginning with the piazza del Duca Carlo and so down to the piazza della Vita, and up the via Rossini to the palace."

I bit my thumbnail, a childhood habit long discarded. Aldo reached forward, and my hand fell instinctively to my side.

"Last year," I said, "or so I was told, the university staff took part and a large audience watched from inside the palace."

"This year," replied Aldo, "only a few privileged people will have seats in the palace. Most of the university staff will be in the piazza del Mercato."

"But that's below the palace," I protested. "How can they see anything from there?"

"They'll hear plenty," replied Aldo, "and be on hand for the final act, which will be the most outstanding."

Someone knocked on the door leading from the audience room to the gallery outside.

"See what it is," said Aldo.

One of the students—Sergio, I think it was—went to the door and talked briefly with the page who had admitted me inside the palace. After a moment he returned.

"The sentries have brought in a fellow prowling round under the western portico," he said. "He had no late pass, and when questioned was abusive. They want to know whether to let him go."

"City man or student?" Aldo asked.

"Student. C and E. A big lout, wanted a scrap."

"If he wants a scrap he shall have it," said my brother. He told Sergio to have the intruder brought in.

"It could be my bully," I said, "a fellow who wanted to

douse me in the fountain after the uproar on Monday. I saw him in the canteen tonight, and he was boasting he hadn't got a pass and didn't care."

Aldo laughed. "So much the better," he said. "He might entertain us. Masks, everyone. And one for Armino."

Giorgio came over to where I stood and gave me a small black mask with slits for eyes, similar to those worn by the two duellists on Saturday. Self-consciously I put it on, as did Aldo and the twelve. When we were all masked and I looked around me and saw how we were lighted only by the flares, the rest of the room in shadow, I realised that to an outsider the effect would be far from reassuring, even startling.

The sentries, masked as we were, entered, bearing the prisoner between them. They had bandaged his eyes, but I recognised instantly the bully from the canteen. Aldo glanced towards me and I nodded.

"Loose him," said my brother.

The sentries threw off the bandage. The student blinked and looked about him, rubbing his arms. All he could see was a dark room lit by torches, and fourteen men disguised and wearing masks.

"No late pass?" enquired Aldo gently.

The bully stared. It was possible, I thought, that he had never entered the ducal palace in his life. If so, the surroundings would seem forbidding.

"What's it to do with you?" he countered. "If this is one of the Arts rags I'd better warn you you'll be sorry for it."

"No rag," said Aldo. "I have authority here."

Nobody moved. The student shifted on his feet. He rearranged his collar and tie, which had become dishevelled during his struggle to avoid arrest.

"What authority?" he asked aggressively. "Do you think by putting on fancy dress you can frighten me? My name is Marelli, Stefano Marelli, and my father owns a chain of restaurants and hotels along the coast."

"We are not interested in your father," said Aldo. "Tell us about yourself."

The question, smoothly asked, deceived the bully into greater confidence. He looked at the rest of us with condescension. "Commerce and Economics, third year," he said, "and it couldn't matter to me less if I'm expelled. I don't need a degree to get a job—I shall take over one of my father's restaurants. He also happens to be a member of the syndicate owning the Panorama, and anyone who sacks me on a flimsy excuse will find himself unpopular with a fair number of influential people."

"Unfortunate," murmured Aldo. He turned to Giorgio. "Is he on the list of volunteers?" he asked.

Giorgio, who had been consulting a list while the questioning took place, shook his head.

The student Marelli laughed. "If you mean the Communist do at the theatre on Monday night, I was not there," he said. "I had something better to do. I have a girl in Rimini, and a fast car. Draw your own conclusions."

Despite my strong dislike of everything about him, from his personal appearance to his attempt to douse me in the fountain, I felt some stirring of compassion. Every word he uttered made his fate more certain.

"In that case, you won't be taking part in the Festival?" asked Aldo.

"The Festival?" echoed the student. "That charade? Not likely! I shall slip home for the weekend. My father's throwing a big party for me."

"A pity," said Aldo. "We could have given you some excitement here. However, there's no reason why you shouldn't have a foretaste of it tonight. Federico?"

One of the bodyguard approached. In their masks they all looked alike, but the lithe build of this one, and the light hair above his mask, suggested to me that he was one of Saturday's duellists.

"Have we anything in the book that would suit Stefano?" asked Aldo.

Federico looked at me. "We had better consult Armino," he replied. "He's the expert."

"Federico's my translator," explained Aldo. "He marked the various passages for us from the German history. Born in a concentration camp, he has a facility for languages."

The unease that had come upon me since the arrival of the captured student grew stronger. I shook my head. "I remember nothing," I said.

Aldo turned once more to Federico, who, drawing a sheaf of papers from his doublet, consulted them. He read them through in silence while we waited.

"The page," he said at last, "the incident of the page would suit Stefano well."

"Ah, yes, the page," murmured Aldo, "the punishment for the page who forgot the lights. To heap coals of fire upon the head of one who would douse in a fountain those smaller than himself would be a fitting climax to a braggart's career. See to it, will you?"

The student, Marelli, drew back at the approach of the two sentries and of Federico. "Now, look here," he said, "if you try any trick on me I warn you that . . ."

But he was interrupted. The sentries seized either arm. Federico, stroking his chin, gave the appearance of one plunged into thought.

"The old brazier," he said, "stored with the iron-work in one of the rooms on the upper floor. It would fit him like a crown. First, shall I read to him the passage from the book?" He pulled out the papers once again. They were copies of the notes I had given Aldo on Sunday. "On one occasion," he read, "a page, who had neglected to provide lights for the Duke's evening repast, was seized by the Falcon's bodyguard. They enveloped the wretched lad in sear-cloth coated with combustibles, and after setting fire to his head drove him through the rooms of the ducal palace to die in agony." He replaced the paper inside his doublet and signalled to the sentries. "Let's to it," he said.

The student Marelli, who not two minutes before had boasted wealth and influence, crumpled between his guards. His face went suddenly grey and he began to scream. The screams continued as he was dragged out into the passage, and they echoed along the gallery and up the stairs to the floor above. Nobody spoke.

"Aldo . . ." I said, "Aldo . . ."

My brother looked at me. The screams died down and there was silence.

"Renaissance man had no compassion, why should we?" he asked.

A sudden horror seized me. My mouth went dry. I couldn't swallow. Aldo removed his mask, and so did the others. Their young faces bore a fearful gravity.

"Renaissance man tortured and killed without compunction," continued Aldo, "but usually he had a motive. Someone had done him a wrong, and he acted from revenge. A mistaken motive, possibly, but that is open to argument. In our time men have killed and tortured for their own amusement and for experiment. Those screams you have just heard, caused solely by cowardice and not by pain, were uttered with just cause day after day, month after month, in Auschwitz and in other prison camps. In the prison-camp, for instance, where Federico and Sergio were born. Romano heard them in the hills when the enemy caught and tortured his friends the partisans; so did Antonio and Roberto. If you had been abandoned, Beo, you might have heard them too. But you were lucky. You were preserved by conquerors, and led a sheltered life."

I tore off my mask. I searched each one of their grave, unsmiling faces, listening at the same time for some sound from the upper floor, but there was none.

"It doesn't work out like that," I said. "You can't torture that student above because of what happened in the past."

"He won't be tortured," Aldo said. "The most that Federico will do to him will be to set a fire-cracker on his head and drive him out. Unpleasant, but salutary. Marelli will benefit from the experience and think twice in future about soaking smaller men in fountains." He beckoned Giorgio to his side. "Tell Beo the true story of the assault on Signorina Rizzio," he said.

Giorgio was one of the bodyguard whom I recognised from Saturday. It was he who had been born near Monte Cassino, his parents killed during the bombing. He was a big, broad-shouldered lad with a shock of unruly hair, and when he had been masked just now had looked strangely formidable.

"The break-in was easy," he said, "and the girls we locked in their rooms were disappointed, so we thought, because we did nothing to them. Five of us went to Signorina Rizzio's room and knocked on the door. She opened it in her dressing-gown, thinking one of the girls had knocked. Then she saw us, all masked and doubtless dangerous, and told us quickly that she had no valuables, she kept nothing of any worth in the hostel. I said to her, 'Signorina Rizzio, the most valuable thing in the hostel is yourself. We have come for you.' She might have thought, from my words, that I meant to kidnap her, but her mind jumped to the obvious. She told us instantly that if it was that we were after we must go to the girls. The girls would be willing. We could do whatever we cared to do to them if we left her alone. I repeated my warning. 'Signorina Rizzio,' I said, 'we have come for you.' Then, luckily—at least, for us—she fainted. We carried her to her bed and waited for her to come round. When she did so, about ten minutes later, the five of us were standing at the door. We thanked her for her generosity, and left. That, Armino, is how the rape of Signorina Rizzio was accomplished. The sequel was what she made of it herself."

Giorgio's face had lost its gravity and he was laughing. So were the others. I understood the laughter, I could appreciate the hoax, and yet . . .

"Professor Elia," I asked. "Was that part of the pantomime as well?"

Giorgio looked at Aldo. Aldo nodded.

"Not my sortie," answered Giorgio. "Lorenzo was in charge."

Lorenzo, a Milanese like the Head of the Department of Commerce and Economics, was half the size of the man he had helped to strip. His manner was evasive, diffident, and he had the veiled eyes of an innocent child.

"Some of my friends amongst the C and E students," he murmured, "have suffered from the attentions of the Professor from time to time. Both male and female. Therefore, after consulting with Aldo we worked out our plan of campaign. Entrance to the house was easy—Professor Elia thought at first that students wearing masks were the prelude to an intriguing game before dining at the Panorama. He soon learnt otherwise."

So I was right. My brother had been behind both incidents. I saw that in his view, and in that of these boys, justice had been done. The scales were balanced, according to the strange laws of Duke Claudio the Falcon over five hundred years ago.

"Aldo," I said, "I asked you this last night and you didn't answer me. What is it you are trying to do?"

My brother looked at his eleven companions and back to me. "Ask them," he said, "what they hope to achieve in life. They'll each give you a different answer according to his temperament. They are none of them totalitarians, you know, or ideologists. And they have their personal ambitions."

I looked at Giorgio, who was nearest to me. "Rid the world of hypocrisy," he said, "starting with the old men of Ruffano, and the women too. They came into the world naked like the rest of us."

"Scum settles at the top of a pool," said Domenico. "If you skim it off you find clear water underneath, and all the living things. Clear away the scum."

"Live dangerously," said Romano. "It doesn't matter where or how, but with your friends."

"Find hidden treasure," said Antonio. "It could be at the bottom of a test-tube in the lab. I'm a physics student, so I'm prejudiced."

"I agree with Antonio," said Roberto, "but no test-tubes for me. There's an answer somewhere in the universe when we explore further. And I don't mean heaven."

"Feed the hungry," said Guido. "Not with bread only but with ideas."

"Build something lasting that won't be swept away," said Pietro, "as the men of the Renaissance did, who built this palace."

"Tear down the barriers that exist everywhere," said Sergio, "the fence between one man and another. Leaders, yes, to show the way. But no masters and no slaves. That goes for Federico too—we've often discussed it."

"Teach the young never to grow old," said Giovanni, "even when their bones are cracking."

"Teach the old what it felt like to be young," said Lorenzo, "and by young I mean pint-sized, helpless, and inarticulate."

The answers came swift and sharp from every lad like successive rifle shots. The last, Cesare, was the only one to hesitate. Finally, glancing across at Aldo, he said, "I think what we have to do is to make the men and women of our generation care. It doesn't matter what they care about, whether it's football or painting, people or great causes, but they have to care, and to care passionately, and if necessary forget about their precious skins and die."

Aldo looked at me and shrugged his shoulders. "What did I tell you?" he said. "They've all given different answers. Meanwhile, on the floor above us, Stefano Marelli has only one thought in mind, and that is to save himself."

The screaming had started once again, and with it the sound of rushing feet. Giorgio opened the door. The rushing, blundering footsteps descended the stairs and ran along the gallery, seeking an exit. We passed through the Room of the Cherubs and stood at the entrance to the gallery, peering into the darkness. A figure came towards us, his hands bound behind his back, wearing upon his head a broken bucket, the bottom of it punched with holes. Squibs had been stuck in the holes, and they were spitting and sparking as he ran. Sobbing, he tripped, and fell upon his face at Aldo's feet. The bucket rolled from his head. The squibs, with a final splutter, died. Aldo bent forward, and with a swift flick of a knife I had not seen cut the cord that bound the student's hands. Then he jerked him to his feet.

"There are your coals of fire," he said, kicking the bucket and the extinguished fire-crackers. "Children could play with them."

The student, still sobbing, stared. The bucket rolled along the gallery and settled. The acrid smoke filled the air.

"I have seen men," said Aldo, "run from their flaming aircraft like living torches. Be thankful, Stefano, you were not one of them. Now, get out."

The student turned and blundered along the gallery to the stairs. The shadow of his loping figure cast by the flare-light on the walls loomed shapeless and distorted, like a gigantic bat. The sentries followed, turning him across the quadrangle below, for he had lost all sense of direction, to let him loose through the great door between the towers. We heard the sound of his shuffling, frightened feet no more. The night enveloped him.

"He won't forget," I said, "neither will he forgive. He'll go back and rouse a hundred others like him. He'll magnify the story out of all recognition. Do you really want to set the whole city against you?"

I looked at Aldo. He was the only one amongst us who had not answered my earlier question.

"That," he said, "is inevitable. Whether Stefano tells his friends or not. Don't imagine I'm here to bring peace to this city or to the university. I'm here to bring trouble and discord, to set one man against the other, to bring all the violence and hypocrisy and envy and lust out into the open, on to the surface, like the scum on Domenico's pool. Only then, when it bubbles and seethes and stinks, can we clear it away."

It was then that the conviction took hold upon me, which I had rejected before through loyalty and love, that Aldo was insane. The seed of insanity had laid dormant in him through childhood and adolescence, and now, ripened doubtless through all he had seen and suffered in war and afterwards, the shock of our father's death, the disappearance and supposed death of our mother and myself, it was strangling his intellectual powers like a cancerous growth. The scum rising to the surface was his own madness. The symbol he took as the world's ills was his own disease. And there was nothing I could do, no way in which I could prevent him from setting alight a conflagration on the day of the Festival which might, figuratively speaking, burn the entire city. His band of devoted students, themselves warped by the legacy of their childhood, would stand by him and question nothing. One person only might have influence, Signora Butali, and she, as far as I knew, was still in Rome.

Aldo led the way back into the audience room. He discussed for some little while further plans for the Festival, the route points, timing, and other technical matters. I barely listened. One thing seemed imperative, and that was to get the Festival cancelled. Only the Rector could achieve it, no one else.

Some time around ten-thirty Aldo rose to his feet. The half-hour had just chimed from the campanile. "Now, Beo, if you're ready, I'll drop you back at the via San Michele. So long, my braves. See you to-morrow."

He went through to the Duke's bedroom and thence to the dressing-room. There he threw off his jerkin and hose, and dressed himself once more in his usual clothes. "Off with the masquerade," he said. "You do the same. Here, in the suitcase. Giorgio will see to it."

I had forgotten—for over an hour I had been wearing the golden wig and the saffron robe. He saw my sudden realisation, and laughed.

"It's easy, isn't it," he said, "to go back five hundred years. Sometimes I lose all sense of time. That's half the fun of it." Now, in his own suit, the disguise discarded, he looked as normal as any other man.

We walked through the Room of the Cherubs and the throne room, and so to the gallery. The page was waiting for us, to light us with his flare down the stairs and across the quadrangle to the side entrance. It was the page who now seemed out of place, a mummer dressed for a pageant, and the walls of the ducal palace, the silent quadrangle, held no more menace than a darkened, dead museum. We went out into the paved way and to the flood-lit piazza Maggiore. The Alfa-Romeo was parked outside the centre door, and beside it, as though to watch for loiterers, stood two carabinieri. I hesitated, but Aldo walked straight on. The men recognised him and saluted. One of them opened the door of the car. Only then did I follow Aldo.

"All quiet?" asked my brother.

"All quiet, Professor Donati," said the man who had opened the door. "A handful of students without late passes, but we've dealt with them. The great majority were sensible. They want to enjoy themselves during the next two days."

"They'll do that," laughed Aldo. "Good night, good hunting."

"Good night, professor."

I got in the car beside him and we drove off down the via Rossini. The street was as quiet as it had been the first night of my arrival almost a week ago. But tonight no snow, no freak reminder of past winter. The air was warm, with a soft humidity about it coming from the Adriatic across the chain of hills.

"What did you think of my boys?" asked Aldo.

"They do you credit," I said. "I wish I had had their chance. No one watched over me when I was a student in Turin and groomed me to act bodyguard to a fanatic."

He paused by the entrance to the piazza della Vita. "A fanatic," he repeated. "Is that really what you think of me?"

"Aren't you?" I asked.

The city was truly dead. The cinema had closed. The city stragglers had all gone home.

"I was," he said, "when I first sought out those boys, and picked them for their birth and background. In each one of them I saw you. A child abandoned on some bloody hill, torn by bullets or a bomb. It's different now. One becomes inured, if never reconciled. Besides, my emotion was wasted, as it turned out. You survived." He swerved into the via San Michele and drew up at 24. "Nurtured by Teutons, Yanks and Torinesi," he said, "to flower finally as a courier to Sunshine Tours. Those whom the gods love live long."

Doubt was with me once again. Doubt and dismay. Doubt that anyone who mocked with so much justice could be mad. Dismay that whatever he had done for those orphaned boys was done for me.

"What happens now?" I said.

"Now?" he echoed. "The immediate now or the hereafter? Tonight you fall asleep and dream, if you care to do so, of Signorina Raspa across the way. Tomorrow you can wander at will about Ruffano watching the preparations for the Festival. You dine with me. After that, we shall see."

He pushed me from the car. As I climbed out I suddenly remembered the letter in my pocket. I pulled it out.

"You must read this," I said. "I found it quite by chance this afternoon. Tucked between the pages of a book amongst the volumes we were sorting in the new library. It's all about you."

"About me?" he asked. "What about me?"

"Your prowess as an infant," I said. "Listen, I'll read it to you, and then you shall keep it as a memento of your lively past."

I leant across the open window of the car and read aloud the letter. When I had finished I looked up at him and smiled, throwing the letter on his knee.

"It's touching, isn't it," I said, "how proud they were of you."

He did not answer. He sat motionless, his hands upon the wheel, staring straight ahead, his face expressionless and very pale.

"Good night," he said abruptly, and before I could answer the car shot away down the via San Michele and round the corner out of sight. I stood there, staring after it.

CHAPTER SEVENTEEN

WHY HAD THE letter produced that effect upon Aldo? I could think of nothing else, either as I went to bed or when I awoke the following morning. I could not remember the letter line for line, but it spoke of "our young fellow's" progress and his promise of good looks, and thanked Luigi Speca for his great kindness during a period of trouble which was happily over. As Luigi Speca had also signed the baptismal register in San Cipriano I judged him to be both godfather and the doctor who had attended Aldo's birth—which, from the double entry, must have been difficult, with Aldo nearly losing his life, and perhaps our mother hers. This would be the "time of trouble" referred to in the letter. But why should Aldo mind? The letter had moved me, but not as deeply as all that. I had expected him to laugh, and even make some quip about having passed for dead. Instead, the hard immobile face, the swift departure.

I did not rush the next morning to arrive at the library on time. We should all be kept there until late, for in the afternoon students and their relatives were to be permitted to view the new library premises, due to be officially opened after the short Easter vacation. I breakfasted alone, my fellow-lodgers having already left.

Just as I had finished the telephone rang. Signora Silvani answered it, and came to tell me of it was for me.

"Someone of the name of Jacopo," she said. "He wouldn't give a message. He said you would know who it was."

I went into the hall, my heart pounding. Something had happened to Aldo. Something had happened because of last night's letter. I lifted the receiver.

"Yes?" I said.

"Signor Beo?"

Jacopo's voice was steady, without anxiety. "I have a message for you from the Capitano," he said. "The plans for the evening have been changed. The Rector, Professor Butali, and Signora Butali have returned from Rome."

"I understand," I said.

197

"The Capitano would like to see you here some time this morning," he went on.

"Thank you," I replied, and before he rang off I said to him "Jacopo . . ."

"Signore?"

"Is Aldo all right? Is anything worrying him?"

There was a second's pause. Then Jacopo said, "I think the Capitano did not expect Professor Butali back so soon. They arrived late last night. The luggage was being taken in when he passed the house on his return home just before eleven o'clock."

"Thank you, Jacopo."

I hung up. A letter written some forty years ago was now the least of my brother's problems. The sick man had got his own way with the doctors and had returned, if not to take active charge at least to be on hand for consultation.

I heard Signora Silvani moving in the dining-room, and left the house quickly before she could start a conversation. I must somehow see Signora Butali before Aldo did. I must urge her to use her influence to try to stop the Festival, how and with what excuse God only knew.

It was half-past nine. After the Butalis' long journey yesterday the signora would probably be at home this morning—ten o'clock might be a good moment to call. I turned into the via San Martino and started walking uphill to the via dei Sogni. The sun was already hot, the sky cloudless. The day promised to be one of those I remembered well from childhood, when the distant slopes and valleys shimmered in a blue haze of heat and the city of Ruffano, set proudly on its two hills, dominated the world below.

I came to the gate set in the wall of our old garden, passed through it to the front door of the house and rang the bell. The door was opened by the girl I already knew, and she recognised me too.

"Is it possible to see the signora?" I asked.

The girl looked doubtful, and said something about the signora being engaged—she and Professor Butali had only returned from Rome late last night.

"I know," I said, "but it is urgent."

She disappeared upstairs, and as I stood there waiting I noticed that once more the atmosphere of the house had changed. The dull vacuum of Monday morning was no more. She was home. Not only were her gloves lying on the table, a coat flung loosely on a chair, but an indefinable scent clung to the hall, a reminder of her presence. Only this time she was not alone. The house, instead of containing her only, and by so doing becoming the more mysterious, the more tempting, so that anyone calling like myself on my first mission, and afterwards on the Sunday, was secretly disturbed and furtively attracted—the house now held her husband too. It was his home, and he was master. That stick placed in its stand was like a totem-pole to tell the world. The overcoat, the hat, a suitcase still unpacked, parcels of books— there was a male smell about the house that had not been before.

The girl came running down the stairs and I heard, in her wake, the sound of voices, the sound of closing doors. "The signora will be down in a moment," she said, "if you would please come in here."

She showed me into the room on the left, the study that had been our dining-room. Evidence of the husband's presence was here too. A briefcase on the desk, more books, letters. And a faint but distinctive odour of cigar, smoked last night on arrival, not yet faded in the morning air.

I must have waited there ten minutes or more, biting my knuckles, before I heard her footsteps on the stairs. Then panic seized me. I did not know what I was going to say. She came into the room. At sight of me her face, though ravaged, tired—for she seemed in some way to have aged within four days—but also expectant and alive, fell in disappointment and surprise.

"Beo!" she exclaimed. "I thought Anna said Aldo. . . ." Then, swiftly recovering, she crossed the room and gave me her hand. "You must forgive me," she said, "I don't know what I'm doing. The silly girl said, 'The signore who was here for dinner on Sunday night,' and in my stupidity and rush. . . ." She did not bother to finish her sentence. I understood. In her stupidity and rush the signore who came to dinner on Sunday could signify one man only. And it was not me.

"There's nothing to forgive, signora," I said. "I have to apologise to you. I heard, through Jacopo, that you and your husband were home, that you arrived late last night, and I would not dream of disturbing you so early and on your first morning home if I didn't think the matter was urgent."

"Urgent?" she repeated.

The telephone rang in the music-room above. She exclaimed in annoyance, and was turning to leave the room with a murmured, "Excuse me," when we heard slow footsteps overhead. Then the ringing stopped and a male voice murmured indistinctly.

"Exactly what I didn't want to happen," she said to me. "If my husband once starts answering the telephone, and talking first to this one, then the other. . . ." She broke off, straining her ears to listen, but the murmur was too faint. "It's no use," she said, shrugging. "He's answered it, and there's nothing I can do about it."

I was wretchedly aware of the trouble I was causing. I could not have called at a worse time. There were hollows under her eyes that told of fatigue and strain. They had not been there on the Sunday night. On Sunday night the world about her could have died.

"How is the Rector?" I asked.

She sighed. "As well as he could be, under the circumstances," she said. "What happened earlier in the week was a great shock to him. But you know already. . . ." She flushed, the colour appearing on her naturally pale face like a sudden stain. "I believe it was you I spoke to on Tuesday night," she said. "Aldo told me. He telephoned me later."

"I have to apologise for that as well," I said, "I mean, for hanging up. I did not want to embarrass you."

She moved the letters on the desk, so that her back was turned to me. The gesture was one of withdrawal, a warning that to probe would be unwelcome. My mission became more difficult than ever.

"You were saying," she said, "that you had something urgent to tell me?" Even as she spoke, the voice overhead grew louder. We could distinguish nothing, but prolonged discussion had obviously begun.

"Perhaps I should go up," she said, anxiously. "So much seems to have gone wrong these last few days. Professor Elia. . . ."

"So you've heard?" I asked.

She gestured, her hands outspread, and began to pace quickly up and down the room.

"The first telephone call this morning was to give my husband an exaggerated account of something that happened on Tuesday night," she answered. "Not from Professor Elia himself, or from Professor Rizzio, but from one of the busybodies in whom this place abounds. In any event, the damage has been done. My husband is greatly distressed. Your brother is to come here later to explain things and to soothe him down."

"Signora," I said, "it is about Aldo that I've come to see you."

She stiffened, and her face became a mask. Only the eyes betrayed awareness. "What about him?" she asked.

"The Festival," I began. "I've heard him speak to the students about the Festival. It's become as real to them as it has to him, and therefore dangerous. I think it should be cancelled."

The anxiety behind her eyes vanished. She broke into a smile. "But that is the whole idea," she said. "It is always the same. Your brother makes the story—whatever it is they act—so vivid and so real that everybody taking part feels himself a character out of history. I know we all did last year. And the result was magnificent. Anyone will tell you."

"I wasn't here last year," I said. "All I know is that this year will be different. It won't take place in the ducal palace, for one thing, but in the streets. The students will be fighting in the streets."

She looked at me, still smiling. Her relief that I had not touched upon her relationship with Aldo was manifest.

"We went in procession in the streets last year as well," she told me, "or rather my husband did, as Pope Clement, with his very lifelike entourage. I was with the ladies and gentlemen of the Court, awaiting his arrival in the palace quadrangle. I promise you there will be nothing to fear, the police are used to it, it will be most orderly."

"How can an insurrection be orderly?" I asked. "How can students, told to be armed with any sort of weapon, keep themselves in check?"

She gestured with her hands. "They were armed last year," she replied, "and surely if any of the students get out of hand it will be easy enough to stop them? Don't think me unsympathetic, Beo, but we have been running these Festivals in Ruffano for the past three years. Or rather my husband has, with your brother to help him. They know how to handle these affairs."

It was useless. My mission had been in vain. Nothing I was likely to say would convince her, unless I betrayed Aldo direct. Told her what I had heard from his lips the night before. And this loyalty forbade.

"I find Aldo changed," I said, trying a different line, "more moody, cynical. He will switch from laughter and chaffing to sudden silence."

"You had not seen him for twenty-two years," she reminded me. "You must make allowances."

"Take last night," I pursued, "take last night in particular. I showed him an old letter of our father's that I'd discovered by accident in one of the library books. A letter to Aldo's godfather, a doctor, I believe, saying what a fine fellow was his son. I thought Aldo would be amused. I read it to him. He didn't say a word, but drove away."

Her patient, rather pitying smile was maddening. "Perhaps he was too much touched," she said, "and didn't want you to know it. He was devoted to your father, wasn't he, and your father very proud of him? Or so I've always understood. Yes, I think I can understand why he forgot to say good night. He may seem cynical to you, Beo, but it's on the surface only. In reality . . ."

She broke off, emotion suddenly breaking to the surface, giving the lie to frigidity, to reserve. That was how she must have looked, I thought, on Sunday night, in the music room above, when Aldo returned to her after bidding me good night, and the vespas spluttered and roared, encircling the city, and the masked students broke into the women's hostel to fake their assault on Signorina Rizzio. "The wife of the leading citizen had been profaned." The question was, which one? I had no doubt about the answer.

"I'm sorry," I said, "I've taken up too much of your time. Please say nothing to Aldo about my visit when he sees you. But warn him to be careful."

"I'll do that certainly," she replied, "and anyway my husband will want to hear all the details of the Festival programme, though he may not be well enough to attend himself. Listen . . ."

The conversation above had ceased. The footsteps moved across the floor to the door and on to the landing. They began to descend the stairs.

"He's coming down," she said quickly. "He's not supposed to walk up and down the stairs." She went swiftly to the door, then turned. "He doesn't know who you are," she said, the telltale spot of colour in her cheeks, "I mean, your relationship to Aldo. I told him someone had called on business, that I was not sure who it was."

Her guilt communicated itself to me. I followed her to the door. "I'll go," I said.

"No," she answered, "there isn't time."

We went into the hall. The Rector was already halfway

down the stairs. He was a man who might have been any age between fifty-five and sixty-five, broad-shouldered, of medium height, grey-haired, with the fine eyes and regular features of one who had been handsome in his youth and was so still, though the grey texture of his skin gave proof of his recent illness. He had the air of authority and distinction of one who must immediately command liking and respect, even affection. My guilt increased.

"This is Signor Fabbio," said his wife as he paused at sight of me. "He came with a message about the library, where he is working as assistant. He was just going."

I realised that she was anxious for me to disappear. I bowed. The Rector inclined his head, wishing me good morning.

"Please don't let me rush you away, Signor Fabbio," he said. "I should like to hear about the new library, if you can spare a few minutes for me too."

I bowed again, the instinctive courier manner taking hold. Signora Butali shook her head.

"The doctors said you were not to come downstairs, Gaspare," she remonstrated. "I heard you answer the telephone. You should have called me."

He descended the stairs and stood between us in the hall. He shook my hand, his fine eyes searching me, then turned to his wife. "I should have had to take the call anyway," he said. "I'm afraid it was bad news."

I tried to efface myself, but he put out his hand. "Don't go," he said. "It is not personal. An unfortunate and very unhappy accident to one of the students, who was found dead this morning at the bottom of the theatre steps."

Signora Butali exclaimed in horror.

"It was the Commissioner of Police on the telephone," he continued. "He has only just heard of my return, and very properly informed me what had happened. It seems," he turned to me, "there was a curfew last night, because of certain incidents earlier this week, and all students, except those with late passes, were warned to be in their hostels or lodgings by nine o'clock. This lad, and possibly others, defied the order. He must have taken fright, hearing a patrol, and run, taking the shortest route, which happened to be those infernal steps. He stumbled and fell the whole length, breaking his neck. His body was found early this morning." The Rector put out his hand for his stick, which

Signora Butali gave him. He made his way slowly into the room we had just left. We followed him.

"This is terrible," she said, "at this moment of all moments, just before the Festival. Has the news been given out?"

"It will have been by mid-morning," her husband answered. "You can't hush up these things. The Commissioner will be here directly to discuss it."

Signora Butali pulled forward the chair by the desk. He sat down. The grey pallor of his face seemed to have increased.

"I shall have to summon a meeting of the university Council," he said. "I'm sorry, Livia. You will have to do a lot of telephoning." He patted his wife's hand, which was upon his shoulder.

"Of course," she said, and gestured hopelessly at me.

"I can't believe the curfew was necessary," said the Rector. "I'm afraid the Council acted out of panic, with the inevitable result that certain students rebelled, and so came this fatality. Was there much disturbance?"

He looked at me. I did not know how best to answer him.

"The various groups were lively," I said. "There seemed to be much rivalry amongst them, especially between the C and E students and the Arts and Education. The sudden curfew caused a lot of dissatisfaction. There was talk of nothing else in the canteen last night."

"Exactly," said the Rector, "and the more high-spirited amongst them were determined to send authority to blazes. I should have done the same when I was a student myself." He turned to his wife. "It was Marelli's boy who died," he said. "You remember Marelli, we stayed at one of his hotels a year or two ago. I don't know much about the boy, a third-year student, but Elia will tell me. What a tragedy for the parents. An only son."

My throat was dry. Whatever Signora Butali said in sympathy I echoed huskily. She was no longer so anxious for me to go. Perhaps my presence made some sort of a diversion for her husband.

"What time is the doctor coming?" he asked.

"He said half-past ten," she answered. "He might be here at any moment now."

"If the Commissioner of Police arrives first the doctor must wait," her husband said. "See if you can reach him, dear, at his home. If he's not at home he'll probably be at the hospital, and he can walk down from there. It's only two minutes away."

She paused a moment before leaving the room, flashing me a look of warning. It could have meant that I was not to tire him. It could have meant that I was not to talk of Aldo. All I wanted was to leave the house before the Commissioner arrived. But first I would have my say.

"This accident, professor," I said, "will it mean a cancellation of the Festival?"

He had taken up a small cigar and was busy lighting it. It was a moment or two before he answered. "Hardly that," he said. "There are something like five thousand students in the university of Ruffano, and to cancel one of their great days of the year because of a regrettable and unhappy accident to one of them would verge on hysteria. It would not be a good thing to do." He drew on his cigar and frowned. "No," he repeated, "you can rest assured that we shan't cancel the Festival. Why, are you taking part?"

The question took me by surprise. The gimlet eyes pierced me. "I'm not sure," I said. "Professor Donati might want me for some minor role."

"Good," he replied, "the more who take part the better. He is due here presently. I shall hear all about it. His choice of this year's subject rather surprised me, but he is sure to handle it superbly. He always does. Where are you from?"

"Where am I from?" I repeated.

"Your home, your university. I take it you are with us on a temporary basis?"

"Yes," I said, my throat tightening again. "I come from Turin. I needed a job to fill in time. I have a degree in modern languages."

"Good. And what do you think of our new library?"

"I've been very much impressed."

"And how long have you been working here?"

"A week."

"A week only?" He removed his cigar and stared. He looked surprised. "Forgive me," he said. "I happened to hear the maid say to my wife that the gentleman who had been to dinner on Sunday wanted to see her. I had not realised she had been giving a large party for the members of the university staff."

I swallowed. "Quite a small party," I said. "It was my good fortune to bring some books from the library for Signora Butali,

205

and she was kind enough to play for me. The invitation to dinner came about after that."

"I see," he said.

He looked at me again. The look was somehow different. Appraising. The look of a husband who suddenly wonders why his beautiful wife should take it into her head to play the piano to a stranger and then invite him to dinner. It was evidently not a usual thing for her to do.

"You are fond of music?" he asked.

"Passionately," I answered, hoping to assuage his interest.

"Good," he said again. Then, abruptly, he fired another question. "How many were there at this party?" he asked.

I felt myself trapped. If I answered half-a-dozen it would be a lie, easily detected later when he might come to question her, and the answer would trap her too.

"You misunderstand me, professor," I said rapidly. "The party was on the Sunday morning."

"Then you didn't come to dinner?"

"I came to dinner too," I said. "I was brought by Professor Donati."

"Ah," he said.

I began to sweat. There was nothing else I could say. He could always question the maid, if not his wife.

"It was a musical evening," I explained. "The idea in coming was to listen to Signora Butali playing. She played to us until we left. It was a memorable evening."

"I am sure it was," he said.

Somehow I must have made a gaffe. Signora Butali, when she arrived at the hospital in Rome the following day, could have told a very different story. She could have said that she had dined alone on the Sunday night, and then, seized with anxiety about her husband, had left early the next morning for Rome to be at his bedside. I did not know.

"In Rome," he said, following a line of thought, "I became very out of touch with life in Ruffano."

"Yes," I said, "that's understandable."

"Although," he continued, "well-meaning friends did their best to keep me informed of everything that went on. Some of them perhaps not so well-meaning."

I smiled. A forced smile. The direct eyes were searching me again.

"You say you have only been here a week?" he reiterated.

"A week today," I said. "That's correct. I arrived last Thursday."

"From Turin?"

"No, from Rome." I could feel the sweat beginning to break out on my forehead.

"Had you been working in one of the libraries in Rome?"

"No, professor. I was passing through. It just happened that I took it into my head to visit Ruffano. I needed a holiday."

My story, even to my own ears, sounded false. It must have sounded doubly false to him. My nervousness was all too obvious. For a moment he said nothing; his ears were cocked to the sound of Signora Butali's voice on the telephone overhead, just as ours had been to the sound of his some minutes earlier.

"I apologise, Signor Fabbio," he said, after the pause, "for asking you such a string of questions. It's only that while I was in Rome I was bothered with anonymous telephone calls with certain allusions to Professor Donati. I tried to have the calls traced, but could only discover that they were made locally. The strange thing was that the caller—who was a woman, for I heard her whispering instructions—did not speak to me direct but through a third person, a man. It just occurred to me—and forgive me if I am wrong—that you might have been the man, and could tell me something about these calls."

This time my look of profound astonishment must have reassured him.

"I know nothing about any calls, Professor," I said. "I think it is best to tell you at once that I am a travel agent. I work with a firm in Genoa, and I was travelling for this firm with a coach-party from Genoa to Naples, via Rome. I certainly made no calls to you. I had never heard your name until after I arrived in Ruffano."

He put out his hand to me. "That's enough," he said. "Please think no more of it. Put it right from your mind. And don't mention the matter to anyone, above all my wife. The calls, like anonymous letters, were unpleasant, but there have been none now for more than a week."

The front-door bell sounded its alarming peal. "That will be the Commissioner of Police," he said, "or the doctor. I apologise again, Signor Fabbio."

"Please, professor," I murmured.

I bowed, and turned to the door. I could hear the girl going to answer the bell and Signora Butali descending the stairs at the same time. I went out into the hall and effaced myself as the front-door opened. The sight of the Commissioner in his uniform made me retreat still further towards the kitchen regions. Signora Butali's figure hid me from view as she showed him into the study. Then she turned to say goodbye to me. The girl who had opened the door still hovered within earshot; I could not warn Signora Butali of the conversation that had taken place between her husband and myself.

"We shall be seeing you again, I hope," she said, reverting to the formal manner of a hostess speeding the departing guest.

"I hope so too, signora," I replied, and then her husband called her into the room and she waved her hand at me and vanished.

I walked down the paved path and into the street, where the Commissioner's car was waiting, a uniformed police driver at the wheel. I turned left, so as not to pass him, and walked rapidly downhill. It did not matter where I went as long as I put some distance between myself and the police car. I decided to return to my room, stay there awhile, and then walk back to my brother's house. The news of Stefano Marelli's death had profoundly shocked me, but I was equally disturbed by what the Rector had said about anonymous telephone calls.

When I reached the via San Michele and started to walk towards the Pensione Silvani I saw that a man was standing before the door, talking to the signora. The figure, the bared head, the face in profile, were instantly recognisable. It was the police agent from Rome, the agent in plain clothes whom I had seen in church on Tuesday.

I was opposite No. 5, and instinctively I ducked inside the open door and climbed to the first floor. I knocked at the door of Carla Raspa's apartment. There was no answer. I turned the handle and found it open. I went in, and closed the door behind me.

CHAPTER EIGHTEEN

I THOUGHT THE ROOM was empty, but the sound of the closing door disturbed someone in the bathroom. A woman came through wearing an apron, a floor-cloth in her hands. She stared at me suspiciously.

"What do you want?" she asked.

"I have an appointment with Signorina Raspa," I lied. "She told me she might be late and asked me to wait for her."

"Very well," said the woman. "This room is ready, but I haven't yet finished in the bathroom and kitchen. Make yourself comfortable."

She turned back to the bathroom and I heard the sound of running water. I crossed to the window and looked down the street to No. 24. The man was still there. Signora Silvani, waxing expansive, was doing most of the talking, and I could see her gesturing. She must be talking about me. She must be telling the agent that I worked every day in the library, that I would probably be there now, that I had been a guest under her roof for a week exactly, that I was a stranger to Ruffano. If he had explained who he was and given proof of his identity, surely he would demand to see my room? Surely he would go upstairs and open the drawers, search the cupboards and my suitcase? He would find nothing of any use to him. I carried my papers on me. But so far Signora Silvani had made no attempt to ask the man inside. They were still talking. Then the cleaning woman came back into the room and I drew away from the window.

"Would you like some coffee?" she asked.

"Please don't trouble yourself," I answered.

"No trouble," she said. "The signorina would wish it."

There was something familiar in the woman's face. She was young and not ill-looking, but with dishevelled hair suggesting an abortive attempt to copy some film-star on a cinema poster.

"I've seen you before, haven't I?" she asked.

"I was thinking the same," I replied, "but Ruffano is not a big city. Perhaps it was in the street."

"Perhaps," she said with a smile and a shrug.

She went into the kitchen and I returned to the window. In the interval the man had disappeared, but whether into the house or further down the street there was no way of telling. I stationed myself by the window, and picking up a magazine flicked the pages idly, keeping the house in view. In a moment the woman returned with the coffee.

"Here you are, signore," she said, "and I've remembered where it was I saw you. You were watching the crowd, near the Ognissanti. You asked me what it was about and why the police car was there. I had my baby in my arms, she was crying. Remember?"

I did. Ruffano was small indeed. There was no escape.

"You're right," I said. "I do remember now. Two people were getting into the car."

"The Ghigis," she said, "and it was just as I told you, they had to identify poor Marta Zampini's clothes. The police took them all the way to Rome—just imagine driving all that distance in a police car! If it hadn't been for such a wretched cause they would have enjoyed it. Neither of them had visited Rome before in their lives. And then the body was brought back and they buried her yesterday. What a crime, though! All for ten thousand lire. The wretch who did it still refuses to confess. The theft, yes, he acknowledges, according to what my husband read out to me from the paper, but not the murder. I suppose he hopes to save his skin by lying."

"Probably," I said. I drank the coffee, one eye still on the pensione further up the street.

"They'll force him to confess," she added. "The police have their methods; we all know that." She stood watching me drink the coffee, conversation making an interlude in the morning's work.

"Did you know the murdered woman?" I asked.

"Know Marta Zampini?" she repeated. "Everyone who lived near the Ognissanti knew Marta. She and Maria Ghigi used to work for Professor Donati's father in the old days. You know Professor Donati of the Arts Council?"

"Yes, I know him."

"They were saying yesterday that it was he who arranged for the police to bring back the body, and he paid for the burial. He's a wonderful man, he's done so much for Ruffano, like his father before him. If old Marta had continued to work for him she would have been alive today."

"Why did she leave?"

The woman shrugged. "Too much of this." She made a gesture of drinking. "She had gone to pieces during the past few months, so the Ghigis said. Always brooding. No one knows what she had to brood about, they took good care of her. Maria Ghigi said she was never the same after the war, when her life with the Donati family broke up. She missed the little boy. She was forever talking about the little boy, the professor's brother, who disappeared with the German troops. Well, that's life, isn't it? There's always something to go wrong."

I finished my coffee and pushed away the tray. "Thank you," I said.

"Let's hope Signorina Raspa won't be long," she said, and then with a sly, long glance at me she added, "She's handsome isn't she?"

"Very handsome," I agreed.

"The signorina has many admirers," she said. "I know, because I often have to clear up after they have been to dinner."

I smiled, but did not comment.

"Ah, well," she said, "I must be going. I have to do my own shopping before my husband comes home for his midday meal. Luckily my mother looks after the baby while I'm here working for the signorina."

There was still no sign of life from No. 24. The agent would have had time to search my room and come downstairs again. Perhaps he was having coffee too, with Signora Silvani. I pretended interest in the magazine. Some five minutes later the woman returned from the kitchen. She had put a cardigan over her dress and was carrying a string bag.

"Well, I'm off," she said. "I hope you spend a pleasant day with the signorina."

"Thank you," I said.

She wished me good morning and went out of the apartment. I heard her go downstairs and watched her walk up the via San Michele. I stayed there, my eyes fixed on No. 24, but no one entered or came out. The agent must have gone. He must have gone some while ago, when the cleaning woman first came in and suggested coffee. Now he could be anywhere, up at the university, perhaps, making enquiries at the Registrar's office or the library. Because of this the library was now barred to me. The Silvani pensione too. There was no refuge left but the apartment

211

in which I sat, and my brother's house in the via dei Sogni. And if I left the apartment and walked up the hill to Aldo's house I might meet the agent on the way. He could even be watching for me to return to the Silvani pensione.

I pulled out a packet of cigarettes and began to smoke. I thought about the student Marelli breaking his neck at the bottom of the theatre steps. It was on those same steps that I had met the frightened boy on Friday of last week. Obviously he had been a student too. There had been no curfew then, but Aldo's sentries must have questioned him, as part of their fantastic, mediaeval game. This time the game had ended in a student's death. Were the scales of heavenly justice finally balanced? Could the game now end?

Aldo, in his capacity as Director of the Arts Council of Ruffano, was a member of the university board. He would thus attend the meeting called by the Rector for later in the day. Like everyone else, he would accept the reason which had been given for Marelli's death—that the student, taking fright, had run from a patrol—but in his heart he must surely acknowledge the true cause.

I looked at my watch. It was twenty-five minutes past eleven. I began to walk up and down the room. I looked out of the window. All was still quiet at No. 24. When Carla Raspa returned, what would be my excuse for being there? I had not seen her since the Tuesday night when I had, so ungallantly and deliberately, walked out on her. It was a strange moment to apologise.

I went through into the bathroom. Jars and bottles were on the shelves, and a dressing-gown had been flung on a stool. A nightgown, hastily rinsed through, hung limply on a hanger above the bath. The bidet was full of soapy water in which a pile of stockings had been left to soak. The sight made me sick. I went back into the kitchen, retching. The disorder, the intimacy, reminded me of hotel bedrooms long ago, in Frankfurt and other cities, when side by side with my mother's underwear, similarly washed and rinsed, would be male socks and handkerchiefs, tooth-brushes and hair-lotion. Streaky hairs would be lying in the bath. As a boy of eleven, or twelve, my stomach had heaved. The stench of lust pursued me across Germany to Turin. It followed me still.

I went and sat by the open window once again and lit another cigarette. I wondered what woman was it who, inspired by jealousy, had put through the anonymous telephone calls to the Rector in his hospital bed in Rome. A discarded mistress of my brother's, perhaps, or someone who had aspired to that position and failed. The woman, whoever she was, must have guessed the relationship between Aldo and the Rector's wife. The calls might have ceased, but Aldo must be warned before he himself spoke to the Rector. I might telephone Jacopo asking him to tell Aldo, as soon as he returned home, to put through a call to me here in Carla Raspa's apartment.

I fingered through the directory and found the number. I asked for it and waited. There was no answer. Jacopo was either out or in his own domain. I put down the telephone and went again to the window. A bunch of students was coming up the street, shouting and whistling, dressed for a masquerade in their coloured hats donned for the occasion, one of them carrying a bag on a stick which he thrust into the faces of passers-by.

"Help the poor scholars' fund," he called out. "Contributions welcome, however small. Every cent given will help some poor scholar to complete his education. Thank you, signore, thank you, signorina."

A man, shrugging, put something in the bag. A girl, pursued with hoots and whistles, did likewise, and laughingly escaped. The students spread out fan-wise across the street. A car coming downhill was stopped and the bag was poked through the window. The student bowed his thanks, flourishing his mediaeval hat.

"Thank you, signore, long life to you, signore."

They continued up the street, still singing, shouting, and turned in the direction of the piazza della Vita. The campanile beside the Duomo sounded twelve, echoed, before the last strokes finished, by the bells from San Cipriano. Noon sounded from every quarter of Ruffano, and I thought how in centuries gone by a fugitive like myself sought sanctuary within a church by the high altar. I wondered, if I did the same today, whether I should find protection, or whether the sacristan in San Cipriano would look at me aghast and straightway run blabbing to the police.

Then I heard footsteps coming up the stairs. The door opened. It was Carla Raspa. She stared at me, dumbfounded.

"I was just deciding," I said truthfully, "whether to remain here in your apartment or seek sanctuary in church."

"It depends on your crime," she said, closing the door behind her. "Perhaps you should confess it first."

She laid her bag and a parcel of books on the table. Then she looked me up and down. "You're about thirty-six hours late for our appointment," she said. "I don't mind waiting one hour for a date, or possibly two, but after that I prefer to find a substitute."

She reached in her bag for cigarettes and lit one. Then she passed into the kitchen and returned with a bottle of Cinzano and two glasses on a tray. "I suppose," she said, "the reason you ratted was that you funked the issue. It's happened before to bigger boys than you. I've usually managed to overcome it, though. There are ways and means." She poured the Cinzano into the glasses. "Courage!" she said. "You never know how good a thing can be until you try it."

She lifted her glass to me and smiled. I had never known anyone more magnanimous. I took the other glass. As I drank the Cinzano I came to a decision.

"I'm not here to apologise for Tuesday night," I said, "or to make good a reputation lost. I'm here because I believe the police are tailing me."

"The police?" she echoed, setting down her glass. "Then you have committed a crime—or are you joking?"

"I've committed no crime," I said. "I happened to be on the site of a murder ten days ago, and I suspect the police want to question me."

She saw from my face that I was not joking. She handed me one of her cigarettes. "You don't mean the murder of that old woman in Rome?" she asked.

"I do," I answered. "I gave her ten thousand lire the night she was killed. My reason for doing so doesn't matter. Next morning I learnt that she had been murdered. No need to tell you I didn't do that, but I gave her the money within minutes, possibly, of the crime. Clearly, therefore, I'm someone the police would be interested in."

"Why?" she asked. "They've caught the man, haven't they? It was reported in the newspapers."

"They've caught him, yes," I told her. "He admits the theft of the ten thousand lire but denies the murder."

She shrugged her shoulders. "So would I," she said. "That's up to the police. Why should you worry?"

I saw that I must explain further. I told her about the English

214

tourists and how I had taken them to the police, but had said nothing about my gift of money, and had left for Ruffano the next day.

"Why did you do that?" she asked.

"Because I recognised the woman," I said, "and to be doubly sure I came to Ruffano to find out."

She finished her drink, and seeing that I had finished mine poured me another. Her manner was still casual, but more guarded than before. "I read in the paper that the woman came from Ruffano," she said. "How was it you happened to know her?"

"I was born here," I said. "I lived in Ruffano until I was eleven years old."

She shot a look at me across the table, then refilling her glass moved to the divan, propping the cushions behind her back. "You've been living quite a lie here for the past week, haven't you?" she said.

"You might call it that."

"And now the lie is catching up with you?"

"Not so much the lie as my omission to tell the truth to the police in Rome," I said, "and the fact that I believe one of their plain-clothes agents recognised me at Marta's burial service on Tuesday. He could hardly have regarded it as a coincidence. An hour ago this same agent was making enquiries at No. 24. I saw him from across the street and came in here."

She lay back against the cushions blowing smoke-rings in the air. "Coincidence or not," she said, "he would certainly think it suspicious. But if they've caught their man in Rome what are they doing here bothering about you?"

"I've already told you," I said. "The man denies he did it. It could be that they believe him, and the search for the murderer goes on."

She considered a moment, then looked across at me. "It could be that I believe him too," she said.

I shrugged my shoulders and moved towards the door. "In that case," I said, "I may as well clear out. You can report me to the police over the telephone."

At that moment the telephone rang. I felt it must be fate— the game was finished. She held up her hand to me to stay, then lifted the receiver. "Yes," she answered, "yes, Giuseppe . . . Lunch?" She paused, looked at me, shaking her head. "No, it's

215

impossible, I've people coming. A student and her mother, due any minute now. I didn't know last night—they only telephoned this morning. I don't know, Giuseppe, I can't make plans . . . If it's possible I'll telephone you this afternoon at the library. So long." She hung up, smiling. "That's settled him for a few hours," she said. "You're in luck he telephoned and didn't walk right in. We had a tentative engagement for lunch which, as you see and I hope appreciate, I've turned down for you. Oh, don't worry. We won't go out. I'll make an omelette." She swung her legs down from the divan and smoothed her hair.

"Then you don't think I'm a murderer?" I asked her.

"No," she said. "Frankly, I doubt if you'd have the nerve to kill a wasp, let alone a woman."

She went into the kitchen and I followed her. She started doing things with pans at the stove and moving dishes from the rack. I sat down on one of the chairs and watched her. My confession had acted like a purge. Our relationship seemed suddenly easier.

"I suppose you want me to get you out of Ruffano?" she asked. "It shouldn't be difficult. I can borrow the car again."

"Not out of Ruffano," I told her, "just up the hill to a house in the via dei Sogni."

"Then you have a friend who knows all about you?"

"Yes," I said.

She hummed under her breath as she broke eggs into a basin and forked them briskly. "Do you mind telling me who it is?" she asked.

I hesitated. I had already committed my immediate fortunes to her hands, and I saw no reason to commit my brother.

"You don't have to tell me—I've already guessed," she said. "You forget, Ruffano is a small city. My daily cleaner lives near the Ognissanti, and I heard all about the murdered woman from her days ago. Old Marta lived for years with the Donati family, and looked after Aldo Donati when he was a boy. Did you visit his home when you were a child, and is that why you remembered her?"

Her guess was ingenious. It was also not quite the truth, but it served my purpose.

"As a matter of fact, yes," I answered her.

The smoke was rising from the pan and she poured in the eggs. "So you went and told your story to Donati?" she said. "And instead of advising you to scamper he suggested you stayed put?"

"That's about it."

"Was this last Sunday?"

"Yes," I said.

"Then it was you who was with Donati all Sunday afternoon and evening?"

"Yes," I said again.

The omelette was done. She slid it on to the dish and brought it to the table.

"Eat it while it's hot," she said, drawing in a chair for herself.

I did as she told me, wondering what she would ask me next. She said nothing while we ate, rising from the table merely to fetch a bowl of salad and a bottle of wine. Her smile was enigmatic. I grew curious.

"Why are you smiling?" I asked.

"The truth has dawned on me," she said. "I should have guessed before, when your noble friend didn't take the trouble to answer my letter. He's not interested in women. A playmate from the past has more allure. Especially a baby-face like you."

This was a curious conjecture which no one would appreciate more than Aldo. I wondered whether to demur or let it go.

"Ah well," she said, "life is full of shocks. I'd never have believed it, though, of him. It only goes to show how wrong one can be. Still, it's a challenge. These escapades can pall." She forked her salad thoughtfully, and stared beyond me. "There's been some curious talk amongst the students," she mused. "Those rehearsals at the ducal palace behind closed doors—they could have been a cover for something else. If they were, Donati had me fooled on Saturday. I'd have followed him to the grave."

Still I said nothing. To comment either way might prove disastrous.

"Did you know a student broke his neck last night?" she asked.

"I heard a rumour."

"It's not official yet, but it soon will be. Defied the curfew, and ran from the patrols. At least, that's the story. A C and E lad in his third year. One wonders what their crowd will make of it. It may be the final straw."

She got up from the table once more and returned with fruit. She chose a pear and began to munch it, holding it unskinned between her hands, the juice running down her chin.

"What do you mean, the final straw?" I asked.

"The breaking-point between their crowd and ours," she said. "If so, God help us all tomorrow when Donati gets his performers into the streets. That concession of his to invite the C and E students to take part in the Festival won't conciliate the rival factions, as he believes—it will have the opposite effect." She laughed, and sucking the pear-core dry threw the remains into the refuse pail below the sink. "Your Arts Director wasn't going to arm his women," she said, "but I can tell you this. Most of the girls I've lectured to the last few days are determined not to miss the battle, and if the C and E crowd attack their boy-friends we'll see all hell let loose. I pity the police."

She rose and stood by the stove, warming the coffee. "Anyway," she said, "they'll be too busy to look for you. You'll be safe and snug in Aldo Donati's hide-out. What's his house like? Monkish or affluent? Deep-carpeted or bare?"

"If you borrow that car and drive me there you might get a chance to see," I told her.

No sooner spoken than regretted. Aldo would have enough to contend with without adding Carla Raspa to the number. Yet I saw no way of getting to the via dei Sogni without her help.

"That's true," she answered smiling. "If I deliver his little playmate to him in person the least the Professor can do is to invite me in."

The telephone rang again. She went through to the living-room to answer it. I stood and listened. Like every fugitive, I expected any telephone call to refer to me.

"No, no, I'm still waiting for them," she said impatiently, shaking her head. "Something must have held them up, you know what the crowds are like already in the streets."

She held her hand over the mouthpiece and whispered across the room at me, "Giuseppe again. He thinks I'm expecting guests." She uncovered the mouthpiece. "You have a meeting. At a quarter to two. I understand. At the Rector's house. Is he back?" She looked at me, excited. "About the accident, naturally. I wonder what he'll have to say. Tell me, will Professor Donati be there? I see . . . Well, you'd better telephone me here when it's over. So long." She came back into the kitchen, smiling. "Butali's back," she said. "He's called a meeting of the university Council for a quarter to two. When he finds out what's been happening this past week he'll have another thrombosis."

She went over to the stove and returned with the coffee. I

looked at my watch. It was just after one. I crossed the room and glanced out of the window. The car we had borrowed on the Tuesday evening was parked below.

"Giuseppe didn't know whether Donati was to be at this meeting or not," said Carla Raspa. "I see no point in dropping you at his house if we can't do it in style with the host there."

"To hell with style," I said. "The important thing is to get me there. Then your responsibility ends."

"Ah, but I don't want it to end," she said.

There was sound of movement from the apartment overhead. Heavy footsteps shook the ceiling.

"My neighbour with the car," said Carla Raspa. She went to the door and out on to the landing. Halfway up the stairs she shouted, "Walter?" The neighbour shouted back.

"Can I borrow the car for half-an-hour?" she called. "I've an important errand that can't be managed on foot."

The neighbour overhead called something in return that I couldn't catch.

"Oh, yes," she cried, "you shall have it back by half-past two."

She returned to the room, smiling. "He's very obliging," she told me, "but naturally I keep him that way. See how it pays. Let's drink our coffee and we'll be off. We may catch your illustrious boy-friend at his lunch."

"Shall I telephone him first?" I suggested.

She hesitated, then shook her head. "No," she said firmly, "he might put you off. I'm not going to lose my one and only opportunity of setting foot in his house."

There was nothing for it but to acquiesce. My hope was that my brother would not be there, and that Jacopo would admit me. We drank our coffee and she went into the bathroom. When she came back the whiff of scent was stronger, the mascara on her lashes deeper.

"War-paint," she said briefly. "Not that I have much hope, but you never know."

I looked out of the window and into the street. There was no one about.

"Come on, I'm ready," I told her.

I followed her downstairs and out of the house. I opened the door of the car for her and she settled herself in the driving-seat.

"I'll be chauffeur," she said, "and you can sit well back.

If the streets are lined with police and agents in plain clothes they won't look at you with me at the wheel."

Her good humour was infectious. I felt like laughing for the first time that day. She started the car and we headed for the via dei Sogni. Our progress was erratic, her driving unprofessional but fast. Twice we nearly hit pedestrians endeavouring to cross street corners.

"Watch out," I said, "or the police will want you too."

She took the long way round by the via delle Mura, so as to avoid coming into the via dei Sogni near to the Rector's house. There was no Alfa-Romeo outside the entrance to No. 2, and I breathed a sigh of relief. My companion got out and looked about her. I glanced at my watch. It was nearly half-past one.

"Lead the way," she said, "and don't think you can throw me off. I'm here to stay."

We passed together through the entrance. I rang the bell of Aldo's front door, praying that Jacopo would answer it himself. He did. But he looked embarrassed when he saw me, and more so when he realised that I was not alone.

"The Professor isn't at home," he said promptly.

"It doesn't matter," I told him. "I'll come in and wait. This lady is Signorina Raspa. I've promised her I would show her the portrait in the living-room—the signorina is interested in pictures."

Jacopo looked more uncomfortable than ever. "Professor Donati already has one visitor waiting for him," he began, but Carla Raspa, determined not to be outdone, brushed past him smiling gaily.

"Then that makes three of us," she said.

I followed her to the door of the living-room, trying to prevent her entry. It was too late. She had already opened the door. A woman was sitting on the settee who, as she saw us, half rose in protest, then, seeing we were upon her, stood silent, saying nothing.

It was Signora Butali.

CHAPTER NINETEEN

I DON'T KNOW WHICH of the two women looked the more surprised, or indeed discomfited. The onus was on me.

"I beg your pardon, signora," I said. "Professor Donati asked me to call, and I'm afraid I'm before my time. May I present Signorina Raspa, who was kind enough to bring me?"

The frigid smile hovered for an instant on her face and vanished. The eyes were distant, looking beyond us to Jacopo with a mute reproach. "Good afternoon, signorina," she said.

Carla Raspa, being the less embarrassed, recovered the quicker. She advanced with a certain brash assurance, holding out her hand. "We've never met, signora," she said, "but then, why should we? Although we share the university life we live in different worlds. I am a humble member of the Arts faculty, and spend most of my time conducting parties of students round the ducal palace. I hope the Rector is better?"

"Thank you," replied Signora Butali, "he is better but still very tired. We only arrived late last night."

"To find all Ruffano in an uproar and the sudden death of a student the climax," said Carla Raspa. "What a homecoming! I'm very sorry for you both."

Her plunge into the burning topic of the hour was ill-timed. Signora Butali stiffened. "The accident was tragic indeed," she said. "I know nothing of any uproar, nor does my husband."

Carla Raspa turned to me with a smile. "Professor and Signora Butali are lucky," she observed. "You and I were witnesses to one riotous event at least. But perhaps they will discuss it at the meeting." She turned again to the Rector's lady. "The librarian, Signor Fossi, is a good friend of mine," she explained. "He told me they were meeting at your house at a quarter to two."

The signora bowed. Comment must have seemed to her unnecessary. An awkward silence followed. Jacopo, who had lingered by the door, now disappeared, leaving the initiative to me. I looked at my watch.

"Don't forget," I reminded Carla Raspa, "your neighbour needs his car."

"It's early yet," she said. "I promised I'd have it back by half-past two. What a charming room!" She advanced further and looked about her, sizing up the décor and the furniture with a rapacious eye. She wandered to the portrait of my father hanging on the wall. "I suppose that's Donati the elder?" she remarked. "Not so handsome as his son, and lacking the Professor's devastating charm. These things must all have come from his old home. Wasn't it the house where you live now, signora?"

She flashed a look at Signora Butali, who, resembling more than ever the gentlewoman in the ducal palace portrait, bowed yet again with Florentine hauteur.

"That is true," she answered. "We are very fortunate in our surroundings."

"I wonder if Professor Donati grudges it?" smiled Carla Raspa.

"He has never said so," came the reply.

The atmosphere, chilly, threatened to become glacial. The signora, who had been first in the room and was the older of the ladies, continued to stand. But my companion ignored protocol and perched herself on the side of the settee.

"If he did, he'd put it deviously," she said, lighting a cigarette and offering one to Signora Butali, who shook her head. "But he'd charm the house out of you in the end by magic means. He has hypnotic eyes. Don't you agree, Armino?"

The smile she gave me was deliberate, the puff of smoke provocative. Remembering what she imagined to be the relationship between Aldo and myself, doubtless she found the present situation intriguing, even enjoyable.

"His eyes are dark," I said. "I don't know about hypnotic."

"His actors find them so, both male and female," she continued, one eye on Signora Butali. "They're dedicated, every one. I suppose, like the rest of us humble members of the university staff, they hope that he will take notice of each of them individually."

There was another pause, then, turning to the Rector's wife, she said, "You're not taking part this year, signora—such a pity. You made a beautiful Duchess of Ruffano last Festival under Professor Donati's superb direction."

Acknowledgement came from the signora, but no more. I felt the expression of agreeable attention already on my features become fixed.

"The rehearsals this year have been so secret," pursued Carla Raspa, now mistress of the scene. "Conferences behind locked doors to all hours of the night. No women taking part. Admission by ticket only to the open meetings, to which I was lucky enough to obtain two tickets from the Director himself, and took Armino. It was a revelation, I can tell you. But then you must have attended one or two of the rehearsals, surely?"

Signora Butali, assured in her own house when she played hostess, looked vulnerable under this roof that was not hers. Even her stance, her hands clasped in front of her, holding neither gloves nor bag—she must have hurried up here on an impulse to waylay my brother before he saw her husband— seemed one of evasion, even of self-defence.

"I'm afraid not," she said, "it wasn't possible. I've spent so much of my time just latterly in Rome."

I saw her furtively consult her watch in a downward glance, easy enough because of her clasped hands, and then with mournful eyes she looked at me, the message one of entreaty. There was nothing I could do. The only hope was for Aldo to return and himself take charge. I had no authority to turn Carla Raspa out of the house, nor had Signora Butali. The interloper, conscious of her power and caring not a jot for her intrusion into what was very obviously a private visit, intercepted the signora's glance and misinterpreted it as being hostile to me.

"Professor Donati must have been held up," she said. "It doesn't really matter to Armino, he can wait here for the rest of the afternoon if he feels inclined. Can't you, Armino?"

"I'm at his disposal," I said shortly.

"Such a pleasant corner of Ruffano this," Carla Raspa went on, lighting yet another cigarette from the butt of the first. "No traffic, no endless parading students, no peering neighbours to gossip about who goes out or who comes in. Your house is only just down the street, signora?"

"Yes."

"Convenient for Professor Donati when he wants to consult the Rector about anything. But of course, as you said, you've been so much in Rome."

The inflection in Carla Raspa's voice was now ironic. One allusion more to Aldo's proximity as neighbour to No. 8, and she might overstep into the realm of direct insult. If she did, I wondered whether Signora Butali would counter with a crushing retort or offer the other cheek.

"Luckily for your music pupils you were able to return to

Ruffano at the weekends," the voice continued. "One or two of them attend my lectures, and they spoke of you most gratefully. I don't think many of them had to miss a single lesson through your absence."

"Signora Butali puts the interests of everybody else before her own," I commented. "She even found a moment to play to me last week."

The interruption did no good. Indeed, it whetted Carla Raspa's appetite.

"The psychologists tell us that piano-playing is therapeutic," she observed, "allowing full reign to the emotions. Do you agree, signora?"

The muscles of the victim's face tautened. "It helps one to relax," she answered.

"It wouldn't work for me," sighed Carla, "though I can see the point of a duet. There'd be stimulation there. Have you tried duets, signora?"

This time the intonation was unmistakable. Had it been last Sunday night and the three of us, Aldo, Signora Butali and myself, at the dinner-table under candle-light, a remark like this would have been accepted as a challenge in the sex-play we were all engaged in. The signora would have smiled, parrying the question with another equally light-hearted. Not so today. This was a thrust, seeking to probe her weak defences.

"No, signorina," she replied. "I leave that sort of thing to children. My pupils study for diplomas, to equip themselves as teachers."

Carla smiled. She was, I felt, gathering her forces for the kill. It was time for me to intervene. But before I could do so the slam of the front door signalled an arrival. There was a hurried murmur from Jacopo in the hall, an expostulation—my brother's —then an ominous silence. Signora Butali turned pale. Carla Raspa intuitively extinguished her cigarette. The door opened and Aldo came into the room.

"I'm extremely honoured," he said, the inflection in his voice warning his visitors that he had expected none of them. "I hope Jacopo has been looking after you, or have you all already lunched?" He did not wait for a reply, but crossed the room and kissed the signora's hand. "Signora," he said, "I was just on my way to your house, and seeing a car here outside which I did not recognise looked in to investigate."

"The car is mine," announced Carla Raspa, "or rather, borrowed for the occasion. Armino lunched with me, and I dropped him here."

"How thoughtful of you, signorina," replied Aldo. "The hills of Ruffano must be hard on a courier's legs." He turned to the Rector's wife with a manner equally detached. "What can I do for you, signora?" he asked. "The meeting called by the Rector hasn't been cancelled, has it?"

The long wait, and the conversation that succeeded it, seemed to have drained Signora Butali of energy, of resource. It occurred to me that she had been unable to reach Aldo by telephone since her arrival home, unless it had been in her husband's presence, and that this was, in fact, their first encounter since they last saw one another on Sunday night. Her eyes searched his to convey a message. The anguish was very evident.

"No," she said, "it has not been cancelled." She struggled bravely to find words that could not be turned by the listening Carla Raspa into food for gossip through the university. "I merely wished to consult you, Professor, on a small matter. It's really of no importance. Some other time, perhaps."

The lie was pitiful. Had the matter been so small she would never have waited for him so long. Aldo looked at me. He must have wondered why I had not gone discreetly, taking my companion with me, the instant I knew Signora Butali was under his roof.

"You'll excuse us, signorina, I feel sure," he said, looking past me to the cause of all the embarrassment. "Liqueurs, Beo, cigarettes, see to it, will you? Signora, I'm so sorry . . . Would you come this way?"

He gestured to the hall and the dining-room beyond. Signora Butali passed through, and Aldo closed the door behind him. I went to the tray of drinks and poured Carla Raspa a liqueur which she did not deserve.

"You behaved disgracefully," I told her. "You'll never receive an invitation to the Butalis' now."

She downed her liqueur and held out the glass for more. "*What* did Donati call you?" she asked, her eyes curious.

"Beo," I said, "short for Il Beato, the blessed."

The eyes grew wider still. "How touching," she murmured. Then motioning towards the dining-room, where supposedly they had gone, she added, "Does the noble lady know?"

"Know what?" I asked.

"About you and Donati?"

The devil entered me. Things had reached such a pass that I did not care. "Oh, yes," I said, "we're quite open about it. But only to her."

"You amaze me," said Carla Raspa. She was so excited that she got up, spilling her drink. I mopped it up with my handkerchief. "But she's mad about him," she exclaimed, "a child could see it. It shrieks to the heavens. Doesn't she mind?"

"No," I said. "Why should she?"

"A woman like that? Avid to be the one and only? My dear Armino! Unless . . ." A world of possibilities filled her mind. Images floated before her. "Livia Butali, Donati, and you. It isn't possible . . ."

Her mind reeled. I took away her glass and put it on the tray. "Now will you go?" I pleaded.

"No," she said, "not after that piece of information. Donati will have to kick me out. Where have they gone, into his bedroom?"

I looked at my watch. "Hardly," I said. "It's ten to two now. He's five minutes late at the Rector's meeting."

"You'll be telling me in a minute that the Rector's in this too," she said.

I shrugged. "He may be, for all I know," I answered.

Voices came from the hall and passed to the entrance outside. Then after a moment or two Aldo came back into the room.

"Who's next?" he asked. "I like to see my clients one at a time."

I spoke before she had a chance to get in first. "The police have been to 24, via San Michele," I said. "I thought it best to take refuge in Carla's apartment. I told her why."

"They've been to the library too," Aldo replied. "Fossi telephoned me. That was what held me up." Then, turning to Carla Raspa, he added, "Thank you for what you did. This fellow could be in trouble. I've stalled them for the time being, and he's safe enough here with me."

The signorina, having gained her ends and confronted her host face to face, was ready to call it quits.

"I was only too glad to help," she admitted frankly, "especially since it gave me a chance to enter your house at last. I've tried often enough. I've called about three times."

"How unfortunate," murmured Aldo. "I must have been engaged."

"You were," she said, looking at me, "with him."

She picked up her bag, and, wishing to show herself aware of the situation which she imagined between us, observed with emphasis, "I had no idea, Professor, that you and Armino were such close friends."

The parting shot fell wide of its target.

"We should be," said Aldo briefly. "He's my brother. We believed each other dead, and hadn't met for twenty-two years until last Sunday."

The effect was startling. Carla Raspa, who had taken my possible status as a suspected murderer without flinching, flushed a deep crimson. Aldo might have struck her.

"I didn't know," she said. "I hadn't realised . . . Armino said nothing." She looked from one to the other of us, overcome, and then, to my consternation, burst into tears. "I lost both brothers in the war," she said. "Much older than me, but I loved them dearly . . . I'm very sorry. Please forgive me."

She blundered towards the door, but Aldo stepped forward and, seizing her by the arm, swung her round and stared into her face.

"Just how lonely are you?" he asked.

"Lonely?" she echoed, the tears blotching her mascara, her skin, now the flush had died, sallow under her make-up. "I haven't said I'm lonely."

"You don't have to," he retorted brutally. "You proclaim it in your body each time you wrap yourself round a different man."

I stared aghast at this sudden violence on the part of my brother. Carla Raspa, by breaking down, had shown herself as vulnerable in her fashion as Signora Butali in hers. Why couldn't Aldo let her go in peace? She stared back at him, and, miraculously, everything collapsed. All pretence and all bravado.

"It's all I have," she said, "there's nothing else to give."

"What about your life?" he demanded. "Can't you lose that too?"

He dropped her arm. She continued staring at him. The running mascara had now smudged both eyes.

"I'd lose it for you," she said, "if you asked me for it."

Aldo smiled and, stooping, picked up the bag that had slipped from her shaking hands.

"That's all that matters then," he said.

He gave her the bag and patted her on the shoulder. He put his finger on her cheek, showed her the smudge of black and laughed. She smiled in answer, and dabbed at it with her handkerchief.

"I may ask for your life tomorrow, at the Festival," he told her, "so remember that you've promised it to me. I may need you at the ducal palace. You will get your instructions some time this evening on the telephone."

"I'll do whatever you want, now, and forever," she said.

He pushed her towards the door. "One thing's very certain," he said, "if you want to die, you won't have to die alone."

As she went into the hall she looked back over her shoulder at me. "Shall I see you again, Armino?" she asked.

"I don't know," I answered, "but thank you for giving me sanctuary."

She glanced enquiringly at Aldo. He gave her no indication of my future, and she passed out through the front door to the double entrance and the street. Through the open window of the room where we were standing came the thin high sound of San Donato striking two.

"I must go," said Aldo, "I'm already fifteen minutes late. I've just telephoned Cesare telling him you are here. He and Giorgio have been looking for you all the morning."

His manner was abrupt, evasive. Whether because of the trouble I had caused him or for some other reason I could not tell. It was as though he did not care to be alone with me.

"When Cesare comes, I want you to do whatever he tells you," he said. "Do you understand?"

"No," I replied, "not immediately. But perhaps I shall when Cesare appears." Then, hesitant, I added, "I don't know if the signora told you. I called at her house this morning."

"No," he said, "she didn't tell me."

"I met her husband," I went on, "and when she was out of the room we had a few minutes' conversation. During the course of it he mentioned—I won't bother with the details now —that he had been receiving anonymous telephone calls while he was in hospital in Rome. The caller was a woman, the allusions to you."

"Thank you," said Aldo. His voice remained unaltered. His expression did not change.

"I thought," I said awkwardly, "it was best to warn you."

"Thank you," he said again, and turned towards the door.

"Aldo," I said, "I apologise for what happened just now— the unfortunate clash between Signora Butali and Carla Raspa."

"Why unfortunate?" he asked, pausing, his hand on the door.

I gestured. "They're so different," I said, "no common ground between them."

He looked at me. The eyes were cryptic, hard. "That's where you are wrong," he said. "They both wanted one thing only. Carla Raspa happened to be more honest about it."

He left the room. I heard the front door slam. The uncertainty of what was yet to come closed in upon me with his presence gone.

CHAPTER TWENTY

I DID NOT WANT to be alone. I sought out Jacopo, who was about to leave for his own quarters across the double entrance.

"May I come with you?" I asked him diffidently.

He looked surprised, then pleased, and waved me on. "By all means, Signor Beo," he said. "I'm cleaning the silver. Come and keep me company."

We passed through to his domain. He led me to his own kitchen —kitchen and living-room in one, the window facing the via dei Sogni. It was cheerful, snug, a canary in its cage singing to the strains of a transistor radio which Jacopo, out of possible deference to me, switched off. The walls were covered with pictures of aircraft, torn from the pages of magazines and framed. Pieces of silver, knives and forks and spoons, dishes and jugs, stood on the centre of the kitchen table in various stages of his cleaning process, some covered with a pink paste, others already polished.

I recognised most of them. I picked up a small round porringer and smiled. "That's mine," I said, "it was a christening present. Marta never would let me use it. She said it was too good."

"The Capitano keeps it for sugar," said Jacopo, "he always uses it with his morning coffee. His own is too big."

He showed me a larger bowl that he had not yet cleaned.

"I remember that too," I told Jacopo. "It stood in the dining-room, and my mother put flowers in it."

Both bowls, Aldo's and mine, were inscribed with our initials, A.D.

"The Capitano is very particular about all the family things," said Jacopo. "If any of the china gets broken, which isn't often, he is very upset, or if anything is lost. He will throw away nothing that belongs to the old days, and to his father."

I put the porringer back. Jacopo took it from me and began to clean it.

"It's strange," I said, "that he should be like that, and respect tradition."

"Strange?" repeated Jacopo, astonished. "I assure you it is

not, Signor Beo. He's been that way as long as I've known him."

"Perhaps," I answered, "but he was a rebel as a boy."

"Ah, boys," shrugged Jacopo, "we are all of us different when we are boys. The Capitano will be forty in November."

"Yes," I said.

The canary started singing again. The song was artless, happy.

"I'm concerned about my brother, Jacopo," I said.

"No need," answered Jacopo shortly. "The Capitano always knows what he's about."

I picked up a leather and began polishing my own small porringer. "Has he not changed at all during the past years?" I asked.

Jacopo considered, frowning a little, as he warmed to his task. "He's more thoughtful, perhaps," he said, after a moment. "He has his moods, as I have mine. It doesn't do to disturb him when he's alone across the way, thinking."

"What does he think about?"

"If I knew that," replied Jacopo, "I wouldn't be here in my kitchen polishing the silver. I'd be like him, a member of the Arts Council, telling other people what to do."

I laughed and let it go. Jacopo had a certain rugged wisdom.

"We suit each other very well, the Capitano and I," he said. "We understand one another. I have never pried into his concerns, as Marta did."

"Marta?" I asked, surprised.

"It wasn't just the drinking, Signor Beo. She became possessive through the years. Her age, no doubt. She wanted to know everything. What the Capitano was doing, where he was going, who were his friends, what were his intentions. Oh yes, that, and a lot else besides. I told your brother, 'If I ever become like that, fire me immediately, I'll know the reason why.' He promised to do so. But he needn't worry. I shan't."

My porringer was clean. My initials shone with brilliance. Jacopo handed me Aldo's porringer and I started to polish that in turn.

"What happened finally?" I asked. "Did he turn her out of the house?"

"It was last November," said Jacopo, "just after his birthday. He had a small celebration for some of the students from the university, and one lady to act as hostess, Signora Butali." He paused a moment, then added, thinking perhaps to explain something that might seem surprising, even shocking, "Professor Butali was at a conference in Padua at the time. And no doubt it would seem to the signora that, as the guests were all students at her husband's university, there would be nothing improper about her acting as hostess to them. Marta cooked the dinner and I served. The evening was a great success. The students brought their guitars and there was singing, and later the Capitano took the signora home. Marta had been drinking and she wouldn't go to bed—she insisted on staying up until he returned. What happened I don't know, but there was some violent discussion between them, and next morning she packed her things and left and went to live with the Ghigis."

"And Aldo?" I asked.

"It upset him very much," admitted Jacopo. "He took the car and went off alone for about five days. He said he went to the sea. When he came back he told me briefly that he didn't want to discuss Marta or what had happened, and that was that. He continued to keep her, though—he paid for her board and lodging, the Ghigis told me. Marta never told them what had happened either. Even when she was drinking, and that was most of the time after she left here, she told them nothing. She did not as much as mention the Capitano's name. But you know, Signor Beo, it was jealousy, nothing more nor less than common jealousy. That's women for you." He whistled up at the canary, who, swaying on its perch, feathers rumpled, was nearly bursting its small heart in song. "They're all the same," he said, "whether they're women of quality like the signora or peasants like Marta. They try to squeeze a man dry. They come between a man and his work."

I held Aldo's porringer to the light. Through the scrolled initials my own face was reflected back at me. I wondered what they were discussing at 8, via dei Sogni, and whether, when the Heads of the Departments left, the Rector would speak to my brother alone, and if he would mention, deliberately or casually, the anonymous telephone calls.

Then suddenly I knew. The woman who had made the anonymous telephone calls had been Marta. That was why Marta had gone to Rome. Marta, dismissed by Aldo after the birthday dinner in November, had pondered and brooded during the ensuing weeks and months, had guessed perhaps that when

232

Professor Butali fell ill in Rome after Christmas Aldo had grown closer to the signora, seen her more often, perhaps become her lover. Marta, her love and loyalty spurned, her mind disintegrating through drink and despair, had sought revenge upon Aldo by betraying him to the Rector.

I put down the silver porringer and went and stood by the window under the canary's cage. The calls had ceased now for more than a week, the Rector had told me. They had ceased for one good reason: the caller was dead. Now, for the first time in the ten days since it had happened, I was glad that she was dead. The Marta who had died was not the Marta I remembered. Alcohol, like poison, had turned her warm blood sour. Her last act, like that of a sick animal, had been to bite her master's hand, and in taking that final journey she had found death waiting for her at the end of it.

In a sense, it was retribution. The slanderer had been silenced, the serpent had died in its own venom . . . Why did I suddenly remember the crazy maxims of the Falcon, quoted by the German scholar in his lives of the Dukes of Ruffano? "The proud shall be stripped . . . the haughty violated . . . the slanderer silenced, the serpent die in its own venom . . ."

The canary's song finished in one last passionate trill. I looked up at it. The small throat quivered and was still.

"Jacopo," I said slowly, "when was my brother last in Rome?"

Jacopo was setting the silver he had cleaned and polished upon a tray to take it across the way to Aldo's house.

"In Rome, Signor Beo?" he replied. "Let me see, it was the Sunday before last—it will be two weeks this coming Sunday, Palm Sunday. He went to Rome on the Friday to consult some manuscripts in the Biblioteca Nazionale, and then he drove back to Ruffano through the Tuesday night. He likes to drive through the night. He was here for breakfast on Wednesday morning."

Jacopo went through into Aldo's house, carrying the tray, leaving the doors open. I sat down on one of his kitchen chairs, staring in front of me. Aldo could have killed Marta. Aldo could have driven past the church even as the touring coach had done and recognised the humped figure lying inside the porch. He could have got out of the car and gone to speak to her. She could have told him then, drunk and in despair, what she had been trying to do. He could have killed her. I remembered the knife that had slipped so suddenly from his sleeve last night at the ducal

233

palace when he cut the bonds that bound Marelli's hands. Aldo could have carried the knife in Rome. Aldo could have murdered Marta.

I heard footsteps passing the window outside the kitchen. They paused by the double entrance, then turned in at Jacopo's door. A young voice said, "Armino?"

It was the student Cesare. He was wearing my light overcoat and hat and carried my suitcase.

"I've brought your things from the via San Michele," he said. "Giorgio and Domenico kept Signora Silvani engaged in the sitting-room, pestering her for a contribution for the university funds. She did not know that I went upstairs and packed for you. I was there less than five minutes. I've come to take you out of Ruffano."

I looked at him dully. His words were meaningless. Why should I have to leave Ruffano now? My thoughts of the last few minutes had left me numb.

"I'm sorry," he said, "those are Aldo's orders. He arranged everything this morning. If we could have found you we should have got you away sooner."

"I thought," I said, "I was supposed to play the Falcon in the Festival?"

"Not now," he answered. "I'm to drive you to Fano and put you on board a fishing-boat. It's all been fixed. Aldo gave no reason."

My brother had worked quickly. Whether he had taken his decision last night when we parted so abruptly, or later, I could not tell, nor apparently did Cesare know. Perhaps it did not matter. Perhaps nothing mattered. Except that Aldo wanted to be rid of me.

"Very well," I said, "I'm ready."

I stood up, and he gave me my coat and hat. I followed him out of the kitchen. Jacopo came through to the double entrance carrying the empty tray. He nodded when he saw Cesare, and said good day.

"I have to leave, Jacopo," I told him. "I've had my orders."

His face remained inscrutable. "We shall miss you, Signor Beo," he said.

I shook hands with him, and he disappeared back into his own domain. The Alfa-Romeo was parked outside. Cesare opened the door and threw my suitcase into the back. I climbed into the passenger seat, and drove out of the city and on to the Fano road.

I was quitting, for the second time in twenty years, my birthplace and my home. Not, as then, waving an enemy flag, but still a fugitive, flying from a crime I had not committed, acting, perhaps—God knows—as my brother's surrogate. Hence my banishment, hence the flight to Fano. I was laying a false trail, away from Ruffano, away from Aldo.

I watched the road ahead, Ruffano behind us now for ever, hidden by the encircling hills, and the brown earth to the left, stubbled with the fast-growing shoots of corn, was saffron-coloured like the Falcon's robe. The road turned and twisted, and later the river ran to keep us company, soon to empty itself, blue-green and limpid, on to the Adriatic shores, already burning under the April sun. The nearer we drew to Fano the more despairing I became, the more angry, the more lost.

"Cesare," I said, "why do you follow Aldo? What makes you believe in him?"

"We have no one else we can follow," said Cesare, "Giorgio, Romano, Domenico, and the rest. He speaks in a language we understand. Nobody ever has before. We were orphans, and he found us."

"How did he find you?"

"By enquiries, through his old comrades who were partisans. Then he arranged for grants for us with the university Council. There are others who have graduated and left—they owe everything to him."

My brother had done this for me. He had done it because he thought me dead. Now, knowing that I lived, he was sending me away.

"But if he has worked all these years for the university and for students like yourselves who can't afford the fees," I persisted, "why does he want to destroy it now, setting one group of students against another, staging these elaborate hoaxes, the last of which ended in Marelli's death?"

"Do you call them hoaxes?" asked Cesare. "We don't. Nor would Rizzio and Elia. They've learnt humility. As for Marelli, he died because he ran. Didn't the priests teach you as a child? He that seeks to save his life shall lose it?"

"Yes," I replied, "but that's different."

"Is it?" said Cesare. "We don't think so. Nor does Aldo."

235

We were approaching the outskirts of Fano, the houses bleak and impersonal like biscuit tins splayed out upon the landscape. I was filled with a terrible despair.

"Where are you taking me?" I asked.

"To the port," he answered, "to a fisherman, an ex-partisan called Marco. You're to go on board his boat and he'll land you, in a day or so, further up the coast, perhaps at Venice. You don't have to think of anything. He'll wait for further instructions from Aldo."

Depending, I supposed, on what transpired with the police, and whether or not the trail was lost. Whether an absent courier, Armino Fabbio, had disappeared without a trace, successfully.

The rounded bay lay blue and still and the great beach, white like an inverted oyster-shell, was already dotted with the black figures of early tourists. Line upon line of bathing-sheds was being painted for the season. Easter was only another week away. The soft air stank of the humid sea. To the right lay the canal.

"Here we are," said Cesare.

He had drawn up before a café in the via Squero at the canal's edge, near where the fishing-boats were moored. A man in faded jeans, his skin burnt black by sea and sun, was sitting at a table smoking a cigarette, a drink in front of him. At sight of the Alfa-Romeo he sprang to his feet and came over to us. Cesare and I got out, and Cesare handed me my suitcase and my hat and coat.

"This is Armino," he said. "The Capitano sends his regards." The fisherman Marco put out a great hand and shook mine. "You are very welcome," he said. "I shall be pleased to have you on board my boat. Let me take your case and your coat. We will embark very shortly. I was only waiting for you and for my engineer. In the meantime, have a drink."

Never, not even as a child, had I felt more completely in the hands of a fate that was not mine to command. I was like a package dumped upon a quayside before being swung by a crane into a ship's hold. I think Cesare pitied me.

"You'll be all right," he said, "once you're at sea. Have you a message to send Aldo?"

What message could I send beyond what he must already know—that what I was doing now I did for him?

"Tell him," I said, "that before the proud were stripped and the haughty violated, the slanderer was silenced and the viper died in its own venom."

236

The words meant nothing to Cesare. It was his comrade Federico who had translated the German history. The manuscripts my brother had consulted in Rome would have borne Duke Claudio's maxims too.

"Goodbye," he said, "and good luck."

He climbed back into the car, and in a moment he had gone. The fisherman Marco was watching me with curiosity. He asked me what would I drink, and I told him a beer.

"So you're the Capitano's young brother?" he asked me. "You're not a scrap like him."

"Unfortunately," I replied.

"He's a fine man," he went on. "We fought in the hills side by side, we escaped from the same enemy. Now, when he needs a change from all his activities, he gets in touch with me and comes to sea." He smiled, and handed me a cigarette. "The sea blows away the dust," he said, "and all the cares and troubles of city life. You'll find it does the same to you. Your brother looked a sick man when he came here last November. Five days afloat— it was winter, mind you—and he had recovered."

The attendant brought my beer. I raised the glass and wished my companion fortune.

"Was that after his birthday?" I asked.

"Birthday? He said nothing about a birthday. It was somewhere around the third week of the month. 'I've had a shock, Marco,' he told me when he arrived. 'Don't ask me any questions. I'm with you to forget it.' Anyway, there was nothing wrong with him physically. He was as tough as in the old days, and worked like one of the crew. Something else had been worrying him, no doubt. Perhaps a woman." He raised his glass in answer to my toast. "Good health to you," he said, "and may you lose your troubles at sea also."

I drank my beer and thought of what Marco had said. It was evident that Aldo had sought him out after the birthday dinner and the quarrel with Marta. She must have railed at him, drunk, as Jacopo said, and outraged, like all peasants who are deeply religious and bound by a moral code. She must have taxed him with starting an affair with a married woman, and that woman the Rector's wife. The quarrel would have angered my brother, which was the reason he sent Marta from the house. But why did he talk of a shock?

Footsteps approached and another man stood before the table.

Short and grizzled, he was burnt even blacker by the sun than Marco.

"This is Franco," said Marco, "my mate and engineer."

Franco stuck out a hand hairy as a monkey's paw, and covered with grease.

"Two hours' work still to do," he said to his skipper. "I thought it best to warn you, as it means delay in sailing."

Marco cursed and spat, then turned to me with a shrug of his shoulder.

"I promised your brother we would be at sea by noon," he said. "That was when he telephoned early this morning. Next, it seemed, there was difficulty in finding you. And now our engine has to give trouble. We shall be lucky if we are away by five." He stood up and pointed along the canal to where the vessels were moored. "See the blue boat there, with the yellow mast and the centre dog-house?" he said. "That's our craft, the 'Garibaldi'. Franco and I will take your case and coat aboard and you can follow us later, within the hour. Will that suit you, or would you prefer to come with us right away?"

"No," I said, "no, I'll stay here and finish my drink."

They walked off along the side of the canal and I sat outside the café, watching until they had climbed aboard. My quarters for the next few days did not tempt me. Marco was right when he told me I did not look like my brother. I was a seasoned traveller on land, but not on water. As a courier I had disgraced myself by being seasick in the Bay of Naples before my clients. The flat oily swell of the Adriatic looked equally repellent.

I sat there, finishing my beer. It was the dead hour of the day. I wondered if the meeting in the via dei Sogni was over. Presently I got up and wandered aimlessly along the side of the canal, but instead of going directly to the boat turned left and strolled on to the beach. Already the sun-worshippers were stripped and lying with torsos naked to the sky. Children screamed and paddled at the water's edge. The bathing-sheds, sticky with new paint, stood in rows, one behind the other, and in front of them, orange and brilliant red, the sun umbrellas spread canopies above the glaring sand. Despondency was heavy within me. I could not shake it off.

A group of children in grey uniforms with hair cropped short, escorted by a nun, came clumping down the beach towards the sea. They pointed to the water, their small faces alight with stupendous surprise, and turning to the nun ran to her, begging permission to take off their shoes. She gave it, her eyes kindly behind her gold-rimmed spectacles.

"Quietly now, children, quietly," she said, and as she bent to gather together their shoes her skirts and wimple billowed about her like a balloon. The children, suddenly released and free, ran with uplifted arms towards the sea.

"They're happy, anyway," I said.

"Their first visit to the sea," answered the nun. "They all come from orphanages inland, and at Easter we have a camp for them here at Fano. There is another camp at Ancona."

The children were knee deep in the water, shouting and splashing one another. "I shouldn't let them do that," said the nun, "but I ask myself, what does it matter? They have so little joy."

One little fellow, having stubbed his toe, burst into tears and came running up the beach towards her. She took him in her arms and comforted him, found a plaster from within her ample robes and placed it on his toe, sending him back again to join the others.

"This is the part of the work I like best," she confided, "bringing the children to the sea. The Sisters of the various organisations take it in turns. I have not far to come. I'm from Ruffano."

The world was small. I thought of the bleak building near to the now resplendent Hotel Panorama.

"The foundling hospital," I said. "I know it. I'm from Ruffano too, but long ago. I never went inside the hospital."

"The building needs replanning," she said, "and we may have to move. There is talk of building us new quarters at Ancona, where the former Superintendent of our hospital died."

We stood together, watching the children splashing in the sea.

"Are they all orphans?" I asked, thinking of Cesare.

"Yes, all," she said, "either orphaned, or left on the hospital doorsteps within a few hours of their birth. Sometimes the mother is too weak to move far, and we find her, and look after her and her baby. Then she goes to work, leaving the baby with us. Sometimes, but very rarely, it is possible to find a home where both are taken in." She raised her hand, and waved to the children not to venture in too far. "That is the happiest answer," she said, "both for the mother and the child. But there are not many people who will offer their home to a foundling these days. Occasionally a young married couple will have lost their first child at birth and come to us to seek another to replace it quickly, so bringing the child up as their own." She turned to me, smiling once more behind her spectacles. "But that," she said, "requires great confidence between the bereaved parents and the superintendent of the foundling hospital. The record remains a secret for ever afterwards. It's better for everyone concerned."

"Yes," I said, "yes, I suppose so."

She took a whistle from some capacious pocket within her skirt and blew it twice. The children turned their heads and stared, then rushed from the water up the beach towards her, scampering like little dogs.

"You see?" she said, laughing. "I have them very well trained."

I looked at my watch. I was well-trained as well. It would soon be four. Perhaps I should go and find my way on board the "Garibaldi" and settle in.

"If you come from Ruffano too," said the nun, "you should call in some time and see the children there. Not these, of course, but those I look after at the foundling hospital."

"Thank you," I lied politely, "perhaps I will," and then, more from courtesy than from curiosity, I said, "Will you move to the new orphanage at Ancona if they decide to build there?"

"Oh, yes," she said, "my life is with the children. Some fifty years ago I was a foundling too."

A kind of pity seized me. The plain, contented face had known no other existence, no other world. She, and hundreds like her, had been dumped upon a doorstep to find mercy.

"At Ruffano?" I asked.

"Yes," she said, "but it was harder for us in those days. The rules were strict, the life was spartan. No seaside holidays for orphans then, despite the kindness of our Superintendent, Luigi Speca."

The children had arrived and she gathered them round her in a semicircle and produced oranges and apples from a carrier bag.

"Luigi Speca?" I repeated.

"Yes," she answered, "but he died many years ago, in 1929. He was buried in Ancona, as I told you."

I said goodbye to her and thanked her. I don't know what I thanked her for. Perhaps it was for illumination from God. Perhaps the shaft of sunlight that fell upon my face as I turned west and walked up the beach beyond the bathing huts was like the blinding stroke that hit Saul upon the Damascus road.

Suddenly I perceived. Suddenly I knew. My father's letter and the double baptismal entry were made plain. Aldo had been a foundling too. Their son had died, Luigi Speca had given them Aldo. The secret, held for nearly forty years, had been betrayed by Marta last November. Aldo, proud of his lineage, proud of his heritage, proud of all he held most dear, had learnt the truth and kept it to himself these past five months. It was Aldo who had been stripped and violated, Aldo who had lost face, not to the friends who did not know, but in his own eyes. The hoaxer had been hoaxed. He who had wanted to unmask hypocrisy had been himself unmasked.

I walked along the canal side in the opposite direction from the boat, and so into the town. My few belongings were on board the "Garibaldi", but they meant nothing. I had only one thought in mind, and that was to go to Aldo. Somewhere in Fano there must be a train, a bus, that would take me back to Ruffano. Tomorrow was the Festival, and I had to be with Aldo when the Falcon fell.

CHAPTER TWENTY-ONE

WHEN I REACHED the bus station I realised that I only had two thousand lire in my pocket-book. I was to have gone to the Registrar's office at the university that morning to receive my salary, but owing to my visit to Signora Butali, and because of hiding in Carla Raspa's apartment, I had never gone. I remembered too that I owed Signora Silvani for my lodging. Perhaps Aldo would have thought of that.

A car to Ruffano would cost more than two thousand lire. I enquired at the bus depot and was told that the last bus for Ruffano had left at half-past three. One was about to leave for Pesaro along the coast, and since Pesaro was some ten kilometres nearer to my destination than Fano I boarded it at once. As the road traversed the canal I looked right, towards the port, and thought of the partisan Marco and his mate Franco working on the engine, waiting for me to join them. When I did not turn up they would go into the town and look for me, enquire in the bars and cafés. Then Marco would telephone Aldo and tell him that I had vanished.

I looked out of the window, trying to make plans. If Aldo had killed Marta he had done so, not because she threatened to betray his possible liaison with Signora Butali, but because she intended to expose the secret of his birth. The Director of the Arts Council was not Donati's son but a foundling, the least of Ruffano's citizens, and this to Aldo meant unendurable humility and shame. What I wanted to do was to tell Aldo that I understood. That I did not care. That he was as much my brother now as always, that everything of mine was his. As a boy he had cherished and tormented me in turn, as a man he did so still. But I knew now what I had never known before, that he was vulnerable. Because of this, at long last, we should meet on equal terms.

The twelve kilometres to Pesaro were soon covered. I got down from the bus and studied the time-table to Ruffano. There was a bus at half-past five. I had just an hour to wait. I began to wander down the street, full of pedestrians, many of them tourists as aimless as myself, staring in shop windows or bound for the attractions of the beach beyond the town. Prolonged hooting sounded in my ear, two vespas swerved close to the pavement beside me and a girl's voice called, "Armino!" There were whistles and shouts. I turned, and there were Caterina and Paolo Pasquale on a vespa, she riding pillion, and behind them the two students Gino and Mario from the Silvani pensione.

"Caught you," called Caterina. "You can't escape. We know all about you, and how you sneaked upstairs and fetched your things, and went off without paying Signora Silvani what you owed her."

They all four dismounted and surrounded me. Passers-by turned to stare.

"Listen," I said, "I can explain . . ."

"You'd better explain," interrupted Paolo. "You can't treat the Silvanis that way; we won't allow it. Hand over the money now, or we'll turn you in to the police."

"I haven't got the money," I said. "I've got less than two thousand lire on me."

We were blocking the route. Someone in a passing car shouted at the students. Paolo jerked his head at Caterina.

"Follow us to the café Rossini," he said. "Armino shall ride behind me on the vespa. We'll get some sense out of him there. Gino and Mario, follow along behind; see he doesn't try any tricks."

There was nothing for it but to do as he said. To have argued further would have meant more trouble. Shrugging, I climbed behind him on the vespa and we shot off in the midst of the traffic to the piazza del Popolo, coming to a stop beside the colonnade beneath Pesaro's ducal palace. Here both vespas were parked, and with Paolo leading the way, and Gino and Mario on either side of me, I was marched to a small café-bar a few yards off. We went in, and Paolo pointed to a table near the window.

"This will do," he said. "Caterina will join us directly."

He ordered beer for all, including me, and when the waiter had disappeared he turned and faced me, his arms folded on the table.

"Now then," he asked, "what have you got to say?"

"I'm wanted by the police," I said. "I had to run."

The three students exchanged glances. "That's what Signora Silvani thought," Gino burst in. "Someone was enquiring for you this morning, but he didn't say why. He looked like a police agent in plain clothes."

"I know," I said, "I spotted him. That's why I ran. That's why I didn't pick up what was due to me from the Registrar's office, and why I couldn't pay Signora Silvani. If you were in my shoes you'd have done the same."

The three of them stared at me. The waiter arrived with our drinks, set them down and went away.

"What have you done?" asked Paolo.

"Nothing," I replied, "but the evidence is strong against me. In point of fact I believe I'm taking the rap for somebody else. If that's the case, I'll go on doing so. The other fellow happens to be my brother."

Caterina arrived, dishevelled and out of breath. She dragged forward a chair and sat between Paolo and me.

"What's happened?" she asked.

Paolo explained briefly. Caterina looked at me in turn.

"I believe him," she said, after a moment. "We've known him for a week. He's not the sort to run without good reason. Is it something to do with the tourist agency where you worked before coming to Ruffano?"

"Yes," I said. Which in a back-handed way was true.

Mario, who had remained silent up to now, leant forward. "Why Pesaro?" he asked. "With only two thousand lire. How do you plan to get away from here?"

They were no longer truculent or mistrustful. Gino handed me a cigarette. I looked at them, and thought how they were of the same generation as Cesare, Giorgio and Domenico. They were all young. They were all untried. However much they differed in their outlook, in their aims, fundamentally they were all eager for adventure and for life.

I said, "I've had time to think, the past few hours. I realise now it was a mistake to leave Ruffano. I want to go back. I was going to take the bus at half-past five."

They watched me silently, drinking their beer. I think they were puzzled.

"Why go back?" asked Paolo. "Won't the police get you?"

"Perhaps," I said. "But I'm no longer afraid. Don't ask me why."

They did not laugh or mock. They treated my admission seriously, just as Cesare or Domenico would have done.

"This isn't a thing that I can discuss with you in detail," I told them, "but my brother is in Ruffano, using another name. What's happened between us, if he's done what I think he's done, is because of family pride. I've got to straighten it out. I've got to talk to him."

This they understood. They pressed no questions. A live interest showed in all four faces. Caterina, impulsive, touched my arm.

"That makes sense," she said, "at any rate to me. If I was suspected of something I believed Paolo had done, even though I might take the blame for it I should want to know his reason. There must be honesty between people tied by blood. Paolo and I are twins. Perhaps that makes us closer."

"It's not just ties of family," said Gino, "it's ties of friendship too. I might take the blame for something Mario did, but first I should have to know why."

"Is that how you feel about your brother?" asked Caterina.

"Yes," I said, "it is."

They drank their beer and then Paolo said, "We'll see Signora Silvani gets her money. That's a small point now. The immediate thing is to get you to Ruffano, and at the same time dodge the police. We'll help you. But we've got to make a plan."

Their generosity moved me. Why did they have faith in me? There was no reason for it. Any more than there had been reason for Carla Raspa to let me hide in her apartment. I might have been a murderer, yet she believed in me. I could be a common swindler, yet the students trusted me.

"But of course," said Caterina suddenly, "the Festival. We just disguise Armino as one of us in the insurrection, and I defy any police agent to pick him out from amongst two thousand others."

"Disguise him how?" asked Gino. "You know Donati told our crowd to turn up just as we are."

"That's it," said Caterina, "in shirts, jeans, sweaters, anything. Look at Armino. That city suit, that shirt, those shoes. He even dresses like a courier! Give him a different hair-cut, and a coloured shirt inside a pair of jeans, and he won't even recognise himself."

"Caterina's right," said Paolo. "Let's take him to the nearest barber and get him crew-cut. Then we'll find him something to wear in the market-place. We'll share the cost all round. All right, Armino, keep your two thousand lire; you may need them."

I became a lay-figure in their hands. We left the café, Paolo paying for the drinks, and I was taken to a barber who transformed me from what I had hitherto believed myself to be, an elegant representative of Sunshine Tours, Genoa, into an undistinguished back-street hipster. This transformation became even more pronounced when they escorted me later to a cut-price store, and there, behind a row of bargain goods, I divested myself of my one good suit—the other was in the suitcase on board the "Garibaldi"—and donned a pair of black jeans, with a leather belt, a jade green shirt, an ersatz leather jerkin and a pair of sneakers. My own clothes were put in a parcel and handed to Caterina, who told me they were terrible, and she would do her best to lose them. They stood me in front of a mirror in the store, and—I suppose it was chiefly the hair-cut—I doubted if even Aldo would recognise me. I might have been an immigrant just landed on American shores, a semi-barbarian already, with only the flick-knife missing.

"You look terrific," said Caterina, squeezing my hand, "much better than before."

"You have style now," said Gino. "Before you had nothing."

Their admiration both baffled and discouraged me. If the object I now was pleased their aesthetic taste, what point in common had we? Or were they merely being kind?

"We'll live it up a little longer yet," said Paolo. "No need to return to Ruffano before dark. Caterina shall catch a later bus, and Armino ride with me. We'll escort the bus on our motorbikes. Let's go and see if the Sports Palace is open. Caterina, you meet us there."

Once again I mounted behind Paolo, and for the next few hours I enjoyed the doubtful pleasure of a student's holiday. We careered backwards and forwards by the beach, by the hotels, up and down the viale Trieste, sometimes racing in company with Gino and Mario, sometimes chasing tourist cars. We patronised the cafés with the loudest radios and the most crowded bars, ending up at a restaurant where we consumed bowlfuls of brodetto, the fish soup flavoured with saffron, garlic and tomato that Marta used to make me as a child. Finally, when it was nearing nine, we took Caterina, still carrying my discarded clothes, to catch her bus, and escorting it on either side, much to the disgust and fury of both driver and conductor, we rode back to Ruffano. What fate awaited me no longer mattered. I had ceased to care, while standing on the beach at Fano some five hours before. I clung to Paolo's belt, and like outriders to the bus we scorched and swerved over the intervening hills.

Ruffano, a celestial city, rose in front of us with a thousand winking lights, the flood-lit Duomo and campanile seeming to shine with a white radiance between either summit. Here from the east the ducal palace was screened by other buildings, but the pale glow in the sky revealed its presence and that of the university beyond, while staring across the slopes directly facing us as we rode towards the encircling wall below would be the lights from my old home in the via dei Sogni, where the Butalis must now be dining.

From one of those windows, impossible to discern amongst its neighbours, Aldo and I had looked across the valley here as boys, feeling ourselves superior to those who lived in the farmsteads beneath, and as I remembered this, clinging tight to Paolo's belt as we approached the porta Malebranche, I glanced up instinctively to the row of lights, uniform and straight, that came from the foundling hospital on the northern hill. There, in that cold building, forlorn, unclaimed, Aldo would have spent his childhood but for my father and for Luigi Speca. There, clad in a grey overall, with close-cropped head, he would have been a foundling boy, and matured, adult, he would have borne another name. I, the only son of my parents' later years, would have been christened Aldo in his stead.

The thought was sobering, even chastening. I should have been different too. Instead of growing up in Aldo's shadow, fearful, overawed, docile to his command, the whole course of my life must have been otherwise. We passed under the porta Malebranche and I knew I would not have it changed. He might not be my brother, he might not be my parents' son, but from the beginning he had possessed me, body, heart and soul, and he possessed me still. He was my god, he was my devil too. Through all the years I had believed him dead my world had been empty, without meaning.

The bus ground to a halt inside the city gate. Paolo and I, with our companion vespa, shot away to the northern summit and the piazza del Duca Carlo. Here, the scene of Tuesday's episode, Duke Carlo, floodlit as he had been then, gazed down benignly on the crowd beneath him. Students and Ruffanesi milled backwards and forwards across the piazza and around the gardens under the statue. The Honours graduates paraded wearing medallions strung on chains, as was the custom, so Paolo informed me, applauded and followed by strings of admiring fellow-students. Extempore music filled the air—mouth-organs, whistles and guitars. Proud parents watched and strolled with indulgent eyes. The inevitable collecting-boxes rattled. Crackers burst and dogs fled howling. Those who possessed cars drove slowly along the piazza, while the vespas, ours amongst them, roared and spluttered in an ever-widening circle.

"What did I tell you?" said Paolo as two carabinieri wandered sedately past us, immaculate in uniform. "Neither those fellows, nor a dozen others in plain clothes, would look at you. Tonight you're one of us."

The largest crowd of students had formed themselves into a group some hundreds strong outside Professor Elia's house, and were shouting and calling for him.

"Elia . . . Elia . . " they chanted, and then, as for one brief moment he appeared and waved to them from the front door of his house, a burst of cheering came from the assembled students. Grouped behind him were his associates and members of his Department, and it seemed to me as he stood there, smiling and waving, that something of self-confidence and bravura had returned, yet not quite all. A momentary hesitation when, on the fringe of the crowd, an unseen student shouted "Where are your bathing briefs?", followed immediately by an explosive burst from a cracker and a gulf of involuntary laughter, suggested, as the professor gave a final wave and then withdrew, that the memory of Tuesday night was with him still.

"Who said that?" cried Gino angrily, turning, with many others, to the back of the crowd from where the disturbance came, and at once the murmur rose from all about us, "It's an Arts man from the other hill. Get him, murder him . . ." In a moment all was confusion, heads turned, the crowd broke up, people began to run.

"A foretaste of what's to come," said Paolo in my ear. "Why worry about him now? We'll get the lot tomorrow."

Once more he set the vespa in motion, and Caterina, appearing suddenly from the midst of the crowd, dashed forward and climbed on to the narrow space between the handle bars.

"Come on," she said breathlessly, "it will take the three of us. Let's see what's doing on the other hill."

We swerved out of the piazza del Duca Carlo, followed by Gino and Mario, and so on to the encircling road on the south-west side of Ruffano, beneath the city walls. Now the façade of the ducal palace shone in splendour, the twin towers paramount, and it was as if the whole edifice was suspended there between heaven and earth, carved out in silhouette against a canopy of stars. We roared down into the valley and up on to the southern hill, but as we topped the rise beneath the students' hostel and the new university buildings we saw at once that the intermediate roads were blocked. A group of students was there, and not only in force but armed.

"What is it? Are the Arts crowd rehearsing?" shouted Gino as we caught the flash of steel. But they were running down the hill towards us, silently, not shouting, and as Gino braked with his foot and swerved a spear came hurtling through the air and struck the ground in front of us. "Come on at your risk!" a voice called. "My God," cried Paolo, "that's no rehearsal!", and braking, like Gino, he turned, before a second spear could follow the first.

We plunged back the way we had come, down into the valley beneath the city walls, braking to a halt on the further side, where we dismounted, staring at one another, while in the distance the floodlit ducal palace shone unheeding and serene. All four faces were white. Caterina was trembling, but with excitement, not with fear.

"Now we know," said Gino, breathing quickly. "That's what they have in store for us tomorrow."

"We were warned," said Paolo quietly. "Donati warned us at the theatre on Monday night. It's a question of striking first, that's all. If we get their forward lines with stones and break them up we can rush them and fight close before they have time to launch those spears or use their swords."

"All the same," said Mario, "we ought to tell our leaders what we've seen. Aren't they meeting tonight in the via dei Martiri?"

"Yes," said Gino.

Paolo turned to me. "This may not be your fight, but you're part of it now," he said. "What about your brother? Is he connected with the university?"

"Indirectly," I said.

249

"Then you had better warn him what he'll be in for if he goes on the streets tomorrow."

"I think he knows," I answered.

Caterina stamped her foot impatiently. "Why waste time talking?" she asked. "Shouldn't we spread the word round amongst all our crowd?" Her small face, passionate and white, looked suddenly distorted under her cloud of hair. "None of us should go to bed tonight," she said. "We ought to bring the others out here into the countryside and dig for stones. We'll never find stones inside the city. They should be jagged, this size," she formed a circle with her hands, "and bound with rope, so that we can swing them with greater force."

"Catte's right," said Gino. "Let's get moving. First to the via dei Martiri to tell the leaders—they may want to issue new instructions. Come on, Mario."

He swung himself on to his machine, Mario behind him, and took the road towards the porta dei Martiri.

Paolo looked at me. "Well," he asked, "what now? Do you want us to take you to your brother?"

"No," I said.

I had made up my mind. To return to the pensione would achieve nothing. Aldo might even hand me over to his students with orders to drive me straight to Fano again. Whereas tomorrow . . . Tomorrow the cortège of the Falcon would leave the piazza del Duca Carlo at ten a.m. What it would consist of I did not know. Nobody seemed to know. But Aldo would be with it, that I felt certain.

The night was warm. The leather jerkin bought at Pesaro was protection enough. I would spend the night in the open on one of the benches in the public gardens behind the piazza del Duca Carlo.

When I told Paolo this he shrugged his shoulders. "If that's how you want it, we won't prevent you," he said, "but you'll join us in the morning, remember. We shall be on the steps of San Cipriano. If you're not in your place by nine you may be stopped. Here, take this." He handed me a knife. "I'll get another out of Gino," he said. "After what we've seen tonight you're going to need it."

Caterina and I climbed once more on to his machine, and we scorched our way up the northern hill again. The crowds had thinned. Townsfolk and students, relatives and visiting tourists, were wending their way downhill to the city centre. I should have the public gardens to myself.

"Don't forget," said Caterina, "to fill your pockets with stones. You'll find plenty there, under the trees. And take your parcel. It will do as a pillow. We'll look out for you tomorrow, and good luck."

I watched them swerve down the hill and out of sight, and as they disappeared suddenly, without warning, the floodlights were extinguished everywhere. The statue of Duke Carlo became a shadow. The campanile by the Duomo struck eleven. The city churches followed, one by one. And when the last note sounded I stretched myself out on a bench in the gardens, the parcel as a pillow, and with folded arms stared up at the darkening sky.

CHAPTER TWENTY-TWO

I DON'T REMEMBER SLEEPING. There were just gaps in time between periods of cold. There was a moment when I stamped up and down blowing on my hands, so stiff and numb that I nearly crept for shelter within the comparative warmth of Professor Elia's portico, but did not do so because my vigil in the open was, in its strange way, a sort of test. Aldo had done this in the past, night after night, amongst his partisans. Romano, Antonio, Roberto . . . the boys brought up in the hills during the Resistance years, they had lived thus as children, but not I. The sleazy furnishing of second-rate hotels, not mountains, formed my background. My ceiling was an apartment room, cramped, confining, not the sky. The adults who spoilt and petted me to win favour from my mother spoke an alien tongue. Their uniforms stank, not of sweat and the clean earth as the torn clothes of the partisans would have done, but of yesterday's spilt wine, of perspiration dribbled out in lust instead of in war. Aldo and his comrades, the orphaned boys and theirs, had the hard ground for bed, or at most a sleeping-bag, while I lay stifled with eider-downs and coverlets in a small room next my mother's, the partition thin; and the night-cries of the hills were never mine, nor the sound of mountain streams, nor the echo of storms, only the sighs of pleasure's aftermath.

Therefore tonight, at least, I would share in fantasy the beauty and the hardship of a reality I had not known. However cold I became, however numb, these sensations made me a partner in what had been. The stiffness of my limbs became an offering, my body's chill belated sacrifice.

As I have said, there was a gap in time between sleeping and waking, and then when the temperature was lowest I awoke and went and stood close to the orphanage gate, and watched the dawn break on Ruffano. First light was grey and cold, a phantom day, a temporary shifting of night's shadows, and then the sky hardened, becoming white, and the shrouded city turned to rose. The sun came up over the sleeping hills. Arrows of gold broke up the patterned valleys, then struck the shuttered windows of

252

the city. The trees in the municipal gardens rustled, and the hesitant birds, waking to another day, stirred and murmured, then, as the light strengthened and the sunlight touched them, sang.

Day after day I had awakened as a child to Aldo's voice, or to Marta calling from the kitchen, but not to this. Then there had seemed security and certainty, morning promised an eternity. Now as the sun turned the city's spires to swords and the rounded Duomo to a ball of fire, I knew there was no promise and no eternity, or if eternity only a repetition of a million ages gone with none to care and all the dead extinguished. The men who had built Ruffano lived in memory alone. This was their epitaph. They had created beauty, and it was enough. They lived for a brief span to burn and die.

I wondered then why we should desire more, why we should yearn to perpetuate ourselves in some everlasting paradise. Man was Prometheus, bound to his symbol rock the earth and all the other undiscovered stars that shamed the dark. The challenge was to dare. To brave extinction.

I went on standing there, watching the sun bring warmth and life to my city of Ruffano. I thought, not only of Aldo but of all those students, now asleep, who in a few hours would be fighting in the streets. This Festival was neither play nor pageant, nor a mock representation of mediaeval splendour, but a summons to destroy. I could no more stop it than any single man could stop a war. Even if the order came at the last moment to cancel the Festival display, the students would disregard it. They wanted to fight. They wanted to kill. Just as their forebears had done through centuries in the same haunted, bloody streets. This time I should not escape, I should be one of them.

It was nearing seven when I heard the horses first. The steady clopping sound came from the piazza behind me, and turning I walked back to the statue and I saw the leading string climb the summit of the hill. They came in pairs, each rider leading a second horse, and they were approaching from the long road leading up to Ruffano from the valley below.

Then I remembered how last night, when we were circling the city on our vespas, I had seen lights in the sports stadium to the right of us, which in the excitement of our ride I had soon forgotten. The horses and their escort must have camped there before sundown, and were now arriving in the piazza to take part in the display. This was the cortège mentioned by Aldo in the ducal palace on Wednesday night.

The riders dismounted, leading their horses to the shelter of the trees. The sun was drawing the moisture from the ground, and it rose like steam from the soaking grass about Duke Carlo's statue, filling the morning air with scent like hay.

I drew nearer and counted the horses. There were eighteen of them, sleek and beautiful, their proud heads lifted curiously to stare about them. None of them was saddled. Their coats shone as though polished, and their tails, whisking at the first flies of the day, were like the proud plumes of conquerors. I went up and spoke to one of the men.

"Where do they come from?" I enquired.

"From Senigallia," he said.

I stared at him, disbelieving. "You mean these are race-horses?" I asked.

"Yes," he answered, smiling, "every one of them. Lent for the Festival, each horse specially trained for this display. They've been training in the hills all winter."

"Training for what?" I asked.

This time it was he who stared. "Why, for this morning's run, what else?" he said. "Don't they tell you what's to happen in your own city?"

"No," I said, "no. All we've been told is that a cortège leaves here at ten for the ducal palace."

"A cortège?" he repeated. "Well, you can call it that, but it's a poor description of what you are going to see." He laughed, and called to one of his companions. "Here's a student from Ruffano," he said, "wants to know what's going to happen. Break it gently."

"Keep out of the way," said the second man, "that's all. The horses are insured, that's what matters to their owners." And then he added, "It was tried out, so they told us, some five hundred years ago, and never since. They must breed madmen in your city. But if he breaks his neck it's his affair, not ours. Here, look at this."

A van had now drawn up by the side of the piazza, and the man beside the driver jumped out and opened the rear doors. They let down a ramp and then, with great care, two men to the shaft and two to the wheels, they lowered a small vehicle painted red and gold. It was a perfect replica of a Roman chariot, and bore upon the front and above each wheel the insignia of the Malebranche, the Falcon with spread wings.

So it was true. The crazy, fantastic feat attempted by Duke Claudio more than five centuries ago was to be repeated now. The pages I had quoted mockingly from the German history to Aldo last Sunday as Jehu's feat, never for one moment thinking that any representation of the event would be other than a staged affair with perhaps two horses—and he himself on Wednesday had spoken of it simply as a cortège—would be translated into fact. Duke Claudio had driven eighteen horses from the northern to the southern hill. There were eighteen horses before me now. It was not possible. It could not be. I tried to remember what the history said. "He was set upon and pursued by almost the entire populace, after having trampled many of them to death beneath his horses' hooves."

Now a second van drew into the piazza, smaller than the first, and from this they lowered harness, traces, collars, ornamented with studs bearing the Falcon's head, and carried these things to the shelter of the trees where the horses stood, and the smell of the leather, polished and bitter-sweet like spice, mingled with the warm horse flesh and the scent of trees.

The grooms in attendance upon the horses began to sort the harness and the other appurtenances, quietly, methodically, chatting amongst themselves. The very orderliness of the sight, the absence of fuss, as if what they did was just part of a regular morning routine, made it the more fantastic, and as the sun rose higher and the horror of what was to happen became more imminent, I felt a sort of terror invade my whole being. It started in my guts and seized my heart, at the same time paralysing thought. Hearing was keener. Every sound was magnified. The church bells had sounded for first Mass at six, then once more at seven, then at eight. They seemed, to my imagination now in turmoil, to be the summons to a city's doom, until I remembered that it was Passion week, and this the Friday dedicated to the Mother of God. When we were young Marta had escorted us to San Cipriano and we had laid bunches of wild flowers before the statuette, which, its painted prettiness veiled, symbolised the seven sorrows that pierced the heart. It seemed to me then, kneeling in bewilderment, that the Mother played a sorry part in her Son's story, first goading Him to change the water into wine, and later standing with relatives on the crowd's fringe, calling to

Him in vain, receiving no answer. Perhaps this was the seventh sorrow that struck her down, which the priests in Ruffano's churches were now commemorating. If so, they would do better to forget one woman's pain and go out into the streets and prevent mass murder.

Now a cordon was being formed around the piazza by uniformed police to keep away the traffic and the early crowd. They smiled and joked, good-natured for this day of Festival, and now and again called out laughing instructions to the grooms, busy with their dressing of the horses.

The nightmare scene became more vivid, more appalling. None of them knew, none of them understood. I went up to one of the policemen and touched him on the shoulder.

"Can't it be stopped?" I said. "Can't it be prevented? It's not too late, even now."

He looked down at me, a big cheerful fellow, wiping the sweat from his brow. "If you've got a seat in a window along the route get to it," he said. "There'll be no one on the streets after nine, except performers."

He had not heard what I said. He was not interested. His job was to see that the piazza was kept clear for the horses and the chariot. He moved away. Panic enveloped me. I did not know where to go, what to do. This must be the fear that comes upon men before a battle when only discipline and training saves them. I had no such discipline, no such training. The desire of a child to flee, to hide himself, to stifle sight and sound, was paramount. I began to run towards the trees in the municipal gardens, thinking that if I flung myself head downward amongst the shrubs and grass the world would be blotted out. Then, as I blundered forward into the splurge of colour made up by the horses and the jingling harness, the gaily-painted chariot and the heedless grooms, I saw the Alfa-Romeo come up into the piazza. The driver must have seen me too, for the car braked suddenly and stopped, and I altered my useless panic course and ran towards it. The door opened, and Aldo sprang out and caught me as I fell.

He jerked me to my feet and I clung to him, stammering, incoherent. "Don't let it happen," I heard myself saying. "Don't let it happen, please, God, no . . ."

He hit me, and the oblivion I had sought for came. Pain brought darkness and release. When I opened my eyes, dizzy and sick, my head swimming, I found myself propped against a tree. Aldo was squatting by me, pouring steaming coffee from a thermos jug.

"Drink this," he said, "then eat."

He gave me the cup and I drank. Then he broke a roll in half and forced it into my mouth. Mechanically I did what I was told.

"You disobeyed orders," he said. "If a partisan did that we shot him instantly. That is, if we found him. Otherwise he was left to rot alone up in the hills."

The coffee warmed me. The dry bread tasted crisp and good. I snatched at a second roll, and then a third.

"Orders disobeyed put other men to inconvenience," he continued. "Time is wasted. Plans are disrupted. Go on, drink some more."

The preparations went on about us, the horses stamped, the harness jingled.

"Cesare gave me your message," he said. "When I got it I telephoned the café at Fano and asked them to fetch Marco to speak to me. When he told me you hadn't turned up at the boat I guessed something of this sort might happen. But I didn't think you would come here."

The panic had gone, whether because of the blow he had struck me, or because the food and drink he had given me filled my craving belly, I did not know.

"Where else should I go?" I asked him.

"To the police, possibly," he shrugged, "thinking by accusing me to clear yourself. It wouldn't have worked, you know. They would never have believed you." He got up, and crossing to one of the grooms picked up a wash-leather, soaked it in a pail of water and came back. "Wash your face with this," he said. "There's blood on your mouth."

I cleaned myself after a fashion, then ate another roll and had a second drink of coffee.

"I know why you killed Marta," I said. "I came back, not with any idea of going to the police—they can arrest me if they want to—but to tell you that I understand."

I stood up, throwing the soaking leather back to him and brushing the earth off my clothes. I had forgotten until then how insignificant I must look, scruffy and unshaven in my black jeans with the jade green shirt, my hair with the new cut shaped like a convict. Aldo, dressed as I had seen him at the ducal palace on Wednesday night in doublet and hose, with a short cape slung from his shoulders, resplendent, elegant, looked part of the background, just as the horses did, parading now beneath Duke Carlo's statue.

"There are two baptismal entries in the San Cipriano records," I said. "One for a son that died, the second for you. The double entries made no sense to me when I read them for the first time last week, nor your sponsor's name, Luigi Speca, nor even the letter I gave you on Wednesday night. It was only yesterday on the beach at Fano that I guessed the truth. There was a nun there, with a little group of orphan boys. She told me the Superintendent of Ruffano foundling hospital, some forty years ago, was called Luigi Speca."

Aldo stared down at me, unsmiling. Then, abruptly, he turned on his heel and left me. He walked over to the horses and began giving orders to the grooms. I watched and waited. The long preliminaries of harnessing began. Each horse was fitted with its own decorated collar, scarlet with golden flanges, and the bridles they had been wearing up to now were changed to others, decorated as the collars were, bearing across the headstrap a medallion of a Falcon's head. Two of the horses were fitted with small saddles close to their collars, fastened by broad bands of scarlet round their chests. The chariot was then drawn up to them and the pole attached to the saddles by golden chains. These yoked horses were the centre pair, bearing the chariot between them, but then I saw that two more horses were being coupled to the centre pair on either side, making six in all, their traces fastened to the chariot front. The twelve remaining horses in groups of four were harnessed in their turn, some distance ahead of the chariot bearers and their fellows, their reins leading back to the arched chariot top. The chariot itself, a featherweight above the rubber mounted wheels, had a semicircular guard around the front and sides and a floor to stand upon. There was space upon the floor for two, no more, and the rear was open without rail or step. Chains, fastened to the front and side like aircraft safety-straps, would bind the riders to the chariot sides. Once fastened and in motion the riders could not fall unless the chariot itself upturned, when the galloping horses would drag vehicle and passengers in their wake, and so to instant death.

Now that the horses were harnessed, and the chariot in place, all movement ceased. The grooms, standing at the horses' heads, were silent, as were the police cordonning off the piazza. Then Aldo moved from the chariot and came towards me. His face was pale, inscrutable, as it had been in the car on Wednesday night.

"I sent you to Fano believing it best for both of us," he said, "but since you are here you may as well play your part. The role of the Falcon is still yours. That is, if you have nerve enough to accept it."

The voice took me back to boyhood days. It was the old challenge, given with the same contemptuous grace, the same tacit suggestion of my own inferiority. Yet, strangely, the mocking tone no longer stung.

"Who would have played the Falcon if I had sailed with Marco?" I asked.

"I intended to drive alone," he said. "There were no couriers five centuries ago. The Falcon was his own charioteer."

"Very well," I said, "then today you can be mine."

My retort, as surprising to myself as it was to him, caught him momentarily off guard. He must have expected my boyhood plea to be spared participation in his adventures. Then he smiled.

"You'll find Duke Claudio's robe in the car," he said, "and the flaxen wig. Jacopo's there. He'll give them to you."

I was no longer conscious of feeling, or of fear. I was predestined to what must be. The decision had been taken. I walked over to the car, and Jacopo was standing there. I had not noticed him earlier when the car arrived, but he must have been beside Aldo all the time.

"I'm going with him," I said.

"Yes, Signor Beo," he replied.

There was an expression in his eyes I had not seen before. Surprise, yes, but it was also respect, even admiration.

"I'm to be Duke Claudio," I said, "and Aldo the charioteer."

He did not comment, but opened the door of the car and handed out the robe. He helped me into it and tied the girdle round my waist. Then he gave me the wig, and I put it over my cropped hair and stared at myself in the mirror.

There was a cut on my mouth where Aldo had struck me, and the blood had dried. The blonde wig framed my white, unshaven face, and my eyes confronted me, pale and staring, like the eyes of Claudio in the ducal palace picture. They were also the eyes of Lazarus in the church of San Cipriano.

I turned to Jacopo. "How do I look?" I said.

He considered me gravely, his head a little on one side. "You look just like your mother, Signora Donati," he replied.

He meant it kindly, but it was the final insult. The humiliation of the years returned. The foolish figure that pattered in bare feet back to the chariot and mounted beside Aldo was not Duke Claudio, not the Falcon it was supposed to represent, but a scarecrow effigy of the woman I had rejected and despised for twenty years.

I stood motionless, allowing Aldo to bind me to the chariot with the safety chains. Then he shackled himself. The guide reins of the centre horses, the guide reins of the leaders, were passed up to him by the attendants across the chariot front. The attendants released their hold upon the bridles as Aldo gathered the myriad reins in his two hands. The horses, feeling the strain, moved forward. The distant campanile by the Duomo sounded ten, echoed by all the churches of Ruffano. The flight of the Falcon had begun.

CHAPTER TWENTY-THREE

We circled the piazza first, proudly, sedately, processing like the triumphant entry of the Emperor Trajan into Rome. The twelve leaders wheeled to the right, obedient to the rein, and then the six in line abreast wheeled likewise, the turning movement like the slow unfolding of a gigantic fan, bearing our painted chariot behind them.

The roads were empty, as the policeman had said they would be, but every window was flung open, black with spectators, and as we paraded slowly before them the gasp of astonishment, of wonder, became magnified into a single cry. The cry rose in the air from multitudinous throats, turning from wonder to acclaim, and then the applause began, with upraised hands sounding as they clapped like the fluttering of innumerable wings. The eighteen horses, indifferent to the thunder, circled and moved on, the burnished metal on their trappings glittering in the morning sun, the jingle of the harness making its own defiant music in opposition to the tumult from the crowds. There was no clatter from the horses' hooves, for all were specially shod, and as they stepped the sound was muffled, dull, an oddly muted note, silent like our chariot wheels.

Twice we circled the piazza, twice the eighteen horses and their charioteer wheeled and straightened in deference to the applauding crowd, and then the attendants approached the horses' heads once more, leading them and us to the far end of the piazza where it was broadest. We turned again, and now we were directly facing the via del Duca Carlo leading downhill to the city. Adjustments were made to the guide reins and the traces, and to the girths of the centre horses. The attendants examined every horse in turn, reporting to Aldo. It took about four minutes, and it seemed to me in those last brief moments, when Aldo gathered the reins and the attendants fell back on either side, that I had reached the peak of fear; nothing, not the final holocaust nor the ultimate crash, could exceed this second.

I looked at Aldo. He was pale, as always, but now with a

tense excitement I had never seen in him before, and the smile at the corner of his mouth was a grimace.

I said to him, "Shall I pray?"

"If it stops the panic in your guts I should," he answered. "The only permissible prayer is a prayer for courage."

None of my childhood prayers was appropriate, neither the Pater Noster nor the Ave Maria. I thought of all the millions upon millions who had prayed to God and died—even Christ Himself upon the Cross.

"It's too late," I told him. "I never had any courage anyway. I depend on yours."

He laughed, and called to his horses. They broke into a trot and then a gallop, gathering speed, the muffled hoof-beats thudding the hard ground.

"Your German Commandant should have quoted Nietzsche to you," he said. "He who no longer finds what is great in God will find it nowhere; he must either deny it or create it."

We came to the front of the piazza and the last of the level ground, and the crowds, seeing the galloping horses, broke once more into a tornado of applause. The cries from the piazza now behind us were echoed by the waiting masses at each window, and for a single moment, here on the summit of the northern hill, I saw the full compass of the city spread below, roof-tops, churches, spires, and away yonder, crowning the southern slope, the Duomo and the ducal palace. Then the via del Duca Carlo opened up beneath us like the descent to hell, and as the street narrowed and curved, and the leading horses wheeled to the guiding reins, never pausing in their headlong flight, their muffled hooves stabbing the cobbles with their muted thunderous note, the houses closed in upon us, leaning precariously from the hill like cardboard shapes with windows all agape, each window spilling out a face, a scream, a terrible tumultuous roar.

There were no cordons here, no uniformed police, the street was ours alone, and when it narrowed before descending to the piazza della Vita in the city's heart the six horses spanning the chariot like a fan behind the leaders reached to the via del Duca Carlo's limits on either side. One check, one startled shy from any of the twelve leading horses, and he would bring his fellows down; they would collapse one upon the other in a sickening, plunging mass, ourselves and the chariot upturned and buried in the midst of them.

262

The street curved and narrowed further yet, the flanking horses must surely brush the lintels of the doors, and as we plunged deeper towards the city's heart I was not conscious of speed, nor of Aldo's voice cheering and calling to the horses, nor of the lurching, swaying cradle in which I stood; but only of the massed and terrified faces at all the windows, of the mounting screams as our headlong pace increased, and in my nostrils the smell of horseflesh and under my clenched hands the burning chariot rail. The church of San Cipriano swam into my line of vision on the left, the steps thronged with students, yelling, shouting, and there were students massing on the converging streets, and down we thundered into the piazza della Vita, every window of every building alight, aflame, with hands gesticulating, mouths that shouted, screamed. The horses, finding level ground again, tore on, the leaders heading for the via Rossini on the far side of the piazza, and so up the ascending hill towards the ducal palace, spurred by their own impetus, maddened and excited by the crescendo of terror and applause.

Looking back, I saw the students break from the streets into the piazza, burst from windows, doors, pour on to the square and cover it in a sudden movement like a massive tidal wave. But instead of the roar of anger I expected, the volleys of stones, the clash of steel, the outburst of pent-up hatred as the opposing factions met and mingled, they started swarming up the hill behind us, shouting, cheering, waving, and they were calling as they ran, "Donati . . . Donati . . . viva Donati . . ."

Now as we mounted the southern hill, up the via Rossini, our painted chariot lurching, trembling behind the galloping horses, the students spilt out of the buildings on either side to join their fellows. The screaming stopped, and the terror too, and the violence that came from all of them was the violence of excitement, of acclaim. All the city shouted, and there was no other sound but this, the roar "Donati . . . Donati . . ." Aldo yelled into my ear "Are they fighting yet?" and I yelled back at him, "They're not going to fight; they're coming after us. Don't you hear them calling you?"

Intent upon the horses he only smiled, and now as the street narrowed and became steeper yet the leaders, feeling the up-ward strain, strove to mount the hill before losing impetus, before the steeply rising street, curving to the right, defeated their attempt to master gravity.

"Arri! Arri!" yelled Aldo, and the cry, spurring the leaders to greater effort, with the thunder of the six abreast behind them, brought them in sight of the piazza Maggiore before the ducal palace and gallantly, superbly, they breasted the last incline. As they faltered, staggered, the students waiting beyond the fountain ran towards them, seizing their bridles. Our curving fan of six abreast, bearing us with them, dared the final slope, and sobbing, with heaving flanks, they felt the check of rein at last, and trembled to a halt where the piazza broadened before the palace doors.

Still the multitudinous cries rang out, and as I stared about me, dizzy, one hand still clutching the chariot rail, I saw that the windows of the ducal palace were black with faces too, as were the houses opposite. People were standing on the steps of the Duomo, they were clinging to the fountain, and now the mass of students who had followed us up the hill from the piazza della Vita came swarming into the square. In a moment we should be surrounded, overwhelmed, but the armed students waiting by the palace doors formed an immediate circle round us, while each of the eighteen horses had a student on either side to hold his bridle. The cavalcade, ourselves amongst it, was now protected by a single cordon bearing swords, each student dressed as Aldo was, in doublet and hose, and I recognised his friends, Cesare, Giorgio, Federico, Domenico, Sergio, and others of his bodyguard. The picture that they made, the splash of colour beside the painted chariot and the eighteen horses, still panting, heaving, from their victorious course, checked the body of emerging students as they advanced, shouting and yelling, on to the square. Once again the cry went up, "Donati . . . viva Donati . . .", echoed from the palace windows, from the houses opposite, from the Duomo steps. I looked at Aldo. He had the reins still in his hands and he was gazing down at the eighteen horses, unmindful of the cheers. Then he turned to me.

"We've done it," he said. "We've done it . . ." and he started laughing, he threw back his head and laughed, the laughter taken up with cheers by the waiting crowds of students and Ruffanesi. Then he unshackled me from the chains binding me to the chariot front, unshackled himself as well, and shouted to the students beyond the cordon, "Here is the Falcon! Here is your Duke!"

I saw nothing but waving arms and tossing heads, and the shouting never ceased but grew ever louder. The students guarding the chariot shouted too, and I stood there bewildered, helpless, a foolish figure in my golden wig and saffron robe, acknowledging the cheers that were not meant for me.

Something hit me on the cheek and fell upon the chariot floor. It was not the stone that I expected but a flower, and the girl who threw the flower was Caterina.

"Armino," she cried, "Armino!" her enormous eyes wide with laughter, and I saw that my saffron robe had come adrift, showing the jade shirt beneath and the black jeans, and wave upon wave of laughter, happy, friendly, rippled above the cheers.

I said to Aldo, "It's not me they want, it's you," but he did not answer, and looking behind me I saw that he had leapt from the chariot, and, diving under the surrounding cordon, was racing to the side door of the ducal palace. I cried to Giorgio, "Stop him . . . stop him . . ." but Giorgio, laughing, shook his head.

"It's part of the plan," he said, "it's all in the book. He's going to show himself to the crowds in the Piazza del Mercato from the palace."

I tore off my robe and the wig, and flung them down, and leapt out of the chariot after Aldo. The laughter and the cheers pursued me—I heard them as I ran. I shook off the restraining hand of Domenico, who tried to stop me, and ran through the side door, along the passage and across the quadrangle in chase of Aldo. I heard him race up the stairs to the gallery above, and I went after him. He burst through the great door to the throne room, and he was laughing as he ran. I was close upon his heels but he slammed the door, and when I opened it he had fled through the throne room to the Room of the Cherubs and beyond.

"Aldo . . ." I shouted, "Aldo . . ."

There was no one there. The Room of the Cherubs was empty. So was the Duke's bedroom, and the dressing-room, and the small temple beneath the right-hand tower. Hearing voices I went to the balcony between the towers, and Signora Butali was there, with the Rector, both of them staring at the Piazza del Mercato far below. They turned in astonishment as I burst upon them, staring at me blankly, the signora in sudden fear.

"What is it, what's happened?" she asked. "We heard them cheering in the city. Is it all over?"

"How can it be over?" said the Rector. "Donati told us himself the finale followed the chariot flight. We've seen nothing yet."

He seemed perplexed, disappointed, cheated of the magnificence he had not witnessed. I went from the balcony through the study to the audience room. It was empty, like the others. Then, as I called Aldo once again, Carla Raspa came through from the gallery beyond. She put out her hands to me, laughing, crying.

"I saw you from the window," she said. "It was wonderful, superb. I watched you both driving behind the horses on to the piazza Maggiore. Where has he gone?"

There were no guardians here today, no guides. The portrait of the gentlewoman stood on its easel unattended, the tapestry was in its place upon the wall. I ran across the room and jerked it back, revealing the closed door. I opened it, and putting one hand before the other on the narrow twisting steps began to climb. As I climbed I shouted, "Aldo!" The sickness and the vertigo I had suffered as a child enveloped me. I could not see, I could only feel the twisting spiral of the steps above. Up, up, forever up, with bursting heart and retching belly, and the creeping dust of years on my fumbling hands. I heard myself sobbing as I crawled, and the tower was forever out of reach, like the pit below. Time was suspended, reason with it. There was nothing left within me but the urge to climb, and sliding, stumbling, I swung between heaven and hell. Then, raising my head, I felt the air upon it, and the door above was open to the balustrade. Once more I shouted "Aldo!", opening my eyes for the first time since I had begun to crawl the twisting stair. The patch of sky, brilliant with the sun, distorted vision. I thought I saw the spread wings of a bird, its body darkening the open door, and crawling blindly on, dizzy with nausea, I gripped the topmost stair and peered about me, recognising nothing.

The door was half the size of the one I dimly recollected from childhood days, and the narrow ledge beyond it, in the open, was not the balustrade we used to climb. The shape was not rounded but octagonal. Suddenly I understood. I had climbed beyond the balustrade. This was the smaller parapet beneath the minaret. The pinnacle rose above me to the sky.

I felt his hands upon me. He dragged me from the stairway to the ledge.

"Lie still," said Aldo. "The ledge reaches between hip and thigh, no more. If you look down, you'll fall."

It seemed to me that the turret rocked. Perhaps it was the sky. My hands fastened upon his. Mine were slippery with sweat, but his were cold.

"How did you find the way?" he asked.

266

"The door," I said, "the hidden door behind the tapestry. I remembered."

The eyes, astonished, searching, turned to laughter. "You win," he said. "I reckoned without that. Poor Beato . . ."

Then frowning, steadying me with his arm, he said, "You'd have done better to go with Marco on the boat. That's why I sent you to him. This isn't your battle. I realised that on Wednesday night."

They were still cheering and shouting in the piazza Maggiore by the entrance to the ducal palace, and now the cry had been taken up from the piazza del Mercato below the towers. Lying against Aldo I could see nothing but the sky. The shouting, coming from beneath us, rose on every side. The students must be swarming downhill from the Maggiore to the Mercato some hundreds of feet lower, beyond the Porta del Sangue and the city wall.

"There's been no battle," I said. "You miscalculated. Your firebrand speeches were just wasted effort. Hark at those cheers."

"That's what I meant," he said. "It could have gone the other way. If we and the horses had crashed, if we had failed, they'd have been murdering each other now, each faction screaming sabotage. It was a gamble."

I stared at him, uncomprehending. "You did it deliberately?" I asked. "You roused them to that pitch of frenzy, dicing with hundreds of lives, your own as well, on the incredibly long odds that Claudio's feat might temporarily unite them?"

He looked at me and smiled. "Not so temporary," he said. "You'll see. They've smelt blood, that's what they wanted. And the city too. Everyone who watched us ride today participated. It's the first and last lesson someone directing any spectacle has to learn: make your audience one."

Still holding me, he brought me closer to the narrow balustrade, and clutching his arm I stared down to the piazza del Mercato below the city walls. The great market-place was black with people, so were the converging streets, and immediately beneath us, on the sloping palace precincts, massed groups of students stood, their heads upturned.

"If by the remotest chance," he said, "my second exploit fails, I've left everything to you. It's yours by right. I made my will on Wednesday night after you gave me that letter, and had it witnessed by Lydia Butali and her husband. The will says that we are brothers—my vanity forbade me to admit otherwise."

The cry "Donati" came now from the piazza del Mercato, as the students from above the palace went to swell those in the crowds below. They must have seen us move on our narrow ledge beneath the minaret, for the cries grew louder, and the cheers, and all the heads were tilted to the sky.

"You were right to suspect my determination not to lose face," said Aldo, "but wrong to accuse me of silencing the slanderer. The thief in Rome confessed. He stole and also murdered. The Commissioner telephoned to tell me late last night. The police weren't after you—they simply wanted to find out whether you knew more than you had told them."

"You didn't kill Marta?" I stammered, astonished and ashamed.

"Yes, I killed her," he said, "but not with a knife—the knife was merciful. I killed her by despising her, by being too proud to accept the fact I was her son. Wouldn't you say that counts as murder?"

Aldo was Marta's *son*. Then it all swung into focus. The pieces fitted. The foundling boy, with his mother to care for him as nurse, came to live under my parents' roof. The foundling took the place of the boy they had lost. The mother stayed, devoting herself to Aldo, then to me. She kept her secret until that birthday evening in November, when on a sudden lonely, drunken impulse she revealed the truth.

"Well," repeated Aldo, "it was murder, wasn't it?"

I thought no more of his relationship to Marta, but of my own mother who had died of cancer in Turin. When she had scribbled me a line from hospital, I had not answered.

"Yes," I said, "it was murder. But we're both guilty, and for the same cause."

Together we looked down at the cheering crowds. The cry "Donati . . . viva Donati!" was for neither of us; it was for a legendary figure which the university students and the Ruffanesi had created in their minds, born of all men's desire to worship something greater than themselves.

"The flight's over," I said. "Tell them it's finished."

"It isn't finished," he said. "The true flight's yet to come. Tested in the hills, just like the chariot drive."

He propped me against the ledge, and groping his way round the narrow balustrade reached down into the parapet for something long and slender, silver-coloured, made up of a million feathers that as he touched them shivered in the wind. The feathers were sewn upon silk, the silk of a parachute, and beneath the material were fibre struts, interwoven and inter-laced. Cords hung from the centre, forming a harness. Aldo lifted them up, standing the whole contrivance on the parapet floor, and he unfolded them, and I saw that they were wings.

"No deception," said Aldo. "We've been working on these all winter. When I say we, I mean my ex-partisan friends who fly glider 'planes today. These wings are designed to a specific formula, identical with the real wings of a falcon. We tried them out in the hills, just as we did the horses, and I can promise you they frighten me far less."

He stood there laughing at me. "On my last flight I was air-borne for ten minutes," he said, "on the western slopes of Monte Cappello. I tell you, Beo, there's nothing to it. The mechanism can't fail. The only thing that can fail is the human element. And after what I've just achieved that isn't likely."

He was no longer white and tense as he had been before the race. The smile on his face was joyous, no grimace. He raised one hand in salutation to the cheering crowds below.

"The landing may be ungainly, not the flight," he said. "I aim to clear the piazza itself, and strike the softer ground where the valley slopes. The parachute behind the wings will open when I release the cords, and become my brake. They told me, when I did it in the hills, that the actual drop looked like a crumpled kite. But you never know. I might soar further this time."

His confidence was arrogant, supreme. He looked out to the distant hills and smiled.

"Aldo, don't go," I said. "It's madness. Suicide."

He was not listening. He did not care. His faith was a fanatic's faith, proved through centuries to bring believers to destruction. Like Claudio before him, he could only die.

Standing on the ledge he began to strap the harness about his waist, buckle the bindings to his shoulders, step into the slots which would enclose his feet. He put both arms into the fibre webbing beneath the wings, raising them aloft. Spread-eagled thus, he appeared to me helpless, even grotesque. He would never free himself from the lashings that encompassed him. The fibre, black beneath the silver, looked like nails.

The crowd, three hundred feet or more below us in the piazza del Mercato, became suddenly silent. The massed heads,

269

upturned, no longer cried "Donati!" They watched and waited while the figure, self-imprisoned, stood motionless on the parapet edge, outlined against the sky.

I crawled closer and put my arms about him, clasping his legs. "No," I said, "no . . ."

I must have shouted, for my voice came back to me in echo, mocking me, and travelling downwards was caught by the crowd immediately beneath, so breeding fear. A sigh arose, swelling to protestation and alarm.

"Listen to them," I cried. "They don't want it. They're afraid. You've proved yourself once. Why in the name of God again?"

He looked down at me and smiled. "Because that's it," he said. "Once is never enough. That's what they have to learn. You, Cesare, all those waiting students, all Ruffano—once is no good. You must always risk a second time, a third, a fourth, no matter what it is you want to achieve. Get out of my way!"

He thrust backwards with his foot and sent me sprawling against the door. I slumped sideways, striking the step with my chest, and, momentarily winded, knelt there an instant, gasping for breath, my eyes closed. When I opened them again he was standing with the wings spread poised for flight. He no longer looked grotesque, but beautiful. As he launched himself into the air the wind current filled the lining of the wings and they bellied out, then tautened, like the sudden jerking of a child's toy. His body was horizontal between the wings, his arms and feet within the slots were part of the structure. Buoyant, effortless, he soared above the crowd, drifting with the wind as he had foretold. The feathers, silver in the sunlight, turned to gold. Gliding south, he would touch down in the valley beyond the market-place.

I watched for him to pull the rip-cord of the braking parachute, as he had described. He did not do so. Instead, he must have kicked his body free, letting the apparatus which he had helped to build drift on without him. He threw himself clear, spreading his arms wide like the wings he had discarded, then, bringing them to his side, he plummeted to earth and fell, his body, small and fragile, a black streak against the sky.

EXTRACT FROM
"THE WEEKLY COURIER"
RUFFANO

PROFESSOR ALDO DONATI, *Director of the Arts Council and a leading citizen of our beloved city, who lost his life in a tragic accident on the day of the Festival, will be mourned, not only by his surviving brother and his friends, but by every student within the university, by his colleagues and associates, and by all the inhabitants of the Ruffano he loved so well. The eldest son of Aldo Donati, who for many years was Superintendent of the Ducal Palace, he was born and educated in the city. During the war he served in the Air Force and won his pilot's wings. Shot down in 1943 he managed to escape, and during the German Occupation he formed a group of irregulars in the mountains and fought amongst his fellow-partisans until the Liberation.*

Returning to Ruffano, he learnt of his father's death some time previously in an Allied prison camp, and his mother's and younger brother's presumed death by enemy bombing. Undaunted though bereaved, Aldo Donati studied at the university of Ruffano, and obtained an Honours Degree in Arts. He joined the Arts Council and devoted the remainder of his life to his work for the Council, for the preservation of the ducal palace and its treasures, and, last but not least, for the welfare of orphaned students. It was my privilege, as Rector of the university, to work with him on Festival productions, and I can only state, without any qualification whatsoever, that his ability in this field surpassed anything I had hitherto seen. He was brilliant, and his enthusiasm so inspired his actors and all who took part in Festival productions that they came to believe—and I speak from experience, my wife and I being amongst the participants until this year—that what they enacted was not fiction but reality.

Whether his choice for this year's Festival production was wise or not need not be discussed here. The unhappy Duke Claudio is not one whose memory we wish to recall; the Ruffanesi of both yesterday and today prefer to forget him. He was an evil man with evil intentions, ill-disposed to all his people, admired only by a narrow circle of friends as ignoble as himself. He left behind him a legacy of hate. However this may be, Aldo Donati decided that he had a claim to fame, if only because of his Jehu feat of driving eighteen horses through the city of Ruffano, from the

271

northern to the southern hill. Whether Duke Claudio actually achieved this feat is still uncertain. Aldo Donati did. The people who watched him do so on Friday morning will never forget the experience.

Had he stopped there, it would have sufficed. What he had achieved was fantastic, even sublime. But he aimed higher still, and lost his life in so aiming. The mechanism was not at fault. Experts have examined the apparatus. Aldo Donati seems to have ignored the elementary rule learnt by every student parachutist—to pull the ripcord. Why he ignored it, we shall never know. His brother Armino Donati, who returned to Ruffano last week after an absence of over twenty years and who will, we hope, remain with us to carry on the work with orphaned students, told me he believed that his brother, in mid-air, had a sudden vision, some sort of ecstasy blinding him to danger.

It may be true. Like Icarus, he flew too near the sun. Like Lucifer, he fell. We, the Ruffanesi who remain, salute the courage of a man who dared.

GASPARE BUTALI,
Rector, University of Ruffano.

Ruffano. Easter Week.